Hang Down Your Head

Hang Down Your Head

A Randy Craig Mystery

By

Janice MacDonald

RaveN
STONE

Published by Ravenstone
an imprint of Turnstone Press
Artspace Building
206-100 Arthur Street
Winnipeg, MB
R3B 1H3 Canada
www.TurnstonePress.com

Turnstone Press gratefully acknowledges the assistance of the Canada
Council for the Arts, the Manitoba Arts Council, the Government of
Canada through the Canada Book Fund, and the Province of Mani-
toba through the Book Publishing Tax Credit and the Book Publisher
Marketing Assistance Program.

This novel is a work of fiction. Names, characters, places and incidents
are either the product of the author's imagination or are used fictitiously,
and any resemblance to actual persons living or dead, events or locales, is
entirely coincidental.

Cover design: Jamis Paulson
Interior design: Sharon Caseburg
Printed and bound in Canada by Friesens for Turnstone Press.

Library and Archives Canada Cataloguing in Publication

MacDonald, Janice E. (Janice Elva), 1959–
      Hang down your head / Janice MacDonald.

ISBN 978-0-88801-386-6

      I. Title.

PS8575.D6325H35 2011   C813'.54   C2011-905982-7

This book is for my good friend Don Whalen.
Without his vision and hard work to create and nourish the
Edmonton Folk Music Festival from its infancy,
I daresay we wouldn't be Festival City.

Hang Down Your Head

1

The trouble with "landing on your feet" is that, while the phrase seems positive, it also indicates that just prior to your happy feline arrival you were plummeting some fair distance, in danger of breaking your neck. Falling, metaphorically or not, is not an action that has any sort of connotative control attached to it. You injure yourself *falling down*; you are out of control during a *freefall*; you are the butt of a practical joke when you *fall for* something. Even the most positive context, *falling in love*, leaves you dizzy and at the mercy of greeting card companies. No, the semantic adhesions to "falling" weren't something I wanted to spend too long contemplating.

I found myself thinking along these lines, though, every time someone mentioned my new career path, which they lately seemed to do with the same frequency as Tim Horton's brews coffee. I appreciated the support of all my friends when they heard about the new job (although I sensed some envy there, too), however, the unspoken part of the statement was that things had indeed been very lean in recent times.

After working as a sessional at the University of Alberta for several years, I spent some time working for Grant MacEwan College's distance outreach section of the English department, delivering rhetoric and communication skills via e-mail and manila envelopes. Truth to tell, there was a lot more e-mail than snail-mail involved. Everyone is online these days, including my Great-Aunt Jessie. Working for Grant MacEwan hadn't been the lean bit, though I could have used some more security and a few more courses. I spent some time working at an online chat site, too, before that was closed down. Once it shut its virtual doors, there wasn't all that much in the way of options, so I did some incredibly creative things with lentils and book reviewing to survive the latter part of the winter.

I didn't mind that too much, either. Since I'd got back together with Steve Browning, he'd done his best to make sure that I ate out at least once a week, at one of our many favourite restaurants. That was another thing that turned out phenomenally well. Even though we'd broken up earlier the year before, Steve and I were now a solid couple, fully expecting to live our entire lives together, to the point of occasionally discussing the M-word, a commitment that had eluded several of my seemingly more deserving friends.

So, I could understand why folks took the news of my appointment to the Smithsonian Folkways Collection Project at the University of Alberta with such surprise and shock. Well, the surprise I could understand. But the shock sort of ticked me off. The job description looked like it was designed with me in mind, after all. It's not as if I don't have the credentials and track record, along with some relatively specialized skills. I was trying to avoid friends with feedback like, "Oh my God, Randy, you landed *that* job?" (Michele Armstrong from Botany); "That's a fantastic post, and the money!" (Sonia Zawarucka from U of A Radio); "They do realize you have no credentials in either Anthropology or Music?" (the ever-so-charming Mary Montgomery, who held a similar foundation-paid position to mine but with the English department's online Orlando Project). Okay, that last one was more of an acquaintance than a friend. Anyhow, it must be the way people who lose a lot of weight feel when folks comment on it. You're happy to acknowledge the good thing you've done, or that has happened to you, but you begin to wonder just what they'd been saying behind your previously substantial back.

The University of Alberta's Folkways Collection, the only full set of Moses Asch's legendary recordings in existence, had been donated to the university by Asch himself, whose son Michael was a professor emeritus here. One of the great visionaries for the preservation of world music, poetry and soundscapes, Moses Asch had been so impressed with the Edmonton music scene every time he visited that he willed his personal collection to the university. It was housed in the Centre for Ethnomusicology, and every now and then a special radio presentation was aired, or a concert took place, to highlight the collection.

At the earliest part of this century, the Smithsonian Institute, which was believed to be the central site for the collection, discovered that their collection wasn't complete. There was much hue and cry and subsequent northern grinning when it was announced that the Smithsonian had to come to little old Edmonton to record the missing sections of the collection. Perhaps to save face, a partnership was struck, and the web presence on the Smithsonian Folkways Collection had a strong linking presence to the Centre up here. There was talk of creating a database searchable by subject of songs as well as by artists and recordings. There was talk of making the collection completely downloadable, given that the copyright on most of the songs had always been in the public domain, and most of the performers were long dead. There was also talk of creating links to research material the likes of Edith Fowke's *Folk Songs of Canada* and some British scholarly works dealing with folk, roots and blues music. The big problem with all that lovely talk, of course, is that input, web design and database construction of that magnitude requires some pretty hefty outlay of both time and cash.

And that's almost where I came into the picture, but not quite. First, out of the blue, an enormous bequest was made to the university, specifically flagged for the Folkways Project. The donor, who wished to remain anonymous, had apparently loved acoustic music and admired Professor Michael Asch. The call went out for people skilled in online writing, with an understanding of university policy and project work and strong communication qualifications. Teaching English, writing magazine articles and monitoring chatrooms had to combine to come in handy somehow, and after a process of three rigorous interviews and the inspired admission that I played the banjo, I was offered the continuity and writing position. I didn't even have to read the fine print: I signed the contract before they could snatch it back and snicker, "You fell for it!"

Summer term at the university was just beginning. Abandoned by all except grade school teachers hoping to escape the classroom by getting advanced degrees and becoming principals, the campus became a lovely place. Suddenly, there was room to breathe, and even occasionally to perch at the coffee outlet of one's choice in HUB Mall, the housing and retail enclosed street extending the entire width of the campus on its eastern, arts-oriented edge. I swear the campus landscapers plant hundreds of new trees every year. It's such a shame that most students leave the campus for summer work or holidays back home just as the U of A is beginning to look like everyone's dream of collegiate life. If it weren't so warm in the July sun, you could almost expect to see a young Jimmy Stewart and Ronald Reagan, stroll past the Dentistry–Pharmacy Building, sporting raccoon coats and striped scarves, shouting "Twenty-three, Skidoo" and singing the "The Whiffenpoof Song."

Speaking of "The Whiffenpoof Song," I was surprised I hadn't found a version of it in the collection yet, since I was finding pretty much everything else as I familiarized myself with the scope of the collection, which my boss Dr. Fuller had advised me to do before getting down to any actual work. The plan was for me to read, listen and make notes for most of the spring, and by mid-summer I'd have enough of a handle on things to write the splash pages to all the sections of the website and have promotional material organized for the tie-ins to the Edmonton

Folk Music Festival's "folkwaysAlive!" stage, where the department would be recording new material for the collection. This
was one of the big things the influx of new money was able to
make happen: Folkways wouldn't be just an amazing collection
of vinyl; it was going to stay a living tool. Moses Asch would
have been so happy.

It was just as well I had all this research to do, otherwise I
might have found myself totally at loose ends. My best friend
Denise was down east all through spring session, doing research
in Stratford, Ontario, and was taking her sweet time getting
home, having detoured in Toronto for some shopping and
shows. Steve, of course, was busy keeping the streets safe for the
rest of us mere mortals, and I hadn't had any teaching work over
the intersession months since things started to dry up for sessionals a year or two earlier. The festival tie-in was fine by me,
too. The only plans Steve and I had made for the summer was
to attend the Folk Festival in early August. I was thinking that,
with this new job, I might be able to write off the cost of the tickets. So, all in all, I was pleased as punch to get the job.

The project made for a very nice working environment.
Everyone, including the classy Dr. Cheryl Fuller, dressed casually, and although I wasn't sure whether it was because of the
nature of the project or the time of year, I wasn't complaining. My protective coloration is campus casual, and I often
get mistaken for a student instead of a lecturer, or in this case,
researcher. It's not that I appear so amazingly youthful; in fact I
am pretty sure I look every one of my forty-two years. I think it
has more to do with the fact that I wear my hair in a long braid

down my back, favour jeans and sweatshirts, and always carry a backpack instead of a briefcase. I look like a student from the Eighties transported by some H.G. Wells sort of magic into the future, only to find my wardrobe has been raided by children less than half my age. Every twenty years or so, my clothes come back into fashion. What on earth would be the point of throwing them out?

I was sitting in the corner of the Centre, headphones plugged into the stereo allotted to the desk I'd claimed, legs crossed yogi style on the institutional tweed stacking chair. I was listening to Carter Family recordings on a Folkways compilation CD, reading along in the newish biography of the first family of American roots music by Mark Zwonitzer and Charles Hirshberg, *Will You Miss Me When I'm Gone*, and trying to take notes on my laptop. From what was coming through my headphones, I figured Sarah sounded like a man when she was singing, a sad man. From what was on the page, I had a feeling that Maybelle would have been someone I'd have liked a heck of a lot if I'd ever met her. The book was extensively detailed in its description of the valley they came from and the times they dealt with.

It struck me that they were living this life around the same time as folks were homesteading in the northern part of Alberta, where I'd done quite a bit of research on the background of a novelist for my master's thesis. It was likely that many of the people I'd talked with up in Grande Prairie and Beaverlodge had been youngsters at the same time as Sarah, A.P. and Maybelle. Somehow their stories of the times seemed of a harsher life, even though we always think the Appalachian hill folks had the worst of it. Maybelle's husband was well off by anyone's standards, and their trip into the nearest major city seemed cosmopolitan compared to a trek from Huallan to Edmonton around that time period. I think James Dickey's *Deliverance*, or at any rate the film version of it, has a lot to answer for when it comes to the way most people think about hillbilly hardship.

I'd been thinking it would be a great idea to work a concordance database that would bring up the music being played in various parts of the world at the same time as the piece you were looking at, to put it in a global context. While I was worried about having too cluttered a screen, I made a note to ask the web designers if it would work. It might be possible to find a way to have a pop-up sidebar people could deselect if they so chose.

So, if folks were trying to understand how "Keep on the Sunny Side" hit the world, they might be interested to know that other songs recorded in 1928 included "Honeysuckle Rose," "Big Rock Candy Mountain" and "Makin' Whoopie." There might also be some room for timelines of important events in the world brought up with each song. Dr. Fuller was interested in it all being international in scope, but within the realm of keeping a unique vision. We didn't want to be spending time and money just to replicate the Smithsonian's existing site.

Whoever the anonymous donor was, he or she had specified that the money was to be used to enhance the Folkways Collection. The Department of Ethnomusicology was doing its best to honour that through the web-accessible database and the MP3 files of all the older songs beyond copyright that were cleared for public domain. That part wasn't my job. Paul Calihoo, the

Centre's one full-time employee, was working his way through the provenance of each recording.

My job, or what it looked like at this point, was to be the creative shaper and the writer on all the copy. While my rudimentary HTML was enough to slot in the elements I wanted to play with, I was just sketching the look of things. Eventually, the material would be pulled into shape by a couple of computer science honour students who needed research projects.

The first thing I had deemed essential was to immerse myself in the entire collection, which was enormous. Think about lining up every single person who attended a folk festival in the past twenty years end to end, and you still wouldn't have a proper idea of the incredible span Moses Asch had established in his vision. There was everyone from Pete Seeger to Allen Ginsberg. There were recordings of mountain music, street sounds and North American frog noises. I had several terrific biographies and music histories to read through, and some of them were already bristling with sticky notes. Two boxes of CDs burned from the original collection sat at my feet, waiting to be organized in their new home after I was through with them.

I was cueing up the next CD and starting a new file on my laptop when I noticed Paul gesturing to me with that peculiar semaphore reserved for people wearing headphones. Pushing them back off my ears so they slid into a collar around my neck, I said, "Yes?"

"The phone is for you on line three." He pointed to the telephone at the corner of my workstation.

"Thanks, Paul," I said, reaching for the phone, and flicking off the power to the CD player for the nonce. It was Steve, who wanted to know if we could swing a dinner at the Blue Chair Café to hear Ben Sures that night. I liked the melancholy quirkiness of Sures's songs as well as his sense of the ridiculous, so I agreed immediately. There was also a platter of nachos there with my name on it.

Moses Asch was right: there was a great music scene in Edmonton—a world-class symphony orchestra; the jazz scene, pioneered by the likes of Tommy Banks and Big Miller, was still going strong; and folk music was a mainstay. Connie Kaldor had lived here, as had Dougie Maclean; and everyone had played here, from Tom Paxton to Sarah McLachlan. Ben Sures was the latest in a long line of strong singer-songwriters to call Edmonton home. The Edmonton Folk Music Festival, while younger than Winnipeg's and not quite so eclectic as Vancouver's, was considered the friendliest and one of the most important on the summer circuit.

So, if you were an old folkie, Edmonton was a pretty good place to be, especially in the summer. Steve was trying to book off the time for the Folk Fest, and I stood in line for weekend passes on June 1, since they usually sold out by about three in the afternoon the first day they went on sale. I'd been to several Folk Fests, but it was especially exciting to think of sitting on the darkened hill and snuggling up with Steve this year. Even if he had to work a shift or two, we'd have some time together. All in all, this had the makings of a fantastic summer.

I turned the music back on, and was coordinating the track number with the liner notes, when I heard the shouting. The first thing that hit me was that I had forgotten to replace my headphones, but before I could, the muffled words in the background became clearer, and way more interesting. I sat very still, which is what you should always do when eavesdropping. I remained as part of the scenery and listened intently to what turned out to be a very heated discussion between Dr. Fuller and two middle-aged people who looked enough alike to be twins. Or maybe they'd been married forever without a dog.

"I don't care what sort of lawyers the university has, this will is not only invalid, it's an embarrassment to my sister and me, and to our father's memory!" I was right the first time, they were siblings.

"Mr. Finster, there is really nothing to be gained by threatening me. I had nothing to do with your mother's bequest to the Centre, but I know something of how university bequests work. I assume that if it has been announced to the world, then the lawyers have ascertained that it has been fully probated and acknowledged as valid. Furthermore, there is nothing embarrassing about the Centre's work. I cannot see how the association of our work and your mother's name, should it be leaked, would in any way inconvenience you or your sister."

"Yes, well, you wouldn't," sniffed the female Finster. "You haven't spent your entire life having to deal with your mother flaunting her torrid affairs in front of her long-suffering husband. My father's money should in no way be funding a celebration of dirty musicians. It was bad enough he lost his wife to them."

This was getting better by the minute. If I had a bead on this

conversation, these were the children of the heretofore anonymous donor to the Folkways Project, who must have been a Mrs.
Finster. The only Finster I had heard of in this town was the car-
diologist, Dr. Manfred Finster. There was a Finster Library over
in the hospital complex, I think. If these two were his children,
and their late mother was his widow, then I suppose having it
known that their mother had indulged a thing for musicians
might be slightly embarrassing. However, since the bequest was
anonymous, I wasn't sure how they could see the connection
coming to light, unless they were determined to stand in university hallways shouting about it, which seemed to be their intent
and, come to think of it, could work.

Dr. Fuller managed to herd them into her office and close the
door. Their voices were muted, partly because the walls in the
Centre were almost completely soundproofed to keep the constant playing of music from overwhelming other researchers,
and partly, I knew, because of the unworldly calm Dr. F managed to instill into everyone who came into her personal orbit.
If anyone could placate this outraged duo, she could.

A dull rock developed in the bottom of my stomach as I
digested all this. If the children of the anonymous donor were
contesting the will, what would that do to my dream job?

I stuck around for about half an hour but no one emerged,
and I needed to pack things up and head home if I was going
to be ready to go out with Steve. There was nothing I hated
worse than missing out on the end of a story, but there wasn't
much I could do about it. Maybe Dr. Fuller would let us all in
on the scoop tomorrow, although I sort of doubted it. She would

probably think gossiping to us about the Finsters was unethical or something. Sigh.

With one more look at Dr. Fuller's closed door, I let myself out of the Centre and headed for home.

2

Steve swung by to pick me up straight from his shift, and he excused himself to clean up a bit in my bathroom and change into a different shirt. While it's marvellous to share a life with someone, sharing a closet brings things to an entirely different level. You have to love a person a whole lot to sacrifice hanger space. To his credit, Steve kept only a few things at my place, mostly shaving gear, but he had left the odd T-shirt or two in my laundry. Those I didn't begrudge. It was easy enough to empty out a drawer of my highboy, since I stored most of my winter weight clothes in my suitcase under my bed, anyhow. It wasn't the clothing that made me realize that our relationship had shifted into a different level, though; that happened when Steve mentioned he had listed my phone number with all the desk sergeants for emergency contact possibility. Nothing says romance like being listed in every police station in town. Oh, the joys of dating a cop.

We were dressed in Edmonton summer evening casual, namely clean jeans and T-shirts. Steve managed to get us a table near the stage, and I was still picking away at the last of my corn chips when Ben Sures was announced. He bounded on to the stage, and immediately commanded it. This was probably surprising to anyone who hadn't seen him before, because he was barely five-foot-four. His twinkling eyes shone past the lights, and his sense of humour, often aimed at himself, was always evident, especially in songs like, "Dear Sarah." In one song he claimed that, in a perfect world, he would be five-foot-nine. No matter how tall he was, I was still happy to support his career by buying CDs and tickets to concerts.

It's impossible to talk when live music is playing, although that didn't stop the people at the table next to us, at whom Steve glared several times. I would have clammed up immediately if his stink-eye had been aimed at me, but the people just continued to yammer. We tuned them out the best we could to enjoy the show, and then paid up after the first set and headed out into the cool of the summer night. I had a sweater, which I immediately buttoned up. Steve's metabolism was set much higher than mine, and he strode along without seeming in the least bit chilly. As we walked down the street to the car, Steve put his arm around my shoulder as we waited for a car to pass, partly for romance, but more for warmth. I was shivering a bit.

"Randy, you could wear a sweater to a steam bath, girl!"

"Well, once the sun goes down it's still pretty chilly. It snowed on the Victoria Day weekend, after all."

"That was over a month ago!" He shook his head. "Nah, summer's here to stay. No snow for at least … oh I'd say we're safe for about twelve weeks."

"You seem pretty sure of that. Have you been sneaking off and taking a meteorology degree in your spare time?"

He laughed. "Call it folk wisdom. You live somewhere long enough, you get to know these things."

His choice of the word "folk" tweaked my memory of what had happened at work that afternoon. I hadn't had a chance to tell Steve about the strange altercation at the Centre. I asked him what he knew of the Finsters.

"Well, there's the Finster Library on campus and the Finster Building over by the General Hospital. Wasn't the guy a heart surgeon or something? He died about ten years ago, and I'm pretty sure his widow, who was sort of philanthropic in the arts scene, just died recently. Or was it one of his kids?"

"I think it must have been his wife, from what I overheard today. His grown-up kids were in the Centre, hopping mad about the bequest that their mother had made, which I am assuming is the Folkways bequest. If they screw that up, I could be out of a job."

"How fair is that? I mean, it's not like some fake maharishi is hovering over a susceptible octogenarian's shoulder here. Why can't everyone just accept that people are allowed to disperse their assets any way they see fit? You say these kids of hers are middle-aged, right? By now they should be able to survive on their own, you'd think."

"I'm not going to survive on my own if they manage to screw up this job for me. Sessional gigs are harder to come by now that everybody wants to be degree-granting. A PhD is turning into the minimum requirement."

"And you're sure you don't want to do a PhD?"

I shrugged, which made me shiver again. "It's not that I don't want it. I just don't want it badly enough, I think. Aside from not being able to afford it, I just can't really picture what I would want to dig into so badly that I could add to the body of knowledge and then be constantly delving into that same area. I'm too much of a generalist, I think." By this time, we were at Steve's car, and I huddled in the passenger seat, trying to warm up my hands by holding them between clenched thighs. Steve put the heater on to help me out, but then had to crack his window to survive, himself. It was this sort of thing that proved he loved me, I figured.

"Well, I wouldn't get too het up about things, Randy. From what you said, Dr. Fuller is right. There's no way the university lawyers would have allowed the announcements to be made and work to begin without that bequest being ironclad. I don't think you have anything to worry about. Besides, your contract is pretty ironclad itself. If the project gets canned, they'll have to buy you out. You'd have a cushion, at any rate."

A cushion is not what I wanted. I wanted the security of a project that could last several years. But Steve was right. It wasn't going to do me any good to worry. It's not like there was anything at all I could do about the situation, in any case.

The car was beginning to warm up, and I slid my hand off my thigh and onto Steve's. There was more than one way to warm up.

3

Paul was right ahead of me as I came down the hallway of the Fine Arts Building toward the Centre's door. No matter how early I came in—and my hours were by no means regular, since I was being paid for the project rather than by the hour—he was somehow always there just ahead of me. It had become a bit of a game I played, trying to beat Paul to work. Good thing I was becoming more of a morning person as I aged.

He had his keys out, which was just as well, since I had a Java Jive coffee in one hand and a newspaper in the other. As he ushered me into the laughably tiny open area with a flourish worthy of a liveried doorman, he smiled and whispered, "That was some fracas yesterday, wasn't it?"

I looked at him and nodded, wondering whether I was witnessing a miracle along the lines of burning bushes and parting seas. Although friendly, Paul wasn't exactly what you'd call verbose. I'd barely ever exchanged a conversation with him worthy of a fellow passenger on a short flight, and we'd been colleagues for well over a month. This seemed downright garrulous, for him.

I wasn't complaining. There's very little I enjoy more than a good gossip. People and their actions and adventures delight and entrance me. I should have been an anthropologist, I guess. Instead, I am just plain nosy.

Since Dr. Fuller wasn't in till noon, we had the Centre to ourselves. Paul opened the mail packet that had been dumped through the slot in the door, and started setting out the brochures for the Baroque Ensemble that had arrived. I went into the staff area behind the reception desk to start the coffee pot; one Java Jive coffee was not going to cut it for me today. Although it was a warm morning, with dew misting up off the lawns, it was chilly in the Centre. It was, in fact, chilly in the entire Fine Arts Building, a dark brick edifice with slabs of uneven grey concrete to relieve the walls of dismal bricks. Most people commented that it was odd that the one building on campus devoted entirely to the fine arts was so unredeemably ugly.

While the coffee pot burbled, I headed back to the front counter to prime Paul for more of his thoughts on the ballyhoo from the day before. He'd been closer to the action, and who knows, maybe he actually knew the players.

"So I take it those people yesterday have something to do with the Folkways Bequest?"

"You'd better believe it. That was Barbara and David Finster, children of the late Dr. Manfred Finster and his lovely wife,

Lillian. Geneticists on the other side of campus are probably shaking their heads in disbelief that two people of the elder Finsters' calibre could produce two such repugnant offspring."

"Did you know the senior Finsters?" I asked. Maybe this whole secret bequest business was a secret only to me.

"Well, I knew of them. My grandmother was actually one of Dr. Finster's patients about twenty years ago, and Lillian was such a staunch patron of the arts around here that you knew her just by seeing her at openings. It's sort of the way you think you should be able to go up and say hi to Colin MacLean just because you've seen him talking on CBC TV in your living room so often."

I nodded; I knew exactly what he meant. I had waved at MacLean once at the Fringe, and probably had him puzzled for five minutes, trying to place me among folks he'd interviewed over the years. It had taken me a few minutes myself to realize that I actually didn't know him personally.

"And the Finster juniors? Were they always with their mother at events?"

Paul shook his head. "Nope, I never laid eyes on them till the time of the announcement. This is the second time they've both shown up here. Old David came on his own once before and I think now I spotted Dr. F talking with Barbara in HUB last week. I have a feeling they aren't music lovers."

"Not from what we saw yesterday. Of course, it might be that they just love large inheritances more than philanthropy."

"Well, I don't suppose we'll ever know. Dr. F will keep this pretty close to her chest, I'm thinking. Ours is not to reason why, et cetera, et cetera, et cetera." With that Yul Brynner impression completed, Paul finished setting the date stamps and headed back to pour himself a cup of coffee. I wandered back to the corner where my headset was waiting for me. It was lucky I didn't have a hairstyle that minded headphones on every day. I chose a CD at random from the Smithsonian sampler for background music while I tried to beat my best time on the cryptic crossword puzzle. The full-time job had lulled me into buying the *Globe and Mail* every morning, and after nearly two months, I could finish it within fifteen minutes four out of five days. I wrote "V.G. 100%" on the top of the finished puzzle for fun, and stretched. Now, with the coffee finally trickling through my arteries and my brain revved up enough to create whole sentences, I was ready to start the day.

I glanced over what I'd been working on the day before, and decided that I'd given enough gloss time to the Carter Family for the moment. I moved on to Mississippi John Hurt, since his was a name I recognized mostly from Tom Paxton's homage song, "Did You Hear John Hurt?" I liked his voice, but I really knew nothing about the blues. I recalled that Karen Hanson, an online friend of mine, had once written a book about the blues scene in Chicago. Maybe reading it would give me some insights and all my previous chatroom time would be seen as worthwhile. If you wait long enough, eventually everything connects.

Everything connecting. That was the beauty *and* the trouble with Folkways. Moses Asch was a visionary, but he'd been almost too far-sighted. The collection included spoken word, porch-front recordings, blues, roots, folk songs and poetry. How do you create an organizing principle for a collection that includes everything from the porch-front party sound of The Carolina Tar Heels to the glorious Sunday gospel of Mahalia Jackson?

The Smithsonian Folkways' re-release of *American Folk Music,* a collection originally organized in the early Fifties by Harry Smith, was turning out to be my yardstick in terms of how this sort of material could be organized. A facsimile of the original handbook came with the six-record set, and it was amazingly detailed. Each of the eighty-four songs had "information on original issues, condensations of text, notes on recordings, and bibliographical and discographical references," and the condensations themselves were often hysterically funny. If I could find a way to create for every recorded Folkways artifact that same delightful thumbnail sketch Harry Smith provided for his selection, then I would have been of use to the project, no matter what else I could provide.

For the time being, what I could definitely bring, was a way to organize. I'm not sure if it was a particular gift, or just what Marshall McLuhan meant when he commented that an artist faced with information overload begins to look for recognizable patterns. This was all a morass of riches at the moment, but I had a sense that I was getting closer every day to seeing a pattern that might work to serve all the material well.

It was barely eleven in the morning, and already I'd filled three pages of my notebook with reminders of people to contact, musicians to group together, and several strange notes to myself, like "What sort of name is 'Eck,' anyhow?" I stretched my arms high and yawned. At the apex of my elongation, I suddenly noticed a movement near the doorway to the Centre. Caught in that position, I immediately got a cramp in my shoulder, and even through my headsets I heard cartilage creak and snap as I brought my arms down sharply. As I pulled the headset down around my neck, David Finster smirked nastily as he glanced at the CD cases on the table, and said, " I see you have the same reaction to folk music as I always have had—utter boredom."

"Oh, no, I'm not bored at all. I just get cramped sitting in one position too long, and need to stretch," I defended myself quickly. The last thing I needed was somebody, especially this man, thinking I wasn't totally enamoured with the job. "I just get caught up in the material and forget to move."

"There's no need to justify yourself to me, young woman. In fact, if you were bored, you'd find a sympathetic ear. I spent my childhood trying to find a quiet place to avoid that sort of music. If it wasn't on the radio, the players themselves would be huddled around the coffee table in the living room, rolling their own cigarettes and strumming beat-up instruments. One summer I even had to give up my bedroom and sleep on the back porch so that some old hillbilly my mother had adopted could rest up and sing about living rough and riding the rails. Of course, the irony completely escaped my mother, as so much did." He sneered his gaze around the room, mentally swiping the surfaces with an invisible white glove looking for grime. Even if I hadn't been aware that this man was campaigning to remove what amounted to my livelihood, I don't think I would have liked him. "I don't suppose your boss lady is around, is she?"

I looked over to the front counter area, but couldn't spot

Paul. Dr. Fuller's office door beyond the counter was closed. With my headphones on all morning and my back to the doorway, I had no idea if she'd come in without me seeing her. If she was in, the door was usually open, unless she was with someone very important, or listening to music. I couldn't hear anything except Frank Hutchison's "Stackalee" coming through my headset, probably even more tinnily than it originally sounded.

"I don't think she's coming in this morning, sir," was all I could think to say. "Did you have an appointment? Perhaps Paul could help you. If you want to press the bell at the counter, I'm sure he'll be right with you."

"What's the matter, don't you work here?" Finster had a really short fuse; he wasn't about to be pawned off, as he apparently saw it. I had no desire to explain that I was hired to a specific project, rather than as a full worker for the Centre of Ethnomusicology, especially since I figured his interest in the place had far more to do with my project than anything else. I decided to hedge.

"Well, I'm researching a particular project, and I don't have access to Dr. Fuller's appointment book. Maybe you'd like me to get Paul for you?" I pulled my headset off my neck, gracefully tangling my braid in the electric cord. As I unbent my leg, my knee decided to give out, so that as I stood I almost tipped right into Finster's arms. This business of getting middle-aged would be fine if your body didn't decide to let you down from time to time. I caught myself just before I lost all dignity whatsover and stood up, face to face with the man who obviously had a personal vendetta against my work. We were almost eye to eye.

While I'm tall for a woman, Finster himself wasn't all that imperious. He probably topped out at six feet, and wore heels to bring himself up to his personal ideal. His charcoal summer weight wool business suit was cut exquisitely, but that didn't surprise me, given his status as the son of one of Edmonton's leading families. What did surprise me was the yellow hard hat he held in his left hand. He followed my gaze and smirked again, which seemed to be his default expression.

"We're the contractors for the LRT stations' additional pedways. I'm expected on site in ten minutes. I just popped in here to see if I could talk some sense into your boss about this ridiculous project my mother decided to toss my inheritance at. It seems, though, that your boss doesn't keep regular hours. What can one expect from a woman in the arts? If she does show up, tell her to expect a call from me. I'm not going to take this lying down, and she'd better be ready."

He strode out of the Centre, making the door shudder in its frame just as Paul appeared from the back vault carrying an armload of sheet music that needed rebinding. His eyebrows shot up inquiringly.

"Mr. David Finster," I said. "He wants Dr. Fuller to know he's not going to take it lying down."

Paul shook his head in disbelief. "I don't know what he thinks he's going to accomplish by getting all tied up in a court case contesting the will. It's not even as if he needs the money. From the signs on the hoarding, it appears as if Finster Construction has a lock on half the new projects in town."

I thought about the light rail transit stations Finster had

mentioned. Those at Health Sciences, McKernan/Belgravia and South Campus had been opened before those at Southgate and Century Park, but the whole south line still seemed like a novelty. The landscaping was just starting to take hold along the line. New elements like tunnels and overpasses were being finessed into shape. The scuttlebutt was that the city was pushing to expand all over the city, northwest to NAIT, into Mill Woods in the southeast and down Stony Plain Road to the west end. Eventually, the dream was to take it all the way to the International Airport. If Finster's company was contracted to build even half the pedways involved in all those stations, he had no need of his mother's money. So, if he wasn't hurting for money, then this was personal. I didn't like the thought of that. Money you could run out of. Hate just went on and on.

The thought of this job going up in smoke was just more than I could bear to think about. I stopped the CD machine at my carrel and tidied up my notes, tossing my notebook into my backpack. I told Paul I was going to take a long lunch, thinking that a walk by the river might clear my head enough to get back to the big picture that was fuzzily just out of reach. Paul nodded, busy with his binding tools.

"If Dr. F comes in, what should I tell her?"

"Tell her I'll be back around two. I'll be in the library after lunch looking for a book on the blues." I shrugged into my hoodie and hauled my backpack over my head and onto both shoulders. The right shoulder I'd cramped up when I'd been caught out by Finster was still hurting.

As usual, it was about ten degrees warmer outside than in the

Fine Arts Building. I held my face up to the sun like a starved flower. There was something so unsettling about the sort of vitriol Finster was filled with, even if it wasn't directly at me personally. I knew that, if Finster had known my actual purpose there, I'd have been flayed alive with his snide commentary. Damn. Why did he and his snooty sister have to come around and ruin what was looking like the best job I'd ever managed to land? I headed toward a bench in the Arts Court where I liked to eat lunch, wishing the world wasn't burdened with the presence of David Finster.

Man, I really should learn to be careful about what I wish for.

4

After finishing my lunch, I cut through the Earth Sciences parking lot and headed west on Saskatchewan Drive and on down the hill, wandering past the statue of Emily Murphy, one of the Famous Five who petitioned for the vote for women, and I smiled at the kids rolling down the gentle hillside of well-tended lawn.

The Edmonton river valley, designed by Olmstead, the same fellow who was responsible for Central Park and Boston's Ribbon of Green, consists of a continuous set of parks running through the entire city. Bike trails, walking trails and cross-country ski trails connect one park with another, and in several places, footbridges span the North Saskatchewan River.

I decided to stay on the south side of said river and head east along the riverbank. I could come up to the university near Kinsmen Park, past the LRT bridge, and return to campus back along Saskatchewan Drive. It would make a good loop, and I could clear my head. I conscientiously tightened my glutes and made little circles with my wrists as I walked, trying to get all the usefulness I could out of my exercise. Sitting for a living was a dangerous thing. Given that we humans are basically a bunch of water and gel in interestingly shaped Baggies, sedentary lifestyles tend to make the innards spread ever downward into an indeterminate blob. I was opposed to that happening on aesthetic principles, and tried in whatever way I could to reverse the pull of gravity.

Gravity was certainly doing its best to best me as I huffed my way up the steep incline and stairs near the south end of the High Level Bridge. It would be nice to get into the controlled climate of Rutherford Library after this. The sun and exercise had pushed my normally chilly metabolism into a bit of a sweat, so I figured my exercise had done its bit. I stood at the top of the stairs, in the rounded turnaround bit of Saskatchewan Drive, and took several deep breaths, with my hands on my hips. I really did need a regular exercise schedule: I was too young to be winded, or at least too vain.

I walked a bit slower past the various university-owned houses along the Drive. The Human Ecology house looked chirpy and shiny, and the Western Board of Music house behind it had piano sonatas floating out a front window. Of course, there on the corner was The House, where I had held an office when I was employed by the English department. After getting my MA, I'd spent a couple of years as a sessional lecturer and really enjoyed the lecturing and connecting with all the diverse students, although one of the best of the lot had been grue-somely murdered. As a direct result of that, I'd spent some qual-ity time in the dark on the basement stairs of that House with a broken ankle. To be fair, the whole adventure had led to meeting Steve, but surely there are better ways to get a date.

I jogged across the street and down the darkened path by the Humanities Building. Two young women in turn-of-the-last-century clothing were playing croquet in front of Rutherford House, while another one was tending some herbs in pots. If my best pal Denise had been in town, we could have gone for lunch, to the lovely restaurant in the sunroom of the historic site. I was missing her a whole lot, but her research in Stratford was likely going to mean at least a book chapter, so I'd just have to suck it up. I turned left past the anachronistic croquet players and headed for the library.

I climbed the stairs in the atrium that bound Rutherford North to its older companion, Rutherford South, where I tried to never go on my own. Those closed-in little stacks are not where you want to find yourself with unfriendly types, as I had once learned. On the second floor of the newer building was the music library, and I figured that, even if Karen's blues book wasn't housed there, I might as well use the computer where people actually knew me. I looked into the corner office area for Carmen, the music librarian, but the plastic and metal gate was drawn across the counter. Maybe she was on lunch, or perhaps this was her day off. Between me being new to the crew and altered summer schedules, I still hadn't managed to gauge when to find people anywhere. All I knew for certain was that Paul

Calihoo would rather be working than practically anything else. I had even caught him in the Centre on his days off.

Carmen was nice to talk with, but at least her absence meant I wouldn't have to haul a box of CDs over to the Centre on my way back. I didn't mind pitching in, but I'd just as soon skip a chore here or there. I pulled a stool up to the computer and did a search of the listings for Karen Hanson's book. *Today's Chicago Blues* was indeed in the stacks, and I scribbled the call number and wandered off to find it.

I love the stacks of Rutherford North. There is something so absolutely right about a library, maybe because it's organized on the principles of everything being in a particular place. Rutherford has clean lines of brick and blond wood, and is hushed without feeling funereal. I had spent long hours in various carrels that were dotted along the outside, windowed walls when writing my thesis, and it made me feel young again, or at any rate, younger, as I walked down the long rows of shelved books.

Pretty soon I was out of the library and heading back to work through the walkway to HUB Mall and the connecting overpass to the Fine Arts Building from there. I stopped at Java Jive to buy coffee for myself, and almond cookies to share with Paul. I checked my watch as I moved back into the gloom of the Fine Arts Building. I'd been gone two hours. Not too bad.

Paul looked like he hadn't budged from his desk. He thanked me for the cookie and turned his attention back to his work. He was in the process of compiling a batch of Indian music for Dr. F to take to a conference, trying to find the best way of maintaining a consistency of sound levels between some pieces recorded in studio and others that were field-recorded using a Nagra reel-to-reel, and still others that had been recorded on cassettes. I backed away to leave him to it, and snuggled back into my corner of the Centre. My notes were as I left them, and it didn't take me long to get back into the mindset I'd left when Finster interrupted me that morning.

I turned to the back of the blues book and found a few of the names I'd been listening to. While I loved listening to the blues, I was never able to keep the players straight or truly understand the subject matter. I guess it's true that you can't have been to a) grad school, b) Disneyland and c) IKEA and sing the blues. I was just too much a child of privilege to really get it.

Bluegrass, Acadian, Celtic and country music in general were another thing altogether. Being a western Canadian of any pedigree at all meant that your grandparents or great-grandparents immigrated to Canada at a time when having entertainment meant providing it yourself, long after the chores were done. Fiddles, banjos, guitars and even a melodeon found their way into the wagons heading ever westward. Nova Scotia fiddle tunes were as familiar to me as nursery rhymes.

I was always fascinated with the collection of traditional music, tracing various songs from their earlier roots in the British Isles through to their cowboy and Appalachian counterparts. I didn't think there'd be any problem writing up the folk strains of Asch's collection. I was grateful, though, for any help I could get on the blues music there.

One of my ultimate duties was to create a through-line for the new concerts on the Folkways stage at the Folk Festival later in the summer. If I could create a playlist for some sort of entr'acte tape to play between sessions, we could publicize the collection and show the range and connections between the contemporary folks we'd be presenting and taping in workshop.

Trying to assimilate connections could be whatever you decide they should be, I was starting to think. Leadbelly's delivery of what now seem like classics wasn't even codified as "the blues" back when he began busking on the streets of Dallas with Blind Lemon Jefferson. So, should I keep Leadbelly with Mississippi John Hurt? Or line him up with the Delta Blues anthologies?

Eventually, I pushed myself back from my desk and pulled off my headphones. Though the room was kept chillier than most places on campus to help preserve the recording tapes, I could feel my ears sweating slightly from being encased in the puffy leather earpieces. I pushed escaping tendrils of hair back from my face and checked my watch. I'd been sitting hunched over the blues book for nearly three hours. It was time to pack things up and head home.

Paul's desk looked as if he was still around, since he usually cleared away everything but the phone and pen holders each evening. He told me he liked to arrive every morning to a new canvas, and I knew what he meant. I shelved the Leadbelly CDs on the wall behind me in their designated L alphabetical area and tidied up my notes and books along the top shelf of my carrel space. In such a cramped area, it didn't do to leave things untidy. My shelving practice was creating a CD formation for the newly burned copies of the collection, which could eventually be borrowed from the Centre. The original LPs would be stored in our new museum area in the old Arts building, as soon as the floors were determined strong enough to take the load of that much double vinyl.

That was an interesting thing about the Folkways Collection. Determined that his records were going to last, Asch had them pressed on double the accepted thickness of recording vinyl. As a result, the grooves were deeper and the sound was still amazingly clear. Even so, the vinyl records had been taken out of circulation, and were going to be stored as artifacts. CDs were burned of every record, and copies made of all the liner notes.

So, my evening tidies were in turn benefiting the Centre by collating and unpacking the boxes of newly burned CDs. Eventually they'd all be here and in active circulation, available to the interested student or alumnus. But they went through me first. You had to love a job like this.

5

I am in no way psychic, but it occurred to me that I might want to grill up the chicken breast in my fridge and slice it up into a salad of romaine and cress, just in case Steve managed to drop by. I knew he was on day duty through the week, but I wasn't too sure whether he was at the station or floating.

It was just as well I listen to the little voices sometimes, because I was folding laundered napkins and thinking about setting the table when Steve knocked and opened my apartment door.

"How many times have I told you to lock this door?" he asked as he shrugged out of his shoes. "Anyone could walk in here on you. This building has next to no security and there have been all sorts of break-ins around campus lately."

"No one ever comes in but you, Mr. Policeman, but I promise

to lock up more," I said, coming into the front room to kiss him. "You're just in time for chicken Caesar. Hungry?"

"Starving." Steve held me firmly, allowing me to lean back in his arms and look up into his face. It was something I didn't think I'd ever take for granted, having this wonderful man loving me. Of course, I probably would—people manage to take the most amazing things for granted, after all. People worked nine-to-five jobs smack dab in the middle of fantastically beautiful places like Vancouver and Hawaii; they assumed their partners would always be there in the same way Edmontonians knew there'd be potholes in the spring. The trouble with all that complacency was that, at some point, a person might not be able to reach out in the dark and find their someone. I knew I'd be tempted to take Steve for granted—after all, that was part of the delicious joy of certainty in one's life partner—but that I never should. Divorce statistics were enough to show me that.

I noticed one of Steve's eyebrows going up and realized I must have been staring. He started to grin and I felt myself blushing. The combination of his being a very good cop and my being a very lousy card player likely told him everything I'd just been thinking. As if he needed any more confirmation of how completely appealing he was to me. I pushed myself backwards from his chest, and motioned toward the dining area.

"It's all ready to eat. I was just about to set the table. Come on."

Steve carried the bowl of chicken and lettuce to the table, and I followed with a loaf of bread on the cutting board and the Caesar dressing. I'd plopped two ice cubes apiece into water glasses and set the margarine tub on the table already, causing Steve to raise his eyebrows one more time.

"Expecting someone?"

"I thought you might be dropping by. Call it woman's intuition."

"Call it sheer luck. I was almost out the door when a call came through about a body being found. I was sure I'd be called back, but when the captain called for Taylor and Georgas, I jumped for the car. That would be the last thing I need, just when the festival season is starting up."

"Why did you think you'd get called back? Was it a body on campus? Where on campus?"

Steve tucked one of the huge cloth napkins I'd snaffled at Value Village into the neck of his shirt.

"Randy, you know I'm not allowed to discuss police business. Let's just say it was close enough for me to worry and far away enough for you not to." While he sawed himself a piece of bread, I tried to think of another conversational gambit, which admittedly was rather difficult with a corpse hovering in my metaphorical peripheral vision.

"Are you still okay to have the time off for the Folk Festival?"

"Not exactly, but I will likely be able to set my hours strategically." Steve slathered margarine on the thick slice of bread with a flourish. "Mostly what I'll be doing is liaising with the security divisions of the Folk Fest to go over their contingency plans, determine how many officers they need to hire, and how many will be provided within the spectrum of keeping the city peace, that sort of thing."

He paused to wolf down some salad, and I popped up to get more water.

"Off-duty rosters are being set up in all the stations now so that officers can sign up to be available for festivals they themselves particularly enjoy. That way everyone wins." He looked at me with a wince of concern, the look he gets when having to admit something, like having broken the bathroom doorknob.

"I'll be on call, just in case. I doubt anything will happen though; it's usually such a calm bunch there, and besides, to boost my karma, I'll be supervising at the Works and the Street Performers' Festivals, and doing some crowd control at Heritage Days. Mmm, this is good."

I pushed the salad bowl at him, which he dug into without demur. That's what I like about feeding Steve. He just loves to eat, and accepts almost everything with good grace. His metabolism must run as high as his temperature, because he stays trim with only a couple of weight training sessions a week, and a run whenever he can fit it into his weekend. I, on the other hand, tend to be pretty lax about my attitude to both exercise and food. While I fluctuate between kicking my weight scale under my bed and obsessively weighing myself every morning, I hadn't been paying attention while ten pounds crept onto my already generous frame. So, I was in a bout of body-consciousness at the moment, which mostly exhibited itself as fretting over eating bread.

"Are you going to eat that or write an ode to it?" Steve pushed some more salad on to his fork with the remains of his bread. I scraped as little margarine as I could out to the edges of the crusts and fell on the sourdough with the sort of soft moans other people might reserve for sex. What the hell. I'd have to find some form of exercise. I wasn't going to do without bread.

We got back to the discussion once the salad was gone and we'd each had another two slices of bread. There were two or three festivals I'd never actually been to, and I was trying to figure out why. It seemed that the Cariwest Festival occurred on the same weekend as the Edmonton Folk Music Festival, so that explained that one, even though I adore steel drum music and the fabulous costumes that the krewes come up with in their parades. I had no excuse for not having attended the Dreamcatcher Aboriginal Festival, though, except that it happened right near the beginning of the school year, when I was always running behind, getting a syllabus organized for printing. I decided to make a point of attending this year, though, and popped up to my calendar to make a note of it.

"It's a nice festival, in Sir Winston Churchill Square, and now that the renovations down there are done you're not always tripping over power cords. The Street Performers Festival, too."

"Not that the Street Performers used a lot of power cords, though. I still hate thinking about how much that renovation cost; I couldn't care less if it was successful or not. Imagine using up all that money when the transit system needs it, or school buildings, or inner-city shelters or low-cost housing. Instead we have fancy electric plugs and a coffee shop on a sterile promontory. It delights not me," I added, really getting into the whole Shakespeare thing, and thinking to myself that the Freewill

Shakespeare Festival in the Park had just started, too. Now there was a festival I could really get behind.

I didn't really want the Churchill Square refit to fail. While I thought the city councillors myopic in their vision of city planning ventures, I actually hoped that things would work out for the best. You can't help it; if you live in Edmonton for a while, you develop a real sense of love for the city. There's something so "little engine that could" about it. Now, if only they could really make the LRT and transit system effective so that parking wasn't such a horrendous issue downtown, they'd have it all worked out. At least the present mayor didn't splash around town in a gas-guzzling SUV like a previous mayor, and I had spotted a couple of councillors riding the LRT.

After supper, Steve and I decided to go out for a stroll. Even though I always tried my best to angle the blinds to avoid the hottest part of the day, my apartment wasn't the coolest place to be on one of the hottest days so far, and Steve had a slight sheen of sweat on his forehead through dinner. Thank goodness I'd gone with salad. If I closed the southward kitchen window and left the east-facing living room window circles open, by the time I got ready for bed, it might be possible to sleep—on top of the coverlet. I never invested in an electric fan since I did have some cross-ventilation, and after all, it usually cooled down nicely every evening but about twelve a year.

This happened to be one of the twelve. While I was immune from it in the tree-laden river valley, the library and then the climate-controlled Centre all day, the temperature soared to nearly thirty degrees Centigrade. There was no way, barring a thunderstorm, that my apartment was going to be livable this evening for Steve. So much for vigorous exercise. I knew I shouldn't have had that last piece of bread.

Outside, we stood looking at the old red-brick Garneau School, faced with the decision of which direction to venture. Steve proposed a jaunt down Walterdale Hill, toward the Kinsmen Fieldhouse, but since I'd already been that way at midday, I opted for a walk southwestward toward the University Farm. A lot of it was getting covered in buildings, but there were still a couple of fields. Steve acquiesced, mostly because the residential communities we would walk through had lovely tree-lined streets, and life would be cooler in the shade. Sweating may be many healthy things, but it's never going to be romantic.

Steve and I were well matched as walking companions. Neither of us had to slow up stride to keep a good talk and stroll pace. Of course, when I sat down, I was much shorter-looking, but the inseam on our jeans was the same length. In fact, the waist measurement was, too. Theoretically, this is all to the good, in that I would have twice as many jeans to choose from should the need arise and our closets completely mesh. It didn't do much for my sense of well-being, though. I wanted to be sylph-like, and one cannot possibly consider one's self to be in the ballpark of naiad when one is able to share trousers with a cop. A really well-built cop with great legs and a gorgeous butt, but a cop nevertheless. I am betting Karen Kain never shared tights with Frank Augustyn, and when push came to shove, I wanted to be at least a size smaller than Steve in the denim department. It helped that his sweatshirts drowned me, but it wasn't quite enough.

I tightened my buttocks as we walked through McKernan, hoping this would somehow add to the burn. I doubted it would. It was too hot to try for a burn of anything, but perhaps the heat could create some sort of melt.

"There's what I managed to duck out of earlier." Steve pointed to some squad cars parked in a cluster in the Neil Crawford Building parking lot, kitty-corner from where we stood on the corner of Belgravia Road. "The body being found. I wouldn't be surprised if it was a kid asphyxiated in a car on a day like today."

"Would that be a criminal charge?" I asked.

"It would if it was a dog," Steve said with a tired shrug. "In fact, if it was a dog locked in a car, there would automatically be an enormous fine, possible jail time. People are more problematic. Remember the case where the guy forgot he was supposed to drop the baby at the daycare and left him in the car seat? Well, that was considered a tragedy and not criminal. No charges laid."

Steve and I crossed the intersection and were almost even with the parking lot by this time. From the looks of things, there was no suffocated infant in a minivan. Instead, the focus of activity seemed aimed at the entrance to the LRT tunnel. There was crime scene tape hung across, and a police officer standing in front of the entrance. A CBC minivan and the City-TV Hummer were parked nearby, and the Global van was arriving at the lot entrance in front of us as we meandered along the sidewalk north of all the action.

"You may be curious, but the minute we go even three steps nearer, you're going to get sucked into all this," I warned. Steve nodded, but just then his pager went off on his belt. He checked the top of it and hauled his cellphone out of his pants pocket.

"I think we might have to postpone our walk, Randy," he shrugged apologetically. "I have to call in, and what do you bet I'm going to be assigned over here?"

"Well, you could pop back in to the apartment when you come to pick up your car," I suggested. Steve nodded, but promised to check for lights on in the apartment before disturbing me. I waited with him while he dialled in. The body language said it all. As he listened to the voice on the other end, his whole torso swivelled to align itself with the entrance to the LRT hole in the ground. Even though the temperature was still just south of a blast furnace, I shivered. Something ugly was unfolding for the man I loved. I was just glad that this time it had nothing to do with me.

6

Steve didn't come back to my place, and I went to bed alone, which was just fine considering the relative humidity and heat in the apartment. Even I didn't sleep very well and called it quits on trying around five-thirty. I checked with the thermometer outside my dining room window; it already read twenty-five degrees. This heat wave wouldn't last; in fact, it would likely rain most of July. However, that didn't make it any less enervating. The worst thing about hot weather in Edmonton is that you feel incredibly ungrateful if you complain about it. So much of the year is spent bundled so that you have no exposed flesh to freeze within ten seconds, that when some hot weather comes—which you really aren't equipped to deal with—you feel as if you can't voice an opinion about it.

I had a shower, sluicing off the layers of sweat accrued during the night. Then I dressed in a pale yellow cotton blouse and white denim capris. My hair was already kinking up as I braided it back. To keep even the small amount of heat generated by the braid off my neck, I twisted it twice and anchored it onto the back of my head with a monster-sized clip. Moisturizer, eyeliner and mascara were all I ever managed in terms of makeup, and today it was an effort even to do that much. However, since it seemed possible that we'd be getting more visitors to the Centre than I'd at first accounted for, I had to make some concessions toward public appearances. There'd been a piece in the paper recently on dressing professionally, and although I didn't think it necessary to power-suit for this sort of research work, it didn't hurt to be as polished as possible.

I packed up a lunch and headed down the two blocks to the campus. The goal of climate-controlled surroundings was fabulously inviting as I could already feel the heat beginning to ramp up another scorcher of a day.

Since most of the houses between me and the campus were university owned or fraternity buildings, there wasn't all that much in the way of gardening on view, but I knew that a block or two over there would be older residents parcelling out precious drinks to plants before the main heat of the day evaporated it all. The birds were singing in the tallest branches of the trees. It was a great day to be alive, even if it was so bright I could hardly see.

It seemed a shame to waste the brilliance of the day hiding out from the heat entirely, so I decided not to cut through the Law Building but moseyed along beside it, toward the front entrance to the Fine Arts building. Everywhere, the core people of the campus were arriving. Up out of the LRT entrance, off

buses in the transit zone, out of cars in the parking lot east of
HUB, came the secretaries, lab techs, researchers, librarians,
custodians, grad students, professors, and service workers. The
university was a small city unto itself in many ways, completely
self-sustaining.

I decided to pop into HUB first to buy a Java Jive, since I figured Paul's coffee pot wouldn't be perking for another twenty
minutes at least. The curly-haired fellow who had been serving me coffee since I was a student smiled and poured fragrant
life-support into my travel mug. At the small tables nearby
were familiar faces, people I didn't know by name but nodded
to out of long-time familiarity. I walked back toward the Centre through the overpass. Somewhere in the building, someone
was already practising a violin piece. I let myself into the Centre
with my key, since Paul hadn't yet opened up. He was in already,
though, and looked up as I entered.

"Oh, Randy! I thought you were Dr. F. She called me at home
and told me to be in early today. You too?"

"Nope, I just figured it would be cooler here than in my
apartment. Did she say why she wanted you in early? I wonder
if she tried to get hold of me?"

My answering machine is sometimes temperamental, and
I hadn't checked my call display to see if anyone had tried to
call. Oh well, if she wanted me, I was here, and if not, I was
here anyway. I moved toward my carrel with the heavy-footed
pace of duty. By ten, I knew I'd be captivated once more in my
research, but at seven-thirty in the morning, it seemed like any
other form of yoke. That's where the crossword came in handy. I

picked up a pen, and went through the clues as I popped the lid off my coffee mug. Within ten minutes, I had seven clues filled in. Dr. Fuller came in just as I was giving up on it, nine-tenths of it complete. I wasn't going to come up with a seven-letter word for "take whatever is left" any time soon. I popped a CD of Pete Seeger singing Woody Guthrie songs, and soon I was humming along to the "what were their names" chorus of "The Sinking of the Reuben James." It seemed Dr. Fuller had no need to speak with me, and although she'd asked Paul to come in early, she still hadn't come back out of her office to speak with him. I looked over at Paul, who was checking out Dr. F's door, looking edgy. He'd been working with her long enough to get a sense of his boss's moods and you could almost see his antennae waving slowly, trying to get a bead on what was up.

He didn't have too long to wait. About twenty minutes later, Dr. F came out of her office, and checked her watch. She waved me to join Paul and her behind the counter, so I turned off the CD player and set my headphones down on the carrel desk. From the looks of it, this wasn't going to be good news.

"I'm glad you're here, Randy. I've got something to share with you both that I've just learned this morning. I think it will likely affect us and our daily work here for a few days, so you might adjust your schedules for that." She took a deep breath. "The police have been on the phone to me at home, and again just now. It seems that they came across a body yesterday on campus ..."

"In the LRT tunnel?" I broke in.

"That's right," Dr. Fuller said, her eyes widening a bit, questioningly.

"I was walking past there last night," I stumbled, feeling awkward for reasons I wasn't quite sure of.

"Well, the police have identified the victim as David Finster, the contractor for the project."

"Finster?" both Paul and I croaked. It was the last name I'd expected her to say. It felt so bizarre to think that someone I'd spoken to just the day before could be dead. Come to think of it, he'd been found dead the same day I'd been speaking to him. I shuddered, much as I had the night before when Steve was called away to the investigation.

"It was murder, wasn't it?" I asked. No one would have called Steve back on duty for a construction accident. "Steve was called in last night," I tried to explain, seeing that Paul and Dr. F were looking at me the way people check out two-headed calves. "He's a detective."

Dr. Fuller nodded. "It was murder. He was found in an alcove of the tunnel under Belgravia Road. He'd been stabbed and then hanged."

"What?" I was about to say that seemed like overkill to me, when the word "overkill" bounced out at me. That sort of thing has always happened to me. I find myself tossing phrases like "couldn't you just die?" and "I could murder a piece of pie" to folks who'd just had a death in the family. With the way Paul's lips were losing colour the more we discussed this, I didn't think I should push it. He obviously wasn't one of those folks who have been inured to death by reading murder mysteries or constant exposure to various permutations of CSI on television.

Dr. Fuller noticed Paul's colouring, or lack thereof, at the same time and offered him a mint from her pocket, putting a hand on his shoulder. I sat, too. I wasn't quite sure what to do. It's not as if there's much etiquette written on how to deal with speaking about people who've just died and with whom you were irritated just the previous day. About the only thing I could come up with was the adage of not to speak ill of the dead, but how was one supposed to think of the dead, especially the ones we'd been thinking plenty ill of so recently?

Well, at least Finster wouldn't be around to cause me trouble with my job. With any luck, his sister would be less inclined to fight the bequest now that she didn't have a partner in her quixotic quest. Dr. F was pouring us all coffee, and Paul's colour was returning to normal. My own heartbeat was calming, too.

"The police called me because my name and number was in his datebook for yesterday. I expected a visit from Mr. Finster yesterday afternoon, but he didn't show up," Dr. F was musing. "I wonder now what it was he wanted."

"He showed up yesterday morning, but I was the only one around. I told him to check back later." I looked at the others. "I'm sorry, I forgot to mention it, Dr. Fuller. Paul caught the tail end of him leaving in a huff."

"What did he want?"

"Mostly he was going out of his way to be nasty. He said some ugly things about his mother giving his room to musicians and then became threatening in an ambiguous sort of way. I got the feeling he wasn't all that enamoured of the Centre or the Folkways Collection, but I guess that was no secret, eh?"

Dr. Fuller sighed. "No, I guess it wasn't. Well, we must have got our wires crossed, because I was sure we were to meet here at one, but he didn't show up. To tell you the truth, I was relieved that he broke the appointment, since I hadn't been looking forward to another session of bombast. I just assumed he'd call and reschedule." She turned to Paul. "He didn't call yesterday, did he?"

"I haven't checked the voice mail yet this morning," Paul replied. "I was in the mixing booth most of the afternoon, so I just left from there. Randy?"

"Well, I got back from the library around two, and there was no one here. I think I went home around four forty-five. Of course, I had headphones on most of the time, so I'm not sure I'd have heard anything anyhow."

"Who knows what the police officers will require when they come to talk with us? Perhaps we should leave the voice mail for them to listen to, if there is any?"

"Police officers? What police officers?" I was asking, but even as my voice rose, the door to the Centre opened and in walked Steve with Detective Iain McCorquodale behind him. I might have known they'd be coming, but for some reason it hadn't computed. David Finster was dead, and the police were going to have to question his movements of the last few days along with people who might have had a grudge against him.

And here I was, one of the people who saw him alive on his last day, one of the people who had the most to lose if he lived and would be better off because of his death, one of the last people who had been personally irritated by his presence. What were the odds?

2

It was a strange way to conduct an interview, I guess, what with me introducing people, and showing Steve and Iain McCorquodale around my new area of employment after they spent time interviewing Dr. F and Paul. There was a sort of theatre of the absurd sensibility to it, as if Ionesco had penned the questions and answers.

"So, this is where you work, is it? Do you leave your laptop here, or does the Centre provide a computer?" Steve was looking at the books lined up across the top of my carrel, while his counterpart was discussing the organization of the Centre's hours and who held keys. While Steve was doing the talking, I wasn't sure whether this was an official interview. On the whole, I hoped it wasn't. The last thing I wanted to do was get in the midst of one of Steve's investigations. His boss was pretty snarky whenever that happened, as it had a bit too often for comfort.

However, I noticed Iain taking surreptitious notes, so I wasn't overly optimistic.

"Well, this is where I work, when I'm not at the library or trundling things between here and the new Collection site over in the old Arts Building. I normally take my laptop home with me, unless I have too much to carry, in which case I lock it up in here." I showed them the large drawer where I kept files, mostly of reprints of liner notes and posters, reviews of albums and online biographies I'd printed off. "I usually put my headphones in there, too, and that's where I keep my backpack during the day. The key's on the same lanyard I keep the Centre key on." I pulled on the cord with "U of A" woven along it in gold against green.

"And what time were you here yesterday?" Steve had his notepad out of his pocket, too, so I guess this was now an official conversation.

"I got here about eight forty-five, and David Finster popped in about ten, I guess. I worked some more, then I went off to lunch around eleven forty-five. I ate lunch and went for a walk before I went to Rutherford Library. I got back here around two. Then I worked some more till about four forty-five, and then I went home. You came by around six and we ate."

"Right. Okay, so you saw Finster here around ten in the morning, but Dr. Fuller says that she expected to see him around one. Now, we can't say for sure that she was here to meet him then, because you were in the library and Paul was in the ... the," he checked his notes, "the recording studio mixing a collection of Indian folk tunes for Dr. Fuller to take to a conference next week. No one saw Finster with you, because Dr. Fuller wasn't yet in, thinking she didn't have to be here till the afternoon, and Paul was where? Oh, yes, he was in the back room collating handouts for Dr. Fuller's conference talk. So, you were all alone with the victim for about half an hour?"

"I doubt it was even that long. He came in expecting to meet up with Dr. Fuller and ended up finding just me. He was annoyed and took it out on me, I think. On the whole, though, I doubt he was a very nice man at any time."

"What makes you say that?"

"Well, he had anger lines on his face."

"Anger lines?"

"You know, the sort of wrinkles that cut up from the bridge of your nose, right between your eyebrows? Two small ones means you squint. Either you live someplace really bright and don't have good sunglasses, or you needed glasses in high school but were too vain to wear them to see the board. If they're deep cuts, or if there's even just one big line shooting directly up from your nose, then you make it a habit to glare at people. That's why they're anger lines."

"And Finster had them?"

"Very deep and very pronounced. Not only that, but he was using them on me big time. The thing is, I wasn't sure if he knew that I was the person contracted to work from the bequest money or not, but he sure had an axe to grind about folk music."

"Well, folk music returned the compliment," Iain chuckled wryly.

"What do you mean?"

"This isn't for public knowledge, of course," Steve's partner tapped the side of his nose in a manner I'd only seen in gangster and con artist movies, "but Finster's body was deliberately staged. He'd been stabbed, strung up from a beam, and a note was hanging from the handle of the knife still sticking into him. It said, HANG DOWN YOUR HEAD."

"Tom Dooley."

"That's the first thing that I thought of, as well," said Steve quietly.

"Yuck. Well, Tom Dooley was tried and hanged for murder. He's the one who 'stabbed her with my knife,'" I said.

"Stabbed who?" Iain looked interested.

"Poor little Laurie Foster."

"Well, this time it was poor little Davey Finster." Steve sounded really troubled, and looked meaningfully at Iain. "Damn, Randy, I wish you weren't involved in this."

"Am I?" I was hoping I wasn't. Being involved with murders is no picnic for me, and it wasn't ever going to be something that grew on me.

"Oh, yeah, I don't think anyone involved in LRT construction has much reason to make references to Kingston Trio music."

"It's a Civil War-era song, popular long before the Kingston Trio. I have a great version by Doc Watson at home."

"You know what I mean," Steve sighed. He wasn't looking forward to Staff Sergeant Keller's commentary either, I was betting. "Look, I have to get Dr. Fuller to come down to sign a statement. You'd better go with her, and sign one yourself. I am not sure when I'll get off tonight. Keller wants this priority one. Finster is as well-known a name as Muttart and Winspear around here. We can't have our top citizens bumped off. So, I'll call you later, but don't wait up for me, okay?"

I didn't expect a kiss, and didn't get one, but it felt odd to see Steve heading away from me without physical contact and acknowledgement. Damn, there were times when I hated his job. Or mine. Or at least the ways they intersected. No wonder Jessica Fletcher never dated, although whenever I caught a rerun, I couldn't help wondering how she could maintain a professional distance from Jerry Orbach. Or maybe that was just me.

8

D r. Fuller and I followed Detective McCorquodale down to the
south side station in her car. I was relieved that she requested
this arrangement, since there is very little I enjoy less than riding
in a police car. You always have to ride in the back, which has
a slight scent of vomit lacing a heavy smell of disinfectant. The
few times I've ridden in a squad car, I ended up washing all the
clothes I was wearing in hot water.

We were seated in the back of the room next to Iain's desk,
reading over and signing our statements when Staff Sergeant
Keller strode in. Honestly, adjectives haven't been created for
what that man does instead of walking, entering or looking at
people. He was larger than life, and used that stature to every
speck of its intimidating value. I'm sure it worked well on hard-
ened criminals, because it made me long for Imodium, and I
usually hadn't done anything wrong. I just hoped that if Steve

and I ever got married, Keller wouldn't be in the wedding party. I had the feeling, though, he might volunteer to give the bride away. Far away.

I suppose I couldn't really blame him. It did seem that the only times he saw me there was trouble happening. Of course, being a police officer, he could likely say that about a lot of people. Come to think of it, the same held true for me seeing him, and I wasn't holding a grudge, whereas one could just look at the anger lines on Keller. I made a mental note to mention Keller's facial grooves to Steve the next time we were talking privately, as prime examples of what I'd been talking about.

"Ah, Ms. Craig." Keller's voice dripped with sarcasm. "How nice to see you again."

I found myself introducing Dr. Fuller to Keller, and explaining a bit of why we were there. Keller held up his hands to stop the imaginary flow.

"I'll read about it in your statements and the officers' reports later, I'm sure. For now, don't let me keep you." He moved on out of the room, and the air got perceptibly lighter.

When we were finished, I led Dr. Fuller out of the warren of halls to the parking lot. She looked across the street to the Swiss Chalet and asked if I was hungry. I looked at my watch. It was past one and I hadn't eaten since seven. Just the mention of food made my stomach gurgle loudly. Dr. F laughed and said, "I'll take that as a yes. Why don't we head across the street? I wouldn't mind talking a bit more about all of this while it's fresh in our minds. Perhaps we can help each other understand what this means, and means to us in particular."

Pretty soon we were ensconced in a booth, eating salads, our orders for the quarter-chicken dinner taken and the efficient waitress on her way. I have to admit a fondness for standardized restaurant chains like Swiss Chalet and Smitty's and Japanese Village. No matter where you go, you know what you'll get on the menu, and you always get what you want.

"Did you ever meet Lillian Finster?" Dr. F asked me.

"No, I wasn't really clear on who she was. Paul told me he'd seen her at various functions, but I doubt I'd be able to point her out in a picture of famous Edmontonians."

Dr. F laughed. "Famous Edmontonians. There used to be a section of the newspaper that would report on that, with photos of people at events. They were mostly people whom very few Edmontonians knew or saw, who somehow formed their own group. It always made me laugh a bit to see the names dropped by that fellow in his column as if we should all be so impressed that he ran a race with this magnate or cooked chili with that tycoon. Now I'm not saying there aren't quite a few wealthy people in this city and even more interesting intellectuals. I think the problem was that he thought he was writing a column for *Majesty* or *Entertainment Weekly*, and it actually read like an old-fashioned town paper that documents great social events like, 'Mrs. Mabel Harris is visiting her sister-in-law Mrs. Minnie McCord this week, all the way from Ladner, BC.' For all its big-city elements, in many ways Edmonton still has a small-town feel. And that's not such a bad thing, in my opinion."

"Well, I can see what you mean about the provincialism, but there had to be a certain amount of international flavour to the music scene for Moses Asch to decide to leave his personal collection to the university, right?"

Dr. F smiled at me, and I wondered if my own provincialism was showing. Sometimes, her grace in the face of lesser mortals was incredibly obvious; most of the time, however, she was so gracious that we lesser mortals never were aware of how much she put up with.

"I think yes, there is a greatness to the music scene here that's aided by the isolation of the city from all the other centres. To have classical music, we needed to provide a symphony ourselves, and an opera company, and a jazz festival, and a folk music festival, and blues and alternative rock. When all those forms of music are built from the ground up, rather than imposed from outside, then there is something vital about the place that grows them. That, I think, is what Moses Asch found when he came here to visit his son. Have you ever met Michael?"

I shook my head.

"Michael Asch was a marvellous lecturer in the Anthropology department and a wonderful colleague. His retirement is something I really regret. Of course, with the Centre and all my travelling lately, I haven't spent much time in the department either, but I do miss him." Dr. Fuller pushed a fry across her plate with her fork. "But it was terrific fun when Michael's parents came to town. He would throw these enormous dinner parties for everyone, and it would always end up with Moe holding court, telling stories about recording various people, about concerts they'd sponsored. His eyes twinkled, you know. I am afraid I have always been vulnerable to twinkling eyes."

I thought of Steve's eyes and blushed. Thank goodness at that moment Dr. F seemed more interested in her chicken than my complexion.

"It was wonderful to receive the collection. I think with it, though, comes an obligation, to continue Moe's vision. The Smithsonian is doing its best to keep the music in circulation, which was part of it. Moe didn't want the music archived; he wanted it flowing out there. That's not our job, of course. For one thing, we don't hold the copyright. But there are a couple of things we can do to help keep Moe's dream alive."

She pushed aside her plate, and leaned her chin on her hands.

"We can cross-reference, and organize the material so researchers and ethnomusicologists of all stripes can use the collection as a resource that no one else could have ever imagined. The other thing we can do is to keep the collection growing. That's the really exciting thing, I believe. We can keep the Folkways Collection alive by doing what Moe Asch did. We can record the performers who collect music, who make the connections between various forms of world music and add them to the pool. That's what makes the collaboration between the Folk Festival and the Centre so exciting, and also what makes this infusion of money to the Centre so wonderful. I will admit to you, Randy, that seeing David Finster and his sister the other day just made my stomach turn. I hope the university president is correct when he says the lawyers have gone over the bequest papers with magnifying glasses and that it's ironclad, because to have all of this dream suddenly possible and then to have it taken away because of pique and resentment is something I am not sure I can bear."

That's what it would be, too, I thought. There was no way Barbara or David Finster needed the money. They not only had settlements from their father, but, as Dr. F painted it, they were both well off in their own rights. David had his construction company, and Barbara owned a set of exclusive boutiques in Edmonton and Calgary catering to women who wore designer labels aimed at the older sophisticate. Dr. F had once been served tea in the changing room at one of the Barbara Shoppes. I wasn't sure how a store could survive on catering that exclusively to the wealthy women in the area, but perhaps Dr. F was right, and there were lots of rich people out there that we hoi polloi didn't even know existed. There must be, or else the Shoppes wouldn't still be in existence, let alone flourishing.

So, since they didn't need the money their mother left to the Centre, it stood to reason they just didn't want the Centre to have money. It was hard to imagine people having something against "Kumbayah," but who knew what evil lurked in the hearts of men, anyhow, besides The Shadow?

Dr. F was mulling over the bill, and waved me away when I reached for my purse. Since she likely made twice what I ever would, I didn't feel too guilty. We headed out to the parking lot, edging past the window boxes of geraniums that were the restaurant's signature. Dr. F dropped me in front of my apartment, insisting that it was pointless to head back into the Centre for just an hour and a half. I didn't object guiltily to that either. Perhaps it was residual shock, but I was feeling just wiped.

I barely managed to get into my apartment and drop the keys before I sank down onto the chesterfield and closed my eyes.

So much had happened in the last, hot, enervating twenty-four hours. I'd been verbally attacked by someone who turned up murdered a few hours later. My boss and I had spent the afternoon at the police station filing statements. I'd had to see Steve's boss, and I was running the risk of being involved in Steve's work once again. I've found myself in danger in the past, being the target of a murderer in a couple of cases and used as bait in another. It wasn't something I cherished repeating.

Suddenly, I sat straight up on the couch, like a corpse in a horror movie. It finally sank in: this afternoon wasn't an exercise in helping the police with their appointed rounds, as in the other situations. I had just filed a statement at the police station because there was every likelihood they were thinking of me as a suspect.

9

Steve phoned me around nine that night to say hi, but there was no discussion of him coming over, or even any idea of when he might have some time off to see me in the next few days. I sketched out my work schedule for him, just in case, but I could feel an edge to things as we were talking. After he rang off, I stood with my hand on the telephone, wondering. Was I already on someone's list of suspects? Was Steve doubting me?

I went to bed with a biography of Allen Ginsberg, but couldn't concentrate enough for it to be worthwhile. Maybe it was the continued heat or the heavy horror of thinking about David Finster's ugly and violent death, but a headache was settling in my temples and my sinuses. I got up in the dark, grabbed a clean washcloth from the shelf above my toilet, ran cold water onto it, wrung it out and took it back to bed with me. I lay there, with only the cotton sheet covering me, and spread the washcloth over my face. It reminded me of when I was young, trying to sleep and thinking of my bed as a pocket on the side of the globe.

Once I learned about the way the planet worked, I always needed my bed to be aligned from north to south, with my head at the north. I would make sure my quilts were tucked in securely, and then I would lie there, snug in my pocket, like the card in the back of an old library book, put away for the night. In this bedroom, the only way the bed could sit was east to west, but I hadn't outgrown the pocket principle.

Well, it was too hot for a quilt tonight. In fact, it was too hot for even a sheet, but for security reasons, I always needed some form of coverlet. As I lay trying to will my headache away, I listened to thunder and felt the lightning more than saw it as it lit up the room through my blind and my washcloth. I waited for the pounding rain to follow, but it was a dry storm, and that likely meant there'd be an even hotter day tomorrow. Oh, goody.

I must have slept, eventually because I woke to my alarm clock at six-thirty feeling only minimally refreshed. My bangs, however, were sticking straight up like those little eavestroughs that teenaged boys like to affect with hair gel. I showered away the sophomoric hairdo and let tepid water sluice over me until I felt moderately awake. I had a feeling this was going to be a day in which I'd need all my wits, but I wasn't sure they were all going to be in working order.

Once dried, braided, and breakfasted, I tried to find some sort of useful armour in my closet, but the closest thing I found was a blue-striped jersey sundress and a white cotton cardigan. I would need the sweater once I was in the Centre, even if it seemed impossible to consider someplace cool at present. I smeared sunblock on my legs and face to protect against a sun that was getting progressively more brutal with every passing summer, and after a quick pickup and clean, I grabbed my pack and my water bottle and headed off to work.

The water was a good idea. I had already consumed half the bottle by the time I'd gone two blocks and hit the corner of 111th Street and 87th Avenue, where the Telus Centre pushed out its albatross glass angles at the world. It was going to be a scorcher. There had been talk on the news of potential tornadoes, but I wasn't overly concerned. An enormous tornado in 1987 had killed and destroyed, and a few other twisters in outlying areas also wreaked disaster, but on the whole we Edmontonians didn't think of ourselves as living in a tornado zone. The whole climate of the world was changing, but it takes a while for us to catch up, I guess. People in England still think they live in a temperate climate regardless of the inches of snow they receive and winter storms they suffer.

I took another swig from my nearly depleted water bottle and headed into the much cooler building, thankful I had my cardigan. I refilled the water bottle at the first electrically cooled drinking fountain, and then made my way around the maze of hallways to the doorway to the Centre. I pulled my key lanyard out of the side pocket of my backpack and opened the door. The lights were already on, so I figured Paul had once again beat me in to work. I couldn't see him behind the counter, though.

"Hello?" I called. It's funny how something like murder can screw with your sense of general well-being. Last week I stayed here in this room until ten one evening, working alone with no fear whatsoever. Now, at eight in the morning, I was nervous because the lights were on. It was with great relief that I heard Paul answering me from the back room. I removed my foot from the doorway and let it close behind me.

Paul had the coffee going, which smelled divine. I set my pack down by my carrel, and my water bottle on the coaster on the bookcase next to the desk. I went back of the counter to kibitz with Paul a bit and pour a cup of coffee.

"I had to head down to sign a statement after Dr. F came back to spell me off," Paul explained. "What a weird process, eh? I've never had to do that before." I thought of all the various statements that I, the most law-abiding citizen I know, have signed over the years, and mentally shook my head in disbelief. "It wasn't much like the movies, though. I was expecting all sorts of guys with shoulder holsters typing with two fingers, you know? It's pretty high-tech there, streamlined."

I wondered what Keller would think of his station being referred to as high-tech. He'd likely be pleased, in that it would strike him as an intimidating thing. Paradoxically, the level of computer efficiency had likely calmed Paul down considerably. It's all in what you're used to, I guess.

I headed back to my little corner of the ethnomusicology world and unlocked my drawer. I pulled out my laptop and its power cord and set it on the table area of my carrel. It didn't take long to go through the initializing, and pretty soon I could download my campus e-mail. I pulled out the crossword from my pack and was filling in "eighty" for "A score less than one hundred" as I waited. As soon as I could get into my word-processing program, I turned on the CD player sitting on the high carrel shelf, and flicked open the CD tray. I pulled out Dave Van Ronk's *Ballads, Blues and a Spiritual*. I have always loved Van Ronk's voice, a sort of gravelly thrumble. I maintain that Tom Waits would be nowhere without Van Ronk to carve the pathway for him. Of course, that could also be true for Rod Stewart and Kim Carnes, who I had long suspected were the same person (of course, once I heard Bonnie Tyler, I realized they were both her). Van Ronk was more melodious on his Folkways recordings than on, say, his renditions of Bertolt Brecht and Kurt Weil songs. There was a decided edge to all his work, though. Irony seeped through his lyrics and styling just as anger swept through Woody Guthrie's phrasing and righteousness through Pete Seeger's verses. Folk music was a breeding ground for revolution, not that anyone seemed to be listening anymore.

I thumbed my way through my copy of *The Whole Folkways Catalogue* issued by the Smithsonian Folkways people in Washington. There was a lot of protest and political flavour to the collection, even down to the choices of what sound effects were recorded. Of course, there were also recordings of the *International Morse Code, The Birds World of Song, Sounds of the Camp, Sounds of the Carnival, Sounds of the Junkyard* and *Sounds of the Office*. I wondered who made those specific choices of commemoration on vinyl. Was it Moe Asch? What exactly was being inscribed for future generations? The sounds of where we got it right as a civilization, or possibly the turning points of where we began to go so terribly wrong?

Pete Seeger's contribution to the collection was immeasur-
able. Of course, if you rounded up all the Seegers and their
friends and relations, you'd likely have over half the entire collection. I wondered what it would be like to actually meet Pete
Seeger. It occurred to me he might be tired of acolytes.

Van Ronk wrote his own liner notes for the songs on *Dave
Van Ronk Sings* and I followed along as I listened, checking to
see if there were any crossover songs I could use to highlight the
essay I was considering about influences within the collection. I
noticed that Lawrence Block had written a parody of an old folk
tune. He was now, of course, more famous for his various mystery series set in New York—I was partial to the Scudder and
Burglar series, myself. Fancy a mystery writer being interested
in folk music. It took all sorts, I guess.

It was almost nine-thirty by the time I looked up again. My
water bottle was empty again and the CD had finished. I had
two pages of notes with ideas for creating a connecting page on
the website for Folkways artists who appeared at the Edmonton Folk Music Festival in the past, with some of their music
available for sampling. Then we could add in the musicians to
be featured and recorded on the Folkways Stage at this year's
Festival. I knew Van Ronk had been here, as had Peggy Seeger.
Sonny Terry and Brownie McGee also played the Festival, along
with Ramblin' Jack Elliott and Doc Watson. There was a link
that people from around here might find interesting, the sort
of thing that I knew Dr. F was wanting. Of course, there might
be people I was missing. I made a note to contact the Folk

Festival office to see if I could take a look at their archives to cross-reference.

In order to avoid the embarrassing knee lock of a couple of days ago, I'd made a vow to stretch hourly. In accordance with that, I got up to refill my water bottle. Paul was hunkered over a magazine of some sort at the counter, while Dr. F was working in her office beyond, with the door ajar, and two strangers whom I took to be students were in the Centre. One was looking through a catalogue at the centre table while the other examined the instruments displayed in glass cases along the main wall near the entrance. I sighed, and leaned over to close down my laptop. I'd have to lock it away in my drawer if I was going to move away from my workstation. While neither of these strangers looked particularly untrustworthy, you could not be too vigilant when it came to your laptop. One unguarded minute could mean two months of research and two thousand dollars of equipment gone. After setting my notebook on top of the laptop, I closed the drawer and gave it a quick tug to make sure the lock was holding.

Since I went to all that work just for a bottle of water, I figured I might as well stretch my legs a bit and head into the mall for a snack, too. Not even ten yet, and I could see the exhaust from the buses waiting in the transit lane curling and shimmering across the street. I was thankful for the air-conditioning I normally pooh-poohed as being too chilly.

But it was hot in HUB, likely because there was no way you could keep a four-block, glass-covered street air-conditioned. I could hear fans whirring in the upper-level apartments as I walked along. I moved past Java Jive to the bakery and bought a butter tart, which I justified as being indigenous to the area, even if it was outside my caloric needs. I wondered if there was a song about butter tarts. The southerners knew how to celebrate their "Shortenin' Bread" and "Jambalaya," but as far as I could think, only Bill Bourne had immortalized "Saskatoon Pie" and I couldn't think of any song extolling the pleasures of bannock, pemmican, Nanaimo bars, butter tarts or fiddlehead greens.

Bill Bourne was someone I hoped the Centre would decide to record. A native Albertan, he had toured with the Tannahill Weavers before settling into a solo and occasional duo career. His was a voice born for the blues, but that wasn't his sole interest. He covered the gamut in terms of musical styles and his eclectic interests in music were eclipsed only by his talent for different styles. I saw him in a coffee shop concert once, claiming that he was just picking up the fiddle and begging us to forgive his efforts. Then he proceeded to play three lovely reels, accompanying himself while he sang one of his own songs. If that was an example of Bourne's learning curve, I figured he could play anything within a week.

I moseyed back down to the Centre, drinking a quarter of my water on the way. I stopped to refill the bottle before heading back into my carrel. I didn't want to have to lock everything back up just for another refill right away. I was wiping the moisture off the bottom of the bottle with a gathered bit of my skirt as I pushed the door open with my back, so I didn't see who was in the room at first. As I turned to release the door, I looked up to find Steve and Iain standing at the counter, looking straight at me. For a moment I froze, and then, realizing my sundress was hitched up, I dropped my hands to my side, almost spilling my water bottle in the process. I swear, I am getting more graceful every day. They'll be reopening the Miss Edmonton contest before you know it, just to honour me.

Iain looked down at his shiny shoes, likely to hide a grin. Steve didn't bother to hide his amusement.

"Hey, Randy," he drawled, "got your own portable waterpark? Not a bad way to counter the heat."

"Hey yourself," I responded. "What are you boys doing back here so soon? Did you realize this is the only place in town with appropriate air conditioning?"

"It's not bad at that," Steve nodded. "I'm assuming it's set this low for the tapes and LPs? How the heck do you stand it?" I pointed to my chair, on which were layered about four different sweatshirts and cardigans. Steve laughed. "Actually, we were wondering if we could drag you away for a little while to aid us in our investigation."

"Aid us in our investigation" was a euphemism for "we just don't have enough evidence to arrest you outright yet"; any dedicated fan of police shows knew that. That interpretation must have flashed across my face, because Steve laughed again.

"Randy, you are not about to be thrown in the hoosegow, I promise. We just need you to help us out a bit in terms of day-to-day time frames for everyone on this end of things."

Paul appeared out of the back area just then.

"If you want," he said, "you can stay here, and we can close the Centre for lunch early. Dr. Fuller has gone out to meet with a graduate student over in the Tory Building and I have to hit the music library before lunch, so you'll have privacy."

I smiled at Paul, silently thanking him for letting me avoid the oppressive heat out there beyond the Centre's hermetically sealed door. Steve and Iain seemed to sense the positive aspects of this arrangement, too, because they readily agreed. Paul offered them coffee before he left, closing and locking the Centre's door behind him. Iain took him up on it, but Steve shook his head.

"How can you drink anything hot on a day like today?" he asked his partner.

Iain shrugged. "It's the same thing as drinking tea in India or the Middle East. You produce a layer of sweat, which cools you; additionally, your innards are at the same temperature as the air around you, rather than at such a different level. It makes it easier to move around and besides, I'm used to it. Myra has a pot of coffee or tea going at all times at home."

"I'll take your word for it," Steve countered. Each of them pulled up a chair at the central table, and Steve indicated I should sit there as well. I was relieved that neither pulled out a notebook right off, or I'd have felt my work sanctum turn into an interrogation room.

"This is about the Finster murder, as you probably figured out," Steve began. "We have two or three lines we're pursuing, but we can't ignore the Folkways connection, especially as there was the purported meeting with Dr. Fuller planned and the impromptu meeting with you that you detailed in your statement on the day he was murdered. So, we'd like each of you to give us as much background as you can on the Centre, and the connections you can see between Finster, his sister, his mother and the bequest that she made to the Centre."

"You really think that Finster's death has something to do with the Centre?"

"Well, I'd be a lot happier if he hadn't been discovered with a reference to Tom Dooley tacked onto his body," Steve said.

"I looked it up," Iain added, "and the story is actually about a fellow called Tom Dula who sounds like a real asshole. He was having affairs with two separate women when this Laurie Foster is supposed to have come and told him she was pregnant. She was a third girl, a mountain girl with no money or name. So he kills her, possibly with the help of one of his lovers, and is tried for it. All this happens during the Civil War, while other men are out getting killed for their country. He gets hanged for the crime, and then ends up immortalized for it."

"That is just one version, Iain. Other historians say that Dula, a Civil War hero, came home to find the love of his life had married someone else and not waited for him. However, the former girlfriend became terribly jealous when Tom took up with young Laurie and killed her, leaving Tom to swing for her crime, which he did because of his undying love for her. Some say he had no idea Laurie was carrying his child."

"Are you sure they weren't glamorizing him for the sake of a good song?" Iain insisted.

"It's no worse than what they were doing in England in their early ballads," I countered. "After all, it's not until the rise of the middle classes that the law becomes a positive thing. Until the majority of folks actually have something they don't want stolen, it's the highwaymen and scoundrels sticking it to the Man who are the folk heroes. Think about it; Robin Hood, Jonathan Wild, Dick Turpin. What about 'The Highwayman'? How many girls saw themselves as Bess, the landlord's daughter, ready to warn her love, the highwayman? There was even a romantic drawing of her in my Childcraft poetry volume, as I recall. It's more than just falling for the Heathcliff bad boys of the world; it has to do with getting back at the overlords and sheriffs who made their lives miserable. I can imagine the Appalachian mountain folk, who would be suspicious of outsiders, would feel pretty much the same way about the circuit judge who came in to try one of their own, no matter what he'd done."

"That's a nice evaluation of the reasoning behind folk ballads, but how does it help us understand the motives behind killing David Finster? Have we checked to see if he was having an affair or three?" Iain made a note, presumably to check into Finster's love life, while Steve wiped his brow, even in this air-conditioned hideaway from the heat. "If anything, he was the overlord. He was worth millions, and from all accounts, he certainly didn't make himself loved by his workers. He blocked efforts at forming a union until it was impossible to resist; he never offered a yearly bonus; he offered the lowest range of benefits possible in the construction business."

It seemed to me an odd coincidence that he was working on the LRT stops that connected the university to the rest of the city at the same time as his mother was donating all her funds to the same university. Of course, he must have had bids in for the contracts long before she died. After all, building projects don't just happen overnight, even though the buildings themselves seem to get slapped up pretty quickly.

Nothing was making the LRT move quickly, though. I had read recently that, if the English-French Chunnel had been built at the same rate as the Edmonton LRT, it would have taken 184 years to cross under the Channel. I shook myself out of my reverie and tried to answer the questions.

I started with Dr. F, with whom I'm sure they could tell I was tremendously impressed. She had offices both here at the Centre and in the Department of Anthropology, and she was a world-renowned expert in Indian music. Her husband, a professor of mathematics, was also employed at the university. She had known both Moses Asch and Lillian Finster, but as far as I could tell, she wasn't personally the reason why either of them made their bequests to the Centre. I figured I might will the university money because of her, supposing I died with money. She was charismatic and highly persuasive, and I could certainly see how she managed to gather the music she did, charming every one she spoke with. I guessed that Edith Fowke and Mike Seeger and the other musicologists who went before must have all had that same talent, to engage the person who would be taped and make him or her feel like the most interesting human being in the world. The trick was to actually feel that way when talking to people, I supposed. Whatever it was, talking with Dr. F was an experience which often left one winded but always rather elated.

Paul Calihoo, whom Steve and Iain had spoken with yesterday at some length, and who just now had so tactfully left us in relative comfort, was a bit of an enigma to me. I knew he came from a long-time Edmonton family. In fact, there was a village of Calihoo, and a Calihoo Road, just west of the city. Paul's great grandmother was a folk musician who recorded various old-time Métis tunes from the area; Paul had been intrigued with the process and followed into this side of the music business when he finished his first degree in music. His instrument was classical guitar, and I knew he gave lessons in the evenings and on Saturdays. Aside from that, I didn't know that much about him. He was newly married, he lived somewhere on the south side, I think close to Bonnie Doon, and he made good coffee.

No one else came into the Centre regularly. People affected by the Folkways collection would probably include Carmen, the music librarian, and the two grad students assigned to the database. Of course, those people likely would manage to get by even if there wasn't a Folkways collection to deal with. When it came right down to it, so could Paul and Dr. F. The only person who was tied solely to the collection and to the bequest money was me.

I winced as this thought came clear to me. Both Steve and Iain saw that this bald fact had only just now occurred to me, and were quick to placate me.

"Don't worry, Randy, there are several other lines of questioning we're following," Steve said, patting my hand.

"Like what? The guy threatens my livelihood and a few hours later he dies. Keller is just going to love this."

Iain grinned, likely thinking of other famous times the entire station had been entertained with Keller's lacerating comments directed at me. Steve glared at him.

"Honestly, the collection is not the only thing Finster was stirred up about, and quite frankly, the guy wasn't the most popular fellow around. As you can see, I haven't been recused from the case, which I certainly would be if Keller were seriously seeing you as a suspect."

Iain joined in with an attempt to console me. "We haven't been able to find one workman who is anything more than merely neutral. Most of them thought he was an outright bastard to work for. The only thing is, there hasn't been all that much construction work happening till recently, so they felt they were lucky to get what they could and just sucked it up whenever he'd pull the shit he pulled."

"Shit like what?" I asked. It seemed that there was little a boss could do that couldn't be dealt with in court somehow, so I was curious to know how Finster had managed to still be a jerk.

"He would find ways to pay the least he could, and was always sending people home with short hours if the weather changed or there was a slow-up on some piece of action further up the chain. While the workers had negotiated for benefits, he managed to swing the very minimum of policies, and refused dental coverage point blank, allegedly saying," Steve flipped his notebook open, "that 'you don't need a twenty-four-carat smile to run a fork lift.' The guy was a real charmer, by all accounts. No bonus, layoffs over the winter rather than holding the crew on a maintenance salary with repair and indoor work to cover the fallow time. He refused to hire back based on seniority, so it didn't matter how loyal you were to his company, you took your chances heading back here for the season to work for Finster."

"Wow, how did he manage to get anyone to work for him at all?"

"For a long time, there hasn't been all that much in the way of construction, and there are certain specialized pros Finster needed who have set union salary scales. The money apparently is always on time, and is exactly what was agreed to, but there's no sense of camaraderie, loyalty or fraternity. It's a job site, nothing more, and Finster never lets them forget that."

"No joy in Mudville," McCorquodale chimed in.

"There is also Barbara Finster to contend with. She and her brother only saw eye-to-eye about hating everything else. They despised each other, and each held the other responsible for the distance between them and their parents. Barbara seemed almost relieved when we told her about her brother's death. Her only words were, 'Are you sure he wasn't hit with a blackjack?'"

"So, what you're telling me is that I'm not a suspect?"

"No," Steve said in a very gentle voice. "What I'm trying to tell you is that you're not the only suspect. There's a big difference." He and his partner stood up, looking tall and burly in the Centre with its glass cupboards housing fragile instruments, and the shelves of shatterable LPs and CDs. It was all so ephemeral, the stuff I loved, and just a breath of suspicion, a slight push of controversy could destroy it. Steve put his hand on my shoulder to comfort me as they left, but it felt like the strong hand of the disciplinary teacher clamping down an unspoken warning.

"Don't leave town, eh?" Detective McCorquodale grinned wolfishly at me as he closed the door behind them.

10

I suppose that when you are being watched by the police as a possible killer, you should appear squeaky clean and above-board in all aspects of your actions and life. We'd all been tense and quiet for three days, and today I felt like playing hooky. It was Poe's Imp of the Perverse in action: well, they suspected me of murder; what would be the harm in racking up a few small misdemeanours while I was at it? It wasn't even lunchtime, but there was no way I was going to be able to concentrate on work today. Humming "Frankie and Johnny," I closed up my laptop, stuffed it into my backpack and locked the Centre behind me after leaving a note for Paul. I had enough music downloaded for research purposes that I could work from home as easily as from the Centre for a week without running out of things to do.

"He was her man, but he was doing her wrong," I warbled as soon as I was sure there was no one in the sculpture garden between the Fine Arts and Law Buildings. This was a nice little courtyard I often came to when having an outdoor coffee break. A small amphitheatre was created with bricks and railway ties, and around it, metal sculpture guarded the pathways. Once, years before, when I was touring my folks around the campus, my mother saw this place and brightly said, "Oh look, they've beaten their ploughshares into ploughshares." While I'd never cared one way or another for the metal sculptures before, they now always gave me a slight laugh.

But not today. Nothing was going to get me out of the funk I was in, except maybe Steve getting down on one knee and saying, "Of course you could never be a murder suspect, Randy. I know you are incapable of ever committing such a terrible action, and it would never in a million years cross my mind that you would even consider such a thing. Forgive me."

And that was going to happen. Sure. We had barely spoken since he and his partner interrogated me at work a few days back, only phoning to let me know the bare basics of what was happening. Him and his damn ethical behaviour, refusing to discuss his work at a time when information could do me the most good. How could he doubt me?

It wasn't that I couldn't see why I might be a suspect. After all, I had access, I had a motive of sorts, and I didn't have any great alibi, since it turned out that, according to the forensic pathologist, Finster had been killed around the time I was wandering alone through the river valley. Of all the stupid things to do— had I but known, I would have taken several bondable members of the young Conservative MBA association along with me, complete with chronometers, digital cameras and copies of the day's newspaper for me to hold in the photos. You never know when you're going to need an alibi. Maybe I should have one at the present moment, too. I felt like stopping the guy whipping past me on the bike to say, "It's eleven-thirty, and my name is Randy Craig. Just remember that in case it's needed."

My anger at David Finster for inconveniencing me by being murdered and my annoyance at Steve for not sweeping it all aside had subsided to simple irritation by the time I kicked my sandals off at home a few minutes later. He was just doing his job, and I'd been on the other side of the scenario often enough to realize that he didn't jump to conclusions or dismiss worries that to another person might seem like paranoia. Of course, this was a man who had saved my life more than once and stood by me through some pretty terrible times, since I seemed to collect trouble like garbage attracts wasps. I owed Steve a lot, so if I had to go through the motions of being one of several suspects, then so be it. I would do more than that for love. Just as long as I didn't become the prime suspect; that I would not stand for.

I ate some crackers and slathered some peanut butter on a rice cake, then cleared away my lunch and breakfast dishes before hauling my laptop out of my backpack and settling in for the afternoon. I turned on my CD player to whatever I'd loaded the day before. Out came the opening tune from *Close to Home*, a Mike Seeger compilation of tunes he'd collected in the Sixties. I pushed myself into the corner of my overstuffed chesterfield, drew my laptop on top of me, and started to compile a list of songs that struck me as being popular inroads into the collection. I was thinking of a series of splash pages for the website, each one based on a particular song to start them off. Perhaps we could organize the folkwaysAlive! stage with the same themes.

"Frankie and Johnny" was still running through my head, so I typed it into a file and started brainstorming. I could go through Pete Seeger's collection of outlaw songs and pick some, along with Leadbelly's "House of the Rising Sun." The other song that sprang to mind, of course, was "Tom Dooley."

I pulled my hands back from the keyboard after typing this last title. Why on earth would someone have done that to David Finster? Not just why would someone have killed him, but why go to such an effort to stage the body? Obviously it was the Tom Dooley reference that really had the police breathing down the Centre's collective neck, but was that the reason for the gruesome scene? To deflect the police to us, or was there really something about the folk scene and David Finster that needed to be examined? Maybe someone should be checking to see if he'd ever got someone called Laurie Foster pregnant.

What was it Barbara Finster had said when told about her brother's death? Something about assuming he'd have been beaten with a blunt instrument instead of stabbed? I wondered what kind of a relationship they had, that she would have previously considered the way in which her brother might be murdered. There were so many times I thanked the stars and my parents that I was an only child.

I looked down at my laptop. Almost without realizing it, I'd opened a new file and had writing various cryptic phrases like:

Tom Dooley, stabbed, hanged, bludgeoned to death(?), pregnant, Barbara Finster, LRT station, trains, midnight special, folk music, university contracts, construction, family, bequests, Centre, Folkways collection, Lillian Finster. As far as I could tell, there weren't all that many obvious connections. Nothing added up. I hoped Steve was going to have better luck with this train of thought. I saved the file as "Murder Case" and turned my mind back to the outlaws.

Harry Smith's *Anthology of American Folk Music* was likely another good place to search for outlaw and criminal ballads. I heaved myself off the sofa and went over to my stereo. One of the best gifts Steve ever gave me was the Smithsonian/Folkways collection, which he'd presented me with when I landed my present job. I opened up the LP-sized box set, and pulled out my own sixty-eight-page Smithsonian booklet and the facsimile of Smith's original liner notes book. "Stackalee" was a possible choice, and Smith also had included the Carter Family's version of "John Hardy was a Desperate Little Man." I had to admit I preferred the Seventies version of "Stagger Lee."

I went into the kitchen to get a glass of water, and on my way back into the living room, I heard Mississippi John Hurt singing "Frankie," his version of "Frankie and Johnny," and stopped still. I wondered if Hurt was the first to record the turgid tale of Frankie who shot her perfidious lover Johnny. It was different from the version I knew best, Pete Seeger's. I always liked the Pete Seeger verse about her "rooty-toot" shooting through the door after peeking over the transom window into the hotel room where Johnny and Nellie Bly were up to no good.

Maybe it was just because Seeger was so loyal to the words that you heard every one. I hit Pause on my CD player, and went into my iTunes to find the Seeger version from *American Favorite Ballads, Vol. 1*. No, I was right, John Hurt spent more time on the aftermath of the shooting and Seeger spent more time on the actual shooting.

That was the fascinating thing about studying folk or roots music: there were so many variants. It must have been amazingly exciting to wander into the Appalachian Mountains at the turn of the century and discover age-old ballads being sung as Shakespeare might have originally heard them. Even more exciting was tracing the line from old version to newer layering. That might not be a bad idea for a theme page, too—the linking of songs through time. I opened another file and stared at the blank white square.

For instance, there was the whole linking of Woody Guthrie's "Gypsy Davey" that became the "Whistling Gypsy Rover" when the Irish Rovers got hold of it. There was another older English version, but its title wouldn't come to me. Steeleye Span had sung it, and so had Dave Alvin. The more I tried to come up with the title, the less it was going to happen. I wrote down "Gypsy Davey" and "Whistling Gypsy Rover" and created a blank line by holding down the underscript button a bit. It would come to me eventually, or I'd stumble over it somewhere.

Doc Watson's voice cut through my reverie. That was the beauty of a CD-changing stereo; I was always being surprised by a song. My machine had a turntable that housed three separate CDs, and I usually changed out only the front disc. Whatever was still on the machine eventually came on after what I'd just loaded, and sometimes the transpositions were odd. This latest surprise wasn't too bad, although as far as I knew, Doc Watson didn't sing about Frankie and Johnny.

I loved Doc Watson's voice; it was as mellow as honey running in the hot sun, even when singing the silly "Froggy Went A-Courtin." I've always loved that song, from the Burl Ives version I heard as a child to the slightly sillier version we'd sung out at summer camp. I particularly liked all of Doc's sound effects. My cousin's daughter once referred to it as "The Mouse's Wedding Song," and it took us ages to realize that this was what she'd been talking about. My mother and aunt and cousin and I had laughed ourselves silly. Wouldn't you know that a man must have named the song? Any self-respecting woman from four to eighty-four knew that a wedding was always all about the bride, not the groom.

Maybe I could make another through-line of variations on "Froggy Went A-Courtin." It could be a whole sideline of the website: the evolution of the folk song. For that matter, I wondered if there were any variants of Tom Dooley other than the Kingston Trio's cleaned-up version. Maybe searching them out would provide Steve with a clue. If folk music was going to be a suspect in all this, maybe it could also be a solution.

I craned forward from the chesterfield to look sideways over to the clock in the dining area office. It was four o'clock. Although I'd been working steadily, I hadn't got all that much done besides figuring out a Murder Ballad page and working up a possible sub-series page, all because of trying to remember the through-line backwards from "Whistling Gypsy Rover" to— "Black Jack Davey!" That was the name of the original English ballad. I knew it would come to me eventually.

Black Jack Davey. Now why did that sound so familiar? Suddenly it hit me. It was what Steve mentioned about Barbara Finster's response when she was told about her brother's death. She didn't say she'd expected someone to bludgeon him to death. She said, when she heard about the Tom Dooley reference, that she "was surprised they hadn't used a blackjack." She was referring to the ballad. I had to call Steve.

Iain McCorquodale answered Steve's direct line, and said that Steve wasn't available. He was sounding a little cagey, so I didn't press things. I asked him to have Steve call me when he had time. I made sure Iain wrote down that it was a matter of business, not a personal call, just in case Steve assumed that I was just calling to make a dinner date. This was important.

It wasn't so important that I was about to try to explain it to Steve's partner, however. He was a very nice guy as police officers went, and I didn't mind sharing Steve with him, but he was really a cop's cop, and I knew he disapproved a bit of Steve's candour with me about work. It's not that I went about blabbing anything or even that Steve divulged confidential information. It was just that I knew Iain would never in a bazillion years speak about precinct work to the women in his life. I knew from Steve that Iain was the son of a cop who was apparently completely mum to Mom, and his mother had never seemed to show any interest in his father's day-to-day activities. As a result, I think Iain was the same way with his wife, and was vaguely suspicious of women who found their man's work interesting.

I tidied up the notes and CD cases, and decided to spend some time in the kitchen. It was still too hot for cooking, but surely I could figure out something yummy that wouldn't require anything more than perhaps boiling water. I stood looking into the open fridge, not particularly caring to decide anything quickly, mostly enjoying the breeze. If Steve decided to drop by, we could make do with salads. I might even have enough in the way of apples, bananas, strawberries and pears to make a fruit salad.

I was tearing up pieces of romaine lettuce when Steve called me back. He sounded really tired. I told him I'd had an insight about something to do with his case, and that I had a cold supper almost ready. He opted to wait on the information and told me he'd see me as soon as he'd navigated the traffic. I put down the phone feeling a bit better about the situation we were in. Steve might be a police officer dealing with a puzzling murder case, and I might be a suspect in that case, but at least we loved each other and he liked my cooking. Things would sort themselves out.

I'd expected Steve to be about half an hour, since traffic down 109th Street—which I figured he'd be taking from the station— tended to back up a bit at rush hour. It wasn't much more than ten minutes before I heard him at my door, though. He did his usual knock before turning the key I'd had made for him, and I poked my head around the dining room corner to greet him.

"Hey! Did you notice it was locked? Just for you, darlin'! I was just setting the table; you were quick."

He unlaced his shoes, kicked them off onto the mat by the door and walked toward me like a circus bear on its hind feet.

"I am so beat. And I should have said, I wasn't at the station. I was actually just down the way at the crime site." "His eyes lit up as he spotted the salad bowls. "Wow, it looks better than a night out at the Keg in here. What's the occasion?"

"I just wanted to do something with my hands, and I couldn't bear the thought of turning on the oven or the stove," I said, sitting down across from him at the small chrome kitchen table. "Dig in. There's a fruit salad for dessert. I'm telling you this now just so you can conserve what room you need if you want it."

"Oh, I want it all right. This is fabulous. All I've had since breakfast was doughnuts. Cliché, right? You know Madeleine Williams? The forensics specialist? She brought three boxes of doughnuts to the LRT site, one for us and two for the construction workers. I think it was to keep them from carping about being held up from work. I assume they'll get paid, though who knows. Their boss is dead, and he allegedly wasn't all that hot on overtime when he was alive. I'm not sure what's going to happen to the station construction now."

"Well, it wouldn't surprise too many people to see construction on that project delayed. I'm thinking the protesters will look at it as a sort of Christmas present—no need to make signs or sign petitions to guarantee another year of inaction."

"Who protests the LRT?" Steve ladled another spoonful of cheese salad onto his plate. "This stuff is addictive, by the way."

"Mostly people whose neighbourhood it would pass through, I think."

"You'd think they'd be happy. Apparently, the traffic noise levels go down exponentially for about four main arterial streets on either side of a train line."

I chewed on some tabouleh, and ran my tongue over my teeth before speaking.

"It's not the noise, as far as I could tell from the last protest, that held things up so long. It's the potential riff-raff coming into their neighbourhood from undesirable areas of town, and the rabbit hole it would offer their teenagers to head toward the undesirable areas of town."

"There's nothing they're going to be able to do about their kids finding trouble," Steve sighed. "Most of the panhandling kids we tell to move on along Whyte Avenue are actually just adventuring suburban kids, not runaways even. They sit around braiding embroidery thread into people's hair and approximating that Haight-Ashbury feeling about fifty years behind the times, and then they head home to Riverbend and Rio Terrace."

"Back to the holdup; will you be done soon? How is it going?" I felt awkward about asking, but I figured that Steve would set the boundaries in discussing his cases, as he always did.

"I think Williams got all she was looking for." Steve shrugged. "Who knows how long it will take? The minute a killer adds something dramatic to the crime scene, things get exponentially weirder. It's worse than just being a premeditated murder, in that the murderer packed in not only a knife, but some rope, notepaper, a Sharpie and a safety pin with which to attach the note. The thought of someone taking another's life horrifies me, but doing all that advanced planning and setting the scene just creeps me out."

Steve's words jogged my memory and popped what I'd been meaning to tell him back into my head.

"Oh! That's why I called you earlier. It occurred to me what Barbara Finster meant about thinking he'd be killed some other way." I gathered our dirty dishes as I spoke, as if somehow declaring my news to a cleaned table would be more impressive.

"Yeah," Steve said, accepting my offer of the bowl of fruit salad from the fridge. "She didn't seem so surprised he was dead, but more shocked that he had been hanged rather than beaten to death."

"Well, something occurred to me today while I was working on ballad lyrics. She didn't say she thought he'd be bludgeoned to death; she said she was surprised they hadn't used a black-jack on him, right?" Steve nodded. "That's because that was his name: Black Jack Davey, just like in the old ballad. I'll bet his mother named him David on purpose."

Steve grinned. "Trust you to find it. He is named that, in fact. On official paperwork his name is Jack David Finster. I'll bet you're right and I'll bet his mother called him Black Jack Davey when he was little. In fact ..." Steve got a ruminative look. "Hang on, I have a hunch. Can I use your phone?"

He leaned over to grab my phone from the cradle on the desk by the window of the dining room, and punched in some numbers.

"Hey, Corinne, it's Steve Browning here. Can you check something for me? I need the complete name for Barbara Finster, of the Ye *Oldie* Barbara Shoppes. Yeah, I'll hold." He grinned at me as he held the receiver to his ear. "Right. Thanks a load. Bye."

"Well?" I wasn't quite sure why he needed details on David Finster's sister, or what he was getting at.

"I've been trying to figure out what those two had against their mother, and folk music in general. I mean, really? Imagine hating folk music. It's like saying you don't like Kraft Dinner or human rights." He picked up his dessert spoon and waved it at my nose. "But now imagine being a Finster with a mother so obsessed with folk music that not only does she open her house to itinerant musicians, but she names her children Black Jack Davey and Barbara Allen?"

"Oh, you've got to be kidding! For real? What do you bet there was Sweet William planted under Barbara's bedroom window when she was a kid? What a burden, especially if Mrs. Finster was anything like my mother, who will occasionally use a family pet name in the middle of something official, like high school graduation dinner."

Steve laughed.

"What was your family pet name?"

I shook my head violently.

"Nope, Copper, you'll never get that outta me. It's too embarrassing for words."

Steve pulled my chair toward him with his feet on the legs of the chair, and gave an experimental tickle.

"We have ways of making you talk."

"You have ways of making me spew fruit salad all over your dress shirt, but I'm still not going to tell you," I said, wriggling to get loose. Steve's grip tightened just a bit.

"I could just wait and ask your mother the next time your

folks come through town, you know. It would be so much easier if you'd just tell me now." He pulled me over onto his lap. I forgot sometimes just how strong he was. Of course, I wasn't actually resisting arrest.

"I may have to tell her about your interrogation methods if you do," I countered, gasping a bit as he licked my neck right under my ear.

"Oh, dear. Well, I guess we're just going to have to move to the mother-doesn't-need-to-know level of discussion." We rose from the chair in a tangle and moved toward the bedroom, working on wayward buttons as we went. After-dinner coffee could wait.

11

There was a sense of release in our relative abandon that had a lot more than chemistry involved in it. While we hadn't been able to get together for almost a week due to conflicting schedules, this was more than that. We made love in a sort of fury, trying to signal to each other with physicality what we couldn't bring ourselves to say in words. I know you're just doing your job. I know you're not guilty of any crime. I love you and trust you to the very marrow of my bones. I have faith in your ability to get me through this. So many things that we couldn't say for fear of offending the other by even admitting to thinking it needed to be said. It all got said. And heard. At least I'm hoping that's what I was hearing. We lay, spent, on our sides facing each other, listening to our synchronized heartbeats, smiling. After about half an hour, with the evening sounds of the city coming in through the open living room windows, we made love again, this time with no need to convey anything but direct connection.

Steve wasn't planning to spend the night, which was fine by me because the heat of the night made lying next to anything warm almost unbearable. Making love was one thing; the thought of curling up next to each other in a twin bed for eight more hours wasn't a charming picture. We decided to share a tepid shower to cool us off, both literally and figuratively, before he headed off to his place. I was towelling my hair, wearing one of his T-shirts since they were looser than my own pyjamas, when the phone rang.

"Hello? Yes, he's here." I handed the phone to Steve, blushing, though it was only about nine-thirty. For all McCorquodale knew, we could have been playing canasta. Of course, we hadn't been. Steve chuckled at the sight of me, and then turned his attention to the call.

"She has? That was quick. Yeah, I'll come get you. Give me twenty minutes and then be outside." He hung up the phone. "The coroner's finished with the autopsy, and some of the forensic details have come through. Iain wants us to go in and collate some of that information with the interviews we've completed to date. Apparently Keller is breathing fire to get a bead on this. Prominent citizens don't get killed in Edmonton all that often, and when they do, we jump to the pump." He tucked in the tails of his shirt and leaned over to kiss me. "Thanks for the oasis, love. I don't know if this is my second wind or my seventh, but I hope it will see me through till two or so. I'll call you tomorrow, okay?"

He was out the door and back to work by the time I padded over to the bathroom to hang up my hair towel. I turned off the lights after straightening the covers of my rumpled bed. Tonight was too hot for any sort of covering. I'd just have to risk not falling off the side of the globe tonight, and I lay down, imagining myself a marble statue carved on top of a queen's tomb—a tomb in a very cool crypt.

It must have been an earlier crash of thunder that woke me, but I opened my eyes to an almost simultaneous flash of lightning and a BOOM of thunder so loud that I thought my ears were going to start bleeding. Another flash of light made everything in my small room show up clearer than usual, since my room was always rather shrouded and dim. Suddenly the rain began, like a rush of snare drums.

I looked at the clock. It was just past midnight. I hoped Steve wasn't caught out in this downpour. While the ground could use the water and the air could use the cooling down, I had suspicions it would turn into hail shortly. Although the thunder was coming about ten seconds after the lightning flashes now, the storm didn't seem to be abating. I lay there watching the ceiling of my bedroom light up intermittently, wide awake.

It's not that I'm frightened of thunderstorms; in fact, I quite enjoy them. I defy anyone to get back to sleep during one, though. It would be like falling asleep in the middle of a Fourth of July fireworks display in Celebration, Florida. I finally gave in and sat up, pulled on the blind cord and leaned back against the wall of my bedroom to watch an amazing light show. Chain and sheet lightning alternated and then flashed simultaneously.

Luckily, it didn't turn to hail. I sat watching the rain a little longer before crawling back under the covers. There were too many residual horror movie effects from the thunderstorm to reimagine myself as a funerary sculpture this time. I lay still and tried to visualize my to-do list for the following day. Before I knew it, I was waking up to my insistent alarm clock. Even with all the interruptions of sleep, I felt better rested than I had all week. Regular sex was sort of like playing the banjo—it felt so good, but it wasn't necessarily something you talked about.

12

Paul, of course, was already sitting behind the counter organizing a box of cassette tapes when I walked in whistling. That's seriously one of the best things about the Centre. Although it resembles a library in many respects, keeping silent isn't necessarily encouraged. My imp-of-the-perverse need to make noise in libraries was easily fulfilled around here. Paul looked up and smiled. I smiled back and headed to my carrel. As I hauled my laptop out of my backpack, I realized I'd been whistling the insufferably cheery "Gypsy Rover," likely because the whole Black Jack Davey connection was still on my mind.

After about an hour Paul came over to tap me on the shoulder. I was interested to notice that he hadn't startled me. Maybe it was just that Paul had an easy way about him, but I certainly didn't have that dents-in-the-ceiling tiles reaction I'd had with

David Finster. Of course, maybe Finster's overtly negative attitude was what I'd been reacting to.

I had a phone call. It was Denise, who had blown back into town the night before and wanted to know if I was available for lunch. I gave a brief consideration of my liverwurst sandwich and apple, and figured they'd keep for supper.

"Sure! Where do you want to meet?"

"How about the Faculty Club at one? The main rush will be over by then." Denise had joined in the previous year, partly to schmooze and network, but also because she calculated how much money she spent eating out, how much she spent on groceries that went bad in her fridge because she couldn't stand to cook for one person, and how much energy she devoted to worrying about whether she was eating well according to Canada's Food Guide. Ever since, she kept milk, bread and eggs in her fridge and ate lunch and dinner at the Faculty Club. Wearing her pedometer, she determined that by walking between the Club and the Humanities Building twice a day five times a week, in addition to her walk back and forth from campus, she managed fourteen kilometres a week in free exercise.

I didn't mind joining her, but I made sure I had some cash to hand her for my share. All that signing for meals could get a person in hock pretty quickly, and I didn't want to add to that possibility for Denise.

I found myself humming again on my way back to the carrel. It was going to be good to see Denise, who was, aside from Steve, probably my best friend in the universe. It helped that we had so much in common, but it was our differences that added the real strength to our friendship. Though we were both English majors, Denise had pushed on for the PhD and was swimming with the sharks in the chum-filled waters of university tenure-track hiring. I, on the other hand, opted to get my MA and try to find teaching work at the college level, which wasn't quite the joyride I'd assumed it might be. While I loved teaching, it wasn't easy to get hired full-time, and the life of a gypsy sessional was just as stressful as that of a freelance writer, which was what I had been prior to heading back into the seeming safety of academe.

It hadn't all been a waste of time, though. I'd met some great people while working on my thesis, especially Denise. I discovered I enjoyed being around universities more than being away from them. I also met Steve through my teaching, though not in a totally conventional way. He was considered the officer most likely to understand university dynamics and had been assigned to a case in which I was involved. So, all in all, life in the ivory tower had been pretty good to me.

Denise and I had gravitated toward each other mainly because we were approximately the same age. While I was out working as a writer for several years between degrees, she did two MAs, one in English and another in Film Studies, before coming to Edmonton for her PhD in English. We were slightly older than the nose-to-the-grindstone kids who were steamrollering through from BA to PhD in ten years or bust, and we were just that much younger than the group of women whose children were finally all in school, allowing them seven hours a day to fulfill themselves at last. Aside from our age and proclivities for literature and film, Denise and I were pretty different. She came from a big, well-off family down east; I was the only child of an Armed Forces family, meaning that we moved every four years. I spent some of my teen years in Edmonton, but bounced around quite a bit until my father finally retired to teach photography at Ryerson.

Denise was also outrageously gorgeous, but oblivious to it. That was one of the things I liked best about her. While she had no false modesty about her looks, she didn't trade on them. She understood the power of the gift, but she was a strong feminist and much prouder of her intellect than of her profile.

I, on the other hand, was sort of a granola-chewing Midge to Denise's paté-munching Barbie. I knew I was not quite what my friend Leo would have called the "standard cutie," but I wasn't so exotic that I stood out a mile from the crowd. I tended to wear clothing as either armour or afterthought, where Denise wore it casually and still managed to make either an aesthetic or a political statement.

Denise had spent all of spring session down east at Stratford doing some research in the Festival Theatre's archives, and then took a quick break to visit her family in Toronto. I missed her, and it would be great to fill her in on what had been happening around here. It would also be great to hear about her adventures. If I knew her, she'd been invited to at least one gala and probably danced the night away with one or another of my theatrical idols.

Of course, since I was looking forward to seeing her at one o'clock, the entire morning seemed to drag. I checked my watch to discover an entire ten minutes had passed since I'd last checked it. I sighed and turned off the Dock Boggs CD I'd been listening to. I might as well fill the time filing CDs. Sometimes, all you're capable of is grunt work. Genius comes into play when you can actually spot those times.

When I finally managed to shuck off the chains of work and hustle over to the Faculty Club, Denise was sitting in one of the wingback chairs in the foyer of the Faculty Club waiting for me. Of course, she looked radiant. While everyone had adopted summer casual, there was still an air of formality to the Faculty Club that demanded something. Denise's orange sandals matched her orange blouse, which was tucked into loose-fitting faded blue jeans. An orange braided cord was wrapped around her head like a hair band and ponytail holder all in one, the way Aphrodite might have done her hair if she'd been around. Denise rose as I pushed through the tall glass door.

"Randy." We hugged, and then pulled back to get a look at each other. She looked tired, but happy. I assumed her research had gone well. Sometimes I really envied Denise her certainty of direction. She was so clearly meant for academe, and so talented in her approach. There never seemed to be any doubts to snag her up or stall her. She knew exactly what she wanted from her span on earth, and was determined to get there. Only her love life was disorganized; when I thought about all the various men she had dated since I'd known her, the organizing principle was less obvious than a patchwork quilt. Every man who fell for Denise, and most did, was totally devoted to her. She, on the other hand, seemed to collect them like other women collect shoes. I watched her wax and wane over a reporter, an engineering prof, a millionaire, and a jazz pianist in the last few years. The amazing thing is that she managed somehow to retain the friendship of every man she dated, so there was never anyone looking daggers across a restaurant toward Denise and her latest swain. I swear, if I didn't know that it cost her at least a hundred bucks a month to keep her hair looking that good, I'd want to trade places with my best friend. As it was, I was perfectly happy to share space.

We nattered about inconsequential things as we moved through the buffet line to collect soup and salads. Denise signed a chit and led me toward a table in the windowed area. Neither of us wanted to sit outside, although there were several people dotted around the grilling area, and a sous chef out there turning silver-wrapped potatoes and taking steak orders. Denise made a mock flourish of setting her napkin on her lap, and then smiled full focus toward me.

"So, what's up? I hear there's trouble brewing over at your end of campus." It always amazed me how quickly Denise could get up to speed with gossip. We in the Centre for Ethnomusicology may have only recently learned of the identity of our anonymous benefactor, but she was back a day and already knew of our connection to the latest murder in town. Of course, perhaps the entire campus already knew.

Although I was so used to not discussing case-specific things with Steve, it felt like floodgates opening to know I could talk to Denise. For one thing, I'd see how an outsider would view the events connected to the Centre. Maybe I was too close to the situation, but I couldn't see any other possibility than what Steve and his bunch seem focused on—that David Finster was somehow killed because of a link to the Folkways collection. Maybe there was another way of looking at the whole thing.

I laid out the general story for Denise, not bothering to emphasize how driven-snow-white I was in the matter. That's another beauty of best friends; I didn't need to justify myself to Denise. She would automatically assume I was innocent, and if it turned out I had done it, then she would assume I had a pretty good reason for doing so.

"So that's the only reason they have for aiming at you? The posing of the body after death to look like a line from 'Tom Dooley' and irritation at his mother's fondness for musicians? That seems like they're really stretching things. After all, he might have been killed because of a shady business dealing, or by a competitor in the construction business. He may have been killed because of a family squabble. Was he married; did he have children? He might have been killed by people driven mad by the LRT warning bells dinging in their back lane, for God's sake. So why are they assuming you would kill to keep a contract job?" Denise took a sip of iced tea and pursed her lips thoughtfully. "Come to think of it, if they're looking at people who would be worried about their jobs because of the Folkways bequest, what about all the university projects that rely on undirected bequests? Maybe someone whose funding was running out saw the chance to scupper the Folkways collection's windfall."

"What do you mean?" This was the sort of Machiavellian

thinking that I was no good at and at which Denise excelled. It was probably all that study of revenge tragedies.

"Think of it. If Finster and his sister made enough of a stink about the folk connection, maybe the university would cave to the point that they'd pull the directive for use, and settle the bequest into the general coffers. That way some of the programs that are timing out, or just not sexy and new, would have access to some of the money. If they could smear the Centre and make the administration uncomfortable, then who knows? If I were you, I'd make a list of all the humanities-based special projects. Forget the sciences; their funding is usually pretty secure, or they're tied to business connections." Denise grinned. "In fact, I'd stick Mary Montgomery from the Orlando Project right at the top of the list. She was the one who told me about the murder when I went in to get my mail yesterday."

"Is the Orlando Project in need of funding?" I asked.

"Everything is in need of funding, especially projects that have been going a long time. Once the glow is off the new aspect of things, it's a fight to keep above water. If you can't show some constant progress, if it's just more of the same, no matter how useful and of long-term benefit, the university admin will find other ways to spend the money. That's the thing that science departments understand, which we in the humanities are just getting the hang of. You have to constantly sell the project and it has to look new and different enough each time you go back to the trough. The science trick is to build a project in seven or eight levels, and sell each one as a separate chapter. That way, each time you go to the cookie jar, you're asking for something new. The moneymen see that as progress, and a useful way to spend money. If you go back year after year to ask for more money to fund an ongoing project to put biographies of all the marginalized writers of feminist literature online, eventually they're going to ask, hasn't this all been done before?"

I sat back, thinking that Denise was depressingly pragmatic. Lucky for the world she was on the side of the angels. She had recently managed to inject new cash into the beleaguered writer-in-residence program and tied it to a long-term investment that would provide a yearly stipend for an invited writer to the campus. Now, all the department had to do was provide an office and advertising, so the program seemed on much more secure footing.

I wondered if the Orlando Project people honestly wanted me to take the rap for murder to keep their funding coming in. It sounded absurd, but of course I'd been hearing absurd theories for the last few days; what was one more in the mix? And come to that, Mary Montgomery sort of scared me at the best of times. I told Denise I'd pass her thoughts on to Steve, and we moved on to discuss her research in Stratford.

"It was such fun. I was trying to work out some dates for modernizations of Shakespeare, to see if I could make some correlations between the choices of layover message to the new works happening in theatre. I started out with playbills, but the real joy was in going through the costume sketch archives. You could see at a glance what the director was aiming for, and some of the sketches are so beautiful—I swear, there's a fund-raising opportunity going to waste. They should be reprinting some of those sketches and selling the art prints as Festival souvenirs. Anyhow, it was lovely to interview some of the costume designers and builders, who've been there for years and years. That's the amazing thing about Stratford, the longevity and close community of it. Actors, designers, directors—they just buy a house and become part of the community. Once Stratford bites you, I think you'd need to be bitten by something as big as *The Sound of Music* to budge you out of there."

Her not-so-veiled reference to Christopher Plummer made me jump tracks into basic curiosity. "Did you meet any stars? Did you see Donald Sutherland? Did you meet Paul Gross?" Denise began to grin. "Oh Lord, you did, didn't you?"

The rest of lunch was taken up in Canadian theatre gossip, which sounded like a real puppy-eat-puppy world when it came down to it. Denise and I tidied ourselves up in the ladies' room before heading back into the hot afternoon. We opted to walk along Saskatchewan Drive back to the Humanities Building, where Denise's office was located. It didn't escape my notice that we were basically following the high-road version of my stroll the day of the murder. Across the road, and down the bush-choked cliff to the edge of the riverbank, to be specific. It was impossible to see for all the foliage. The denizens of Saskatchewan Drive had a better view in the winter, once the leaves had fallen. I doubted any of them wished the summer gone for all that. Moreover, I was sure that no one walking up here would have been able to spot me down there, giving me any kind of alibi.

Denise was talking about attending a campus film series at

the Tory Turtle on Monday evenings. I wasn't sure I'd be able to get to all of them, but I figured Denise wouldn't have any trouble giving my ticket away any given Monday, so I agreed to go. Actually, it sounded sort of interesting, music biographies in the movies. There were a couple I'd seen already, but some of the others seemed as if they'd fit right in with my research: *Bound for Glory* and *Coal Miner's Daughter*, for sure. I'd seen *Shine*, *Ray*, *Walk the Line*, *The Glenn Miller Story*, *La Bamba* and *The Buddy Holly Story* already, but I loved the music in them. I always meant to see *Bird*, *Selena* and *Immortal Beloved*, and I had never caught Jessica Lange's version of Patsy Cline in *Sweet Dreams*. I figured Dr. F would approve of my leisure-time choices.

I walked Denise to the midway door of the Humanities Building, but decided not to head up to the HUB passageway. I hugged her goodbye and passed straight through and across the hall to the access to the parking lot. My carrel was waiting for me across the breadth of two parking lots. I wandered alongside HUB mall, in the shade of the long building. It was so good to have Denise back in town. I hadn't realized how lonely it felt not to have her around while all this had been happening.

It was about two-thirty when I pushed the Centre door open to return to my work. Thinking of watching the Woody Guthrie story made me want to listen to some of his music, so I pulled *This Land Is Your Land* from the shelf beside my carrel instead of cueing up the next cut on the Dock Boggs CD I'd been listening to before lunch. Something I'd read in Pete Seeger's collection of writings, *The Incompleat Folksinger*, had really struck me;

Woody Guthrie may well be the only modern songwriter whose songs would live on past more than one century. I guess when you have the talent to write over a thousand songs, you have a fair shot at immortality. I wondered how many one-hit wonders ever looked at "This Land Is Your Land" and deflated their collective egos.

I was making putt-putt noises along to "The Car Song," which I'd always known as "Take Me Riding in the Car-car," when the door blew back on its hinges. I pulled off my headphones, and I saw Paul stand to attention behind the counter. We both focused on the tall man standing in the doorway, grinning at us.

"Hey, y'all," said the stranger, dropping a leather satchel suitcase inside the doorway, "I'm Woody."

13

I know it had a lot to do with what I'd been listening to and thinking about just prior to his arrival, but there was something about Woody Dowling that I was predisposed to like from the start. While Paul was busy trying to locate Dr. Fuller to let her know that a specialist from the Smithsonian Center for Folklife and Cultural Heritage had arrived, I was roped into showing him around the Centre and taking him across the street to check him in to a suite at the Campus Tower Hotel.

I offered to wait in the lobby for him, but he wouldn't hear of it, insisting that I come up to the tenth-floor suite with him, to inspect and approve it.

"After all, how would I know whether I was getting the works unless someone from hereabouts looks out for me?" He had a point. Besides, there was something so outrageously larger than life about Woody that I just moved in some sort of magnetic orbit behind him toward the elevator. Part of me flashed on Edith Wharton warnings from *House of Mirth*, but this was the twenty-first century, after all. Popping up unchaperoned to a man's hotel suite wasn't grounds for suicide anymore.

Woody dumped his suitcase in the bedroom and bounded across to see the view from the west window. His suite was on a corner, so he got a nice view all the way out to the mall, and from the north-facing bedroom window he had a view all the way to the river valley. Bits of the Legislature Building could be seen peeking through the trees. It was a shame they didn't light ours up with fairy lights like they did in Victoria. I turned back from the bedroom doorway as Woody called out, "Catch!"

He already had the complimentary fruit basket unwrapped and tossed me a huge Gala apple. I caught it instinctively, and Woody whistled appreciatively. "'Okay, some of them are going home!' You know, you looked like Geena Davis in *A League of Their Own* just then. Do you play ball?"

I laughed, I couldn't help myself. So far I had known the man for three-quarters of an hour, and already he'd covered his allergies, his reverence for Thomas Pynchon, the state of the bathrooms on the airplane he'd been on, whether e-learning was ever going to be appreciated by institutes of higher learning, the new paint colours of his office at the Smithsonian, whether or not ceramic tiles were the best thing for kitchen floors and the genesis of his name.

"Everyone I meet through work figures I was named for Woody Guthrie, of course, but my name is actually Sherwood, and not for any high cultural reason like being named after

Sherwood Anderson. No, my mother was a real Errol Flynn fan, especially Errol Flynn in tights. I think my father vetoed her first choice of Robin as being too girlie for his tastes. So, she called me Sherwood for Sherwood Forest. It got shortened to Woody when I was in kindergarten, and pretty soon I learned that the best way to avoid any joking about my name was to head 'er off at the pass." Out of the blue, he rattled off a perfect imitation of Woody Woodpecker's signature giggles. "I'll bet you got teased about your name, too, right? Matter of fact, probably the same sort of teasing as me." To his credit, he didn't stop to take in my blush, but had turned to unpack his computer from his bag and plug it into the cable line indicated on the wall of the living room area of the suite.

"I just have to check in with my bosses, let them know I'm here safe and sound, and then I'm all yours. Well, as long as you give me five minutes to splash some water on me."

He rattled a quick e-mail and hit the Send button with what I was beginning to recognize as a characteristic flourish.

"I swear I won't be five minutes. Help yourself to the fruit. In fact, you can take those kiwis with you, if you want. I'm allergic to them, too."

I sat down on the sofa and decided to place a call to the Centre just to let them know that I hadn't lost the Smithsonian guy on the way over. Paul put me through almost immediately to Dr. Fuller, whom he'd called away from a tutorial to meet up with a Woody who wasn't there when she reached the Centre. She didn't sound too happy about things. I told her we'd be back in a few minutes and that he was just freshening up from his trip.

I cupped the speaker of the phone close to me, because I suddenly realized that the background sound I was trying to speak over was Woody yodelling in the shower. The man was having a shower, obviously with the bathroom door wide open, while I was sitting there in his hotel suite! I stammered something unintelligible to my boss and hung up the phone as quickly as I could. Then I stood up and tried to find the most innocuous place, barring standing outside in the hallway, that I could wait for a now presumably naked man to get dressed and reappear.

Just thinking about him being naked in the other room was a bit over-stimulating. The man, after all, was somewhat dishy by anybody's standards. He must have been at least six-foot-four, unless he wore heels, since he towered over me, and I'm no slouch in the height department. He had the kinetic grace of Hugh Jackman, the frame of Tim Robbins, and the eyes of Joseph Fiennes. All that would have been easy to deal with if it hadn't been mixed in with what could only be described as charisma. He had that star quality you see in certain politicians and movie stars, the sort that you might not notice on TV, but which startles you on the street or in airports when you run into them unexpectedly.

Oh God, and he had the abs of Kenneth Branagh in Frankenstein, I realized as he wandered into the living room with only a towel wrapped around his nethers. I leaned back against a wall, which was several inches further away than I had calculated. Attempting to appear as if I had meant to do a backward press-up against the wall occupied my urge to babble, and I managed not to embarrass myself too much as he smiled at me and headed back into the bathroom with his shaving kit in one hand and a pile of clothing balanced on the other.

"Five minutes, I swear," he sang to me, and this time, closed the door to the bedroom. I sank down on the closest chair, and took a few deep breaths. I had the feeling this was going to be a complication I could certainly do without.

He was true to his word. A scant ten minutes later we were crossing 87th Avenue, back toward the Timms Centre and the Fine Arts Building. Woody was appropriately appreciative of the Timms' architecture, and raised a quizzical eyebrow as we reached the Fine Arts Building.

"I know," I said. "I think maybe it was an attempt to be so neutral that any student piece created here would shine in relief." We swooped into the building on the force of Woody's laughter.

It was obvious within minutes that Dr. Fuller was just as susceptible to Woody's charms as I was. I reluctantly pulled away from the discussion when it veered from specifics to the Centre for Ethnomusicology in general. I figured they'd get back to me when they needed me. It took about half an hour.

"Randy," Dr. F leaned on the top of my carrel, "would you come with us to the mall for coffee? Woody thinks we should discuss the implications of this terrible situation for the collection, and I think you should be privy to all this."

Woody smiled from near the counter. I wondered fleetingly if including me had been his decision or Dr. F's. Then I found myself wondering why it would matter to me whose idea it was.

Instead of settling into the middle of the mall at one of the central tables, we took coffee in La Pasta, one of the sit-down restaurants in HUB, and sat upstairs in the corner. Woody sat in the very corner, with his back to the window.

"I think I must have been an outlaw in a former life," he apologized, as he manoeuvred himself into place, folding down into the corner chair. "I cannot for the life of me sit with my back to the room or the door."

"I must say, this is an unexpected pleasure for the Smithsonian to send you, Dr. Dowling," Dr. Fuller started out, sounding for all the world like she was beginning a board meeting. "While we're not certain the situation is as problematic as you folks might think, we certainly appreciate the solidarity."

To me this sounded like diplomacy. It occurred to me that Dr. F wasn't pleased in the least that Washington had sent anyone up here at all. I had a feeling there were a few rough edges in the partnership between our collection and the Smithsonian Folkways collections down south.

Woody caught the drift immediately, too. "Please, Dr. Fuller, call me Woody. Everyone does. And please don't think of me as trying to muscle in on your territory in any way. I'm just the pro from Dover, here to help in any way I can and wangle a free trip out of the deal. While I'm here, I'll be liaising with the Edmonton Folk Music Festival folks to work out all the logistics for recording from the Folkways Stage, but the powers that be figured I might be of some use to y'all up here now, so here I am, at your disposal. Believe me, I know how problematic things can get when large sums of money are involved. How you can deal with that, as well as fending off police investigations and possible murder charges, at the same time, well, that boggles the imagination." He took a big swig of coffee. "Of course, it makes it sort of exciting, too, doesn't it?"

Dr. Fuller, who trekked into some pretty remote areas in Nepal and India to collect songs, probably didn't have the same concept of excitement as Woody, and I had very few romantic notions of how much fun being involved in a police investigation could be. On the other hand, I knew nothing about Woody's background. Presumably, since he too had a PhD in Ethnomusicology, he may well have been involved in some adventures in the pursuit of his work. Or he may have been seconded to archival research for the Boston Pops for all I knew. It didn't do to presume too much. I vowed silently to keep an open mind.

Dr. F and I told Woody about the questioning we received from the police, and what we deduced from their line of questioning. With a very small hesitation, which I figured I'd analyze later, I mentioned my connection to Steve, which gave me a few more insights into the investigation than we might otherwise have. I also went over my meeting with David Finster for what seemed like the seventeenth time.

"Man, it sounds like the real mystery was how did that guy manage to stay alive as long as he did?" Woody drawled, to our startled amusement. "I mean really, how can anyone hate folk music? It's un-American!"

Dr. F smiled a very tight smile, and Woody winced visibly.

"Oh shit, I'm sorry. That sounds like I'm some sort of redneck hick, doesn't it? I was trying for satirical and ended up sticking my own foot in the mess I was trying to point out. I do realize y'all are a distinct and separate country with ideas and ideals of your own."

"We even have different words to 'This Land Is Your Land,'" I grinned, enjoying his discomfort. To his credit, he laughed and blushed. There is something sexy about a man who has both the ability and the grace to blush. Or maybe there was just something sexy about Woody Dowling.

"What I was trying to get at, in my blunderingly boobish fashion, was that this David Finster sounds like a candidate for ugliest soul around."

"Don't forget he has a sister," said Dr. F in a low-key delivery. I practically spewed coffee through my nose, gagging a guffaw.

"Oh yes, Barbara Allen. Have y'all heard anything from her since that first time when the two of them barged in on you?" Dr. F and I both shook our heads. "And did you really have no idea about the source of the funding before they introduced themselves to you?"

Again, Dr. F shook her head. I shrugged, abdicating myself from the discussion since I was just a hired gun, with no background on the project. In fact, until I had been hired, after the bequest had been announced, the only thing I had in common with the Centre for Ethnomusicology was a guitar, a banjo and five of the remastered Smithsonian Folkways CDs in my music collection.

While Woody and Dr. F spoke in what seemed like code, but was really some form of administrative lingo known only to those who actually deal with large sums of research funds on a daily basis, I hauled my datebook out of my backpack and checked the dates with what Woody had been talking about. The bequest had been announced in January, I'd been hired in May, and David Finster and his sister came to see us in late June. This coming long weekend would mark the beginning of July with Canada Day celebrations. I was sure I'd heard when Lillian Finster died, but couldn't recall whether it was September or October of the previous year. I guess it had taken time to probate the will and for the university lawyers to guarantee the bequest as valid before it was announced.

So why had it taken so long for the Finsters to figure things out and go on the rampage to us at the Centre? Had they known all along? Or did they just find out recently? I had a feeling that would be worth knowing. And when did the Smithsonian Folkways folks get involved? I knew they were underwriting the Folkways stage recordings at the Folk Fest in August, but just why was it deemed useful for Woody Dowling to appear on the scene now, riding in like a cowboy on a palomino?

I shook myself to clear my head and returned to the conversation. Dr. F was describing the eventual housings of the collection in the main floor of the old Arts Building.

"As you must know, the storage of vinyl records is something that can really test the structure of the flooring. We need to consider that, as well as accessibility to students and scholars, and the chance of expansion. We have a mandate to keep the collection up to date by purchasing all new recordings produced by Smithsonian Folkways, and we also have plans to expand by means of recording up here. That, of course, you know about as well." She smiled graciously at Woody. "We are engaged in the database at the moment, and the means of bringing the collection we have to the level where it is internationally accessible online for scholars. Randy is bringing the written aspect of that to life, by finding the appropriate entrances to the collection. While the database will eventually be elastic enough to suit even the most esoteric reaches of specialist research, we're hoping to pre-guess the average needs of the generalist. Randy's approach is to find the likeliest needs of the collection, and create entry-level content for the website at each doorway."

I felt Woody appraising me, as if by checking me out physically he could tell whether or not I was cerebrally up to the job. Just in case he could, I found myself sucking my stomach in a bit more. I grinned self-consciously, the way I used to when my mother was speaking to her bridge friends about my plans for courses in the coming school year.

"Sounds like a great project. So Randy, have you connected with anyone in Washington in terms of your project?" His question sounded innocuous, but I could feel Dr. F stiffen beside me. I braced myself to tread warily in the dark.

"Well, not yet. I'm still in the composition and research stage. We haven't committed anything to the website yet. I think I want to keep some distance till I have a clear vision, so as not to co-opt the overall site. I mean, I'm certainly not anxious to reinvent the wheel, and I'm aware of what your website does, but there's not going to be any competition. More of an enhancing connection, I'm foreseeing."

Woody was nodding easily across from us, but I could still feel the tension in my boss. It was making me feel awkward, since I wasn't sure if it had anything to do with the website collaboration idea, or whether something else was bothering her. Whatever it was, I wanted to be gone. I made an obvious show of surreptitiously checking my watch, only to discover that it really was way past my work hours. I normally knocked off at four, and here it was already a quarter past five. To emphasize things, my stomach suddenly gurgled very loudly in the otherwise quiet restaurant. Woody laughed. Dr. F looked a bit startled by my body noises, and masked it with comments that we really had gone overtime, and did Woody know how to find his way back to his hotel? He assured her that he would be fine, that perhaps he could impose on me to point him in the right direction?

"As long as you don't mind going back via the Centre," I agreed. "I have to put some stuff away and pick up my laptop."

Dr. F shook hands with Woody and nodded to me and left the restaurant before us. She was a distant figure heading north to the Tory Building by the time we reached the mall level. I pointed us to the south, and Woody loped along beside me.

"Where is she going?" he asked.

"Dr. F has an office in the Anthropology department, and that's in the Tory Building—the tallest building on campus. Or she might be headed to the new Centre in the Arts Building—or her car." Woody nodded. I felt as if all bits of information that he received got stored carefully away for future possible use.

When we got back to the Centre we found that Paul had already left and turned out the lights. I told Woody to hold the door open, and rummaged for the cord to my laptop in the ambient light from the hallway. I set the books on my carrel neatly in a pile on the desktop, not bothering to put them back up on the upper shelf. I could clean up in the morning. I wanted my laptop, though. Ever since I got it a few months ago, I'd got acclimatized to working from my chesterfield rather than the desk in the dining room. Besides, if I worked on my folk essays in the evening from home on the laptop, there was less chance of dallying on a conference site or checking eBay for bicycles and mandolins.

Woody held the door wide, and ushered me through with a sweeping gesture.

"So you're now done for the day?" he asked.

I shrugged. "Technically. Chances are I might do a bit of research still. I have some books I'm trying to work my way through, half for pleasure, half to make the pictures all come clear in my mind." Woody nodded.

"And your police officer friend will be meeting you for dinner?" My danger antennae leapt up to attention. What should I answer? Why was he asking? Maybe he just wanted someone to take him out for supper. That was natural. It was his first evening in a strange city. I was surprised Dr. F hadn't organized something. Of course, I was still wondering if Dr. F had even known Woody was coming at all, let alone early. That might be the source of the tension I had been sensing.

"Well, I think it's likely he'll be up to his ears in this case still," I admitted. "When something like this is on the books, Steve's hours get a lot more irregular." The truth, of course, was that I wasn't sure how much Steve was going to be fraternizing with me till the whole case was concluded, but I wasn't about to go into all that with a perfect stranger.

"In that case, can I lure you into dinner out with an almost perfect stranger?" Woody smiled winsomely, which tempered my being startled by his use of the very words in my head. He'd very likely learned that smile when apologizing for breaking windows with his slingshot or baseball. He just had that all-American boy sensibility to him, wrapped up in a grown-up package. I found myself grinning back at him and agreeing to join him for supper. As long as I could drop my backpack off at home and pick up my mail, I wouldn't mind eating something I hadn't cooked myself.

"Sure. Where do you live?" Oh God, that was going to mean bringing Woody into my apartment. What had I done? It's not as if I could tell him to wait out on the street for me. As we walked down the three short blocks from his hotel to my apartment, I worried about the wisdom of both letting him know where I lived and allowing him to see how I lived. There's something so intimate and personal about one's living space; I am loath to invite people I don't know well into my home. After all, what we choose to place on our bookcases, what we surround ourselves with in terms of art or decoration, says a lot about us. A friend of mine who did grad studies in abnormal psychology said that you could tell more from someone's record collection than you could from the first four months of therapy. So what was I doing breaking my cardinal rules of not allowing strangers into my inner sanctum, especially this man, who I had already sensed was relatively dangerous to my equilibrium? Man oh man, I was playing with fire.

Woody was appropriately appreciative of my art deco building and the lovely Persian hall runner. He stood in my apartment doorway, nodding and taking it all in greedily, as if reading the book that was me. I wasn't mistaken. This man was interested in me.

"I'll only be five minutes. Don't even bother to take your shoes off." I saw slight confusion cross Woody's face, and it occurred to me that perhaps people in Washington didn't automatically take off their shoes in other people's homes. If that was the case, he was a quick study, because he stood obediently on the welcome mat while I dropped my backpack in the dining room, hauling out my wallet and keys. I called Steve's desk number and left a message for him, which I hoped Woody would overhear.

"Hey, it's me. It's almost six and I'm heading out to dinner with a fellow from the Smithsonian Institute who's in town to deal with the recording issues for the Festival. I shouldn't be too late out. Call me after ten if you have time, 'kay?" I hung up the phone, and turned to face Woody. "Okay. So, how do you feel about Greek food?"

"You're a mind reader! I was just standing here wondering where I could get a great moussaka." Woody grinned. "Is it far? I take it we're going to walk?"

"Do you mind?"

"Not at all. It's a great town for walking in, as far as I can see."

I took us down 109th Street to Whyte Avenue. Normally, I'd have cut cross-country through the Old Strathcona neighbourhood maze of one-way streets and walk-up apartments surrounding the old houses pulling themselves up and sticking their verandahs out proudly at the progress going on around them. However, I wanted Woody to get a sense of where he was in relation to things.

We heard the bouzouki music from half a block away. Woody's eyebrows shot up as I ushered him through the doors of my favourite Greek restaurant in town, Yianni's Taverna. Marina, the hostess, came out from behind the bar when she saw us. She squeezed my hand, and said, "Randy! It's so good to see you. We've got the avgolemono soup tonight. It's lucky we do. You didn't call." She turned to Woody and looked suddenly puzzled to note that he wasn't Steve. I jumped in quickly before she could say anything.

"Marina, meet Woody. He is a colleague from Washington, DC, who wanted to know where to find the best Greek food in town." Marina beamed and led us to a table near the front of the restaurant, which opened out on Whyte Avenue. Woody commented on the charming decor, which further endeared him to our hostess. We ordered the starter platter, a combination of feta cheese, Greek olives, kalimari, tsatsiki, hummus and dolmades. Woody ordered a bottle of Amalia wine as well.

"Everything Greek goes with red wine, I figure," he said.

"You're not allergic to the histamines in red wine?"

"Nope, lucky or what? I know it sounds like I'm some sort of bubble boy, but it's mostly avoidable stuff—not essentials like wine." Woody tipped his glass rim toward mine. "Here's to colleagues and getting to know all about them."

I clinked and repeated, "To colleagues."

"You know, I volunteered to come up here. Not that it was

billed as a hardship task, but I've always had a fascination with the North, and I thought it might be possible to drive to Great Slave Lake from here."

"It's not impossible, but it would take you a couple of days' driving and you'd have quite a detour in the summer. In the winter there's an ice road that cuts the time down. Lesser Slave Lake is here in Alberta, and it's about four hours north. Do you fish?"

"No. I just wanted to collect all the Great Lakes, to be able to say I'd seen them. I have been to Lake Winnipeg once, you know. Why, is fishing all there is to do there?"

"Of course not. You could canoe, or speedboat, or water ski. Or you could drive a quad around on the dunes. There's a heck of a lot of nature out there to spoil if that's what you want."

Woody shrugged. "Maybe just a drive in the country would be enough."

"Have you ever been to the Canadian Rockies?" I asked. Again he shook his head. "Well, in my opinion, that's where you should go. Just three hours west of here on good roads, and you're in the most amazing scenery you'll ever see. Wild animals wander about everywhere. The glacier-fed lakes are the craziest blue-green colour. There are hiking trails, and camping areas, and cabins to rent, and hot springs. It's beautiful up there."

"It sounds great. Maybe I'll be able to swing a trip there. I suppose I should rent a car while I'm here."

I nodded. Our transit system was good when contractors weren't getting murdered in it, but if Woody was going to be here for a few weeks, then he'd want to get out and around at his leisure. Besides, Edmonton and northern Alberta in the summertime were wonderful places to explore; I was all for promoting that to anyone.

"Well, my expense account will allow for a car rental," Woody continued. What sort of car would you like to drive?"

"Me?"

"Yes, after all, I'll need someone from the Centre to be my guide, won't I?" He attempted to bat his eyes, which made me laugh.

"The trouble is, I'm not technically an employee of the Centre so much as an employee of the Folkways collection."

"All the better! The Smithsonian could lean on the Centre to allow for your liaising with their representative here. I'll need someone to help me connect with the Folk Festival crowd, and to show me around the city. I may even need someone to drive me to the mountains." I wasn't sure how to read his look, and I wasn't sure I wanted it clearly interpreted.

Just then our food arrived and I busied myself trying to avoid wearing too much flaky phyllo pastry while devouring Marina's husband's spanokopita. It looked like Woody was enjoying his meal, too. We didn't speak much for about ten minutes while we dug in to the food-laden plates in front of us.

When I sat back for a breath and a drink of water, it occurred to me to ask Woody what he had meant by something he said to Dr. F earlier in the day.

"What's a pro from Dover?" I asked. Woody chuckled.

"It's a line from the novel *M*A*S*H**," he explained. "When Hawkeye was younger, he would play golf for free at various clubs by introducing himself as the pro from Dover. He would then be invited by the club pro to try the course gratis. So, in the midst of the war, he and Trapper John and some other character I can't for the moment recall head off to a base hospital to cadge some equipment, and they refer to themselves as the pros from Dover. Miraculously, or because of their sheer nerviness, they walk out with what they need, no questions asked."

"So, are you faking your qualifications?"

In answer, he pulled out his wallet from his back pocket, and produced both his driver's licence and his Smithsonian picture ID. I picked up his driver's licence. The picture was better than most. I noticed in the statistics that he was indeed six-foot-four, and he weighed two hundred and twenty-eight pounds. He must work out, because there wasn't a spare ounce of fat obvious on him.

"I think I used the term mainly because of the Smithsonian connection. Maybe you'd have to work there or at least hang out there a bit to get what I'm trying to say. It's a huge place, and it's the repository of the entire culture, classic and popular, of the United-States-of-America-of-thee-I-sing. Working there means that you validate that concept, whether it's something like the front porch song collections of Alan Lomax, or Fonzie's black leather jacket from *Happy Days*. For better or worse, the Smithsonian has it detailed and recorded. So, when it comes to venturing out as a rep of the Smithsonian, I feel as if I've become a representative of all that is both good and hokey, if not downright silly, in American culture." He swirled the heel of wine left in his glass, and stared at it sparkling with the candlelight behind it. "I have to admit, it's awful hard to be an American these days. At the same time as I am tremendously proud of so much of what has gone into the making of America, I am well aware that we have squandered bushels of good will and taste and potential in the last few years. We can't figure out why the world hates us. Heck, we can't figure out why the people living in our inner cities hate us. We spend more money on making one summer movie than most African countries put together have as a yearly budget. We claim to love nature and then we drive out to it in our suvs and scrape it off our grilles on the way home." He grinned a bit weakly. "You've uncovered my Achilles heel, Randy. I'm the pro from Dover, I guess, because I find the only way I can operate as a cultural representative of the greatest-country-in-the-world is ironically."

I nodded.

"I can understand what you're saying," I said. "But there are a lot of wonderful things about the United States that people tend to forget about. Look at the Smithsonian as a case in point." Woody toasted me with his glass, encouraging me to maunder on. I should know better than to have more than one glass of wine. "Look at the amazing art that has come from the us, as good as or better than anything else in the world. So much of the world's art comes out of a cry of oppression. It's fascinating to see where man can go when he's not oppressed or hungry or in need. *Citizen Kane*. The Chrysler Building. *Catcher in the Rye*. The Golden Gate Bridge. *Angels in America*. *The Sopranos*. The geodesic dome. *Love Medicine*. Batman. *Buffy the Vampire Slayer*."

Woody smiled. "The thing is, you have to include Las Vegas,

the Manhattan Project, Three's Company, Milli Vanilli and Batman and Robin. Talk about cancelling out. You are very lucky to be Canadian. There are so many people down where I live who look up at y'all and wish they could be you. You are like the ideal American—all the potential realized without any of the bullshit associated."

It was my turn to shrug. "We're not as great as we think we are. It's only in comparison to you folks that we come out looking as peaceful and caring as we do. There are influential people here crying out to end all of our social safety programs. So, I'm not sure we either are or would care to be considered ideal Americans, if you take my point."

Woody grimaced and nodded. "Far be it from me to paint y'all as the fifty-first state! Well, I figure we've saved the world enough for one night. Shall I get the check and you can lead me back to where it is I live?" We tussled a bit over who should pay, but Woody's claim that he had a daily stipend for meals that exceeded what both meals combined cost, and that he intended to get in some groceries to his suite and therefore keep the meal cost down throughout the trip mollified me, and I was happy to watch him charge it on a platinum-coloured charge card. For all my talk about socialism and need, it was always extremely nice to go out to a lovely restaurant and have my way paid to boot.

We headed out into a pleasantly warm summer evening. It was still daylight, of course, as our concept of twilight is dusk falling around ten o'clock. Short but intense summers, that's what we're famous for. And we make the most of it. Woody and I watched a bunch of teenaged girls in short shorts wheeling down the street on in-line skates, and a group of people stopped ahead, listening to a busker playing classical guitar.

It took us a bit longer to walk back home than to the restaurant, but that's usually the way of things when you're satisfyingly full and having a pleasant conversation. Woody demurred when I offered to walk him all the way back to his hotel, saying that he could almost see it from the sidewalk in front of my apartment, and that he wouldn't be likely to get lost walking in a straight line.

"Thanks, Randy, for a lovely evening. You've proved that the whole tradition of Western hospitality is alive and well. I'll see you in the morning." With that, he squeezed my upper arm with one large hand and loped off into the dimming light. I stood there and watched him go. At the end of the first block, he turned and waved, as if he knew I'd be watching.

14

There was no message from Steve on my machine when I got home from my dinner with Woody. I went to bed and dreamed about US–Canadian relations in one form or another. While I didn't recall my dreams in detail, there was enough residual heat to make me feel a bit guilty.

I showered and dressed with a bit of care, given that I'd apparently be representing my country as well as doing my job. A pink cotton blouse tucked into a clean pair of pale blue jeans was the best I could manage. The pink pom-poms on my ankle socks sticking out over top of my white sneakers tied the ensemble together, as far as I was concerned.

After rubbing moisturizer into my face and sliding mascara over the tips of my eyelashes, I braided my hair and stared at myself in the mirror over the bathroom sink. Did I really want to analyze why I seemed to be taking extra care getting ready this morning? My reflection shook her head at me, so I decided to follow her advice and just get on with the day.

Just in case I was surprised by visitors again, I rinsed out my breakfast bowl before heading out the door. You just never knew. I grabbed up the bills I needed to mail, hefted my backpack onto my shoulder, and set off for work.

The weather that had been so oppressive the week before was now mild and beautiful. The air had the smell of damp dirt and big trees that I've always associated with summer camp time by the lake. The oddest thing was that, while it struck me that this was the calmest time of year on campus, it was always the most productive for me. The only rival times I could think of were those moments in the fall when you could discern the scent of the previous evening's bonfire on the air; that to me was the palpable smell of kilts and knee socks and new pencil crayons.

I wondered if anyone else connected times to smells as much as I did. I know that psychologists have determined that smell is the most important sense for memory, but for me there's a real connection between things and smells that actually don't emanate from the things themselves. Plastic binders smell to me like Christmas, calamine lotion recalls canoe trips; peanut butter is the scent of my old tree house, and the smell of tangerines reminds me of hair salons. I supposed I was lucky. My mother had next to no sense of smell at all. If she was cooking dinner, she had to remain in the kitchen or the beans would be burned to the bottom of the saucepan in no time. While it qualified her as the person least likely to mind cleaning out the fridge, her inability to discern whether the broccoli was turning was usually what made the fridge need cleaning in the first place.

The Fine Arts Building smelled ancient, which was odd, since it couldn't have been more than about thirty years old. There were plenty of older buildings on campus that didn't have that scent o' crypt about them. It probably had something to do with FAB having hardly any windows. Or maybe it was the colour of the bricks. The Law Building was nearly the same vintage, as far as I could tell, and it had a far livelier sensibility to it. Of course, it seemed to have more ambient light, too.

The lights were on, and so was Paul's computer when I got to the Centre. I couldn't spot Paul, though. I went behind the counter to see if he'd also had the good sense to begin the coffee. No such luck. I was thinking of dropping my backpack at my carrel and popping over to Java Jive when I noticed that Dr. F's office door was ajar and the lights were on there, too. That was unusual. Planning to ask her if she'd like a cup of coffee, I moved toward the office. As I got closer I noticed something else odd on the floor in the doorway.

I think we're just hardwired not to understand visions of violence. It took me what seemed like forever to puzzle out what it was I was looking at. Why on earth would I be seeing the bottoms of Paul's boots staring back at me? I finally realized it was because they were still attached to Paul and he was lying still, stretched out on his stomach in the middle of Dr. F's office, his head in a pool of blood.

15

I couldn't have been frozen there too long before calling 911, because the police and paramedics arrived in what turned out to be only about half an hour after I'd left my apartment. By the time Steve and Iain began to question me, I was no longer standing in the doorway, but sitting at the library table once more, in the middle of the Centre. Paul, by this time, was being whisked through the emergency ward at the University Hospital and Dr. F was heading in to the Centre after being called by the police.

She wasn't going to like what she saw in her office, I knew that for sure. It had been royally trashed. Madeleine Williams, the forensics specialist, was going over it while I sat there, numbly listening to Steve speak to me from the far end of a long, long tunnel. It took a great deal of effort to focus on what he was saying. I figured out from the inflection of his voice that he was asking me a question. So what else was new? I made an effort to pay closer attention, and he repeated himself.

"Do you think Paul was looking for something in the office and was surprised by an intruder, or was it the other way around?"

"Is he going to be okay?"

"It's hard to say, Randy. It sounds like he took a pretty hard blow to the head, we're not sure with what yet. Lucky for him, you got here shortly after it must have happened. Lucky for you, you didn't get here any sooner than you did. I don't think you missed seeing the assailant by much, kiddo."

I shivered. This was reminding me too forcefully of the time my old office had been trashed, only a couple of blocks from where we were now standing. While it had been those events that had resulted in my meeting Steve, it wasn't something I wanted repeated. It was just my dumb luck that it took acts of extreme violence and prejudice to bring interesting men into my life. That suddenly reminded me.

"Woody!" I exclaimed. Steve looked quizzical.

I filled him in on the arrival of the "pro" from Washington who had breezed in with such aplomb yesterday to work on liaising with taping for folkwaysAlive! at the Folk Fest next month. While I didn't think Woody had anything to do with the events this morning (after all, why would he?), it occurred to me that not only did he need to know about the situation, but that his arrival may have had something to do with this focus on the Centre. Steve agreed that I should call him at his hotel and have him come over.

Woody's warm greeting on the phone turned businesslike immediately when he heard about Paul. I tried to be as discreet as possible on the phone, and he agreed to head over to the Centre right away. He arrived in five minutes .

I introduced him to Steve. Iain was helping the forensics woman measure angles from the doorjamb, and a uniformed officer was spreading grey powder all over papers on Dr. F's desk. I hoped the fingerprinting powder didn't get into any tape boxes or adversely affect the CDs piled on the shelf behind the desk. I also hoped that someone else would be buttonholed to clean up the mess the police would leave behind. It was bad enough that I was going to have to wash the fingerprint ink from my cuticles several times before it disappeared. I have had my prints taken for "elimination purposes" in the past, and knew it had to be done, but it still felt invasive and awkward.

It's bad enough that criminals trash things. When the police arrive and cover the scene with powder and chemicals and yellow tape and plastic, they just add to the mess. There's probably a real growth market in cleaning up after crime scenes. Not that I'd want to branch out into it. I have enough trouble cleaning out the tub drain after a shower, let alone sticking my hands into the effluvia of dead strangers.

Steve was writing down Woody's particulars and studying his identification around the time Dr. Fuller burst in. I expected her to take one look at her office and burst into tears, but she was made of sterner stuff. She stood in the middle of all that scrambled evidence of work, and shook her head in disgust.

"My field tent in Kenya was once scuttled, we think by stampeding water buffalo, and it was neater than this," she remarked drily. "At least the animals had no vested interest in our culture. This, on the other hand …"

"With the attack on Paul Calihoo, this is officially a crime scene, Dr. Fuller," Steve said, breaking in on her vision of a lengthy cleanup. "I'm afraid we have to ask you not to touch anything. If you could, though, eyeball the area and see if there's anything missing? That would help us determine if this was a robbery that became an attack, or an attack that turned into an act of vandalism."

"Right," she said. "How is Paul? Has there been any word?"

"Intensive care," answered Detective McCorquodale. Dr. F sucked her lips inward over her teeth, and bit down, obviously willing herself to remain businesslike and not break down.

"We'll have to contact his family. Has anyone called Laura, his wife?"

I hadn't even thought of doing so. I told her I would get right on it, and went to the front desk phone. There were ten programmable numbers per phone in the Centre, and I checked each out by pressing the corresponding number. The call display area announced whose number was chosen. Laura's work number was #4. I clicked the Dial button and waited through several rings. I was just about to give up when a very professional voice answered, "Nojack Press, Laura speaking."

"Hi Laura, this is Randy Craig calling from the Centre."

"Hi?" She sounded puzzled and cautious, since I doubt in a million years she'd ever expected to speak to me on the phone.

We'd met only once, in a movie lineup about two weeks after I'd been hired.

"I'm calling to let you know that it seems like Paul surprised a burglar here in Dr. Fuller's office, and he's been taken to the emergency at the U of A. Apparently he's in intensive care."

"Oh my God. Is he okay? I'll be right there, I mean the hospital." She hung up on me, which is probably how I'd have reacted under the same circumstances. I moved back to Dr. F's office in time to hear her say, "I'm quite certain they were here. I wouldn't have left them out in the general room of the Centre." Iain edged the office door closed so that I couldn't figure out by body language what she had been referring to. She didn't sound too happy, though.

Maybe it was a robbery. Campuses make a pretty easy target, all in all, especially in the summer months when most of the renovations happen. There are work crews unfamiliar to the security staff everywhere you look, and much less in the way of hallway traffic. I had heard that the overhead DVD/video projectors, newly installed in many of the classrooms in Grant MacEwan's South Campus, had been stolen within three weeks. Now the replacement machines sat in welded cages cobbled together by Facilities personnel.

It would be good if it had been a random robbery and not a personal attack on Paul Calihoo. I couldn't imagine Paul generating enough antagonism in anyone to warrant that being the objective of the attack. I was sure he had surprised someone who had then hit him to keep him from stopping or catching the unknown assailant. Likely it was someone who figured the

Centre had some form of petty cash that could be easily lifted. Why they thought petty cash would be in Dr. F's office was beyond me, though.

I must have been looking particularly blank, for me, because both Steve and Woody approached me with concern on their respective faces.

"Randy? Are you going to be okay?" Steve cupped a steadying hand on my elbow, and it felt as if his strength was the only thing actually keeping me standing. "Maybe you should go home. There's not going to be much peace around here to work today. Can you make it home on your own?"

"I could walk her there," offered Woody, "unless you still require me for the moment. I'll get you settled with a cup of tea and then head back here." Steve took a bit more of a look at Woody than he actually needed to, but agreed that it would be a good idea to have me ferried home like a semi-invalid. He told me he'd call in on me later, and then to my great surprise he kissed me on the forehead, in front of his crime scene cronies. Woody lifted his left eyebrow just slightly, but bobbed his head to Steve as he took my arm. I had the presence of mind to grab my backpack by the counter where I must have dropped it when originally spotting Paul. Out we went, back the same way I had walked what now seemed like hours ago. When we got outside, I was surprised to realize it was still morning, quite early out.

"What time is it, anyway?" I asked Woody, who was still holding my arm, taking his St. Bernard role very seriously.

"Ten to ten," he answered, after swivelling his left arm around to read his watch face, bringing his elbow into lock with mine and supporting it with his right hand, making me feel as if we were in some bizarre square dance, promenading home. "Just the right time for a cup of tea."

Before I knew it, we were at my apartment, and I was fishing into my backpack pocket for the keys. Woody loomed in the shadowy dark of the shotgun hallway once more, admiring the Persian runner and the hardwood. While I can't take credit for the decor, I am always proud to acknowledge I have the good taste to live where I do. We kicked off our shoes, and I dropped my backpack in the dining/office area. Woody moved past me to the kitchen, and began filling the kettle, then bustling about with the teapot and caddy. I left him to it, and wandered back into the living room to collapse on the chesterfield. What a bloody morning.

My phrasing, even though I hadn't actually uttered it out loud, was enough to make me shudder. Woody had just reappeared in the living room and must have thought I was in some level of shock. Who knows, maybe I was. He pulled out the folded quilt that I kept tucked behind a couch cushion and wrapped it around my shoulders, chafing my arms through the blanket.

"The tea will be ready soon, but you should stay warm." Ironic, the heat wave had just broken, and here I was already shivering again at the thought of Paul lying there in his own blood.

Surely there was nothing in the Centre that was worth coshing a man unconscious for. The whole scene kept hanging behind my eyelids like a puzzle picture where you have to figure out what's wrong, but it all seems perfectly normal. Of course, this picture didn't seem normal at all. I must have shaken visibly once more, because Woody pulled me over to him and wrapped his arms around me. I leaned into his chest and began to cry.

16

Eventually I got myself together. It would be more accurate to say that Woody got me together, really, since he was the one who got me tea and cookies—which I had forgotten were even in my cupboard—and alternated between companionable silences and cheerful chatter. He had a knack for being optimistic and easy without appearing callous to the events that had just occurred. I wasn't sure, but I figured that had to be an uncommon talent.

Steve called around noon, but Woody was the one who talked to him, in muted tones, so I couldn't quite overhear them. By that time, I was curled up on the couch, sliding in and out of a nap. Woody roused me with a tray he placed on my coffee table, and offered me a hand so I could swing myself up and around to have some lunch.

He had made tomato soup and cheese melts. It was such a

nursery comfort meal that I almost burst out crying again, but instead my stomach gave a cheerful growl and I decided just to tuck in. Woody smiled in approval and retrieved a tray of his own from the kitchen. He sat in the chair across from me, balancing his tray on his knees, and slurped his soup happily.

"My mom used to make me this very meal when I had to stay home sick from school," he offered, between slurps.

"Mine, too," I said.

"No kidding? Maybe there's less to this forty-ninth parallel than meets the eye. I mean, you've got your proto-Japanese shoe removal at the door, and all that nitpicking business about universal medicare, and don't get me started on the Queen, but when it shakes out, we have a lot more in common with each other than say we would with citizens of Yapp or Burkina Faso."

"Don't say that too loudly in some quarters. There are heaps of Canadians who can only identify themselves as non-Americans. Just think what would happen if they couldn't do that. They might just spontaneously combust."

"You see, that's why I think the Folkways project is still such a vital one. Moe Asch's vision of a heritage of sounds of the entire world does a lot more to indicate lines of similarity rather than lines of demarcation. More soup?"

I declined, and so Woody went into the kitchen to finish off the remainder. The soup was settling me down nicely, or maybe it was Woody's presence. I decided to test my land legs and unwrapped myself from my quilt. I followed Woody into the kitchen with my now empty tray and found him starting a sudsy pan of dishwater in my sink. I leaned against the edge of the built-in sideboard and watched him. I'd never seen such a tall man look so natural in an apron before, but Woody just seemed to fit in wherever he went. He calmly reached for my soup bowl and started humming as he splashed his hands into the dishpan.

It took me a minute, but I realized that what he was humming was "I've Been Working on the Railroad." I started to laugh, thinking of who was in the kitchen with Dinah. It was likely my banjo in the corner of the living room that had put it in his mind. It was amazing how many songs actually mentioned banjos in comparison to, say, piccolos or lutes.

"Fee fie fiddle dee oh, strumming on the ole banjo," we both warbled in questionable harmony and ended up laughing, which I suppose is what music is supposed to do. I know I felt a bit lighter.

"Thanks, Woody," I said, picking up a tea towel.

"My momma raised me to always do the dishes, or at least offer," he replied, making room for me to get to the drying rack beside him on the counter.

"I don't mean the dishes, although I must say, I admire the way your momma raised her children. I mean taking care of me this morning. I feel like I've really interfered with your work. I had no idea I was going to get so swacked out by things, but I am sure glad you were around when you were. I think Steve is likely relieved, too, not to have to worry about me while he's busy trying to get his job done."

"Don't be too sure about that. Of course, your Steve there is a very perceptive fellow. However, that is what I'm here for, to take care of the Folkways' interests in the midst of upheaval, problems and muggings. Since you represent Folkways' interests here in Edmonton in more ways than one, I figure I'm following my directives to the letter." He turned and smiled at me. I could swear a space heater had just been turned on me full blast. I felt like a magnet being drawn closer, but forced myself backward and turned to pick up another handful of cutlery in my towel. I could feel Woody's eyes on me still, but I studiously avoided looking at him, concentrating on getting the knives as dry as possible before setting them into the cutlery drawer beside me.

Finally I heard him rinsing the tea mugs, swooshing the wash water into the low white sink, and rinsing the pan itself. I handed him the tea towel to swipe out the dishpan before he hung it back up on the hook I'd glued to the side of the fridge. He dried his hands on the apron and then removed it.

I led the way back into the living room. Both of us seemed to have moved back into work mode. We were Folkways employees, and something was attacking our livelihood. While I had complete faith in Steve's ability to read a crime scene and solve the murder and the attempted murder, it couldn't hurt for Woody and me to find some sort of pattern or link between the two, if indeed there was one. I considered grabbing my laptop and opening my murder file, but figured a fresh perspective would happen by starting fresh with Woody. I grabbed a notepad and pen from the coffee table, and Woody began to list out some of the issues we were facing.

"David Finster is killed. We know he had discovered and was objecting to the Folkways bequest his mother made. We likely can't find out whether there was trouble in his own personal life, or in the construction business, but we'd need to before we can assume that Folkways was sufficient cause for his death."

"I'm sure Steven and Iain are working all the angles."

"Of course, that's what the police are brilliant at. What we can be brilliant at, I hope, is figuring out whether or not there is someone targeting Folkways in particular, by working from the inside outward. I have to think that, given the attack on Paul this morning, there's something to be said for Finster's death being Folkways-related. I can't get my head wrapped around the idea that Edmonton is somehow a hotbed of physical danger, especially around the university campus. It just doesn't compute."

I nodded. It wasn't totally unheard of to hear of fights and even killings in the news, but when they did occur, they happened in the less salubrious parts of town. I couldn't recall anyone ever being mugged inside an actual university building before this morning.

"So, if we are to continue along the logical progression, whoever killed David Finster likely also attacked Paul Calihoo. It is also possible to infer that this mysterious person was looking for something associated with the Folkways collection, since that seems to be the only point of intersection between the two men, right?"

So far Woody was making sense, although I wasn't absolutely sold on the idea that it was the same attacker in both cases.

"If it was the same person, do you think maybe Paul's attack happened just because he was in the way?"

"Why do you say that?"

"Well, for one thing, there wasn't anything extra brought

along to make it into a folk song." I went on to describe as much detail as I had gleaned about the scene of crime folk tableau found with David Finster. "So there isn't any of that stuff around Paul. He's just lying there, oozing blood. Now, maybe there is a folk song about someone hit on the head in his own place of work, and left for dead, but it's not springing to mind."

Woody looked contemplative for a few minutes, and then shook his head. "Nothing as clear as your Tom Dooley reference, that's for sure. The only thing that actually springs to my mind isn't even a Folkways recording and that's Jim Croce's 'You Don't Mess Around with Jim.' He shook his head even more forcefully. "And that won't do, it's about a knife fight."

"Well, maybe whoever didn't expect Paul to be in the office so early was there to steal something. I think I overheard Dr. Fuller telling the police there was something missing from her office, but I have no idea what it could be. We should ask her. Maybe Steve will tell me later, but I wouldn't count on it. Of course, if the intruder knew anything at all about the workings of the Centre, they'd realize that Paul would be in, like clockwork, at eight."

"Do you think they came in after Paul, or did he walk in on a robbery already in progress?"

I wondered that, too. If he opened the door to the Centre at eight as usual, wouldn't he have been able to see anyone inside? He'd have been able to see all the open area, from my carrel corner to the counter to the right. If the intruder was already in Dr. Fuller's office, with the door closed, then perhaps he wouldn't have any hint that there was something wrong. The climate-controlling main door closed heavily as one walked into the Centre, so the intruder would have been warned of Paul's arrival. All he or she would have to do was wait inside Dr. F's office till Paul rounded the counter and turned toward the main part of the room. If the intruder wasn't waiting to attack Paul specifically, and I supposed we couldn't rule that out, then he or she would have to incapacitate him somehow to escape Dr. F's office unscathed.

It would really help to know what was missing from Dr. F's office. I wondered if Steve would be forthcoming with that sort of information. I wasn't sure where I stood in terms of receiving information about this case at all, given that I was supposedly on the list of suspects in the Finster murder. I didn't see how I could be considered problematic in Paul's attack, but then again you never knew. One general rule of thumb is to suspect whoever finds the body and calls, and that had been me.

Woody made us more tea, and then we decided to go for a walk. He had a cellphone, and I had been excused from work for the entire day, so technically it wouldn't be skipping out of duties. Nonetheless, I felt sort of guilty as I strolled across the High Level Bridge with Woody, as if I'd called in sick to school and was taking a Ferris Bueller day.

Woody was easy to talk with, and seemed to have no end of interest in things he saw. He managed to make polite noises about our Legislature Building and reflecting pool, even though he came from Washington, where the most famous reflecting pool of all time shimmered. I took him down Jasper Avenue, which was starting to emerge from its thirty years' slumber into a relatively interesting place. Give it a few more bistros and bookstores, and we might actually revive the downtown. We then wandered over to Sir Winston Churchill Square, where they were setting up for the Taste of Edmonton food festival beginning the next week.

"How on earth do you keep track of all the festivals? It's like the summer arrives and you folks go into party mode." He danced a few steps of an impromptu conga.

I laughed, which was probably Woody's intention in the first place. All part of the cheer-Randy-up campaign.

"Honestly, though, I love it. In fact, I'm going to have to race around back home to get everything done in time if I have a hope of getting back here for Heritage Days."

"You're heading back to Washington?"

Woody nodded.

"Yes, I got a call this morning, right before you called me over to the Centre about Paul. Once the police are ready to let me leave, I'm going to have to head back home to see about expediting the movement of some of the Smithsonian Folkways recordings through Customs in time for the Folk Festival sales tent. Apparently, I alone am qualified to handle the paperwork on that, which in other words means I must have lost a bet somewhere. If I can get all that done sooner rather than later, it'd be all to the good. I figure it will take me a week, not more than two. Sorting out the Folk Fest requirements will need to be handled from here closer to the time and Heritage Days sounds like a fun time."

"You bet! Eighty-three varieties of meat on a stick." I grinned.

"Actually, I like it a lot. It's about the only festival here in town where you get a complete cross-section of the populace. Besides, Heritage Days is set in the park, and it's so much nicer to walk around on grass than on tarmac or concrete."

"Well, if you don't resent me deserting you as you deal with all this turmoil at work and the upcoming Folk Fest, I promise I'll be back to escort you to Heritage Days." He grinned at me and put out his hand. I shook it and we pronounced it a deal. I led us past the CBC windows and the Made in Canada store, which Woody insisted on popping in. He bought a birdhouse shaped like a grain elevator, and had it wrapped up as a gift. I looked at earrings, waiting. I wondered who the gift was for back in Washington, but didn't really want to find out. I took us past the Telus Towers, across the patio, and along Macdonald Drive to see the river valley view. Then we crossed over to wait for a bus in front of the *Edmonton Journal* building on the corner of 101st Street. There are times when enough walking is enough walking.

We got off the bus in front of the Garneau Cinema and Woody left me at the entrance to my apartment around the corner.

"I'm flying out day after tomorrow, as soon as I've had it okayed with your Steve. I have a feeling he'll be just fine with me leaving," he smiled, and leaned over to kiss me on the cheek.

I watched him lope down the avenue toward his hotel. I had a feeling he was right about Steve.

17

The day after Woody left, Denise called me to see about a day out. The police still had the Centre cordoned off, so there was very little I could do at work. Dr. Fuller called me the evening before and asked me to keep track of my hours working at home, but not to "push myself," as she put it. I was taking that to mean that three or four hours of work on the laptop would see me square on the job for the next little while. Steve was keeping a pretty low profile, too, at least from me, which had me feeling troubled. I was all for taking my mind off things, and besides, aside from our one quick lunch, I'd been without Denise for two whole months.

Denise picked me up outside my apartment. She was driving her baby, a Volkswagen Beetle convertible in a creamy off-white colour with black leather interior. With her shiny blond hair and penchant for basic black clothing, the car seemed like an extension of her ensemble. It made me wonder what sort of car I could consider an appropriate accessory—perhaps a Pacer: out of date, almost transparent and dependable, with plenty of storage room. I was better off with a bus pass.

I slipped into the passenger seat and buckled up. Edmontonians with convertibles are almost all optimists by nature. We have so little in the way of actual summer, even though the days are long, and it seems like more of those days are taken up with umbrellas these past few years than before. Denise had a hard shell for her Bug, but tended to park it in a heated garage for most of the winter and take the bus, thereby avoiding the cost of university parking, higher insurance rates and offensive drivers on wintry streets. She had bought the car a year and a half ago and it still looked showroom shiny.

Denise had a plan for the morning, with several stops to make, but aside from an idea for a nice lunch spot to introduce me to, she had nothing much planned for the afternoon. My suggestion of hitting a Barbara Shoppe was met with incredulity.

"Does Steve know you're detecting, Randy?"

"How do you know I'm not just interested in seeing how the other half lives?"

"Half? More like other five percent. What the heck, I have nearly new underwear on, sure. We can go to the one in the west end. It's near the lunch place I was thinking of."

We popped into Lee Valley for fruit fly traps, which Denise swore by, so I obediently bought a box of two as well. The place was like home-project porn for gardeners and woodworkers. All the tools and canny devices listed in their catalogues were set out for inspection. I could see at least seven items that would improve the quality of my life, but the predominant improvement would be the ensuing lightness of my pocketbook, so I restricted myself to daydreaming.

"You can dream all year long," Denise confided, as we waited for our numbers to be called and orders filled. "Now that they have your name and address in their computer, they'll send you their delectable catalogues."

After Lee Valley, Denise headed us south to the Callingwood Shopping Centre, which is actually an extended strip mall anchored by a Safeway that also hosts a farmers' market twice a week. We, however, were here to have lunch. Denise had discovered The Bagel Bin a while back when helping a friend move. The bakery was on site, and everything on the menu—written on chalkboards behind the counter—was made from scratch. I chose the lox and cream cheese on a country bagel with an order of cream of wild rice soup. Denise had a grilled veggie panini. The food was delicious, and another mark of its excellence emerged when we each admitted that we were a little sorry we hadn't chosen what the other had ordered, since it looked so good.

Denise scooped a taste of my soup with her coffee spoon.

"Mmm, it's sort of like clam chowder without all the fishiness! I swear, everything on the menu is great. I should just sit here and try it all."

"It's a bit out of the way, but that's probably a good thing, considering how much cream might be in this soup," I said, pulling my bowl proprietarily back toward me. Denise nodded.

"No doubt. But it would be worth it to get fat on this sort of diet."

We spent the next few minutes digesting in silence, the mark of truly great food or inordinately hungry people. With half a bagel to go, I took a sip of water and sat back for a bit.

"So, Barbara Shoppe is next, right? Is it very, very swanky? Am I going to be embarrassed to walk in there dressed as I am?"

Denise raked a clinical eye over my ensemble, which consisted of red jeans, red Birkenstock rubber clogs, and a white and red striped T-shirt. She was wearing a sleeveless black polo-necked top tucked into black slub linen trousers, with black strappy sandals showing off a beautiful pedicure and discreet silver toe ring. Denise would always look classically appropriate wherever she went. She nodded, and said that I looked as if I'd been hauled away from my prize-winning perennial garden and had a sort of Katherine Hepburn disregard for fashion.

Since I actually bought the T-shirt brand new rather than as my usual thrift shop find, I was a bit put out by her assessment, but was so pleased to be compared to Katherine Hepburn I didn't let it get to me overmuch. As long as no one looked askance at me in the store, I didn't mind.

Denise laughed at my obvious nervousness over our upcoming sortie and seemed so jazzed by the idea of spying out the woman who might be making life miserable for me that I didn't have the heart to call it off. Besides, what possible harm could it do to go into the store?

We got in the car and drove to a small shopping plaza near the zoo, halfway back toward the centre of town. The Barbara

Shoppe was snuggled in between an Italian bakery and a wine-making supplies store. There was another bistro-style restaurant at one end of the strip, and a small pharmacy at the other. All the cars in the ample lot looked either brand new or classic. It occurred to me that I'd never actually seen this place before. I guess I just don't move in the right circles.

I'd read an article in the paper a couple of years ago that made me laugh about where the "working rich" lived in Edmonton, as opposed to both the middle class and the idle rich. It just never hit me that there would be idle rich here. After all, if you didn't have to work for your livelihood, why wouldn't you take yourself to somewhere more climatically hospitable? However, it seemed there was a coterie of trust fund babies who ambled about on various curves of the riverbank and never had to bother to ask how much anything cost. This had the look of a place they might frequent. I was starting to regret the whole idea.

Denise turned to me as she removed her driving sunglasses and checked her hair in the mirror behind her sun visor.

"Ready, Randy? Just remember, these women can smell fear. Just try to look bored and we'll be just fine."

"I'll let you do all the talking."

"That would be best. Okay, ready set—charge it."

The carpet in the Barbara Shoppe was thicker and softer than most mattresses. While the door didn't chime when we walked in, I think it must have set off some sort of announcement, because a well-tailored woman in her mid-forties appeared from behind a mirrored wall. She smiled a welcome from her position behind a highly polished French-styled table desk, which held a ledger, a small collection of pens in a crystal tumbler, another crystal saucer with assorted pins and elastics, and a large vase of flowers. The clerk, or manager, or whatever she was, feigned arranging the already perfectly arranged orange gladioli and burnished bronze eucalyptus leaves, which I was betting she had chosen to complement her own light auburn hair and creamy complexion. The scarf around her neck had orange and rust colours winding through a cream overprint, along with an almost brown tone that matched the shade of her dark linen skirt. She would have looked right at home in Buckingham Palace, or even Monaco, and her cultured voice matched her looks, I realized, as she spoke to us.

"I'm so relieved the weather has decided to calm into merely pleasant. My garden was about to frizzle up and admit defeat last week."

"Did those lovely glads come from your garden?" Denise moved forward into the circle of conversation. She'd obviously been born knowing the right thing to say in any situation. The woman lost her veneer of forced charm and smiled honestly at her.

"Yes, they did. I've been very lucky with my gladioli these last few years. My mother said she found them too 'insistent' but I've always loved their vigour." She dusted imaginary garden soil from her perfectly manicured hands and turned full face to Denise. "Was there something special you were hunting for, or are you having a pleasure jaunt?"

I don't know what it is about some people's ideas of pleasure. I have never found shopping to be much of a joy, but I know of lots of people who see it as a diversion. My grandmother used to love to shop, and she counted it a major victory if she returned home with nothing.

Denise assured her new friend that we were just browsing, and we were left to our own recognizance. I looked at the price tag on a pair of gabardine trousers and lost the capacity to breathe for a moment. Denise's hand on my elbow shocked a gasp back into my throat.

"It might be a good idea to try something on. Salespeople tend to talk more if they think you're serious about their merchandise. Do you want to try things or should I?"

"I'm not sure they'd have my size; aren't they all size 2 at the country club?"

"Don't you believe it. In order to survive, a place like this has to have sizes for the dowagers who are rich enough to not have to worry about tennis lessons. The real beauty will be that you will find yourself mysteriously fitting into sizes about one to two sizes less than you would in your average chain store. Extreme wealth means never having to say you're plus sized."

Denise was right. Aside from the rack of camel-hair skirts and jackets from Jaeger in London, most of the sizes were skewed slightly larger than I was used to. She and I randomly chose skirts and dresses to try on. I had to call for help from the saleslady when I discovered that I was swimming in the size 12s and 14s I'd picked out. Soon I was decked out in a full-skirted silk dress slightly reminiscent of the Fifties, twirling in the three-way mirror in the dressing room common area. Maybe it was worth $600 to claim I was a size 9.

Denise came out of her dressing room looking like a blond Jackie Kennedy minus the pillbox hat.

"Chanel is reinventing itself," the saleslady, who asked us to call her Pia (though I was certain she was going to say Grace), purred approvingly. Denise's suit was wheat coloured, with black and gold piping around the edges of the boxy jacket and the pocket flaps. Black and gold military buttons marched down the front. Pia pulled a black suede headband from behind her back and offered it to Denise. She was right. It was perfect, pulling back Denise's blond hair and declaring it part of the ensemble. "Now that suit will take you to the opera or to the steeplechase. In fact, if you wanted to try a pair of black trousers with the jacket you can see how easily this becomes a staple classic for your wardrobe."

Denise allowed her to go searching for a pair of trousers with which to make her point, and turned to examine my dress.

"That style looks great on you, Randy. Actually, most of the Fifties and Sixties styles look great on all women. I think Twiggy and Mary Quant should be taken out and shot for what they bequeathed the rest of us."

"Sure it looks great, but did you see what it costs?" I hissed, so that Pia wouldn't overhear my ingratitude for being considered petite.

"No one is going to force you to buy it, kiddo. Just enjoy."

I shrugged. Maybe I was missing some essential shopping gene. I just didn't get it. I turned to head back into my changing room, which was probably the most luxurious room I'd ever seen outside a stately homes tour. There was a Louis XIV-style chair and table in the corner, and a huge gilt mirror on the wall. A coat rack with a fluffy white housecoat stood in the other corner. Terry-towel slippers sat under the housecoat. At the side of the louvred doorway was a small framed sign hanging over a set of doorbells, similar to that of a small apartment building. The sign indicated that one should ring the bell next to our particular sales lady's name if we required any help, but to feel welcome to don the robe and venture out into the shop if we wished.

I probably could have managed the back zipper on the dress, but I had a hankering to see what Pia's call bell would sound like. A muted "Ode to Joy" sounded somewhere out beyond the change area, and the super saleswoman appeared almost immediately. She had trousers for Denise, and was more than pleased to oblige with the zipper.

"I have a middy blouse I think you would just love. Would you care to try it?" I wasn't all that sure what a middy blouse was. I nodded to Pia and popped back into my red jeans in the meantime. I silently thanked the gods of lingerie that I was wearing a relatively new brassiere that didn't have that dingy look most of my bras took on just before the underwire decided to work its way through the lining and stab me.

The mirror in the changing room had to be rigged like a funhouse mirror. I swear I looked twenty pounds thinner when I looked in it. Maybe I should just move in, and let Pia run out for my meals.

Since we were all alone in the store, I risked opening my door and calling out to Denise. She had the trousers on now, and appeared in the doorway of her change room.

"Don't you love it? I wish I could handle having only about four classic pieces in my wardrobe and letting them become my signature silhouette. The trouble is, I have enough budget to get one suit and a pair of trousers, or four blouses, three pairs of jeans, two wool jumpers, a black skirt and four mix-and-match pieces of power-suit dressing—but not both."

"I could shop for two years at Value Village for what that dress cost," I replied. Denise laughed, and then nodded.

"The thing about this kind of wardrobe is that you're a lot more likely to come across pieces like it at Value Village than you are to find blue jeans. People eventually grow bored of their clothing, I think, and this sort of thing is just way too good to cut up for rags or sew into a patchwork quilt." She grinned. "Take me with you on your next foray and I'll see what sorts of labelwear I can find."

Pia reappeared at that moment and flourished a sailor top in front of her. It was made of a thick, cream-coloured polished cotton, and navy piping was worked into two lines around the squared-off sailor collar. My mouth must have hung open because Pia beamed with a look of self-congratulation. She had my number but good.

I walked into the change room holding the middy blouse in front of me. I didn't bother looking at the price tag, knowing that I had to try it on, and not wanting to be dissuaded before I could feel it on my skin. I closed my eyes and slipped it over my head.

It was perfect. It hung just to the right length to make my hips seem controllable, and felt like silk against my skin. The long sleeves ended in cuffs that looked tailored, but somehow hid an elastic, making them easy to slide into. With my hair drawn back into a braid, I looked like a young Victorian girl ready to recite "The Boy Stood On the Burning Deck" for my mother's tea party, or to be Anne Shirley's bosom friend, Diana. I loved it. I turned to the door, and opened it. Denise and Pia were standing there, waiting, and both of them clapped spontaneously at the sight of me.

"Tell me it's not too expensive, Denise," I begged, holding up my hair so that she could scoop out the price tag from the back of my neck.

"It's not too bad, depending on how much you love it."

I took a deep breath. "Tell me," I said.

"One hundred and fifty dollars."

"Oh, dear."

"It is on sale, dear," Pia rode in to the rescue, although God only knows what the word sale meant in this environment. "It was in our spring offerings, mostly for cruise wear, we thought. Maybe it was just too young a look for some of our clientele. Let me go check the books."

Denise and I looked at each other. While she could walk away from a Chanel suit with a laugh and a shrug, I wasn't sure I could leave this top behind.

Pia was back in a minute.

"It is marked down to ninety-three dollars." Ninety-three dollars? For a shirt? I couldn't do it. I shook my head and went back into the changing room. In a minute, I was standing near the door with Denise, back in my red striped T-shirt. Pia smiled and offered a parting shot.

"Check back with us in another month when all the summer clothes go on sale. Our spring wear will be even more reduced then."

I promised to return in late August and pulled the door open. The air was palpable on our skin; it had warmed up that much while we were in there.

"Careful of the seatbelt buckle," Denise warned as we slid into her car. "So, that's the Barbara Shoppe. No sign of Barbara Finster, no obvious element of folk music haters. Did you get anything at all out of that visit, besides a longing for the sea?" she laughed.

Easy for her. Everything looked good on her. I was going to be dreaming about that blouse for a long time to come.

18

While I had been salivating over the middy blouse, apparently Denise actually got some information out of Pia about what it was like to work for "the formidable Barbara." She'd been with the Barbara Shoppes for twenty-two years, and a couple of the other salesladies even longer, lured over from Johnston Walkers when it went the way of the dodo.

"The first Shoppe was in a basement under a music store on Jasper Avenue, around the same block as the old Paramount Theatre, from what I could figure, give or take a block. Pia started talking about having to stop meeting for coffee and butterhorns at the Silk Hat Restaurant because Barbara had determined that it wasn't seemly that her ladies would be seen frequenting a greasy spoon. Now, I know the Silk Hat is still there, in a new configuration as a fancy bar, but precious little else is."

"Twenty-two years selling overpriced clothing to wealthy women?" Knowing that, I couldn't imagine how Pia could plaster on a smile in the morning, and her smile had seemed genuine enough.

Denise shrugged.

"It's a living. You would be amazed at what sorts of livings people eke out all over the place, Randy. Look up from your books once in a while."

I felt ashamed. Denise was right. Someone had to keep the world as we knew it ticking along. Just because I didn't see a particular need for a certain job didn't mean it wasn't necessary. After all, without clothes boutiques and artisan bakeries, perhaps the streets would be overrun with gangs of truculent members of the Junior League, looking for trouble.

Denise went on: "So Pia and the other ladies assumed that when Ms. Finster expanded the business to three Shoppes, two in town and one in Calgary, as well as moving from the original location, that the commensurate profits would be reflected in both their pay and benefits packets. It's about this time that the picture gets a little less rosy."

"God! When did she tell you all this? I swear I was only in the dressing room alone for a minute or two."

"You were mooning over that sailor top for at least half an hour," Denise laughed. "It's almost two-thirty, you know."

I looked down at my wrist to check and realized for the first time that I'd forgotten to wear a watch. There was proof positive that I trust Denise as a true friend. Having allowed her to control the shape of the day, I left it all in her capable hands.

Two-thirty? I couldn't imagine that we'd been breathing that rarified Barbara Shoppe air for over ninety minutes. Maybe I was catching a glimpse of the magic of entertainment shopping.

We were by this time zooming over the one-lane bridge that merges traffic onto the Whitemud Freeway heading southbound. When Denise got back on solid land, she changed to the middle lane, which meant she didn't intend to take Fox Drive exit to the university off the bridge. Like any good annoying passenger, I was immediately on the defensive, wondering out loud where we were headed.

"There's another Barbara Shoppe out in the southwest end of town. I thought you might be interested in seeing if they had your sailor suit on a deeper discount." I was about to protest when I caught on that she was joking. Damn if she didn't look just like the Cheshire Cat when she grinned.

"I thought it might be a good idea to hit both of the Shoppes here before they begin to compare notes and get back to the boss lady, what do you think?"

I thought that Denise, who had always bemoaned my propensity to propel myself into dangerous situations, was actually getting bitten by the detective bug herself, and I told her so. She laughed out loud.

"I will admit that if it comes to trying on clothes and gossiping about the active rich, then I am all over this. Guns and bad guys I will leave to Steve and his pals. I just can't see Steve in a Chanel suit, though, you know?"

I laughed, too. All in all, this was not a bad way to spend a free day. I felt like I was tuning into an important feminine wavelength. This wasn't likely what Gloria Steinem had in mind for me, but what the hey.

"Speaking of gossip," Denise broke into my feminist reverie, "I ran into Mary Montgomery again a couple of days ago." I cocked my head slightly, indicating, in that way that dogs and small rodents do, that this was something worthy of note. Mary Montgomery had been in one of my grad seminars back in my MA days, and I seemed to recall that she and Denise shared an office at one time. She was sort of a rival of Denise's in that they both wanted full-time security in the English department, but since they were each carving their own way to it, I didn't think the rivalry was too furious.

Of course, you never knew with Mary. What she reminded me most of was a Valkyrie, tall and strong and squarely built. She had wild, curly auburn hair that hung down her back, and she strode everywhere purposefully, even when she was merely headed to Java Jive for a cup of coffee. She was blunt almost to the point of brusqueness, but I don't think that, for the most part, she meant to be rude.

While Denise had moved into becoming the administration's darling for running the writer-in-residence program while teaching a full course load, Mary had seen the future as a paperless world and jumped on the bandwagon of the Orlando Project, which was an English department venture to secure under-known and consequently undervalued feminist texts and biographies online in a set-up complementary to the Guttenberg Project. Mary did research associate work for the project all through her PhD work, and parlayed her familiarity with the software program and the project's templates into a full-time position that turned into an elongated post-doctoral placement. Aside from the fact that Mary hated teaching undergraduates, which was a necessary evil when working in a university environment, she was mostly content with her lot in life as the Orlando Project overseer.

"It seems Mary's none too happy with the influx of money for the Folkways project," Denise continued.

"What does it have to do with her, though?" I couldn't see the connection that Denise seemed to think obvious. I could sense her impatience with my denseness.

"Mary thinks the university should be endowing the Orlando Project with more sustained funding. It's a proven entity, it's entirely the baby of the U of A, and her life would be a whole lot easier if she didn't have to stop every three years and go cap in hand for grants to keep it going."

"But what does that have to do with the Finster bequest? It's not as if the late Mrs. Finster had a crush on *Mrs. Dalloway*. She wanted to support folk music, not any old university project. And when it came right down to it, she wanted to support something that would fly in the face of her husband and children, from the looks of things."

"Feminist literature might fit that bill just as easily as fiddle tunes," Denise replied. "Anyhow, that's the way Mary sees it. The thing is, she sounded as if she knew all about the bequest, which makes me think that you and the Ethnomusicology Centre folks might have been out of the loop a lot more than you think."

I was a little bemused by the thought that Mary Montgomery

might see my job as some kind of an obstacle between her and the accessible funding money she craved. More than just bemused, I was also a little frightened. It didn't do to get on the bad side of Mary. She might dress you down in public in her precisely enunciated, clearly projecting voice. Or she might tackle you to the ground; you just never knew. Being even taller than me, she was the sort of person for whom the word "loom" existed. The thought of Mary Montgomery seeing me as an obstacle was not a pleasant thought.

It occurred to me that my job as the shaper of the Folkways online image was somewhat akin to Mary's job with the Orlando Project. I don't know why that hadn't connected for me before. I guess I hadn't started out thinking of my appointment as any sort of political step or judicious move on the professional ladder, the way I knew Mary thought about her position across campus.

Denise's gossip had taken some of the warmth out of the day for me, and I was so preoccupied with what she had said that it was a shock to realize that we were already turning into yet another parking lot.

The second Barbara Shoppe was located in an otherwise nondescript mall that housed a hair salon, an organic grocery, a dance school, a pet boutique, a wine shop and a Caribbean takeaway. The parking lot offered a much more mixed bag of rolling stock than the other location, as well. There were a couple of vintage muscle cars near one end of the lot, and several more minivans. The mall was partly strip, and partly covered, with tall glass doors leading to the interior where one found the dance school, salon and Barbara Shoppe, while the other businesses were located discreetly along the main sidewalk.

It was a nice touch, having the store there. I was betting all the patrons of the salon and clothing shop dreamed of their lither days as they elbowed their way among the bun-headed ballerinas. It probably worked both ways, with the little girls learning to breathe in the rarified air of Joy perfume before they knew just how much an ounce of it would set them back.

The same bell system must have been installed in all the stores. We were hardly six feet into the store when a tall, brutally slender woman, who had to be this store's equivalent of Pia, appeared from the back room. She was dressed in black ballet flats and a knee-length, pencil-thin tweed skirt. She wore a loose smock-styled top over it, and something was scratching at my memory for the look she evoked. It took me a moment, but when she welcomed us in a pseudo mid-Atlantic accent, I almost shouted it out. She was trying for Audrey Hepburn in *Funny Face*; I'd stake my last five dollars on it. So, we had Grace Kelly and Audrey Hepburn. This was like a road-tour version of *L.A. Confidential*. I wondered if Barbara Finster had thought this one up all on her own.

Denise exchanged pleasantries and I stifled a giggle when she told us her name was Holly. I'd just bet it was. This woman had a serious Audrey Hepburn fixation. Truth was, at her age, she should have been aiming for Audrey as an older Maid Marian, instead of Holly Golightly. I suspected that her name was probably Jane but that she'd changed it legally when she was eighteen, after seeing *Breakfast at Tiffany's* for the eighty-seventh time.

My mind was running along the lines of whether or not Mickey Rooney's racist stereotype of a Japanese national actually ruined that movie or only partially ruined it, when Denise waved me over to the sales rack Holly-Audrey had led her to.

There was no sign that said SALE on it. That would have been too easy. Instead there was a grouping of summer weights and spring colours all in one small area, rather than spread around the store. For instance, there was more concentrated pink and white in this rack than anywhere else in the Shoppe. It seemed that pink was on its way out and some sort of olive drab was now the "new black."

Denise held up my middy top, to taunt me, or so I thought. I moseyed over to them in time to hear Holly-Audrey say, "We just simply couldn't match it identically, so that's the reason for the pricing."

Denise held out one of the cuffs to me.

"Can you spot the button that doesn't match?"

I looked. All three buttons seemed to be similar brass buttons with anchors embossed on them. Holly-Audrey placed one long French-manicured nail next to the middle button.

"The rope on the anchor leads off to the left instead of the right, and it's not top drawer brass, I'm afraid. It's the closest we could find."

"Holly says that the button went missing the first week the blouses were in stock, and the manufacturer was out of them. They tried to match it the best they could, but this blouse, and this blouse only, is reduced to reflect the imperfection." Denise was grinning at me, and nudging me to look at the price tag. My mouth felt a bit dry. I turned the tag over in my hand and read, "Forty-nine dollars." I could feel my face forming into a grin, and I realized right then that we all have a price at which we are willing to jump. I knew, for example, that my price for silliness at a flea market is three dollars. Anything above that seems too much to me. A good price for a meal is eighteen dollars. If I go over that, there'd better be violins and free valet parking. And now I knew what I'd spend for an impulse piece of clothing.

"Would you like to try it on?" Holly-Audrey purred, and I suddenly found her affectations endearing rather than pretentious.

"Maybe I'd better." I checked over to Denise, who nodded and moved off to look at some silk dresses. Holly-Audrey led me through the portal at the back of the store into a room dominated by a Henry Moore statue. She left me in a changing room more spacious than my own bedroom and once again I fell under the spell of my new blouse. Eventually, although it seemed like just moments, I drifted back out carrying my prize.

"It's perfect. I tried it on in your other Shoppe, but it was still out of my price range. This is like a minor miracle for me." I could hear myself babbling, so I just busied myself with my debit card.

Holly-Audrey smiled with just a tinge of spite. It made me wonder if there was a quota system organized between the various Shoppes. Somehow, my buying the blouse here, even discounted as much as it was, put her ahead of Pia. I wondered if she liked Pia, or got pitted against her by the boss. I wondered what Barbara was like to work for.

Denise was on my wavelength and three steps ahead of me.

While I looked for my debit card, she leaned on the table where Holly was folding the blouse in tissue paper, with far more delicacy and care than I usually take over fragile Christmas presents to precious people. She obviously loved her job, and I admired her for it. If you are going to do something for a good portion of your life, you might as well put zest into it.

Holly was ringing through my debit card and being lulled almost into a gossip with Denise, who was admiring the light fixtures, of all things.

"Are these the same as the ones in the other Shoppe? I thought those had the look of actual crystal. I'm not saying these aren't very nice, I just assumed there would be some uniformity throughout the shops."

Denise had hit a nerve, and it was an old wound, from the sound of it.

"Miss Barbara had told us that we'd all be equal, but that it didn't necessarily mean the same. Her idea is that the clientele will be moving from Shoppe to Shoppe, instead of having a loyalty to one particular place. I don't mean to doubt her thinking, but my ladies tend to be very loyal to this site. I wish we'd received the chandeliers like the west end Shoppe, but Pia had first dibs because she worked in the original Shoppe. Instead, we got the statue in the dressing room foyer." Her shrug toward the back of the shop was dismissive. "It's supposed to be something special, but Miss Barbara isn't the one who has to deal with it day in and day out. You can go back and look at it if you want."

Denise lifted an eyebrow to me, and I grinned and nodded. Retrieving my card and accepting my shiny, blue paper-handled shopping bag, I moved toward the changing area with her. I knew what to expect, but was anticipating Denise's reaction to the Henry Moore nude lolling back on her elbows in pride of place.

Denise snorted a polite chuckle beside me. "Now I will bet you any dowager seeing those hips is going to feel svelte in comparison! What a great idea."

I nodded, noting that Holly had draped a gauzy scarf across the nude's lap. I might have to give Miss Barbara Finster more credit for a sense of humour than I'd previously considered her to have. Of course, she might have just done it to irritate the help.

Speak of the devil and she appears, my grandmother used to say, as if I was personally responsible each time her blithery neighbour popped by to borrow her angel food pan or some walnuts. It was uncanny, of course, how Mrs. Archibold would show up usually right after I'd done my impression of her, which was razor sharp in the manner of twelve-year-olds who haven't yet been stung with cellulite, acne or empathy. It seems I hadn't lost the touch in the intervening years, though I was hoping I'd become somewhat more diplomatic. As we turned back into the central part of the Shoppe, who should be blocking the doorway to the mini-mall but Miss Barbara in person, looking strong enough to have posed for Henry Moore herself.

She looked at me with the vague smile we reserve for people whom we are sure we've seen somewhere before but can't place in a different context. I know the look mostly because I tend to use it on old students from two or three years previous. I gave her a noncommittal smile in return, and Denise and I scooted past her and into the relative freedom of a swarm of frothy pink fairies stomping down the mall in tutus, hoodies and hightops, swinging enormous pink gym bags over their slight shoulders. We didn't talk till we reached the car.

"So I take it that Maleficent as portrayed by Bea Arthur back there was Miss Barbara herself?" queried Denise, as we buckled up and started toward home. I laughed.

"I was thinking of her as rivalling the backroom statue, but that's an apt image, too. There's just something about her that makes me leery of letting her into a dressing room with me, you know? How did she ever create a set of exclusive dress shops, anyhow?"

"Oh, I doubt she ever deigns to actually wait on anyone. She just hires these vassals and then looms over them, haunting their dreams and nursing their fantasies. Speaking of fantasies, who do you think the Calgary manager is trying to be, if we already have Grace Kelly and Audrey Hepburn?"

I hooted with the release of my own wicked thoughts. "My money's on either Catherine Deneuve or Lauren Bacall. How could we find out?"

"I wish I could drive down there, but I don't honestly have time right now," Denise sighed. "Maybe we can head down to check her out next weekend? Who knows, you might decide you want to pick up the sailor pants that match your top."

"That's going a bit overboard, I think. This top can go with a skirt for dressy, or with jeans for everyday work. I think it's a classic. Maybe that is the way to shop, one or two classic pieces in your wardrobe that will last for all time."

"Classics are houndstooth, Chanel suits and pearls. A sailor suit is nursery wear."

"Ouch, that's not fair."

"I'm not saying there's anything wrong with it. I'm just saying you have to acknowledge that your concept of style has more to do with the playroom than the boardroom."

I thought about the various pieces of Winnie-the-Pooh lingerie in my drawer at home and had to admit that, if nothing else, Denise actually knew me. Instead of feeling insulted, I felt oddly pleased to have been considered by my friend at such a minute analytical level. As Oscar Wilde might have said, there's only one thing worse than being thought about, and that's not being thought about. However, given how I was about to be run through the rumour mill, I have come to the conclusion that Wilde is no longer the final word on everything in my philosophy.

19

Denise refused to come in for tea and zoomed away down the alley from the apartment building's back entry where she'd let me off, waving without looking back. I turned back into the comfortable gloom of the hallway, hugging my glossy Barbara Shoppe bag to me like a guilty treasure. My mother wouldn't believe that I'd even entered a store like that, let alone bought something. I made a mental note to call my parents, and kicked off my clogs at the door to my apartment.

The message light on the answering machine was blinking from across the room, and as I neared I could read the numeral four. I clicked the ALL button on my way through to the tea kettle. Every single message, barring one electronic voice telling me my reserve request from the library could be picked up, was from Steve. I didn't even bother checking the caller ID as I picked up the ringing phone, while pressing erase on the message machine.

"Randy, where the heck have you been? And when the hell are you going to get a cellphone? I have been trying to reach you all day."

"I was out with Denise," was about all I could squeeze in by way of explanation before he was off on another mini-tirade. He had tried to get hold of me through the Centre, and was told we weren't holding regular hours because of the crime scene embargo, so he assumed I'd be home at my computer busily doing whatever it was I was supposed to be doing. And now it turned out I'd been out all day with a girlfriend.

It was beginning to sound a lot like envy rather than worry or censure to me, but I let him vent. Pretty soon, he ran out of steam and I asked him why he'd needed to get hold of me.

This was apparently not the thing to ask one's boyfriend, especially not in the aftermath of an attack causing a coma in my fellow worker. Steve had been worried about me and now he was angry with me for having wasted his concern.

"But I'm delighted you were worried about me! This wasn't emotion in vain. Play your cards right, and this is worth more than candy and flowers."

There was a pause on the other end of the line. "Sometimes I think I'm getting close, but then I realize I will never understand women as long as I live."

I made soothing noises, and he suggested we go out for supper. I hung up the phone, smiling. It was nice to be worried about. Not that there was anything to worry about. Then for a minute, I began to worry that perhaps he was more worried about not knowing where I was than he was actually worried about me. As in not knowing where his chief suspect was. Ah, worrying could get you into too much trouble.

I took my new blouse into the bedroom and lovingly pulled it out of its bag. I found a hanger in my closet to slide it onto and pushed the assorted hanging oddments to either side so that it wouldn't be crumpled settling in among its new surroundings. I then pulled out the tissue and folded the blue bag reverently, thinking it might be good to carry shoes or lunch in when I wanted to impress someone with my fashion savoir faire. I slid it down between my dresser and the wall.

It was just turning five o'clock and Steve wasn't coming by till seven. I grabbed an apple to tide me over and figured I would get a couple of hours' work done before he arrived. Even though I had explained to Steve that Dr. F hadn't been expecting me to put in full-time hours from home, it did feel sort of funny to be taking a holiday because Paul's head had been bashed in.

I took a jump drive to my laptop and transferred some of the documents from work over to my desktop computer in my office/dining room. I figured I could listen to some of the Folkways tunes while searching various databases for ethnomusicology papers on folk music and the collection of folk music. To my way of thinking, Moses Asch had been the twentieth-century Childe, and it wouldn't hurt our folkwaysAlive! site to have some evidence that corroborated that claim. I Googled Childe Ballads and wasn't surprised to see over 2,590 hits. The whole concept of searching out and recording for posterity is the connection I wanted to highlight, and I was looking for a good biography.

I reserved seven books at the Edmonton Public Library and

two more were going to be interlibrary loans through the NEOS system. I doubted I was the first person to consider the connection between Asch and Childe, and there were likely to be more supporters of people like Alan Lomax and Mike Seeger and Edith Fowke as the North American stand-ins for the historic collector of English ballads. However, it wasn't a bad comparison, and Moses Asch was certainly a visionary with a scope beyond the imaginations of most. To determine from the beginning that everything recorded would always be for sale and in circulation, and to have that written into the agreement with the Smithsonian Institute when they took over the collection, was truly a great accomplishment. In most contemporary recordings and publications, it isn't cost-effective to reprint a book or remaster a disc. Novelists published by small publishers often find it impossible to reprint a book, since the money has to come straight from the publishers' own pockets instead of some grant for their new list. One Canadian publisher went bankrupt when a book of poetry won the Governor General's Award and became a bestseller, requiring a reprint. Joseph Heller would have had a field day with Canadian publishing.

Steve called from his cell as he was getting into his car, telling me to get ready as he'd only be about ten minutes. I ran into the bathroom to wash my face and hands and check my hair, grabbed a light sweater and my handbag, and went to the back door of the apartment to wait for him. Steve was going to pick me up in the alley, rather than double-park on the busy road out front.

At seven, the sun was still pretty high in the sky. It would continue to be daylight till around ten-fifteen, before the hazy beginnings of evening drifted into twilight. Even though we had to endure darkness at four-thirty in the winter months as a result, I revelled in our long summer evenings. It felt as if you could accomplish anything in this place where you'd been given longer days in which to do it.

Accurate to his word, Steve rolled up almost exactly ten minutes later and I got into the passenger seat and buckled up.

"Where to?"

"I have an outrageous urge for bread pudding," he admitted.

"Colonel Mustard's it is," I nodded. "I wonder what their soup is today."

We made it over to the north side via the Groat Bridge, and Steve whipped up the first exit ramp and onto 107th Avenue with the panache of someone who regularly drives flashing, marked police vehicles. I settled back in. The sun on my shoulders and the company made me feel like singing. I'd been considering all the tribute albums to various Folkways artists, and wondering where I might put links to them on the website. Maybe that was what made me start into "Mary Don't You Weep," having just been listening to Springsteen's masterful rendition. I turned to look at Steve, who was smiling indulgently while keeping his eyes on the road.

"Sing along!" I urged.

"You know I don't sing, Randy."

"Not even on rowdy old camp songs? Not even in the shower?"

"Not even in my dreams," Steve stated, turning left onto 124th

Street and revving up to speed before he had to slow down a couple of blocks away. I pushed my back into the passenger seat and willed myself not to brace my feet on the floorboards or work my imaginary brake pedal. I am not averse to speed entirely; there are just times when I get nervous about hurtling through space in a ton of steel and plastic. Mostly, this feeling occurs when there's a lot of traffic around, which wasn't actually the case here. Maybe I was just tense from everything that had been happening lately, or perhaps my body had just had its quota of riding about in cars for the day. Maybe Steve needed to do less speeding and more singing. I just couldn't understand why he didn't feel the urge to warble from time to time. It was one of the major differences between us. He loved concerts and music in general, but he had no predisposition to making music of any kind himself, whereas I couldn't imagine life without it.

We made it to the restaurant within minutes, and lucky for us there was a parking spot open alongside it. Steve pulled in sharply and smiled the grin of the successfully landed pilot. I swear that he became a cop just because of the toys. We got out of the car and headed to the door of Colonel Mustard's. I loved this restaurant, which combined a chic sensibility with hearty home-style cooking. We were waved in to a free table, where I snaffled the wall seat, making Steve pull out a chair across from me. The waitress handed us the menus clamped to their little clipboards and went off to get us a bottle of water.

The soups listed were tomato basil and carrot curry. I opted for the tomato basil, with bread pudding for dessert. Steve ordered the meatloaf and, of course, bread pudding. I think there would be serious consequences if the owners ever considered taking Steve's pudding off the menu.

A look usually seen only on Raphael's cherubim appeared on his face with the first bite.

"This is all you really need, you know? Think about all the permutations and combinations of pastry and sugar confection that go into various desserts, but all you need is warm, sweet, melt-in-your-mouth bread pudding. The added consideration that it's helping you to use items that would only get stale and go to waste anyway is a bonus. Why does anyone bother with anything else?"

This pronouncement took quite a while to deliver, since he kept stopping to dig in and then to savour spoonfuls of his dessert. I happily ate along, nodding, although anything that even emitted a vague resemblance to an argument tended to trigger a knee-jerk reaction in me.

"There's no chocolate in it, of course. Lots of people would say the perfect dessert required chocolate," I pointed out.

"Lots of women, you mean." Steve waved his spoon at me to make his point more forcefully. "What is it about women and chocolate, anyhow?"

"Serotonin, isn't it? Eating chocolate releases serotonin in the brain, and serotonin makes you happy, so you eat chocolate and you don't mind being fat."

Steve laughed, and I bowed my head slightly to receive my due. He wasn't done, though. "Not bad, Randy. Triptophan, I think, is what is in chocolate, along with some other compounds that elevate your happiness quotient with endorphins and stimulate your nerves much the same way as good sex. The thing is, though, that given the choice between good sex and Bernard Callebaut chocolates, very few men would choose the chocolate. I'm not so sure about women."

"Maybe we want sex with Bernard Callebaut."

"Seriously, I can't imagine any guy I know getting that sort of cult-worshipper look in his eyes when discussing chocolate."

"I don't go crazy for chocolate," I countered.

"That's true, you don't. Of course, you are unusual in so many ways. You're one in a million, Randy Craig."

"You're just saying that because you want the rest of my bread pudding."

"Well, it would be a crime to leave it."

"And you took an oath to prevent crime, after all."

Steve polished off what was left on my plate, which admittedly wasn't much, and we took ourselves out. Steve didn't have any calls on his pager, so we headed back to my apartment, where we sublimated any desires for chocolate I might have had for quite some time.

20

As Steve had to be up for early report, he didn't stay over on the grounds that he didn't want to disturb me in the morning. Perversely, I woke early anyhow, full of energy. This sort of vim should never be squandered. I figured that even though the Centre was temporarily closed, I could take my laptop over to the music library in Rutherford and listen to some of the CDs of the Folkways collection while working on some content sections for the website.

I wandered into Rutherford from the ground level, since it had seemed too nice a day to spend one minute more inside than I needed to. The girl at the information booth in the atrium smiled at me as I walked past her and up the main staircase. I entered the library on the second level, which had been the main door when I'd been in grad school. Old habits die hard. The music library was all located on the second floor, anyhow.

I headed back to the corner where Carmen's office was located, and came face to face with the wobbly but effective plastic and metal barricade. Somewhere down the line I must have known that the music library's summer hours were now officially from one to five but it hadn't registered with me that morning. So, I wasn't going to be tuning into the dulcet tones of Dave Van Ronk while I worked this morning, after all. I stood in front of the counter, probably looking as blank as I felt. Heaving a sigh, like Algernon the Mouse at a dead end, I tried to rethink my proposed day's schedule.

Deciding that a quiet place to work was a positive thing, I headed over to the north wall, where a line of study carrels sat under windows facing the Arts Court. With the music library closed and summer session resulting in a bare five percent of the students normally found on campus, I could choose whichever carrel I preferred, a luxury not possible from September through April. Maybe I would start at one end and move every hour, taking advantage of every empty space. Maybe not.

I sat in the last carrel, closest to the east corner, thinking that if I were still here when Carmen or her assistant Bill arrived, I could easily pop up and check out a CD or two. The chances of me sitting in the same place from eight-thirty till one were unlikely, however. It wasn't that I couldn't get caught up in reading or writing or research for long periods of time; I had been getting lost in books since I was three. These days, though, my distractibility had less to do with the power of words and more to do with bladder control. More and more, I was turning into someone with a forty-five-minute bladder in a fifty-minute lecture world.

Here is the inherent problem with portable computers. We are given the ability to carry our work with us anywhere, making life such a smorgasbord of possibilities, and yet it now becomes impossible for us to stop what we're doing to run an errand or hit the toilet without having to pack up everything and move it with us. Portable means easily stolen. So, while my laptop made life nicer in some ways, it sometimes ended up being an albatross for me to lug everywhere. At least I didn't have to explain my purchase of it to every wedding guest I happened upon, like some contemporary ancient mariner. Thank heaven for small mercies, or I'd never get to the bathroom on time.

I had worked on five or six paragraphs dealing with some of the peculiarities of Asch's recording choices before I acknowledged to my inner plumbing that I had to move. If I had to pack up everything to move across the stacks to the washroom, I figured I might as well turn the expedition into a full coffee break and head for HUB afterward. A little voice in my head commented that maybe the core of my haulage problem could be linked to the amount of coffee I drank, but I quickly silenced her by hitting the hot air hand dryer button.

I ducked under the shoulder strap of my carryall, and slung it behind me the way Robin Hood would wear his quiver. I felt sort of like Jane Russell in one of her bra ads, with the strap diagonally across my chest, but it made hauling the "lightest" laptop around a whole lot easier. Technically, it flattened out my left breast, Amazon-style, the way Wonder Woman would actually look if drawn by women. I made a quick check of my hair and teeth in the mirror and headed out for HUB.

There's a turnstile installed in the exit area of the second floor of Rutherford North that is made of interlocking bars all the way up to the ceiling. It reminded me of a zoo exit, or perhaps the entrance to a maze, something so incongruous about the image of all those bitey metal cogs and teeth being encased in a hedge somewhere had obviously implanted itself in my subconscious. For what it was worth, it might have been an image I'd lifted from an old episode of *The Prisoner*. Being mildly claustrophobic, I was always afraid of getting stuck in the turnstile, so I chose to take the service stairs back down to the ground level of the library.

I scanned left and right, trying to decide from which stairwell to access the mall level of HUB. Because it was summertime, it didn't make all that much difference, as there would be room to stroll rather than be swept along in the sea of humanity that marked class change times in the fall and winter terms. I opted to head north and went in by the old Arts Court stairs, which were now the A&W stairs. I moseyed toward the home baked treats of Java Jive, thinking I might as well fortify myself while I was at it. All this walking and computer-lugging probably should entitle me to a cinnamon bun without fear of embedding calories.

I was almost to the glass case when I heard my name. I stopped and scanned the area. It was a good thing Denise had filled me in yesterday on Mary Montgomery and her beef against the Centre, because there she was, sitting in front of my destination, stirring a piece of biscotti into a foamy cup of coffee. I figured I would just pretend I had no inkling of her disfavour and bluff my way through on hearty bonhomie. The trouble is, I am painfully transparent when I put on any kind of act. I probably looked like Oliver Hardy trying to sneak a cookie.

"Mary! How are you? Gee, it's been ages." I smiled and felt my cheeks crack with the pressure. I immediately stopped smiling. Mary looked a little alarmed, but it was most likely the vision of me looking like some sort of automaton greeting her. She probably expected me to next proclaim, "Thunderbirds are go!"

"So, I hear there may be trouble on the Folkways Project," she said matter-of-factly. That was Mary, no beating around the bush for her. It reminded me of what one of my professors once said about a particular Canadian playwright: "She'd never use a door if there was a wall handy." I hesitated. What did she want me to say? I decided to keep playing naive until I got the general feel for what she was after.

"Oh, I don't know about that."

"Haven't the police closed the Centre?"

"Well, there is that. But my work can be done pretty much anywhere, for instance, Rutherford Library. I'm just grabbing a coffee, and then it's back to the grindstone." I smiled manically once more. It wasn't going to work. She motioned to the other chair at her table.

"Get your coffee and join me."

It felt like a command more than an offer, but I was feeling too feckless to find any easy way out of it. It wasn't as if I could head back to the Centre with my coffee and cinnamon bun, and I couldn't take food or drink back into the library and Mary knew it. If Mary walked south toward the library after I'd declined to join her and found me sitting there scarfing down my pastry, she would really have reason to hate me. Right now, as far as I knew, she only disliked me in principle, and that made me uncomfortable enough. Heaven knew what would happen if she felt I'd somehow personally scorned her.

I smiled and walked over to order my coffee and cinnamon bun, although I wasn't sure I would be able to swallow, given the sudden departure of appetite due to apprehension. Pretty soon I was sitting across from Mary Montgomery, who looked the way real Amazons looked, even when she wasn't wearing a book strap across her chest, a sort of redheaded Brunhilde thing going. She was a tall woman even when she sat, which I've always admired. I, on the other hand, seem to carry all my height in my legs, so that when I am sitting down I am inevitably the shortest one at the table. This tends to surprise short men at cabarets and wedding dances.

It was Mary's intensity that always sort of scared me, though. I felt like those knights in Monty Python having to answer skill-testing questions in order to cross the medieval bridge, wherein failing to state one's favourite colour resulted in being flung far into the abyss. It paid to stay on your toes with Mary, which never made for a relaxing time.

"How are things going over at the Centre?"

"Well, what have you heard besides the fact that we're closed for the moment?" I thought I was being superbly discreet.

"The attack on Paul Calihoo? Yes, I heard about that. Scary stuff."

How did everyone hear these things so quickly? If I hadn't

actually walked in on him I probably would still be in the dark, even if Steve had been assigned to the case. Come to think of it, how the heck did Mary know Paul by name? I'd never met him before going to work for the Centre. I pulled my cinnamon bun apart. It didn't pay to wonder about Mary. She had a sixth sense for nosing out gossip.

"So, are they putting a hold on things till they get all that ballyhoo about the Finster money settled?" she prodded.

I couldn't help myself. "How in heck do you know about all this? I thought it was supposed to be completely anonymous in the first place and very hush-hush still."

Mary looked smug.

"It's a very small world, Randy, especially when it comes to university money and foundations." For whatever reason, she seemed to take pity on me and throw me a crumb. "I heard his company was bidding on the project to reinforce the Arts Building floor to make way for the Folkways Collection and heard the precise amount of the bequest the Centre had received. He put two and two together and hit the roof. I think he and his sister tore a strip off the president before heading for Dr. Fuller. Who knows? All this negative publicity for the university may make the president rethink the specificity of the bequest, eh?" She crumpled up her now empty styrofoam cup, and stood, hovering over me like a fearsome Emma Thompson in *Angels in America*.

"I've got to head back to Orlando. Things are really chugging along there. Nice to see you, Randy."

Was it my imagination, or had that been a stronger inflection on the word "there"? Was this a challenge? A threat? Or just another jolly holiday with Mary? I swallowed the last of my coffee, and wiped sugar and cinnamon from my lips, watching her stride off toward the Humanities Building and the office of the Orlando Project.

21

You have to understand, I am totally in awe of the work that has been achieved by the Orlando Project at the University of Alberta. The database created about female writers—paying close attention to their travels, politics, health concerns, placement in birth order, number of children they conceived, number of husbands they buried and contents of their libraries—made for some glorious inferences on influences in their writing.

I had nothing against Mary Montgomery's work. I was hoping she could say the same for me, though, because I truly didn't want her for an enemy, especially while I seemed to have some pretty effective antagonists already setting me up as a suspect in one murder and one assault.

Now there was something else I couldn't fathom anyone believing: that I would want Paul Calihoo's job so much that I was willing to bash him over the head to get it. From having covered his tasks for the last few days, I couldn't see what was so fantastic about his position. Mostly it involved answering Dr. F's e-mails, making sure that everything was catalogued properly, that everything was seen to on the paperwork front, and kept organized enough to tick over seamlessly. Dr. Fuller herself seemed to glide through her life and work, to some internally generated and no doubt indigenous drumbeat, but after working Paul's gig for a couple of days, I could tell that she wouldn't look half so effortlessly elegant without the back-up player.

I went back to the music library carrels and spent almost two hours working on the Introduction about Moses Asch's vision for the company. I figured it would be worthwhile setting this out on the website close to the entrance to the database. If a music scholar wandered in but wasn't quite sure what he or she was looking for, having an inkling of the scope Asch envisioned and the actual swath he managed to carve out would likely be of benefit. Just as I was calling it a day and packing up my laptop yet again, I heard the plastic/metal curtain being pulled back and saw Carmen opening the music library desk. I considered popping over to say hello and gossip a little bit about Paul's injury and the police closure of the Centre, but decided against it. If I discovered one more person less out of the loop than I was, I figured I'd scream, and that was so not a done thing in libraries. I walked quietly to the big corner staircase, out of sight of the desk, and was soon on my way back to my apartment.

Once I moved out of the shadow of the trees running the gauntlet between Rutherford Library and HUB, I could tell that the hottest part of the day was truly upon me. The diagonal bar of the strap across my chest felt sticky by the time I passed the Law Building, and by the time I'd made it down my back alley two blocks further, I was ready for another shower. It was as if the heat of two weeks ago had returned, ramped up past max to another higher setting, Hades, maybe.

My apartment was shrouded in blind-drawn shadow. I opened the kitchen window a crack, noting that the north end of the building was still in shade. The temperature inside the apartment wasn't quite as bad as out on the sun-pounded concrete, but I couldn't find a draft anywhere to move the air past my skin. I peeled off my trousers and shirt and tossed them on the laundry pile. Then, in a fit of industry, I shrugged on my terry towel robe and hauled my laundry across the hall to the wash.

I don't do hot very well. It probably comes from not having much need to acclimatize, since we Edmontonians don't get that many terribly hot days, but heat does seem to sap me of all energy. I was glad I'd headed off to the climate-controlled library early enough in the morning to get some work done, since I couldn't imagine doing too much quality work after whatever late lunch I was going to manage.

While the sandwich I slapped together was satisfying, the simple preparations for lunch had made me tired. I got up from the table with less energy than I'd brought to it. I calculated that, although I'd stopped for a tense cinnamon bun earlier in the morning, I hadn't actually taken any other break, and a nap might be in order. I switched off the bell on the telephone as I passed by, and I turned the message machine to silent record.

People in Latin countries who practise siestas have the right idea. There is absolutely nothing more civilized than an afternoon nap in a hazily lit room. The paper blind in my bedroom, which was always drawn, was once red. Though it was now faded to almost pink, it still offered a peaceful ambience in the small bedroom. I drifted off, trying to establish a list of reasons why I didn't live in Spain. It was going to be hard to come up with anything past number one: I don't speak Spanish.

I woke up around five-thirty. I knew this instinctively, not because I was an ace Girl Guide, able to gauge the time from the angle of light, but because my upstairs neighbour was jumping around on her floor above me. She came home and did a half hour of Richard Simmons' sweating aerobics without fail. Today, she probably got her first pint of sweat onto her headband just bending over to get the VCR going. I mentally applauded her dedication, and then cursed her disregard for her neighbours, as usual.

My mother had always been so adamant about not wanting to live in an apartment, or condo, because she feared the possibility that a late-night bath might annoy people who had to listen to her water pipes clanging and gurgling. She, of course, had no idea of the basic indifference of man any more. She had been raised in an age of manners and etiquette, which is something we have somehow managed to lose along the way to the twenty-first century. I thought about what we'd gained in compensation, and couldn't see how microwave ovens and cellphones held up their end of the bargain. The world was just more and more rude and irritable each day. There were reports of knifings, shootings

and road rage happening in Edmonton, which had to be one of
the more laid-back cities in North America. In fact, most people
still ambled when walking along the sidewalk or window shopping in the malls. Cut someone off, or get in their way, though,
and you risked your life.

I thought about the gormless girl on the floor above me, hopping along to the oldies, totally heedless of other tenants and their
needs or schedules. For all she knew, I could be a shift worker
who needed my sleep. Of course, if she did consider me at all,
she probably didn't think I'd be at home napping at five-thirty.
Normally I wasn't. Most of the time lately, I was barely even home
by now. I silently forgave her trespasses and took back my unkind
wishes that she might sprain an ankle or retain water.

I sat up on the side of my bed and took a couple of deep
breaths. I had no real desire to wake up but I knew that if I
didn't, I'd be up at eleven with no ability to sleep through the
night, and I'd ruin my chances at a productive day after that. So,
it was up and at 'em time.

I trudged into the bathroom and splashed cold water on my
face. There were slight pillow marks on my right cheek, always
an attractive look. I was about to scrub my face when I decided
that the path of least resistance would be to step into the shower
again and hose off. It was a relief to feel the initial spray of cold
water, and I didn't bother waiting at the foot end of the tub till
the hot water kicked in. I was squeezing my hair and stepping
out by the time it had barely reached tepid. I rolled my hair into
a towel turban and patted myself off with a hand towel. I didn't
bother to rub myself dry. The cool sheen of water was a gift.

I found an oversized white cotton shirt and pulled it on, flipping the cuffs up to my elbows. I pulled my damp hair up into a high ponytail, and dug out some pink capri pants I'd picked up at the Bissell Centre thrift store a few weeks back. I was going for a Gidget sort of look, on the grounds that Sandra Dee didn't perspire and therefore I too would remain cool and collected.

I wandered into the kitchen, and spot-washed the few dishes with a Kurly Kate and some squirted dish soap. I had no desire to eat anything more, and no real alternative. After putting the kitchen to order, I drifted back into the living room and collapsed onto the couch. Maybe it was more than the heat. Maybe I was coming down with something. I hoped not; summer colds were the worst thing, especially in Edmonton. It feels as if you're wasting the good weather if you take time off to lie in bed, sweating and coughing up a lung. February was a much better time to contract consumption.

It probably was the heat. I wondered if this was anywhere near the sort of heat and oppressive weather that Raymond Chandler had meant when he wrote about the Santa Ana winds and the urge to kill people. Maybe whoever killed David Finster would use that as his alibi. I couldn't recall anyone ever using our chinook winds, which, of course, came in the middle of winter and merely sucked away the snow, as a murder defence, but there was a first time for everything.

Not that I wanted to kill, of course. I wasn't even miffed at anyone, although I sort of resented whoever it was that clobbered Paul and loaded me up with the extra work. I guess I was a little bit ticked off at Woody for running off, as well. I had a feeling that a lot of his bright ideas about the folkwaysAlive! stage were going to just end up meaning a whole lot of more work for me at the last minute.

Thinking about work reminded me to turn my phone ringer back on and check my answering machine. It was a good thing I did, since it told me that six people had been trying to reach me while I'd been sleeping.

Three of them were hang-ups, then there was a brief message from Dr. Fuller reminding me to check my e-mail for a list of things to do for the Folkways folkwaysAlive! stage. What can I say? Sometimes I marvel at my psychic tendencies. The fourth call was also a hang-up, which I find irritating. If people would only hang up as soon as they hear the answering machine begin, the call wouldn't even register. The fifth call was from Steve, wondering where I was. The sixth call was also from Steve. He sounded a bit more urgent and asked me to call his pager immediately.

I dialled his pager, hung up and took the phone with me into the kitchen while I made a pot of tea. I needed the caffeine of a high-test cup of coffee if I really wanted to wake up, but I wasn't all that committed to the idea. Tea would be fine.

The kettle clicked at the same time as the phone rang. I answered, and stuck it between my ear and my shoulder, hoping my cheek didn't press some awkward button by mistake. Multitasking was so much easier in the days of rotary dial telephones.

"Randy? Where have you been?"

"Hi, yourself. I was sleeping. I turned off the ringer so I could get some rest. How are you? Are you still at work?"

He sounded grim. "Yeah, I'm still at work. Listen, stay there, and I'll come by as soon as I can, okay? I think we need to talk."

I agreed, and he broke the connection, leaving me to wonder what the heck was troubling him. It was pretty obvious something was, and I was afraid it had something to do with me. For the life of me, though, I couldn't figure out what I could possibly have done to make Steve tense at work. Something to do with Paul's attack? Something more to do with David Finster's death? As much as I liked my Folkways job, I was beginning to wish I'd never heard of the bloody Finsters.

I turned on the computer to access my e-mail. There was the promised list of chores from Dr. F, twenty-five pieces of spam offering to increase my "package," decrease my weight, grant me an easy PhD, and pay off my mortgage, and an e-mail from Woody. I deleted the spam and clicked on the Smithsonian header.

He started off with a description of his flight home, making it sound like something out of an Adam Sandler film. The third paragraph, though, had the gist of the message in it.

"The word here is that we can consider a recording session for everyone signed to the folkwaysAlive! stage, as long as they all sign off on the deal. There'll have to be the standard anthology contract, and we can't pay big bucks, but the main hurdle is contacting everyone prior to the event so we can determine timetabling and recording potential. I think recording live through the sound feed would be feasible and in keeping with the concept of the project but I'm willing to be persuaded of other ways. I'm going to be arriving back there in a couple of days with boilerplate contracts and a list of needs for a capable sound engineer.

"Can you find it in your heart and schedule to get me a list of at least three recording engineers to speak with on Friday? I need someone with portable equipment, a sense of adventure, a track record in outdoor recording if possible, and an abiding love of folk and world music.

"Aside from that, Mrs. Lincoln, how has your week been? I miss you.

"Love, Woody."

The "Love, Woody" bit didn't startle me all that much. I had a feeling Woody was the sort of fellow who would sign letters to his bank manager "Love, Woody." What floored me was his assumption that I would be able to round up even one sound engineer, let alone three, within the time frame he was proposing. There was more to this whole music-ethnography thing than just listening to recordings and thinking up opening essays for database sections.

Seeing as Paul was out of commission and Dr. F likely had a list of chores twice as long as the one she had sent me, I guess it really would be up to me to flush out some recording engineers. I grabbed a pad of foolscap and the Yellow Pages, then plonked myself down on the floor in front of the coffee table. I felt as if I was back in Grade 11, doing a social studies project on "understanding your community" or such like. I'd never even considered the possibility that there were recording engineers in Edmonton, although on reflection I suppose there had to be, given the number of local singers. I couldn't find a listing for

Engineers, but there were twenty-four Recording Studios in the area. One had to have some form or other of portable studio. I wasn't banking on three, but I pegged Woody for an optimist the minute I met him. I decided to write down the names and numbers of the ones with the most professional-looking advertisements.

I was just jotting down Woodbend Music's number on my list when Steve appeared. I looked up at his figure framed in the doorway and my heart fluttered, just like one reads about in cheap romance novels. Now there was a question for the phenomenologists: Did we have romantic physical manifestations before they were spoken about in books and pop lyrics, or did the culture reflect the already established reality? All I knew was that whenever I caught sight of Steve in a crowd after not seeing him for a while, my heart literally banged on the inside of my ribcage. Would that happen if I hadn't done a class in the Romantics? I wasn't sure.

I smiled at Steve, who was still in the doorway, looking at me as if I'd somehow wrecked his appetite. I felt my smile fade, and suddenly it seemed stupid to be sitting on the floor. I scrambled to my feet, banging my knee on the side of the coffee table in the process. I stood half bent over, rubbing my knee and looking at Steve. "What is it? Is there something wrong?"

"I've been trying to get hold of you all afternoon, Randy. Where have you been?"

"Here."

"I called you and you didn't answer."

"I was having a nap; I turned the sound off so I could sleep."

"Were you here all day?"

"No, I got up early and went to the music library to work."

"Oh good. And there were people there who could confirm this?"

"Well, no, it turned out the music desk wasn't open till one, so I just worked at my laptop in one of the carrels in the stacks." This comment seemed to sadden Steve. I wasn't sure how to cheer him up because I wasn't clear why he seemed so fraught with the ins and outs of my schedule for the day. All I knew was that somehow I was responsible for this mood and I had to think of a way to lighten it.

"I worked through till, I don't know, around nine-thirty or ten, and then I went out into the mall and had a coffee break run-in with Mary Montgomery," I recalled. "After that, I went back into the library to work for a couple or three hours and then I came back here, made myself some lunch, and had a nap. I've been working on Folkways stuff since I got up." Steve, by this time, had come into the living room and sat himself down on the sofa. I shuffled together the papers, phone book and pens and took them to my desk, and then came back and sat at the other end of the couch.

"So why is it so important where I was today? Was there something I was supposed to do? We weren't supposed to have lunch today, were we?"

"The reason I was hoping you would be taking part in a large, coordinated group activity is that at some time in the early part of the morning, someone set fire to the Barbara Shoppe on the south side, and we have tentatively identified the body discovered in the back area as Ms. Barbara Finster. Given your connection to her brother's death, I was hoping there wouldn't be anything to question you about in this situation."

"Do you mean to say that you think I killed a woman and torched her store?"

"No, I am not saying I believe that. I am not saying any of the detectives I work with would believe that, either. I'm sure that even Superintendent Keller doesn't believe it. What I am saying is, if you don't have an alibi for the time when Barbara Finster was killed, then it makes us look lax if we don't at least question you."

"I don't believe this! I'd never even heard of the Finsters till I got this job. I hadn't even been in a Barbara Shoppe before yesterday."

Steve groaned.

"Oh God, Randy, tell me you weren't in the Petrolia Mall Barbara Shoppe yesterday."

I felt like a teenager caught with cigarette smoke on her breath. The only defence seemed to be silence. Yes, I had been in that Barbara Shoppe. I had likely left fingerprints all over the changing room area. I could recall touching the Henry Moore, and I wondered if I'd rung the bell for the attendant at that store or just the one on the west end.

"Well, what if I was? I have people who could vouch for me. Denise was with me, and the serving woman who looked like Audrey Hepburn—Holly. They saw me there, so they could confirm that I touched things yesterday."

"Or they could help make the point that you were casing

the joint in order to return early this morning and kill Barbara Finster."

"Why would I want to kill Barbara Finster? Why on earth would anyone believe that?"

"Randy, you would be amazed at what people will believe if you spin it correctly. You could be trying to save your job from the woman who's trying to pull the money away from the university. You could be somehow exacting vengeance against whomever you perceive to have attacked your colleague, Paul. You could be striking a blow against the fall line, for all I know. If someone wants you to be the fall guy for this, then you've done your level best to help him out."

"Well, if I am avenging Paul then I can't be suspected of braining him; I suppose that's some consolation."

"Don't be so sure. You could be covering up the first crime with the second. But the fact that you had coffee with someone on campus is probably enough. What was her name again?" He pulled out his notebook and pen.

"Mary Montgomery. But you can't be serious, Steve. Have you really come here to question me about murdering a woman?"

"I shouldn't even be here, truth to tell. I have a feeling the dots haven't been joined yet in the Finster thing. Just hearing that name set off alarm bells for me. So far, there are two different crowds working three different crime scenes—David Finster's murder, Paul Calihoo's attack, and the fire at the Barbara Shoppe. You're the only link between all three that I know of, so I came to see if we could effectively eliminate you before any shit got stirred up in the first place."

"I can just imagine what Keller is going to say the minute he sees the pattern," I moaned.

"Not to worry. We just get this Montgomery woman to swear she saw you, verify when she saw you, and describe what you were wearing. You don't smell of smoke, so case closed."

I must have signalled dismay somehow because Steve stiffened. "What?"

"I came home and threw my clothes into the wash since I'd sweated through them. They're still in the washer across the hall. So, no matter what Mary says I was wearing, if she even remembers, you can't say that they did or didn't smell of smoke. Or me either, since I had a shower after my nap."

"Damn it, Randy. It's like you want to be framed for this."

"Well, pardon me. I didn't wake up this morning thinking, 'Oh boy, better make sure I have an alibi just in case some old battle-axe gets herself burned up today.'" It was partly the anger, and partly the heat, but mostly the image I conjured just then of Barbara Finster, so towering and domineering, being a charred corpse—that made my stomach lurch and churn. No question of perception and language there. I rose and stumbled to the bathroom just in time to lose what was left of my lunch.

22

Steve was technically off duty, so he made hot, sweet tea while I cleaned myself up and then held me while I settled. Apparently, iced tea doesn't cut it as an antidote to shock, even on sultry summer days. Good thing we don't get too many of them— hot days or shocks. I don't throw up easily. I think I've done it a total of about twelve times in my entire life and it always leaves me shaking and crying, even when it's connected to flu rather than horrors. Come to think of it, Steve's been with me two or three of those times, too. And yet he still sticks around. It must be love.

Eventually I was calm enough to consider more sustenance than tea. Steve and I decided to walk over to the local sushi restaurant, as the thought of raw fish sounded more tempting than anything hot. Steve ordered a big bowl of chirashi and I settled for a California roll and some miso soup, which calmed me even more, and I was finally able to think and talk about something other than arson and murder.

"Woody e-mailed me and asked me to find him a recording engineer for the Folkways stage at the Folk Fest. I have a list of people to call, but I have to phone the Festival bunch and see what the procedures are and what equipment is already at hand. There might be a way to take a pretty decent recording off the mike feed, for all I know. Anyhow, that's on top of coming up with a playlist and a compilation of music to organize for the PA between sets. Dr. F wants Folkways recordings emanating from the speakers at all times when live music isn't being played on the stage. The feeling is that we need to sort out music that would complement the acts that have already been and those upcoming on the stage. She hasn't got the complete lineup yet, although the Festival has already apparently gone to print with their program book, meaning there should be a list available. It's up to me to get that list and start choosing what to put on our master mix tape."

Steve smiled. "Sounds like fun."

"It is fun, you know. The hassle is working from home, and working without Paul. If he were around, he'd be doing the mix tape and I could concentrate on the recording of the new stuff and the coordination with Festival staff. As it is, I have to do it all from my phone line and laptop."

"Well, if anyone can do it all, it's you," Steve said and gallantly toasted me with a piece of raw tuna.

"Just don't go arresting me or none of it is going to get done," I growled.

"I'll see what I can do to give you an alibi for the next twelve hours or so," Steve smiled. I blushed, I'm sure, and looked around to see if anyone had heard him. He laughed, and reached over to cover my hand on the table. "No one could ever accuse you of hiding your thoughts, girl."

It was still inordinately hot when we got out of the restaurant, so we decided to take a walk. On the premise that water cools people down, we wandered out on to the High Level Bridge footpath. Others seemed to have the same idea, and we nodded to people passing by as we strolled out to the middle of the bridge. There was no breeze, no relief. The black metal of the bridge was hot to the touch. The riverbanks looked sandy and wide. We stood leaning on the handrail, watching some birds that were immobile on a sand bar. The cars behind us on the bridge seemed slower, more subdued than usual. All around us, the whole city was being pushed into the pavement by the heat. We all stood there sweating, praying for rain.

23

The next morning was still stiflingly hot. Steve and I both woke up grumpy, either because of his probable distrust of me and my wounded honest pride, or more likely, from the assumption that we'd have been cooler had we been in a larger apartment. We wouldn't be any cooler in the middle of the cavernous Agricom Building in this weather, but we were still snippy until both of us showered and managed to down one cup of coffee. Then things looked a bit brighter. As if we needed bright in a heat wave.

"Have you ever noticed how difficult it is to remember being really frostbitten cold in the middle of the summertime?" I had been trying to think cool thoughts, but it wasn't working.

"Yeah, I think there is some sort of psychological amnesia that occurs so the seasons offer a miraculous renewal, or so we can bear the thought of yet another winter. It's probably the same amnesia that makes women forget the pain of childbirth until they have the next baby. As a species, we need to put certain things out of mind."

"So you think it would be harmful to me psychologically if I could recall the feelings of a minus forty degree day with a wind chill factor of minus sixty? I was just thinking it would make me thankful for this scorcher of a day if I could think of the alternative. Instead, all I can think of is pleasant times when it doesn't drag you down just to stroll around the block."

Steve shrugged. "Maybe we're not supposed to be comparing. A Zen master would tell us just to live in the sweat of the moment."

"Wow, that is so beautiful—I should embroider that onto a cushion."

"Smart ass." Steve poured himself another cup of coffee and topped up my mug. "So, what's up with you today? Where are you going to be?"

I sighed.

"I'm just asking, Randy. You aren't under suspicion from me." I was mollified until I thought about the qualifier. I could just imagine Keller sticking my photo on a squad room bulletin board. However, it was too hot to pick a fight, so I decided to just answer my man.

"Well, I have to find Woody a recording engineer who is willing to work outdoors for three days at the Folk Festival. I then have to sort through a playlist for the interregna, and then head over to the music library this afternoon with the list. I am not sure if they have the capacity right there to burn things to CD, or whether that's going to be a last-minute chore once you let us back into the Centre. I know the set-up there, at least."

"You might get back into the Centre sometime tomorrow, for all I know. I don't think the crime scene people have any more need of it. Want me to check?"

"Sure, although I will have to call Dr. Fuller before heading over in any case. There's no way I'm going in there all by myself with no one knowing where I am."

"Good plan. In fact, the more people who know where you are these days, the better. I'll keep my ear open about the Barbara Shoppe fire, but don't be surprised if I can't keep you out of things. There are bound to be connections made, especially since they'll be focusing on who'd been to the store recently."

"Okay, I am duly warned. I admit I was curious about the woman, naturally enough, seeing how she and her brother were tampering with my livelihood. Denise and I just decided to go check the places out. Oh! Did I show you what I bought?"

"You bought something at the Barbara Shoppe that was later torched? Oh this just gets better and better."

I decided to ignore that and went to get my middy blouse. I pulled it out of the closet and smiled all over again at how glorious a piece of clothing it was. Steve wasn't as impressed.

"You'll look like a CGIT girl."

"A what?"

"Canadian Girls in Training; my sister was one. We used to call them Canadian Girls in Training Bras. They were sort of like the Girl Guides, only connected to the United Church of Canada. My sister wore a middy and a navy skirt, and made stuffed animals for kids in hospitals during her spare time, and went camping every summer. She played guitar and made macramé plant hangers for our mom, and organized bottle drives to help the food bank."

"Are you talking about Gloria, the stock analyst?"

"Yeah, well, she was a CGIT once upon a time, what can I say?"

"So, my lovely new top looks like a girls' club uniform?"

"It could be worse. You could look like a Boy Scout."

I chuckled. "Yeah, you're right. Things could be worse. What the heck. I love it."

"Well, then I'm glad you found it. If you hear Gloria whistling 'Taps' when you wear it around her, you'll just have to understand."

I tossed a cushion at him, which he fielded masterfully. As I was hanging my sailor middy back into the closet, Steve tidied up the kitchen and met me back in the centre of the living room. He pulled me into an enveloping hug, and kissed the side of my neck, which he knew would make me squirm.

"Be good, get lots done, stay in touch, and try not to get framed for any murders today, okay? I have to head out now; I'll see you soon."

"Right. Be careful out there." Somehow, I never get that authentic *Hill Street Blues* tone, but Steve always obligingly laughs.

"I swear, this weekend, we are going to get you a cellphone. My treat."

"Oh lord, so I'm to be dragged into the twenty-first century, am I?"

"Kicking and screaming, girl, kicking and screaming."

"You wish."

"Hoo-wee, is it getting hot again in here, or what?"

"Hit the mean streets, Detective. I have work to get to."

"You bet, sweetheart." Steve headed off down the hall, doing his best Adam-12 impression. You'd think Steve Browning spent his entire childhood glued to the screen of a television from the pop culture references he was able to toss out at any given moment.

Speaking of pop culture, I was wishing for a bit of cartoon overdrive to speed me into a bustle of activity. I didn't think it was going to happen though, at least not in this heat.

I spent the rest of the business hours leaving messages for or talking to recording engineers all over the city, along the way learning enough from each conversation to ask more pertinent questions. Woody may have been overly optimistic in his desires, but I managed to sort out four people he'd likely want to talk with for the folkwayAlive! stage recording project.

I stayed home, folded laundry, made a point of saying hello to Mr. McGregor in the hallway while going to get my mail—because you just never knew who might be getting murdered at three that afternoon—and called it a day around five o'clock.

Steve called, sounding fond but distracted, so I let him get on with things. I settled down to a bowl of popcorn, a pitcher of iced tea and *Labyrinth* on DVD. There's just no mood that David Bowie and some Muppets cannot improve.

Maybe it was the film's Escher-like staircases, the oppressive heat or just my jumbled state of mind, but my dreams were twisty and tense. I woke enervated, with no recollection of any storyline but with a heaviness that was hard to shake, even with a shower and coffee. I took it easy, sorted through more websites and made sure my levels of vitamin C were topped up. I made it to bed early again, and a second full night of sleep seemed to do the trick.

I was up with the birds and ready to head back to work. However, the last thing I wanted to do was head to the Centre unheralded. I called Dr. Fuller's home number. We spoke briefly about my recent efforts, and the possibility that the Centre would be open later that day. She agreed that pulling a bunch of songs appropriate to the music that would be next up live on the stage was the best format. I had a working list of performers from the Folk Fest website, and a good idea of what about half of them were about. I figured I'd research the other half online before heading over to the music library after lunch.

I packed up my backpack, including my laptop—I figured I could drop it at the Centre on my way to the library—and headed out. It was warm, but either a breeze had come up or I was acclimatizing, because it didn't feel quite as evil as the day before. Still, I dodged into the first air-conditioned building I came to.

I hummed my way through the Law hallway that led to the pedway through to the Fine Arts Building, just because with all that brick and glass, the acoustics make anyone sound great. One of the great perks of working on campus in the summer months is that there is all this wonderful echoey space and no one around to hear you make a fool of yourself.

I used to sing show tunes almost exclusively when walking, but since working at the Centre I'd taken to mournful folk music in a big way. "Poor Wayfarin' Stranger" was my latest favourite for walking-along music. I hit the double doors around the start of the chorus: "I'm goin' there, to meet my mother, I'm goin' there, no more to roammmmmm …"

The door to the Centre was wedged open, and from inside I heard an answering baritone voice singing: "I am just going over Jordan, I am just goin' over home." I stood in the doorway and saw Woody sitting at the central table, smiling at me.

"Hi, Randy! Surprised to see me?"

That would be putting it mildly.

24

Woody wasn't supposed to be in Edmonton; I mentally had him safely ensconced in the Smithsonian Institute, far, far away. I expected him to be calling me this evening to arrange a pickup from the airport in the next couple of days. What was he doing here, and if he was already here, why did he e-mail me, asking me to do local chores for him? How long had he been back, anyhow?

His guileless smile didn't get me far. The man was born to play poker. I had a feeling I wasn't going to learn anything about Woody's schedule that Woody didn't want me to learn. I walked over to my desk and opened my backpack to pull out my laptop in a bit of a daze. He watched my every move by swivelling slightly on the table and sitting cross-legged like some medieval tailor.

"Cheryl Fuller tells me you have the inter-act music well in hand. Have you found me a recording engineer yet?"

I told him what little I'd uncovered. The best recording engineer in the region was a rather famous musician and composer himself, but he didn't operate outside his specially designed and hand-built studio on an acreage west of town. Of the good engineers who were willing to be portable, three had previous engagements that weekend, leaving Woody with a choice of two names. I plugged in my laptop and opened the file I'd made. I had to head behind the counter to access the printer that was spitting out the addresses and phone numbers, bringing me close enough for him to reach out and touch my arm in passing. I felt a jolt, almost like an electric shock, pass through my arm from his hand. I stopped.

"Randy, you're upset with me. How come?" Woody sounded like the same happy-go-lucky fellow I enjoyed spending time with just a week and a half ago. Now, he felt dangerous, and I wasn't totally clear why. I had no reason to suspect him of doing anything wrong, but I'd been through too many bad situations, both recently and in the past, not to listen to my instincts. Whatever his explanation for being here where I didn't expect him to be, I was intending to be a little wary of Mr. Dowling.

"Not upset, just wondering why you didn't let me know when you were coming to town. I would have offered to pick you up at the airport."

"But you don't have a car."

"No, but I could have been there to meet you, brought you up to speed on what's been happening. When did you get back, anyhow?"

Woody's eyes took on a bit of a vague look.

"Oh, you know," he said, looking at his wristwatch, "a little while ago now."

I knew it; I wasn't going to get a straight answer out of him. He might have just arrived this morning, or he could have been here a day or two without my knowing it. Maybe he hadn't actually left Edmonton at all, just made sure I hadn't run into him. Who knows, maybe he was another potential suspect for the arson at the Barbara Shoppe.

I was just getting carried away now, I chided myself. Just because he hadn't let me in on his plans and moves, I was hurt. That was all. Well, it was no skin off my knees if Woody Dowling wanted to be mysterious. Two could play that game. Of course, one of the two couldn't be me. I was about as mysterious as paint.

I handed Woody the list of sound engineers and told him about the ideas for tapes of existing Folkways music in the same style being played while the stage was struck and the sound crew was working to set up the next act.

"Of course, we can't project it up the hill, because that would interfere with the sound crew, but a small speaker aiming downhill behind the stage, focusing on the people passing by along the path or waiting at the porta-potties, shouldn't be too much of a disruption to the levels of the stage crew. Dr. F and I figured that if it was going to act as an incitement, we should concentrate on the act to follow rather than the act that just appeared. Don't you think?"

Woody grinned, nodding his head.

"You're all over this project, girlfriend! Sounds good to me.

Can we get a tape of quality good enough for our purposes from the machinery here?"

"It's good enough for Dr. F to take to international music conferences; it should be good enough for a scratched-up speaker at an outdoor festival."

"So be it. I'll leave that part of the project with you. I have to tackle the Festival organizers today and see about bringing in one of these two fellows to record the workshops and mini-concerts on our stage. By the way, you are planning to be at the Festival the entire weekend, aren't you?"

"We've had our tickets since June 1, Woody."

"Tickets, schmickets." He pulled a lanyard with a plastic ID card hanging off it from out of his briefcase. "This will get you fed like royalty whenever you feel like it, access to the backstage of our little stage and the evening main stage, through the door to all the after-hours parties, and onto the free shuttle bus from the hotel. It will also get you onsite all through the week prior to the Festival during the set-up, but I doubt you'll be required to head over there until Friday morning at the earliest. After all, we're not doing a Thursday evening set at the folkwaysAlive! Stage."

The pass had my name on it, along with a thumbnail photo of me—the same one that appeared on my university ID, which I thought had been a one-off. The whole thing was laminated, which made me think this plan of Woody's had been in the works for some time, although this was the first I was hearing the fact that I would be working the Festival rather than sitting on a tarp on the side of the ski hill, enjoying myself.

Woody must have heard my inner thoughts, unless I'd unwittingly said them out loud.

"Don't worry; you won't have to work the whole weekend. And it will be fun, being part of the in-crowd, believe me. Well," he untied his legs from the crossed knot he'd had them in and slid gracefully to the floor, "I'd best be running. I'll get back to you later in the day, to let you know which of these guys we'll be working with and what else has come up, okay?"

It was as if I had somehow been keeping him from his appointed rounds, rather than his having hijacked *my* afternoon. Still, I smiled and waved him off. I couldn't help liking Woody. I just wasn't sure I trusted him.

25

Woody hadn't actually taken up too much of my time, a fact I realized once I came out of the hazy fog he seemed to wrap me in whenever we were together and looked at my watch. I still had the whole day ahead of me, and a whole slew of music to go through. There were two sets at the folkwaysAlive! Stage on the Friday evening before the mainstage concert began, and I had set myself the goal of finding music to augment those concerts by the end of the day.

The first set was an instrumental workshop, comprised of a fellow I hadn't heard of on a Chapman Stick; Bryan Bowers, the autoharp maestro; and a sitar player and actor from Central Alberta, Larry Reese. No problem. All I had to do was find some classical, eclectic Indian music. If only Harry Manx had recorded for Folkways.

I headed off to the music library, after making sure to leave a note for Dr. Fuller. From here on in, I was going to signal all my turns and make sure everyone knew where I was at any given time. It was bad enough someone was getting away with murder; I was damned if they were going to have an easy patsy in me anymore.

I was just passing a soup and sandwich place when I realized I hadn't packed any lunch. The reserve energy bar in my backpack just didn't seem too appealing, what with the smell of beef barley soup and fresh bread wafting toward me. I retraced a few steps and stood dutifully in line to get a large bowl of soup and a small roll. There was no place to sit right by the restaurant in HUB mall itself, so I took my food and headed into the Rutherford walkway. I perched on one of the seats, using the concrete table beside me as a makeshift dinner table.

When the university is in fall or winter session, a person could sit in the spot I'd chosen and see practically everyone she knew on campus. Of course, the odds were against you a bit, since this was the time of holidays and conferences, but it wouldn't have surprised me to see someone I knew passing through. It wasn't exactly Piccadilly Circus, but then again, neither was Piccadilly Circus anymore. I therefore wasn't all that startled when Mary Montgomery plopped herself down across from my concrete table and said, "Well, we meet again!"

"Hi, Mary," I managed, between spoonfuls of soup. "How goes the battle?"

"You know the drill; hurry up and wait. I've been waiting sixteen weeks for a book on Maori customs from interlibrary loans. It's the final icing on a Katherine Mansfield section I've been working on all year. It ties right in with that last book by Janice Kulyk Keefer, too. But there's some holdup and no one will tell me why. I tell you, it would be cheaper, considering my time, to just order the book from the publisher. If only we had the budget for that sort of thing." I wasn't sure if that was a deliberately meaningful look on Mary's part or not. I was just glad I was obviously on my way to the library so she couldn't make comments on my spending more liberally on my grandiose budget than she could on her meagre allotment.

I wasn't so sure her allotment was all that meagre, either. Of course, it likely was nowhere near a science research budget, but the Social Science and Humanities Research Council grants seemed to be more and more respectable as the years went on. Besides, as I tried to tell myself every time I got resentful of full-time lecturers when considering my term status, it sure beats having to punch a time clock at a humdrum job for a living. Being paid to do research and think and talk and write about writers—or, in my case, musicians—and to be able to march to the beat of the university instead of the outside bustle of the commercial world was a great and glorious gift for which I tried to be consistently grateful. Just as long as I didn't need a root canal, it was a good life.

Mary was still sitting there, pensively drinking from her violet-tinted water bottle. I always feel awkward about eating in front of people who aren't, but it's very hard to share soup. Maybe if I could get her talking, I thought, I could finish my slurping and we could once again be on an even footing.

"So, are you doing any of the festivals this summer, Mary?"

As conversation gambits go, this was as standard in Edmonton during the summer as, "So, is it cold enough for you?" is in the winter. Mary grimaced with the likely repetitiveness of it, but answered anyway.

"Jessie and I are probably going to do our regular Fringing later in August. We each pick a play, then we pick one from the critics' picks, and finally we pick one just by guess and golly. Then we figure out how to hit the beer tent in between them all. What about you? Folk Festival, I presume, eh?"

"Well, this year I get to work the folkwaysAlive! stage, so I'm getting in for free. Of course, I had been planning on making that my break time."

Mary laughed harshly. Of course, that could just have been her laugh. I hadn't heard a lot of it. "That's the one big trouble with pursuing what you love as a career. Leisure starts looking a lot like work, and parties become seminars with pâté."

I nodded, chewing on my roll. It was true. The drawback to having a vocation was you never actually got a vacation.

Mary rose gracefully from the padded bench seat and saluted.

"Back to the grind. See you later, Randy."

I waved and wiped my mouth with the paper napkin the roll had been wrapped in, scrunching it into my now empty soup bowl. Even though I hadn't been planning to take that much time to eat my soup, and she had been idle exactly the same amount of time as me, somehow Mary made me feel as if I'd been slouching while she was on a tight schedule. What was it about her that set me on edge every time we met? Could it be chemical? Or was it just a by-product of Denise's warnings that

Mary was out to scoop my grant monies? Whatever the case, now was no time to sit and ponder. I could barely make out her back, striding down HUB Mall. And I was still here, lolling about. Time to get on to the music library.

I made it to the library corner just as Carmen was pushing the plastic retainer curtain aside. She nodded as I leaned over the counter to grab a mimeographed copy of the Whole Folkways Catalogue. I needed some instrumental string music. With luck, I might find an anthology album, thereby saving myself a whole heap of time on taping.

It wasn't as easy as flipping to "instrumental" recordings. Everything was listed by country of origin, with the largest selection coming from the United States. Within the States, it was broken into such categories as American Folk, Bluegrass and Old-Time Country, Cajun/Zydeco, African-American Traditions, Gospel, Blues/R&B, Jazz, Rock, and Hawaiian. That took up fourteen pages of the catalogue, then came nine more pages from other countries, and then seven pages of recordings organized by subject matter: American Popular, Historical and Political Song, Soundtracks-Musicals-Radio, Children's Recordings, Christmas and Holiday, Euro-American Classical, and Contemporary Classical and Electronic. Then followed six more pages of Spoken Arts Recordings: Drama, Poetry, Prose, Humor, Historical, Instructional, Music Instruction, Science and Nature, Psychology and Health, and my favourite, Miscellany, a category that held diverse items like an interview with Timothy Leary and another with Alfred Fuller, of Fuller Brush fame, on "Careers in Selling." I wondered if Arthur Miller had ever listened to that record. It would be fun to make some *Death of a Salesman* references when I was dealing with that section.

I checked my watch and decided to pack up for the day; trouble was, I could just sink into this stuff forever if I let myself. Time now, though, for instrumental strings to connect to the Chapman Stick and the autoharp. Sadly, I flipped back toward Recordings from the United States.

I made a few notes and then went back to find Carmen. She told me to help myself to the shelves. I guess she trusted me to put things back where I'd found them after watching my behaviour over the last month or so. The Collection was one of Carmen's great joys. There's no way she would ever be too busy to maintain order in it. I wondered how she would feel when it left forever to be housed in the Arts Building. Would having a lending set be enough after serving as the Lord High Grand Protectoress? After all, Carmen currently had the right to decree who could or couldn't sign in to the listening area, and no one had been able to borrow the actual LPs for nearly a dozen years now. In fact, some CDs were off limits till the Smithsonian allowed for another pressing. Ever since the agreement signed with Washington, the music library was no longer allowed to burn CDs from the existing LPs.

Carmen waved at me as I carted a stack of CDs into the listening room along the east wall of the music area. I had a few ideas, but I wasn't totally sure about some of them. I had to check out how many straight instrumental tunes there were on the Iron Mountain String Band recordings, see if Uncle Dave Macon's solo album could be used in its entirety, and check out the Mike

Seeger collections. I had a feeling I'd have to edit the latter; he was always letting someone jaw on about making dulcimers out of barn parts or wailing along with a musical saw in the middle of his recordings. I imagined Mike Seeger as the quintessential Folkways collector, though; totally delighted with everything he came upon, and equally respectful of it all.

Chet Parker's *Hammered Dulcimer* was a great find, and I figured we could use a good three-quarters of it for the luring music. Maybe I could salt it with some Doc Watson instrumentals and a couple of mountain banjo tunes from the Mike Seeger *Old-Time Country Music* collection. I signed three CDs out after carefully reshelving the others. Carmen handed me another full box of tapes to haul back to the Centre, and pretty soon I was contentedly retracing my steps from earlier in the day.

Wax on, wax off. There was a lot to be said for the comfort of the humdrum, after all. Maybe that's what was wrong with my life. I couldn't seem to retain enough of the humdrum to keep me going.

26

After a pleasantly humdrum evening, I woke to a pleasingly humdrum morning. I ate a moderately ordinary bowl of oatmeal, washed up and headed off placidly to my nice, if more than ordinary job.

When I got to the Centre, the door was unlocked, and sitting at the central table were Steve and Iain. Since no one else was around, I gathered they were waiting for me. They didn't have the look of wanting to take me for an after-work beer, either.

"Don't tell me there were more than two Finsters," I sighed. Steve snorted and Iain looked askance at my bad taste.

"No more bodies, Randy. We just want you to come with us to the precinct to look at some pictures."

"Okay. Pictures of what, though? Bodies? Suspects? Folk musicians?"

It was Iain's turn to snort.

"Actually, we want you to look through some pictures of clothes that may or may not have been at the Barbara Shoppe while you were there," Steve explained, looking a bit uncomfortable. As well he should have. He knew me well enough to know I am not fixated on fashion.

"I'll try," I shrugged, "but you might try asking Denise. She would be better able to tell you."

"We will be talking with her, as well as the store manager."

"You mean Holly who thinks she's Audrey Hepburn?" I grinned as I locked up the door to the Centre behind us. I had left the box of tapes on the table, and checked my backpack to make certain I had laptop, notes, instrumental CDs and the Folkways book I'd meant to get before Woody's appearance had startled me the other day.

"I mean the manager, Holly Menzies, who is on holiday somewhere incommunicado," Steve answered. "We haven't been able to track her down yet. Supposedly, she left for somewhere near Puerto Vallarta a couple of days ago."

We were approaching the unmarked Crown Victoria in the parking lot by the Law Building. I wondered why "undercover" police cars still always look so much like police cars. I figure they'd catch a lot more speeders and other assorted bad guys if they drove around in souped-up minivans. Then they'd be truly unremarkable in the crowd.

Iain drove and Steve turned halfway in his seat to continue to talk with me in the back of the car.

"We're going to ask Denise to come in tomorrow if it's

convenient. We'll pull in Grace Galbraith from the west end and Eve Sampson, the manager from Calgary after that."

"Eve? Are you sure it's not Lauren or Ava?"

"Nope, it's Eve."

"Maybe she's Eve Arden."

"Who?" asked Steve.

"You know," drawled our driver, "*Our Miss Brooks*. Tall and ascerbic with a beauty mark." I looked in amazement at Iain McCorquodale, and, it seemed to me, so did Steve. I guess you can be partners a long time and still get surprised from time to time.

"It really makes you wonder if people are born and raised to do the jobs they find in life, doesn't it?" I pondered. "Or do they wend their way to jobs that make their peculiarities somehow validated?"

"If that's the case, can you figure out how he and I came to be cops?" Iain muttered. Steve laughed.

"Don't even try answering that one, Randy," Steve cautioned.

I wasn't going to. We'd arrived at the station, and even though I'm the most law-abiding citizen I know, police stations always make me nervous. It's all those buzzers and locking doors, I think. Or maybe all those uniforms. Unless a uniform has a smiling tooth on it holding a toothbrush, I'm leery, and even then I'm not all that at ease. I took a deep breath and followed the team of McCorquodale and Browning into the precinct.

Steve and Iain led me to a room beyond the open area where their desks sat nosed in against each other amid others. This room had a door and white boards along the walls. Photos were stuck up along one wall, and various notes were written in blue and black whiteboard pen. There were a couple of desks with phones and files stacked on them, but what seemed completely incongruous was a wheeled clothes rack in the centre of the room. It was the sort of thing I'd seen in movies set in New York, where people pushed these racks along in the garment or fur district. This one, though, gave off a pungent reek of fire.

"This is what we managed to salvage from the fire at the Barbara Shoppe, Randy. What we'd like you to do is look at each item and then mark the letter on its tag to where you recall it being in the store on this map." Steve handed me a clipboard with the basic layout of the Barbara Shoppe I had visited in Petrolia Mall. Iain handed me a pen.

It was tough for me in one way, because I'm not much of a shopper, but I tend to be pretty good at spatial recall. I took a look at the beaded gown that was Exhibit A and then closed my eyes. I'd been riffling through the sales rack near the back of the store while Denise wandered along the side wall, checking out the power suits. Where were the evening dresses? I mentally walked my way through the store, heading to the Henry Moore. Suddenly I remembered the alcove of evening gowns, tucked into the corner near the manager's fine wood desk. I put an A in the corner and moved on to the Chanel suits, much like the one Denise had tried on in the other store. They were on the side wall opposite the evening wear, about halfway down. I marked B, C, D, E and F there. I had no idea where I'd seen the next few really dressy mid-length dresses hanging, but they were exquisite. I figured that even if the campfire smell never came out of them, they'd be wonderful to wear somewhere.

The wool suits in winter white and pale butter yellow, with their double-breasted buttons imitating sailors' pea jackets, were at the front of the store, near the window. I had checked the cost of the jackets and nearly swooned at the time. I marked K, L, M, N, O, P at the door and pushed them to the left. Some hand-tatted lace nightgowns had survived, though they no longer had the pristine look of bridal whiteness they'd had in the store. I recalled seeing lingerie hanging close to the archway to the changing rooms, so I marked my R, S, T, U, and V there. I had absolutely no recollection of where the chinchilla jacket was, but I petted its sleeve for a bit before moving on to the last few items. There were three dresses that looked like sacks on their hangers. I recalled the Rita Rudner routine where the salesclerk tells her a garment looks "really good on." "On what?" she replies. "On fire?" I snickered nervously, because that scenario was too close to reality. Actually, I had seen these dresses, since they were hanging rather close to the sales rack where my precious middy was housed. While they weren't as heart-stoppingly expensive as the wool suits, I recalled that they were pricey. Their elevated price must have had something to do with the designer label. I figured that particular designer must really hate his ex-wife and was now taking it out on women in general. I marked their corresponding letters by that rack and pushed through the once-jazzy-looking raincoats, which I recalled being featured in the window but was uncertain where they were hanging in the store. That was about it. Not a lot left of what had seemed a thriving business.

"Is this all that was salvageable?" I asked when I was finished.

Iain nodded. "The rest was just cinders, aside from the big stone statue in the back. That looks like it could be scrubbed up and plunked down in a park, good as new."

"Holly didn't like that statue; she would rather have had the crystal chandeliers that the west end store got," I recalled.

"I don't suppose Barbara Finster was too fond of it near the end, either. That's where we found the body, draped across the statue."

I shuddered at the thought. Steve reached for my clipboard.

"So this is where you recall these items hanging?" he said, changing the subject.

"As best as I can recall. As I said, Denise can probably zone in on the right inch of rack space. It's weird, though."

"What's weird?"

"Well, it seems odd that these things would make it through and other stuff on the same rack would burn up. After all, the store was full, and each rack was full. For instance, there had to have been twenty-five evening dresses on that first rack, and only one was saved. Do you think it had something to do with the sort of fibres? Maybe there was some kind of flame retardant on this material?"

"Nope, I think it had a lot to do with conservation of expensive or favourite items. These clothes were hanging in the back storage area on this rack. They weren't out in the main area. We figure we can get the forensic team to check for residual material in the areas we pinpoint with the maps you folks make for us, and then we can see if there were corresponding items still in the store. Maybe we can write this off as some sort of exchange that was planned with another store, or clothes that had been tried on or returned and were going to be touched up before being put back on the sales floor."

"Well, you can cross off the idea that they're try-ons. For one thing, that rack was situated right across from the Henry Moore, to your right as you walked into the change area. For another thing, you just wouldn't get all five sizes of a wool suit being tried on by the same woman, right? A try-on rack would be a lot more diverse in one way and common in another. Same sizes across the board, and similar types of things, but not the same outfit in all the sizes it comes in. For one thing, Holly could probably peg a client's size as she walked in the door. There might be occasional divergence, but not by much. For another, there was just so little business in those stores that I can't imagine Holly letting the try-ons get that far behind in rebuttoning and rehanging. When Denise and I were in there, we were the only ones shopping, in both stores, and we spent quite a bit of time in each one."

"So what do you think this rack represents?" Iain asked, with a tone in his voice that let me know that he likely felt even more uncomfortable than I did in high-end women's clothing stores.

"Since I saw pretty much the same wares in the other store, and there was no offer to get something sent over from another Shoppe when we were trying things on, I think these women run their stores like jealous little fiefdoms. Most of these clothes were new stock, ready for the fall. Their summer stock was already on sale, weirdly enough, but I think that's par for the course in retailing anymore. So I doubt this rack was going any-where, either to another Shoppe or returning to the distributors. If I were of a suspicious mindset, I would check the stockbooks and see if these weren't the highest priced items in the store. Maybe someone was making sure these clothes wouldn't be ruined in the fire."

That sounded good, but there was something wrong with it.

"If that's the case, though," I continued, "whoever saved these is the person who set the fire. But my theory that they were sal-vaging the good bits would only work if it was an insurance scam where these clothes were taken away from the store before the fire, then claimed as part of the burned-up inventory. The only person who would benefit from that would be the owner of the insurance policy, who I am figuring was Barbara Finster, right?"

"Right," Steve grimaced. "You're thinking along the exact same lines as we have been. Someone moved this merchandise, readying it to be removed from the arson site. Maybe Barbara Finster herself was doing this, when she was snuck up on and killed. Then whoever killed her could have just continued to fin-ish what she had started, hoping to cover their work."

"Unless she was overcome by the fumes of her own fire and got caught in it," offered Iain. "We're waiting to hear back from the medical examiner about cause of death, and from the arson boys about patterns of accelerant."

"But surely she'd have hauled the rack of clothes outside to a truck or a van first, before doing anything," I pondered.

"What we'd like you to find out, Randy, is if there are any folk songs that correspond to this crime scene in any way. We have some holdback information that I'm afraid we can't let you in on, but could you research women dying in fires they've set themselves, dying in clothing stores, dying in factories? I'm wondering if we can tie this to the tableau effect of David Finster's murder in any way."

"I can try. I'm not sure there are all that many folk songs about rich women in boutique clothing stores, but I'll look. Is that all you want from me, then? Because if so, I'd like to go home."

"No problem, and thanks for this. That store's an enormous pile of ash; this helps us narrow down where to expend our forensic efforts. None of those tests come cheap, so any narrowing down we can do helps the budget enormously." Steve stood up from the desk where he had filed my map. "Iain, I'm going to drive Randy home. Call Denise Woolf and see if she can come in to give us a map, too. Randy, give Iain Denise's phone number. I'll go sign out and get you home."

It wasn't till I was outside in the parking lot that I realized I'd been inhaling the smell of fire-sale clothes so much that the smell had all but disappeared for me. Now, out in the fresh air, I caught a whiff of it in my hair. A shampoo would be first on the list of things to do as soon as I got home, along with washing the clothes I was wearing. I didn't know how firefighters did it. It was a relatively benign smell, until you coupled it in your mind with the charred images of destruction, and then it took on such a powerfully dangerous sensibility.

Steve caught up to me and I leaned into him briefly as he unlocked the passenger side door for me. He, too, had the smell of fire and death on him. I nibbled his ear.

"Want to join me in a shower at my place?" I murmured.

"Best offer I've had all day," he hugged me briefly, "but I'm going to have to take a raincheck. The day isn't ending for me yet."

We drove back to my place in silence, partly because of the rush hour traffic, which seemed to start earlier and get worse every week, and partly because there seemed to be something hanging between us—something neither of us had the energy or the will to tackle. When we got to my back door, I leaned over to kiss him briefly on the nose, and jumped out of the car before I had to listen to him hem and haw about whether he wanted to make time to be with a murder suspect on his time off.

27

Over the following week, Steve and Iain interviewed a dozen or more women who had recently shopped in the now-torched Barbara Shoppe—including Denise, who was able to give them a nearly complete inventory and layout. I'm not sure how she manages to keep all that information in her head along with having most of Shakespeare memorized and ready to spit out at unruly students.

Meanwhile, I managed to get quite a bit done on my master tape for the Folkways Stage. Woody had hired a sound engineer, and the two of us arranged to go down to the Festival office to meet with the executive director and the site manager. The permanent office for the Festival was in a very central location—at the bottom of Bellamy Hill, which led to the downtown core of the city. Even so, it was sort of hellish to get to, with all the one-way streets and busy six-lane freeways we had to cross and dodge to get there. Woody rented a car this time round, and was happy to drive as long as I navigated. Of course, as long as he stuck to bus routes, I was fine. It was his desire to quickly find locations and subsequently to achieve parking spots that was driving me crazy. I stared death and the angry driver of a massive SUV in the eye as we darted across two lanes of traffic to make the turn into the area of townhouses where the Festival offices were located.

I was still shaking as Woody calmly got out of the car and waited for me to join him. Instead of commenting on our near escape, he pointed his key ring at the car and smiled at me as the doors locked electronically. I smiled back. What the heck? We were alive.

The executive director was waiting for us, which was a nice thing. Of course, he was a Folk Festival director; he had to be perceived to be nice, right? It took about twenty minutes of jolly banter about Edmonton, Washington, folk musicians, recording labels and beer before Woody and the director, Aric Skurdal, got down to business. Woody wanted access badges for his sound engineer, announcements from the main stage to let people know that the performances on the Folkways Stage would be recorded for folkwaysAlive!, and some assurances that noise bleed from the afternoon mainstage concerts could somehow be minimized.

"There's nothing going on at the other stages when the main-stage matinees are scheduled," Skurdal smiled. "There's no need to worry about that point at all."

Woody shook his head. "I've heard tell that encores can push through more than fifteen minutes longer than they're allotted. If that happens, we'll end up with over twenty minutes of relatively unusable recording time, what with sound bleed and crowd movement noises. What I'm asking, I guess, is some way of guaranteeing that the matinees start on time and end on time. Maybe we could talk to the people you've booked for those slots and explain what it is we're trying to do across the bushes from them? Or maybe you could mention it to them?"

Skurdal wasn't looking quite so folksy anymore. "I'll see what we can do. Maybe we can fit some baffles in between the tree belt there to help mitigate. You have to understand, though, that the whole concept of the Festival is that you go with the flow. If the crowd calls for ten minutes of encores, you can't just turn off the speakers."

Woody nodded. "I hear you."

I laugh inwardly whenever I hear the phrase "I hear you," because from what I've seen it always means, "I see you talking but you can't come in." Woody wasn't going to give on this point, I could just tell. Thing is, what could you do about a festival that had so many acts booked it required two major matinees to satisfy the main stage time for them all? I thought the names we had listed appearing at the folkwaysAlive! Stage were incredible, but compared to some of the names listed for the mainstage and evening lineups, we were relatively small potatoes. Luckily, we were small potatoes with the full clout of both the University of Alberta and the Smithsonian Institute behind us.

Woody and Aric Skurdal hammered out particulars. I let my mind wander a bit, surveying the posters lining the walls from previous festival years. Skurdal was about the fourth director, but the festival seemed to be pretty similar to its original concept—only much, much bigger than it had been in the early years. It used to start on a Friday evening, then run all day and evening Saturday and Sunday, with lots of people buying tickets for just the evening concerts.

Now it began on a Thursday night, continued Friday night and through the full weekend. Instead of being a festival in which all the performers got mainstage billing and shuffled about in various workshops during the daytime hours, many of the day slots were now given over to solo concerts to accommodate all the people booked to play. I had yet to meet one person who came away from the hill having seen everyone they wanted to see, and the magic of the weird combinations of musicians that were created in the workshops had almost completely disappeared.

That potential for weird magic was one of the wonderful things about the folkwaysAlive! stage. Woody and Dr. Fuller had maintained the workshop layout. Several of our musicians were featured more than one time on the stage, and some of the combinations were either totally outlandish or amazingly inspired. We had four one-hour concerts booked through the entire weekend. The rest were workshop combinations of those four major names, in and around other groups and musicians booked from the Festival in general.

We had dispensation to record it all, and the glorious thing was that everyone had agreed to work for scale. I guess the Asch guarantee that you would never go out of print went a long way to getting to people to sign onto an anthology album.

If things worked out and Nathan Lamothe, the sound engineer Woody booked to handle the recordings for the folkwaysAlive! stage, was all he was cracked up to be, we would end up with five albums for the Smithsonian folkwaysAlive! label. Dr. Fuller had told me on the q.t. that she'd still be happy if we ended up with just two albums from this year's venture. I figured that modest goal was a good thing, because the way things were going, who knew what we'd end up with?

I came back to Reality Central just as Woody and Aric were shaking hands, which I figured had to be the signal that the meeting was over. Aric looked pleased with himself, Woody a little less so, but his diplomatic veneer seemed to be covering up any problems he might be nursing.

As we got out to the parking lot, I asked him how he felt it had gone.

"Great! It was a piece of cake organizing all that. Skurdal isn't a bad guy to work with. Remind me to tell Nathan he has free rein all the way to the fences at the top of the hill, in case he wants to cover the background noises and crowd ambience. The idea behind any great live album is to mike the entire hall, you know. So that's what we were trying to get dispensation to do."

"What about the bleed from mainstage? Won't that affect things?"

Woody shrugged. "Marginally. We'll just have to schedule for sacrifice acts right after the mainstage material and toward the end of each day's session. That's the one sad bit. Things tend to get really rolling along toward the end, but if the sound checks start up on the other side of the treeline, our music may not make it to the anthology album." He grinned. "We'll have seventeen hours of music to choose from, though, so I don't think we need to worry overmuch."

"So why did you look like Aric had won some sort of pissing war on our way out of there?"

"Did I?" he asked. I nodded, putting on my sunglasses. It was a good thing I did. He smiled, and I swear his teeth sparkled just like the villain's pearly whites in a melodrama.

Woody began to hum softly. It wasn't until I closed the car door that I realized he was humming "The Battle of New Orleans." So Aric Skurdal qualified as "the bloody British" in Woody's mind? I wondered who else might fit that billing. The Finsters? Paul Calihoo? Me? I tried to think back to see if Woody had been finessing me at any time in the past few weeks, but it was too hard to tell or sort things out with all that had been occurring lately. I asked if he'd mind dropping me at the corner of 109th Street and 87th Avenue so that I could grab a bite to eat at home before heading back in to the Centre for the afternoon, and he whipped into the High Level Diner parking area so I could access the back door of my apartment building. He waved his arm out his open window as he drove off down the alley. For someone from Washington, DC, who had only been here a couple of weeks, he certainly had a firm grasp of the area.

28

I spent most of the weekend working on playlists for the Folkways performers. Most of the folks had submitted them by
e-mail, though there were one or two who were holding out
for more spontaneity and a couple whose grasp of technology
extended only as far as fax machines. Steve was busy doing festival patrol at Heritage Days, but promised he would come over
some time on Sunday afternoon, once he had signed out.

It was eight-fifteen when Steve knocked at the door. I walked
out of the kitchen, wiping my hands on the front of my shirt. I
wasn't quite sure why I didn't just yell out, "Come in," but maybe
I was acting on the same instinct that kept him from using his
key and just sauntering in. He stood in the hallway, head cocked
to one side, looking at me.

God, he was handsome. I took one half-step toward him and
he met me in the middle. He smelled of warmth and health and

easy feelings. I loved this man, and that was brilliantly clear to me. Woody Dowling could just stay on his side of the table and across the room. When we had to work the Folkways stage the following week, I was going to make sure I was professional but cool. Nothing was going to jeopardize this relationship if I could help it.

Steve responded to my extra-tight squeeze with one of his own, and then pulled back to look at me. "Are you going to let me come in?"

I grinned and pulled him into the apartment. "I've made black currant iced tea, want some?"

"Sounds good," said Steve, untying his shoes and setting them on the mat beside the door. He padded after me to the kitchen, but I poured tall glasses of tea and herded him back into the living room area to the sofa.

"So, does Iain have any new info on the Finster murder? Or the attack on Paul?" I tried to persuade myself I hadn't put on a flirty look in order to lure information out of the man I loved.

Steve shook his head. "You know the drill. Keller would have my scrotum for a tobacco pouch if I discussed the case with anyone, even you. The only thing I can tell you is that tomorrow we're releasing a statement to the effect that we think the attack on the Barbara Shoppe may be related to the murder of David Finster."

"You think? Gee, a brother and sister are murdered within days of each other after making threats to contest a huge bequest to the university. And the police think that *may* be related?"

"Randy, there's nothing more I can say without getting into

trouble professionally. I pulled the Barbara Shoppe arson, which is now connecting to the Finster murder, from which I had recused myself principally because of the connection to you. I figure the only reason Keller hasn't pulled me from the arson is that it's the middle of summer and we're short-handed with all the family guys claiming their furlough."

"You mean that I'm a suspect, right? I knew Keller had it in for me."

"Be reasonable. Keller is not trying to frame you for the murders of David and Barbara Finster. It's just that you are one of the people who stands to gain from the university keeping the money. You have to see how that makes you involved."

"Well, of course I am involved. John Donne and all that—'each man's death diminishes me'—but that shouldn't de facto mean that I am somehow left in the dark and suspected of involvement. I could help if you'd let me."

Steve kissed me. It was a great kiss, one of those lip-tingling sorts that make you pity the women who have to pay to have their lips puffed up chemically.

"What was that for?" I asked as we came up for air.

"It was either that or a primal scream. You have got to be the most stubborn person I've ever come across, and if I weren't crazy about you, you'd just drive me there."

I grinned. He had a point, I suppose. I guess I didn't mind Steve not sharing every little minute of his work day with me most of the time. It was just that lately every little minute of *my* work day seemed to be the object of his attention. In the interest of social harmony and justice, I supposed I should do my part. I told him about my time at the Folk Fest office, leaving out my musings on Woody's Machiavellian manipulation of Aric Skurdal.

Steve told me that Paul, who had come out of the coma early in the weekend, was going to be moved out of intensive care. It would likely be another week or so before they released him. That meant it would be me working the folkwaysAlive! stage all on my own, although Dr. F was planning to close the Centre for the coming week and I was sure I could count on her to do more than her share of running and schlepping. With Woody along, we should be able to manage. But really, some people will do anything to get out of manual labour. Next time, I should think about a convenient coma.

Steve and I snuggled in and watched a bit of the news on TV, and then he decided he could likely stay the night if I promised to set the alarm for five-thirty. I thought that was a ridiculous time to wake up during a bank holiday weekend, but Steve had more duty on Heritage Day patrol and needed to head back to his place for his uniform before heading down to Hawrelak Park for nine. As long as I was going to have to get up early, I might as well think about heading to Heritage Days as well. I wouldn't be able to pal around with Steve, and there was no way I was going to risk going anywhere social with Woody, especially with Steve and half his friends on the force watching, but I didn't feel like going around the world in eighty tents all alone.

It was almost ten o'clock but I risked calling Denise to see if she wanted to do Heritage Days with me the next day. Luck was in and so was she. She didn't seem too ticked off that I'd called so late, and she hadn't yet been down to the Festival so she was willing to be talked into it. We agreed to meet down there at the Korean tent at eleven a.m. I was hoping Korea wasn't set up too far from where I'd recalled it being last year.

By the time I hung up, I had finished a quick tidy in the kitchen. I just never can sit still while talking on the phone. I turned out the kitchen light and the living room lamp and wandered into the bedroom where Steve was already pushing the comforter to the end of the bed. I set the alarm for five-thirty as requested and then popped into the bathroom to wash my face and brush my teeth. By the time I came out, Steve was already under the cotton sheet. Asleep.

Not too deeply, as it turned out.

29

I figure I will eventually be rewarded in heaven for joining Steve for breakfast cereal and coffee the next morning. My initial reaction was to pat his arm and roll over to sleep in when the alarm rang, but his suggestion of sharing a shower was more intriguing than another hour of sleep. Eventually I found myself shampooed and tingly clean, scooping coffee into the drip maker.

Steve was gone by seven, and I was fully awake. By nine-thirty I was hungry again, but I'd made the date with Denise for eleven, and it occurred to me that we'd eat lunch down at Heritage Days. After all, choosing where and what to eat was most of the fun.

I was particularly fond of the honey cakes at the Korean pavilion, the jerk pork at the Caribbean tent, and pad Thai at the Thai pad. I munched on a handful of almonds and packed

my backpack with a water bottle and some sunscreen. I decided
to head out right away and take my bike, so I could detour past
SUB to hit an ATM sponsored by my bank on the way to the
park. I wasn't sure they'd take a debit card for food tickets at the
Festival, and I knew that few of the craftspeople would. I figured
I could have a good time on fifty bucks, but of course, I'd have
to push it to sixty, since the bank machines spit money out in
multiples of twenty.

That was the best thing about working for Folkways: I didn't
have to budget like crazy in August for the first time in almost
ten years. Sessionals get paid pretty well for what they do, but
the money all stops in April or, if you're lucky enough to land
a spring session course, June. You could live okay through the
summer if you were a canny budgeter and had saved all year, but
I didn't know anyone who could manage September. You had to
start up for fall session with a new haircut, at least one new item
of clothing (so you wouldn't be pitied by returning students
who had failed your class the year before and knew your entire
wardrobe by heart) and of course, shoes, not to mention all the
file folders, cue cards, purple marking pens and photocopying
I usually had to pay for out of my own pocket, since Printing
Services was always backed up like crazy. I didn't know how
married people or parents did it, but I knew loads of them who
covered school fees, various lesson and club fees, insurance,
school pictures, school outfits, lunch boxes, school supplies and
more by stacking up enormous credit card debt against when
they were finally paid at the end of the month.

So it was kind of wonderful to have steady employment

through the summer months and on into the fall. This must be
how regular people felt. I got one of those "hey I'm a grown-up"
twinges that happen only occasionally. It was so thrilling not
to have to budget on a feast-or-famine schedule anymore. Of
course, given the precariousness of my job in light of the murders and attack at the Centre, I might be wise to consider cutting
back on my spending. I shrugged off the thought; I wasn't *that*
mature.

I popped over to SUB and used the ATM, then headed back
to 87th Avenue toward the park. I passed the new Edmonton
Clinic, next to the renovated Jubilee Auditorium where I went
to see travelling musicals, the opera company and major concerts. I scooted over to bike along the side road on the south
side of the avenue, in order to be on the correct side of the
divided road when I got to the hill heading down to the park.
I didn't want to share the road with cars speeding down the
hill toward the Groat Bridge. I would drive accommodatingly
slowly behind pedestrians and roll my bike down the trough
built alongside the wooden steps down to the back entrance to
the park. I am a social bike rider, not a dedicated daredevil, and
I try to avoid thoroughfares and stick to bike paths as much as
possible. After about three more blocks of residential area lined
with the homes of retired professors and assorted wealthy families, a traffic circle at the top of the hill made crossing traffic a
bit of a nightmare. Thank goodness most Edmonton drivers are
scared of traffic circles and slow down for them. I popped across
on the crosswalk with a few families heading the same way, and
rode the brakes down the hill behind an older couple dressed

alike in orange T-shirts, khaki shorts, navy blue, wide-brimmed Tilley hats and Birkenstocks. They both had small backpacks and walking sticks. They were holding hands as they walked, and I wondered if Steve and I would look like that someday— a matched set, still very much in love. That thought made me wonder about Steve in general, and I scanned the sea of people I was descending into to see if I could spot any red striped legs. I didn't have any luck, but then, I hadn't really supposed I could instantly find someone I hadn't organized to meet here. Heritage Days is probably the best-attended festival in the city, and the one that attracts the most diverse cross-section of people. Many of them are in national costumes, even if they're not volunteering at a tent. The tents are run by various cultural societies and are set out all around the enormous park. While a set program takes place on the permanent stage in the middle of the park, most of the tents have an adjacent stage of their own. Loudspeakers compete against each other all through the grounds to broadcast music for dancers and choirs.

I tethered my bike and clipped my helmet to a strap of my backpack before heading to the information tent to pick up a map. A quick perusal revealed that the Korean tent was very close to where I was standing. I lined up to buy some food tickets, and then headed off to meet up with Denise.

I'd barely been at the tent long enough to read the odd yet encouraging phrases on the little notebooks for sale in the crafts area, when Denise popped up behind me saying, "Boo!"

"Great timing." I greeted her with a hug. "Do you want a honey cake now, or should we come back for them as dessert?"

"Oh, we'd better buy them now. I've heard they're already out of bannock taco pies over at the Métis Society. Graze as we find it should be our motto." We each bought one of the deliciously gooey sweet pancakes, and headed clockwise around the world while munching. We watched some tiny tots hula dancing, and then some Métis dancers doing what looked like a modified sword dance around two leather belts. I lusted after an alpaca wrap at the Peruvian craft tent, but realized it would be too lightweight for anything but the mildest of fall evenings, and my chances of heading to the symphony on a mild fall evening were low to nil.

We soon joined the crowd watching an amazing display of dance and balance at the Philippines stage. Five young women balanced half-filled glasses of water on their heads as they swirled around without spilling the same amount in the glasses they held in each hand. They danced, twirled, sat down, stood up, moved about the stage, smiling thousand-watt smiles the entire time. Denise was totally entranced. Something familiar about someone walking nearby registered in my peripheral vision. I turned to see Woody arm-in-arm with Dr. Fuller, heading past the Hong Kong tents and toward the Ugandan pavilion, beyond the tree break halfway along the perimeter of the park.

Now, I wasn't actually suspicious of anything between Woody and Dr. Fuller. In fact, Dr. Fuller was by all accounts superbly happily married to Mr. Dr. Fuller over in Romance Languages, who was probably here, too. It would be the most natural thing in the world for her to have invited Woody to accompany them to Heritage Days. After all, he was a guest in the city, and we were a notoriously friendly bunch out here in the Canadian West.

I was just more than naturally curious about whatever Woody Dowling decided to do, given the whole business of him mysteriously being in town at a time when I'd been led to believe he was back in Washington, DC. I turned back to Denise, who was clapping for the Philippina dancers, and tipped my head to the right in the universal signal of "want to get a move-on?" She nodded and we strolled off—along with the half of the crowd who were going around the world our way, occasionally dodging the half who decided to tackle the fair counter-clockwise.

"Have you ever noticed that this is the only festival in Edmonton where you see an actual total cross-section of the city attending?" Denise mused.

"Yes, Steve and I were commenting on that, too. Jazz City is mostly guys of a certain age. The Street Performers' Festival gets the urban crowd, and The Works caters mostly to the visual artsy crowd, naturally."

Denise continued with the festival chronology. "Klondike Days, or whatever they're calling it now, gets the blue-collar crowd and teenagers. The Cariwest Festival gets the African-Caribbean crowd, and the Anglos all go to the Folk Festival. The Fringe gets mostly the university and drama crowd, and of course, the drinkers. Heritage Days gets everyone. When it comes down to it, for the percentage of Asians in Edmonton, it's so odd that this is the only festival where I would guarantee a demonstrable turnout of them. Maybe Chinese New Year festivities are enough for them?"

"You wouldn't think so," I said, pointing at a group of dancers in silk and shantung in front of the Borneo stage. "Not when they get to dress up like that; those look like pretty serious party clothes to me. Maybe the Dragon Boat Festival is predominantly Asian-attended?"

"Well, whatever. I'm glad we have Heritage Days. It's nice to have a few days a year when we all mix it up together. Good for the system, I think. Ooh, look, the Nigeria pavilion!"

"Puff puffs!" we both crowed in unison, and went to join the appreciative line.

I hadn't spotted Woody and the Fullers since, but I was still trying to keep an eye out. Just as I popped a lovely hot ball of fried Nigerian bread into my mouth, Steve appeared on a sturdy-looking mountain bike. He relieved me of a puff puff, gave Denise's shoulders a little squeeze of hello and kissed me on the forehead.

"We have to cover the perimeter on bikes and Segways, but it's better than sitting in the police motorhome in the centre by the stage; the shift yesterday blew the air conditioning and it's sweltering in there. Are you just starting, or halfway along or what?"

We pointed back to the vicinity of the Korean tent where we had begun, and Denise mentioned that she was hoping to get a green onion cake up at the Chinese pavilion around two, since two former students were performing a Wu Shu demonstration then.

"It's sort of like the martial arts they performed in *Hero* and *The House of Flying Daggers*, apparently. Anyhow, these fellows are both national award winners, so it's bound to be pretty spectacular."

Steve checked his watch. "I'll try to make it over to that end around two. See you then!" He pushed off on his two-wheeled steed.

"There's just something about a man in uniform," muttered Denise, nodding him off. I looked at her and we managed to keep our faces solemn for about thirty seconds before giggling like Wilma Flintstone and Betty Rubble. It was a good thing Steve had firm muscles and great legs, because even he had a hard time pulling off the bike helmet and red-striped shorts uniform of the bike detail. We turned to see a magnificent Indian man walk past in a creamy linen salawar kameez and trousers, covered head to toe, and the juxtaposition made the bicycle cop uniform even more *Boy's Own*. It took us all the way to the Chilean Pavilion to calm ourselves.

We were seated by the Chinese display area, munching on heaping plates of pad Thai, when I spotted Woody once more. He was wearing a coolie hat and had a huge pair of bright blue wooden shoes strung over his shoulder. He carried a plate of green onion cakes in one hand, and had a three-foot carved giraffe tucked under the other arm. It was nice to see visitors getting into the spirit of Heritage Days, I thought, trying not to laugh. I glanced around to see if I could spot the Fullers, and just as I found them, sitting in the shade a few feet away from us, Denise tugged on my arm. Her former student had appeared in the performance area, in a gloriously bright red silk uniform that the announcer informed us was in the northern style. He was joined by a girl in pink, another fellow in orange and one in green. They moved into position solemnly, and began a series of movements choreographed to look simultaneously balletic and deadly. As soon as they bowed with one fist clasped in the other hand, they ran off the stage, leaving the boy in orange in the centre of the roped-off area. He stood and then, without any warning or crouching to create a spring effect, he did two backflips in the air and landed in an attack position. It was amazing stuff. Watching these students, it was possible to believe the fight scenes in *Crouching Tiger, Hidden Dragon* hadn't been done with wires at all.

After he left the stage, a group of adults in white silk outfits entered. This was the tai chi class, and they began the fluid movements that I loved to watch. A man walked the perimeter of the stage offering brochures from the tai chi college, and I took one. You never knew.

Woody must have been watching the exchange; as we turned to leave the area, there he was. I introduced him to Denise, and it said a lot for both his charm and her tact that they managed a civilized exchange even though he looked like a clown covered in all his purchases. He invited us back to see the Fullers, who were dusting the grass off themselves and getting ready to mosey further on to the German tent. Denise knew my Dr. Fuller through an arts council group they'd both sat on a year or two before, and apparently Mr. Dr. Fuller had been the external examiner on her dissertation, so it wasn't necessary to introduce her. As we walked en masse toward the bratwurst, Woody and

I found ourselves falling in behind Denise and the Fullers, who sandwiched her.

"I saw your knight in shining Kevlar today, peddling along the highways and byways. I'm not sure he recognized me."

"What had you bought by then?"

"Oh, I think I had the hat. The shoes came later. Aren't they great? I figure in a flood I could just float along in them."

"Maybe he recognized you and was just trying to avoid you?"

Woody laughed. "You could well be right. That's the beauty of heading into middle age. As John Hiatt once said, it gives one the right to dress like a clown with impunity. Oh well, it would have been nice to say hello to Steve. Has he had any leads on the murder and the break-in?"

"Not that I know of, and I don't think he'd tell me if he had." I hoped I didn't sound as bitter as I felt. Woody had managed to zone right in on a sore point between Steve and me. I wondered if he meant to.

"Well, we can hope that whatever is going on has nothing to do with the Folkways Collection, right? We'll just mosey along, record our artists, run our stage and launch our website. Oh my gosh, will you look at those shirts!"

I lost Woody to a discussion of Polish soccer shirts for a bit. I stood outside the pavilion, watching Denise and the Fullers amble toward us, and considering what a pretty, manicured park this was. The fountain splashed high in the middle of the pond, and Canada geese hugged the shoreline, despite the crowds of small children running toward them, trying to either herd or stomp on them. The geese just hopped into the water and floated away, leaving the children screaming happily, proud to have rid their imaginary country of this terrible pestilence.

Woody emerged with a red bundle in his hand, which I assumed was a Polish soccer shirt. I was wrong. He presented me with the bundle as if handing over a coronation jewel. It was a crocheted ladybug tea cozy. I must have looked puzzled, because he hurried to explain.

"It's for personalizing your bicycle helmet! Let me." He unlatched my helmet from my backpack and stretched the tea cozy-like monstrosity over my helmet. Antennae bobbled and wobbly eyes looked at me. It was insanely ridiculous, of course, but anything would be an improvement on what bike helmets look like in general. I put it on, in the spirit of international harmony. Denise and the Doctors Fuller rejoined us and commented on my gift with near-hysterical laughter. Perversely, I decided to keep it on and bobbled my antennae fiercely in response.

Denise was taking the shuttle bus up to the university stop, where she'd parked, and Woody and the Fullers were heading to the Irish stage to see the Irish-African fusion dance, so we said our goodbyes before the next set of tents began along the west side of the layout. I figured I would walk Denise to the shuttle stop and wait with her.

It wasn't a long wait, and I waved to Denise as the bus took off. Wearing my bobbly ladybug helmet, which was getting far more attention than I figured it deserved, I reclaimed my bike and rode to the park entrance. I decided to push my bike up Emily Murphy Hill and pedal home past the Faculty Club and the Tory Building.

Festivals are a lovely part of Edmonton summers. They're just a little hard on the hamstrings.

30

The next four days flew by, what with all the preparations for the Folk Festival, along with having to man the phones and do all the filing and taping that Paul was normally responsible for.

We heard from Paul's wife that the doctors were cautiously optimistic that he would mend up fine, and that the police had been in to see him, but he still couldn't really communicate anything of use. They figured it was partly traumatic amnesia and partly the angle of attack. It was very possible that he had no advance notice of who or what hit him from behind.

Dr. Fuller was almost as excited as she would have been heading for a field excursion to India. It turned out that she had nursed a huge fan crush on Tom Paxton since her university days and was thrilled to be meeting him. Apparently he and his small entourage were touring the province, heading down from Jasper to Banff, and then over to Drumheller to see the Royal

Tyrrell Museum. He would be back in town on Friday after-noon, and Dr. Fuller was going to take him out to lunch before the Festival began. She was glowing as she sorted through her business. Waiting behind her at the photocopier, I was certain I heard her singing "I Thought You Were an A-rab" under her breath.

Her excitement was contagious, or maybe it was Woody's enthusiasm for everything, or perhaps just the whole fun of heading down to the river valley with thousands of other would-be and former hippies. I was perfectly willing to get caught up in the glow, and too busy to notice that Steve wasn't all that forth-coming about work when I actually managed to see him. I think that first week of August was likely the least amount of aggregate time I'd spent with him in over three years. If I had had more time to think, I might have been worried.

The Edmonton Folk Music Festival is held right in the heart of the city, on what is, in the wintertime, a ski hill. The stages are set at the bottom of the runs, and the crowds sit on tarps and blankets and low-slung lawn chairs up the hills, in a nat-ural amphitheatre that has one of the most famous and least acknowledged skylines as a backdrop. In fact, I'd been told that Edmonton's pretty cityscape was often used in movies as a stand-in for cities that didn't quite measure up.

Woody and I averaged two or three trips to the Festival site per day, lugging equipment for Nathan the sound guy, setting up liaisons with the stage crew and regular sound man for the folkwaysAlive! stage, and helping to sort out airport pickup and hotel arrangements for our designated artists. By the time

Thursday morning rolled around, I was already pretty sick of the sight of lines of blue porta-johns, and the four-day marathon was just beginning. Luckily, Thursday and Friday were evening-only events. The daytime workshops began on Saturday and ran through Sunday as well. I knew that by the time the Sunday evening concert began, every muscle and joint in my body would ache from hauling me and my stuff up and down hills in the constant outdoors. Although I knew from experience that a melancholy would flood over me with the final chords of Sunday evening's traditional last song, "Four Strong Winds," I don't think I could handle the Festival being any longer, or more often than once a year. Maybe this was a sign of actually getting old.

I was hauling two covered plastic bins filled with moist towelettes, bandages, antiperspirant, throat lozenges, duct tape, masking tape, writing paper, permanent markers and Folkways hats. The hats had been my idea, and I thought they turned out beautifully. Shaped like an actual Folkways album (the same double thickness), they were made of foam and cut in a basket pattern in the middle to create a crown when pushed up. The brim consisted of the outer platter of the "record." On an average-sized head, it stuck out enough to provide anti-glare for eyes and neck shade behind. We were going to wing them out into the crowd like Frisbees in the hope that they'd publicize the folkwaysAlive! collection and the Smithsonian Folkways label. Woody was thrilled with them, and swore he'd be promoting the idea that Washington make them a staple for festival tents across the continent.

We chose two different record labels to print, one on each

side of the platter: Woody Guthrie on one side, Leadbelly on the other. I thought that combination was appropriate and would resonate with the largest group of people.

"You've earned your keep by thinking up this hat, Randy," Woody gushed, in earshot of Dr. Fuller, which made me especially chuffed. She nodded beatifically and pulled one of the hats on at a rakish angle, making her seem even more like a bemused angel wandering about the earth. She stopped as her cellphone played the opening strains to "Scotland the Brave," and turned her back from us slightly to answer it. It had to have been Tom Paxton's party calling, because she lit up as she listened and nodded several times as she responded. Clicking her phone closed, she turned back to us and made her apologies.

"They've arrived at the south end of town and aren't too sure what the game plan is. I'll head out now to sort them out, and I'll bring them down to the site for four-thirty or five, okay? He's expressed an interest in seeing what we're doing with today's recordings. I'm sure you two can manage from here, right?"

Not actually waiting for our response, she strode off. Our stage wasn't far from the volunteer and performer entryway, and I knew her car was parked on that block, so it wouldn't be long till she achieved her goal to meet with Paxton et al. Woody and I continued to sort out the backstage materials. We wanted our performers to feel like they were receiving a certain level of care above the rest, even though they weren't getting mainstage evening concerts. The recordings were one thing, but we wanted the atmosphere to be really special around the folkwaysAlive! tent. With most of the funding aimed at the recording, preservation and promotion of the original collection, we needed word of mouth to cover the shortfall to performers and industry insiders. I was hoping a battery-operated massage chair pad, a cooler full of bottles of ice water, and funky Smithsonian hats might help.

We had two hours till the first two of our hour-long sessions took place. After that, the evening mainstage concert would send the crowd back to the main hill. Woody was schlepping cable for Nathan, hauling it up the hillside along the snow fence boundary. A couple of the volunteer sound guys for the Festival were bemused, since no one before had ever recorded except through a clean feed from the monitors. Woody and Nathan were adamant, though, that an authentic sense of the performance could only be achieved through microphone placement all over the hillside.

Nathan was shinnying up a medium-sized tree in the brush between the two stages. I wasn't quite sure how he got up as far as he had with his utility belt full of wire, tape, and who knows what else, with the cable looped round his right shoulder. Of course, I'd been in the back of the tent and wasn't even sure how he managed to get on the other side of the snow fence. I was, however, pretty sure the Festival guys weren't going to approve of this stunt. Sure enough, the next thing I knew, Aric Skurdal was striding up the hillside to speak to Woody. It appeared to be a rather heated discussion, but Woody's charm seemed to hold up against the onslaught. Skurdal eventually moved back down the hill, pausing only to bark a terse comment to Nathan, who gave a nodding salute. He didn't even bother to acknowledge me; given the glower on his face, that was just as well, I figured.

"When he hears the mix, he'll be apologizing all over the table," Woody grinned as he nodded after Skurdal. "Innovative methods take time to absorb, but I'm sure he'll come around. After all, the man loves music enough to shoulder the headache of a summer festival every year, right?"

"How exactly are all these mikes going to work again?" I inquired.

"Well, Nathan has them connected to three different recording boards, alternating so there isn't any bleed between the adjacent mikes. When he gets to the studio, he realigns the tracks so the hill is recreated placement-wise. No matter where you sit on the hill, listening to that recording will give you a dyed-in-the-wool accurate version of the performance. All you have to do is move between your speakers relative to your seat on the hill."

Woody seemed enthused and Nathan was too taciturn to elaborate, so I figured I'd just leave it all to them. As a fellow I knew used to say, "That's not in my job specs." Technically, none of this was in my original job specs, but with Paul's attack and the effervescence of Woody, it seemed perfectly logical that I would be putting a hold on the website and database content, and pitching in with the Festival process.

Steve came round the side of the tent just as Woody was heading back up to the other side of the hill.

"Hey Officer, where's your trusty steed today?" Woody waved as he trudged up the hill, cable threading out behind him.

"No bike tonight," smiled Steve in his even, dealing-with-the-public voice. We stood and watched Woody until he was about halfway up, then I shook myself and invited Steve to see what I'd managed to create in the backstage tent. He whistled when he saw the massage chair, and nodded at the boxes of supplies I had hauled.

"Pampering the talent?" he grinned.

"Something like that," I acknowledged. "Not that they don't get pampered in the dining tent and at the after-parties, but we wanted them to feel that being folkwaysAlive! performers makes them something more, if you know what I mean."

"Sure, well they're the ones getting tagged for being original, creative and worthy of preservation. Why shouldn't they feel special?" Steve reached for a cookie from the tin, and I let him. It helps to have the police on your side. Besides, they were his favourite monster cookies with Smarties baked into them.

"So, what's the game plan for your time tonight?" he mumbled, his mouth full of cookie.

"I have to be back here minding things while the sessions are on, and then it will take about an hour to lock up everything for the night. After that, I was thinking of heading up the main hill, above the screens, for the concert. What about you?"

"I have to patrol the site for about another three hours, focusing mainly on the beer tent, of course. Then I figured I would take up point at the top of the hill, so I can watch for people trying to sneak in contraband and still hear the concert. Do you have a ride home?"

We agreed that I would head to the top of the hill to find him at the end of the evening concert. This was good, because it meant I wouldn't have to fend off the idea of heading to the post-concert party with Woody. I kissed Steve briefly, catching a whiff of deodorant, sunshine and the starch the cleaners put in his uniform collars. I watched him head out, looking tailored and trim. There was just something about a guy in a uniform, for sure. While Steve much preferred a detective's plain clothes, he agreed with the thinking that had all festival personnel in uniform for easy identification, not to mention low-grade intimidation. If the cops were near, the jerks tended not to act up in the first place. For what it was worth, he looked a whole lot more intimidating in his long pants today than in his bike shorts from Heritage Days.

I finished in time to crack open a bottle of water before anyone showed up in the backstage tent. I held the bottle against my temple to cool down. The weather wasn't killer hot, but the combination of hard work and the close confinement of the tent had me sweating.

"Getting a case of the vapours?" Woody inquired in his best Scarlett O'Hara. I jumped, even though I had been halfway expecting him. He was just a little too fleet of foot for me. You never knew when he was going to appear right behind you.

"Nathan should be back any minute now. He's said ambient noise won't bother him because he'll be wearing a headset, but I still think we should keep the noise down back here during the sessions, all right?"

I had a feeling this meant I was supposed to play bad cop and tell people to shut up while Woody schmoozed, but nodded and drained a bit more of my water bottle. I could see the hillside beyond Woody, and considered that this might be the last time I saw it bare and green all weekend.

"What's he doing up there?" I asked, looking at Nathan clambering to the top of the sound booth halfway up the hill. Woody turned to look, then shrugged.

"He's putting up a digicam that will take in the entire stage. Apparently it won't be too clear, but it should be enough to let him watch what they're doing on stage so he can manually adjust the tracks as he's recording."

Nathan was back down and heading toward us, smiling. "Ready to rock and roll," he announced, and took off his leather work gloves. "Now for the fine tuning." He motioned to the two tables covered in metal suitcases. "I'm going to be over there, Randy. That gear won't be in your way, will it?"

"Not at all, Nathan. I've got all the room I need here, and I'm going to try to keep folks on this side of the tent, anyhow." I held out a bottle of water to him, which he cracked and downed in one long slug. Woody checked his watch.

"I've got four-thirty, what about you?"

I glanced at my wristwatch. "Yep, the gates are opening right about now. Bring me your sweaty, tie-dyed masses."

Woody grinned, and Nathan hooked up his laptop to the grid of recording track boards, humming something under his breath. I couldn't make out what it was, but I had a feeling it wasn't folk music. Oh well, most musicians I knew found something of value in all sorts of music. It was only the rest of us who created either/or positions on country versus classical, and roots versus rap.

Dr. Fuller bustled in with Tom Paxton, who greeted Woody as if they were old friends. No wonder he was such a star, with that sort of memory for faces and names. I hoped Woody had mentioned to Nathan that Paxton was just as much a raconteur as a musician, but I needn't have worried. The man himself was over talking with Nathan within a few minutes, giving him a copy of tomorrow's set list and mentioning possible idiosyncrasies that might crop up. Nathan walked him outside to the stage, after showing him the set-up on the computer.

"I'll be watching you and listening, too. Don't worry; all of this will be mixed later. Right now I am just trying to get as many tracks as possible cleanly picking you up from various points on the hill. The idea is to have the Festival experience of Tom Paxton, not the studio experience."

"Great stuff," Paxton nodded. "I'll be looking forward to hearing it. It always strikes me that the most sincere version of the song is the one that comes from the sun-drenched stage of a festival." It occurred to me that he seemed as fascinated by the bells and whistles of Nathan's system as Woody had been. Honestly. Boys with toys.

Just then, boys with instruments began to arrive. I turned on my pre-show mix tape and welcomed Bryan Bowers and Larry Reese backstage. They were dressed to go, and pretty soon were out front, setting up their instrument stands and talking things over with the stage crew. Leo Gosselin showed up with a long case that looked like it might hold an extra-fancy pool cue, but it turned out to be his Chapman Stick. In minutes he, too, was out on stage, mucking in and doing sound checks on his mike.

I gave Dr. Fuller the script I'd printed up for her introduction, and she was scanning it distractedly. She looked extra nice, even for her. The long lines of her linen sundress enhanced the select strands of silver in her hair, making them look planned by her rather than Nature. Her Birkenstocks were a stylish variety, with thin bands of leather over the toe and sliding up her arch at an angle. The old water buffalo sandals of our youth had gone high-tech and healthy. She looked as much a star as Paxton, and just as gracious.

I set out a few more bottles of water on the beach towel I had brought as a tablecloth, and poured some cold McIntosh apples into a plastic bowl. A couple of Festival personnel had come along, ogling Nathan's set-up backstage and helping themselves to apples. I diplomatically shooed them out to the side chairs that had been set up for what passes for dignitaries at events like this.

Beyond them I could see people beginning to claim spaces up the hillside. A couple of girls were setting out an elaborate gourmet supper, with gauze platter covers over the plates they were laying out. I hoped there weren't any ants up the hill. They were wearing showy sunhats and gloves, and I think the idea was to outdo the other festival patrons. Well, I don't know if it was going to make people trade in their T-shirts and cut-offs for lawn party dresses, but I was willing to bet there would be a load of people salivating over what looked like a platter of Camembert and green grapes, and a whole plate full of dolmades.

That was one of the things I loved in particular about the Folk Fest. It was everyone's personal festival, whatever they made of it. Whole tribes of people formed at various places on the hillside, identifying themselves to their kin by mounting huge stuffed green frogs on poles to mark their site, or by spreading out specially striped tarps to indicate their place. Some people aimed for the same place on the hill each year. Others had a special wardrobe they wouldn't dream of wearing at any other time, or of wearing anything else come Folk Fest weekend.

Some folks spent their whole Folk Fest in the beer tent; others never left the kids' area. Some followed one particular entertainer everywhere; others plotted their workshop days based on musical preferences. Still others aimed for the mainstage and stayed there.

I was amazed at how trusting people seemed to be on the hillside. I suppose the thinking was that no one would risk stealing something in front of so many onlookers, but really, how could anyone on nearby tarps tell that you weren't part of a group, coming to pick up their cooler or umbrella or backpack and take them to another stage? People didn't seem as cautious as I was, though; they would pitch a tarp in the morning and leave foodstuffs, cameras, sleeping bags, down vests, and all manner of other portables, trusting to the good hearts of people who knew all the words to "Blowin' in the Wind."

You were supposed to pick up your tarp each evening, allowing others a chance at good viewpoints the next day, and Festival staff went around and tossed anything left overnight before they let the crowd in the following morning. Aside from the Gold and Silver tarps, which were prizes offered in the Festival sweepstakes, everyone had to take a new shot at a place on the hill each new day. I suppose it was as fair as any system could be.

Dr. Fuller cleared her throat beside me, bringing me back to reality.

"Wish me luck!" she whispered, and moved up the two steps at the back of the stage to introduce the first workshop and the whole folkwaysAlive! concept. Woody and I grabbed a couple of handfuls of hats each and headed out to either side of the stage. As Dr. Fuller finished explaining that we'd be recording all weekend at the stage, she welcomed anyone who wished to make history to clap and cheer as loudly as possible, and then buy the album to hear themselves. We took that as our cue and started flinging hats like Frisbees into the crowd. They were a great success, and people put them on right away, preening in the reflection of their friends' sunglasses to see themselves.

Nathan was nodding as he monitored all the mike feeds and matched them to what was happening on stage. Woody was swaying along to the music and tapping his hand against his key-filled pocket. It seemed I was the only one awake to the fact that Bill Bourne had arrived and was unloading what looked like the same number of instruments as had been enough for three musicians before him.

Woody got my whispered hint as I rushed to help Bill, and we crept back and forth from his golf cart behind the stage, bringing in his equipment. He was dressed in black trousers and vest, with a white poet-style shirt and his trademark idiosyncratic top hat. He was availing himself of a bottle of water by the time Larry, Bryan and Leo returned to the backstage area. The stage crew swarmed the stage; Tom Paxton gave Dr. F a peck on the cheek and a thumbs-up to Bill Bourne, then he went out with the first musicians to grab a ride to the mainstage area on the golf-cart and get side stage seats for the evening show.

More people were clambering up our hill to see Bourne, a local boy who had made his mark internationally. He was someone who came to mind whenever I thought of the ultimate in musicians. Every time I saw him he was trying something new, sort of like Joni Mitchell in a top hat. This evening he was playing a solo show, and going by what he brought out on stage, he'd be playing two guitars, mandolin, harmonica, and fiddle. My favourite of all his songs was "Dance and Celebrate," but there was nothing he played that I wouldn't listen to happily. I was really pleased he was part of the folkwaysAlive! recording list, especially considering the workshop possibilities on Saturday.

There would be no one else on our stage after he finished, but from the work he put into his act, I had a feeling Bill would be very thirsty after the performance. I set out three bottles of water, put the rest back into the cooler, and hefted it into the bottom of the locker. If this balmy weather kept up, I'd likely be schlepping more water into the backstage by Saturday afternoon. As it was, I had enough on hand to keep us rolling through the morning workshops, as long as I didn't forget to bring along more ice for the cooler.

I tidied away the hats and napkins and general paraphernalia into the locker, and went to the side to watch the finale. It was great to see the concentration on the audience's faces as Bourne sang a wordless song redolent with primordial rhythms and joyous primitive ritual. Who knows, maybe that was the closest we'd come to tracing back to the first music—sounds of joy and transport. Maybe our ancestors' ancestors had sat out in the open on a hillside and listened to music much like this. That sort of continuity to history often floored me. It was like you were walking along a shady path most of the time, admiring the wildflowers by your feet and the trees around you, but every once in a while you came to a high clearing and could see how far the path wound behind you and how far ahead it cut through the forest. It wasn't earth-shaking, but it just adjusted your perspective for a short time.

Thunderous applause marked the end of the concert, and pretty soon Bill was backstage, chugging the water I'd laid out and smiling the smile of the just. Woody was congratulating him and briefing him on the setup for the recording through the weekend workshops, so I just gave him a thumbs-up and kept working. I bundled up the soaking wet beach towel that had covered the table and popped it into a plastic bag for laundering at home, set the combination on the locker, and waited for everyone to precede me out so I could close the tent flap behind me. Woody helped Nathan pack up most of his equipment, as no one carried enough insurance to leave it all on a hillside overnight. He was going to help Nathan haul it to his van, which was parked near the volunteers' entrance, and then meet me back at the food tent before I went up to find a place to watch the evening performances. Nathan would then head back to monitor a few ambient feeds he wanted to leave running to get hill noises.

Woody planned to watch from the performers' side stage seating, but that notion didn't seem authentic to me. There was joy to be found up the hill that I didn't want to miss out on just because I was working the Festival. I wandered over to the food tent and got into line for some amazing-looking fare.

Soon, laden with a plate of chicken wings, three different salads, cornbread and homemade chutney, and balancing a bowl of bread pudding on top of a cup of coffee, I inched my way across a flooring of grass and cables to find a place at a table that seated more than one. Woody and Nathan would be back soon. It felt like I was back in the high school cafeteria trying not to look too pitifully alone and vulnerable.

I steadied my plate on the edge of the table and pushed it in to safety, and then moved my pudding, sloshing only a little scalding coffee onto my wrist in the process.

"My mother used to say, 'The lazy man's load is the overload,'" Woody's smug voice drowned out my muttered curses.

"Damn it, I am going to have to put a bell on you," I growled. I was thankful I hadn't still been balancing pudding when he snuck up on me or I'd likely have been wearing it. "Where's Nathan?"

"He decided he didn't want to sit outside all night, and he wasn't hungry. Can you believe it? I wonder if you could just sit here all day and eat? What a spread. Save me a spot, I'll be right back." I was halfway through my potato salad and started on the Greek when he returned with a plate even more loaded than mine. I looked pointedly at his three pieces of cornbread.

"Oh, one of them's for you. I noticed you'd only taken one. Well, girl, you cain't eat but one piece of cornbread!" And with that, he plonked a piece down on my plate. I ate them both, and the pudding. So much for trying to act the part of the svelte young thing. I was destined to be a big-boned girl from Northern Alberta, to paraphrase k.d. lang.

Woody matched me bite for bite, and it was half an hour before we got up and cleared our plates. I looked at my watch and realized that the opening act of the mainstage performances had already begun. It was a ska group from Winnipeg—not really my cup of tea, but it would likely energize the early hillside denizens. I walked with Woody toward the mainstage and left him to head into the backstage area. I turned left and headed for the rows of portable latrines. There was no way I wanted to slog up and down the steep hill more often than absolutely necessary.

The second act was just starting as I joined the constant line of people trudging up the hill. My red-striped tarp was in place about halfway up the hill, just past where the huge video screens were set up. I couldn't see it from where I was yet, but I had no doubts it would be there. Occasionally, large groups of people crowded the next person's tarp and overflowed into their personal space, but I had never heard of anyone actually moving or totally usurping someone else's designated area. It's not for nothing that every Canadian kid reads *Never Cry Wolf* in Grade 8 or 9. We know how to mark our territory and how to recognize the next guy's.

Sure enough, there was my tarp, my denim backpack, and my folded short chair. I scanned the people around me. I spotted Brian, who ran CKUA, and his wife, Frances, who suffered me to jog with her whenever I was feeling virtuous. I waved, and she spotted me and waved back. Denise wouldn't be here. I'd dragged her to the Festival one year and she had been like a fish out of water, a fish sitting primly on the edge of a tarp slathering sunscreen on her arms and cocking her head to try to digest the lyrics to rockabilly songs, with that same look people have when trying oysters or curried squid for the first time.

So, I wouldn't be seeing Denise on the hillside, but chances were I would see someone or other I knew. To that end, I had shoved a tiny pair of opera glasses into the bottom of my pack. They were mostly for watching Ricky Skaggs pick or Jerry Douglas play, but at the moment, Son Egal, a French-speaking, reggae-styled group from Senegal were dancing and leaping on the stage energetically enough that I didn't need the glasses to enjoy them. So, instead, I turned the glasses on the crowd.

I tried looking right down in front of the stage but I was too far away to see who won the Golden Tarp this year. Besides, they had their backs to me. I checked to see if I could spot anyone on the sinewy line of people walking up and across the hill from the record tent side of the stage. I saw Jim De Felice, whom I knew slightly from the Drama department; he was a playwright and retired professor of directing who always made a point of taking the time to walk posters for Drama shows down to the English department and over to the Education Building. I liked the widened sense of collegiality he showed. Not everyone was like that. A lot of people saw the university as a set of connected fiefdoms rather than a whole. Perhaps now that Grant MacEwan College was fully degree granting, the University of Alberta would band together against a common foe instead of spending so much time with the infighting.

Something caught my eye; someone looked familiar. Stupidly, instead of moving the lenses back and forth to recapture the moving shape I took them away from my eyes. I had no idea where I had actually been looking. I tried once more to focus but the flow of people was continuous, and it had only been someone's back and hat-covered head I'd seen, anyhow. Not much to go on. It was just something about the way he or she moved that looked familiar, if that wasn't too ludicrous.

My moment of detective-like behaviour had me wondering about Steve's whereabouts. He would likely still be at the beer tent, though he might head up the hill via my side of the mountain. I settled back in my chair to look at my spiral-bound Festival program. Now was a good time to read through all the biographies and details about performers I didn't know so I could make some informed choices for my infrequent off-duty moments this weekend. Well, it would have been, except that James Keelaghan began his set just then, which had me swept up in historical cameos, from the Hillcrest mining disaster to Louis Riel's lonely librarian dying alone in New York. If there was anyone who could shake Canadians up and make them feel proud of their own history, it was Keelaghan, who until recently we could count as an Alberta boy. I made a mental note to discuss the possibility of him being signed onto the folkwaysAlive! crew for a fall concert.

The rest of the evening went by in a blur, but I think that was because I was so gosh-darned tired. We had literally lugged in everything for the folkwaysAlive! tent ourselves, and Woody, Dr. F and I had been clocking fifteen-hour-plus days all week. My week still wasn't over by a long chalk, but I had this evening, and my body just decided to avail itself of that fact by conking out on me. I actually think I fell asleep through most of Harry Manx. Either that or he only played one very long song, which just didn't seem possible.

I shook myself, tidied things up around me so I'd be able to grab everything up easily in the dark at the end of the concert, and pulled my woolly sweater over my head. With it out of my backpack, everything else could fit inside. I could easily lug the tarp in one hand and the chair in the other on my way up the hill. The final act of the evening, Tanglefoot, were being introduced. They bounded out on the stage, looking like long-haired gypsy pirates. I loved these guys. They wrote rousing songs dealing with Canadian historical events, and had started out touring Ontario schools. Now they were a much bigger deal than that and could sell out a folk club in ten minutes. As Al Parrish spun his enormous double bass, they launched into their hit, "Secord's Warning," which had even enjoyed airplay on the space station when Chris Hadfield was up there. In my book, that was truly making it.

Although they played a solid set of more than nine or ten songs, it seemed far too short. That was the one trouble with Festival concerts: if you were in the mood for one particular sound, then you likely wouldn't be satisfied with just a taste of it among the rest of the potluck on your plate. From the sounds of people around me, Tanglefoot had made themselves a hillside's worth more fans with this performance. With any luck, I could catch a full evening of them sometime this winter, if rumours of their impending retirement weren't true. Someone would no doubt be booking them, after the ovation they'd just been given.

The overhead lights designed for night skiing came on to light the hillside for people rolling up their tarps and gathering their empty water bottles and detritus. I hurried to catch the wave of people heading to the upper exit rather than having to fight those heading downward. Why feel like a spawning salmon if you don't have to? I made it up to the top with my backpack on, my chair slung over my shoulder, and my tarp under my arm. I spotted Steve standing and eyeing the crowd near the Nut Man's booth. He lit up when he caught sight of me, which did more to warm me up than the hot coffee he handed me.

"I figured you might need this," he said. "I'm off duty, so we can head out now if you want. Hand me the chair."

We wove our way out the exit and down the street. Steve had parked across Connors Hill Road, just past a church parking lot, earlier in the day before his shift. It felt great to sit in an engineered car seat after perching on the hillside all evening. My heart might belong to folk music, but my skeletal system was starting to tell me it might be time to stay home and listen to Mantovani records.

Steve asked if I wanted to come to his place for the night, but I had stuff to get from my apartment in the morning, so I regretfully decided to be mature and head for my own place. He dropped me off at the back door, kissing me on the forehead.

"Sleep well, Randy. I don't have to be on duty till five, but there's stuff I'd like to see before then."

"Why don't you bring your uniform down and I can lock it in the backstage locker at the Folkways stage? Then we could mosey around between my sessions? Woody's responsible for the stage from two till five."

"That sounds good, as long as you'll have room for the bike backstage. I'll see you around one-thirty at your stage, dollface."

I don't even remember opening the apartment door, but somehow I managed to get inside, drop my stuff in the entry-way, and head for bed. If I was lucky, I'd be able to squeeze in seven hours of down time before I had to be up and lively.

31

I wasn't born lucky.

I bashed my alarm clock against my dresser, but it still wouldn't stop ringing. Finally, just as I heard it make the sick noise of innards coming loose from the casings, I woke up enough to realize I was actually hearing the phone ringing.

My eyes felt as if they were glued shut, and my fingers got stuck in my hair when I tried to comb it back out of my face. I stubbed my toe on the coffee table as I made my way to the desk to stop the ringing. I still wasn't compos mentis enough to think about actually speaking to whoever had caused this state of affairs.

I picked up the handset and stared at the buttons for a minute, trying to recall which one to push. Finally, I hit the left button and it lit up; blessedly, the ringing stopped.

"Hello?" I barked, stupidly hoping the listener wouldn't

know I was still asleep. Why I should care about that, I'll never know, but I would usually rehearse a hello or two before picking up, just to make sure I didn't croak or give away my sloth at still being asleep at whatever time this was. I had broken my clock before registering the time. I reached over to turn on the light so I could see the kitchen clock, recoiling like a vampire from the sudden brightness.

"Randy? Randy? Are you there?"

I'd forgotten I had a phone in my hand. "Yeah? Who is this?"

"Randy, this is Woody. I am so sorry to wake you up, but I really need you to help me out."

"Where are you?"

"I'm about to be taken downtown for questioning. Can you call Dr. Fuller and maybe someone in Washington to let them know? I'm hoping they can fund some high-powered local lawyer for me."

"Say again? You're being taken downtown for questioning? For what? The Finsters?"

"Nope. It seems they found a body on the hill early this morning, when they were clearing up the leftover tarps. That's all I know; these officers won't tell me anything. They've only given me enough time to dress before we head downtown. Maybe you could call Steve and see what he knows?"

"What time is it, anyway?"

"I've got five a.m. by my wristwatch. They knocked on the door here around four-thirty. I'm calling from my cellphone, and it took forever for you to pick up."

"Yeah, well, it took a while to get to the phone. Okay, I can't call Steve but I will get hold of Dr. Fuller and I'm sure she will call the Smithsonian for you. Do you want me to come downtown, or would I be of any use to you?"

"Maybe you should call Nathan and just run things at the hillside for me, as long as you get hold of Dr. F."

"Okay, Woody. Hey, did you say they found a body on the hill?"

"Yep, that's what they tell me."

I stood there with the phone receiver in my hand, not sure what to do. No wonder people talk about shaking themselves. Some of these metaphors aren't so far out. I actually tried a little shimmy to get myself in gear. I had to call Dr. Fuller, and then I figured I would call Steve to find out if he could actually tell me anything. Then I thought maybe I should call him first; that way if there was anything he could tell me, I could pass it on to Dr. F.

Steve answered on the third ring, which made him a candidate for morning person in a way I would never be.

"Did you know that Woody was arrested for a murder of someone on the folk hillside?" I demanded.

"I've just heard something, but I'm not too clear on details. Iain called me and told me I was needed downtown. I'm heading there now. What did Woody tell you?"

"He didn't tell me anything, just that he was being escorted downtown, and there'd been a body found on the hillside, and that I was to tell Dr. F and then co-ordinate things with Nathan today in case Woody wasn't let go in time."

"That sounds like a plan, Randy."

"Do you know who was killed?"

"I don't know anything yet, sorry. Call Dr. Fuller. She'll have some contingency number or other. Besides, she's the one to report to. Then get down to the hillside as soon as you can. If it's something to do with Woody, you can bet the forensic people and detectives in charge will be wanting to crawl all over your backstage area."

Oh lord, that hadn't even occurred to me. Steve said goodbye, and I hung up the phone, trying to think of what to do first. I dialled Dr. Fuller's home number, which I had on an emergency card she'd given me after Paul's attack, and then with the phone tucked between my ear and my shoulder, I went into the kitchen to pour some water and coffee grounds into the dripolater. Dr. F picked up just as I was hitting the On button, so I walked back toward my bedroom as I conveyed the gist of what Woody had told me.

We decided to divide the work along the lines that Steve had suggested. I would get over to the Festival site; she would head to the Centre to call the Smithsonian, and then go down to the police station with one of the university lawyers in tow.

"Be careful down at the stage, Randy. We don't know why they've arrested Woody, and we have no idea what they're thinking. We don't even know who was killed. But if this has anything to do with folkwaysAlive!, you could also be a target."

That was just what I needed to hear. I assured her I'd be careful. There I was, hardly awake, not even showered, and already I had agreed with three people that I should watch out for murderers. Boy, it was looking to be a banner day.

I was out of the shower, dressed and braided in seven minutes flat. It was imperative that I get to the hillside, and the quickest way I could think of was to bike, so I tucked my jeans into my socks and tossed my backpack over my shoulder. My helmet was hanging from the coat tree by my door, and I grabbed it on the way out. It still had the silly ladybug cozy on it that Woody bought me, but I had no time to remove it. With the access to the river valley trails right behind the High Level Diner, I figured I'd make it to the Festival site before Dr. F got to the Centre. Just to be on the safe side, I hooked two separate coffee travel mugs into my bike basket. I had a feeling I was going to need to be wide awake.

The Festival had a bike lock-up area that wass supervised, but I had a lock anyhow, even though I suspected more people would laugh at my particular bicycle than attempt to steal it. A kicked-about ladies' one-speed, with a white wire basket on the front and mismatched tire, it claimed to be a Triumph, but the only thing triumphant about it would be its longevity. Still, it got me places and held quite enough groceries in the basket and hanging from the handlebars to suit me.

It was early enough that I didn't meet many people en route. Most of the diehard folkies would have been lined up at the hillside for a couple of hours by now, and the rest of the city had the sense to sleep in on a lazy Saturday morning. I zipped around Kinsmen Park, under the Walterdale Bridge, up through Skunk Hollow—which had got increasingly upscale since I'd last been through—and along the hill behind the Old Timers' Cabin. I could see the Festival site, but I was still a whole cloverleaf of roadways away. I opted to head for the Edmonton Queen paddle wheeler dock, and used the pedestrian overbridge to get toward the Muttart Conservatory. By now, I was only two blocks from the main gate, and I could hear the hum of people already patiently waiting in line. The policy was to let a hundred people in at a time so there was no mad stampede for the best tarp places on the hill. By the time I navigated through the crowd— which snaked through a cattlepen and continued across the road, along the sidewalk, around the corner and down the next block—it occurred to me that no one at all was moving yet. No wonder I could hear the crowd muttering. I was betting they weren't letting anyone in till the crime scene investigators were done with the hillside. The entire hillside, I wondered? Lord help them.

I locked my bike, got a ticket to prove I had reason to go back into the compound to retrieve it later, and headed back past the crowds. I could walk down the other street to the performers' and volunteers' gate, flash my pass, and with any luck would get through without a hitch. Steve's comments about investigators picking apart my tidy backstage area had me spooked.

I had no trouble getting in, although there was a police officer there to write down my name, affiliation, and where I intended to be for the next few hours. I pitied his notes when it came to listing the environment crew or the 50/50 draw folks, who traversed the entire site several times a day.

I stared up at the hillside as I went past, along with all the other rubber-necking volunteers and two excited zydeco musicians who seemed to think it was all just as entertaining as a TV drama. The investigators appeared to be concentrated on an area straight up from the sound booth, about four or five tarps back from the height I'd been sitting at, but in the geographical centre of the crowd, whereas I had been on the periphery. It was a fitting place for me, all in all. I felt like a pinball being slammed about from unrelated bumper to bumper. Nothing about this summer was making sense, this least of all.

"They've taken the body away," I overheard a Hospitality crew member say to an Instrument Lock-Up worker. "They told the Gate crew that it would be about another hour till we could let people in."

"Wish I had a hot chocolate and coffee truck out selling to that crowd," replied her friend. "You'd make a killing catering to them right now."

I moved on toward the folkwaysAlive! stage. Somebody had already made a killing in this crowd, as I saw it.

32

I undid the combination lock on the side of the tent. It was a formality, of course; anyone with a box cutter could slice right through the tent wall and waltz in. The point was, no one had. Nothing seemed to have been moved at all. That calmed me down a bit. Maybe the police were on the wrong track with Woody; maybe this murder had nothing at all to do with the Folkways collection.

Yeah, and maybe the rural vote would swing to the NDP in Alberta. This latest crime had to be connected with what we'd been going through. In fact, I was pretty sure I would be more relieved to know it was connected than to find out there were random killings happening all over the city, impinging on my personal space.

I figured I'd better get busy setting things up while I had the time. If the police really were going to swarm the place, there'd be no time later to get ready for the performers. As far as I knew there would still be performers. The old saw about the show having to go on must apply to folksingers as well as tap dancers. The ice in the coolers had puddled to liquid but the bottled water bobbing around was still cold. I hauled out the bottles, tipped the coolers away from the cables on the grassy floor, and replaced all the bottles but one, which I opened and took a long drink from. I checked my watch. It was barely ten o'clock. and already looking to be a scorcher of a day. I hoped the golf cart guy with the bags of ice would be along soon. I set out some sun-hat disks and taped up the players' timetables, complete with their submitted playlists, in front of Nathan's table.

Nathan himself appeared just then, hauling in silver suitcases full of his recording equipment.

"Need some help?" I asked, hoping he would be chauvinist enough to assume I couldn't heft the soundboards.

"Sure," he said in an irritatingly enlightened way, "there are three more on the cart outside, along with your ice bags. They told me I had to haul them too if I wanted the ride."

"Great," I sighed. Yesterday I had managed to get the driver to bring the ice bags right in to the cooler corner. Today, it looked like I was going to have to tote my own barge, and lift Nathan's bales as well.

I was hauling a suitcase soundboard with very sharp corners into the tent when the Centre's cellphone began to ring. Woody had set the ring tone to "In-A-Gadda-Da-Vida," which I had thoughtwhile wildly inappropriate for a folk music phone, but at least it was easy to hear. I was almost late answering it, though, because I'd left it in the locker that I hadn't yet opened. Nathan kindly brought in the ice while I scrambled for the phone and answered breathlessly.

It was Dr. Fuller. "How are things down on the hill?"

"They let us come in to set up, but we haven't seen any of the performers here yet. Of course, we're not recording the first workshop of the day anyhow, so no worries there. Ferron is on here at noon, though, and we've got to be prepped for that. Are you downtown with Woody?"

"I've just come out of the police station. Woody is still there, assisting them with the investigation, if you can hear my quotation marks. The Folkways lawyer is also down there now, so there's not all that much I can do at this point. I'm going to be at the hill as soon as I can. Is there anything I need to pick up?"

I couldn't think of anything in particular besides a big cup of coffee for myself, and I could likely slip away to the kitchen tent for one of those once Dr. F was here. I quizzed Nathan, but he too was fine.

"Nope, we're okay, just awaiting the onslaught. By the way, have they let anyone know who the victim was yet?"

"That's the reason why they're tying it to our troubles, I guess. It seems it was a woman who managed one of the Barbara Shoppes. A Pia Renshaw. Any connection to those damned Finsters makes us part of the picture."

"Pia Renshaw? Is that the woman who runs the west end shop?"

It had to be the Grace Kelly woman who had been so instrumental in me getting the middy blouse. I had more trouble imagining her sitting on the Folk Festival hillside than I did imagining her dead, for some reason.

"Yes, that's the one. Apparently, she was a real folk music fan, although I doubt that it was something she discussed with her boss," Dr. Fuller chuckled ruefully.

No, I couldn't imagine Barbara Finster being overly happy to know that one of her employees harboured a fondness for guitars and harmonicas. Of course, it would be one place where you'd know for sure you wouldn't be running into your boss. Maybe that was part of Pia's reason for attending festivals. But none of that explained why she would be leaving the hillside in a body bag.

Dr. Fuller hung up, and I returned to the ice task. I had just refilled both coolers and crumpled the empty plastic bags into a larger black plastic refuse bag when the police finally showed up. I checked my watch. They were twenty minutes ahead of the workshop start. The two police officers came in at the same time as the sound guy and the stage hands. I hadn't met either of them before, but most of the cops I was familiar with came from the south side division. I had a feeling these guys were from downtown. I introduced everyone, and then made an executive decision. Since the stage hands were needed immediately to set up for Tim Hus, Mike Stack and John Wort Hannam, the southern Alberta boys who were going to head the first workshop, I suggested the police get what information they required from the stage crew first. Nathan wasn't required till noon, but he was busy setting things up for recording the hour of Ferron we'd be hosting. I'd be around all day. It only made sense to have the police wait and talk to me after they dealt with everyone who had to be in other places with more urgency. They agreed, which surprised me, considering that my experience with police officers other than Steve had been that they rarely enjoy being told what to do. Maybe they were just happy to come across someone on the site able to prioritize. There was something about folk festivals that tended to bring out the lackadaisical hippie even in otherwise button-down personalities.

They were done questioning the stage crew in very little time, and soon the music started up. There were fewer people at our little hill than I'd have liked, but I had a feeling people were still being let in through the gates due to the holdup of the investigation and that the area in front of the stage would fill up throughout the workshop. I had whispered as much to the musicians before they stepped on the stage.

Tim patted my shoulder. "Don't worry, I've played to crowds that would have made a Volkswagen feel spacious. This looks good to me."

After tossing out some sun-hat flying saucers to the crowd, I disappeared back into the tented area backstage to see what was happening with the interviewing. The officers were talking with Nathan and trying to get a bead on what our whole project was.

"So, you're recording everything?"

"Technically, yes. We've got the rights to use only certain aspects for pressing and distribution, but we have the archival rights to record everything that's produced on the folkwaysAlive! stage this weekend, and Dr. Fuller has asked that we get as much of it as possible. I'm just ramping up now for the present workshop since it took so long to get in on-site this morning what with everything, but," he paused to tweak a dial as he listened to one of the headset pots he held against his ear, "as of this minute, we're recording the complete ambience of the hillside as well as the stage."

"Did you say you were recording the hillside?" said a familiar voice behind me. I turned to see Iain McCorquodale striding into the tent. The other officers nodded to him with the deference given to plain-clothed detectives. I just smiled at him. Nathan gave him a quizzical look, but I quickly made introductions and Nathan deigned to answer his question.

"Yes, this whole hill is miked to give us a better sense of the ambience. Once I mix it in the studio, we should be able to approximate the real hillside experience. I based it on the principles of miking an opera house, to make use of the acoustical bounces from the back balconies and chandeliers and all. The purpose of digital recording has to be to fulfill the complete potential of the listening experience."

Iain was enough of an expert interrogator to hear a technical rant beginning, and he cut Nathan off before he could get full-swing onto his favourite hobby horse. "So these mikes on the hillside, how much spill do you think you'd have through the trees there to the mainstage hill?"

I was starting to see where Iain was going with this line of questioning, and so was Nathan.

"You think I captured the murder on tape? Like in *Blow Out*?

"You mean the Antonioni film? Wasn't that a photographer?" Iain McCorquodale's breadth of background never failed to amaze me. I knew he was knowledgeable about jazz music and Eve Arden. Now it seemed he was also a foreign film buff.

Nathan was no slouch, either, it seemed. "No, that's *Blow Up. Blow Out*, the Brian De Palma version, uses a sound engineer looking for the perfect scream. Otherwise it's very much the same film." So maybe he was more into that since it was about his chosen profession. Or maybe everyone just had hidden depths.

"Well, whatever the case, if you could isolate some of the mikes that might have caught some bleed from the mainstage, it might be useful. How late were you taping last night?"

"For about four hours into the mainstage act. Partly, I was hoping to create a background wall of sound to play the folkwaysAlive! concerts against, just in case there were some crud noises I had to peel, like teenagers effing and blasting too close to one of the hill mikes during an official Folkways session. The idea was just to have some extra crowd sounds, just in case of whatever."

"We can't pinpoint the time of death yet," said Iain, who appeared to be understanding Nathan in a way I wasn't, "but it would really help to listen to the ambient tapes from last night. Can you sign them over to me now?"

Nathan looked stricken but quickly calculated with me that it would be better for him to be disconnected from his monitors for a few minutes now than it would be in twenty minutes' time when Ferron was playing. He directed me to watch the levels on two tracks, and to bring them up slightly if more sound was heard, and then he and Iain removed themselves to the back of the tent to go through his masters from the day before. He was leery about handing them over completely to Iain, but he compromised by logging into a satellite Internet provider and e-mailing the files to Iain's computer.

The transfer took a few minutes because of the large size of the files, but pretty soon Nathan was comfortably back in the control seat and I was flitting about preparing for Ferron. Dr. Fuller had just made it into the back of the tent, carrying extra-large Tim Horton's coffee cups, bless her soul. I filled her in on what was happening with Nathan's recordings, and she brought me up to speed on happenings with Woody.

"They've sprung him for now and he's heading down to the hill immediately, as far as I know."

"Good. Maybe he'll have some idea of what's up with the police and the Folkways connection."

"I was listening to the news on the way here, and it doesn't look all that good," she said, frowning. "Already the announcers are making Finster/Folkways connections. I can't imagine the provost of the university enjoying this sort of notoriety."

"But there's not much they can do, is there? After all, the money was willed to the Folkways collection, and the people contesting the will are both dead. So there shouldn't be any problem with the collection getting the money unless the police somehow prove that one of us killed the Finsters to keep the money."

I laughed, but Dr. Fuller didn't. In fact, the look she gave me was weird, sort of halfway between looking nauseous and about to cry. Who knows, maybe she believed Woody was guilty of killing the Finsters. The police surely couldn't though, or they wouldn't have let him go, I figured. And let him go they had, because he was suddenly in the doorway to the backstage area, ushering Ferron in with enough of the Dowling charm to have her laughing as she entered.

He was all in denim, looking straight out of a chain gang in *O Brother Where Art Thou*, but since I was pretty sure Alberta put prisoners in day-glo orange, it was likely his own clothes. On closer look, his shirt was pressed neatly and his faded jeans fit nicely enough to be tailored for him. He looked up at me and winked, making my face get hot. I swear, that man could read my mind.

Ferron was working solo today, without the cellist she'd recently been touring with. I moved forward to welcome her and show her the lay of the land, leaving Dr. Fuller to deliver the front stage thank-yous. The hill was getting more crowded, but nowhere near what we'd been hoping to draw with a name like Ferron on the bill. I wondered if the lineup was still being let onto the grounds, or whether the radio news covering a murder on the hillside was keeping some of the folkies away. Ferron was taking it in stride, though, and seemed delighted to be recording for folkwaysAlive! She asked if we wanted any preamble and how much between-song banter we were up for. Nathan told her to play it however she wanted to, and that final editing would be seamless whatever happened.

"Moses Asch had all sorts of spoken word records in the collection, so the idea of speech in a musical recording isn't anything new," he enthused. "After all, have you ever listened to any of Dave Van Ronk's recordings? Talky! Another thing to remember is that you have liner note freedom too, in case there's anything you want to add about any song, or the feelings you get performing it now or every time."

"Cool," said Ferron, "this feels like a good thing to be doing."

"I'm so glad you feel that way," smiled Dr. Fuller, coming into the circle. "We're certainly very pleased you've agreed to be one of the folkwaysAlive! performers."

"Indeed," concurred Woody. "The Smithsonian Folkways Collection is equally pleased and I hope the connection will be equally beneficial to us both."

"Spoken like a true American," laughed Ferron. "Don't worry, I mean that as a compliment."

They went on bantering like that for a few minutes while the crowd responded enthusiastically to the high-spirited boys from Southern Alberta. Ferron was soon chatting with Hus, Stack and Wort Hannum as they poured into the backstage area, pumped up with the energy a good set gives a performer. Tim Hus poured the contents of the water bottle I handed him over his head and shook himself like a Newfoundland dog, all over me. It was a darn good thing his good old boy grin made for such disarming protective coloration. Next thing I knew, Dr. F was out on the stage, introducing Ferron, who was standing at the edge of the tarp curtain, hands folded on top of her guitar. She reminded me of an old wise woman, though she couldn't be more than ten years my senior. There was just something so centred, so rooted about her. She was totally comfortable inside her own skin, and that ease emanated out from her like ripples in a pool. She stepped forward into the applause as if moving toward the warmth of a campfire, and I knew it was going to be a magical recording.

I stationed myself near where Ferron had just been standing, except two steps down on ground level, behind the risers of the stage. From there I could see her and a good portion of the hillside, but it was unlikely anyone could discern more than that there was a shape where I stood, because of the shadow and the contrast to the brightness of the daylight beyond the tent. People were still streaming up the sides of the hill, still coming from other stages, or perhaps drawn by the power of "Shadows on a Dime." The applause was tremendous, and Ferron moved right into her next song.

I decided to see if I could gauge the number in attendance. Steve had once told me how to estimate a crowd by making a headcount of a set square of people and then determining how many of those squares would be in the total area. I had got to two hundred and forty when I spotted someone I knew, which immediately threw off my estimating. Why the hell was Mary Montgomery here, harshing my mellow? Of course, I supposed if she was going to be anywhere on this site, it would be at the Ferron concert. It was just that I thought of her as too judgmental to be a folkie, and I'd really been hoping she hadn't managed to score a ticket. On the other hand, I still couldn't imagine Pia Renshaw as a folkie, and there was irrefutable proof that she had been caught dead on the hill. You never knew who you would run into around here.

Some people came for the music. Others came to reclaim,

one weekend a year, the whole "summer of love" sensation. Still others were playing hippie despite being too young to have even been born to parents who would conceivably name them Rainbow or Sierra. I came because I loved the music, and admired the skill of the musicians working acoustically and immediately to achieve what popstars only managed in the digitally sweetened mix anymore. So why would someone like Mary Montgomery, who seemed to have a real hate on for the folkwaysAlive! project, be sitting here grooving to Ferron on a Saturday afternoon? I had no idea. I'd given up trying to figure out what made that woman tick.

Ferron asked people to take out their keys and jangle them for percussive effect. The whole hillside immediately sounded like finger cymbals and rain sticks, and it blended into the song gloriously. I tried to shake off the feeling of Mary hovering in my world, and went back to counting people. By my shaky approximation, there were over five hundred people on the hill.

"So what do you think, about five hundred?" Woody's voice sounded soft in my ear, spooking me. Whether it was his uncanny ability to sneak up on me and pinpoint what I was thinking, or that he was until recently "helping the police in their inquiries," I couldn't be sure. I hoped my edginess didn't show, but I turned and moved back a couple of steps so that we were no longer in the doorway to the stage.

"Yeah, I think. More people are coming all the time."

"I'd better tell Nathan he can open up some of the upper mikes, then." He didn't move though. I looked at him. Even in the half-light of the backstage area, he looked weary and haggard. There must be something marrow-sucking about jail, even momentary incarceration. Or maybe the whole responsibility of keeping the folkwaysAlive! business safe and on track was taking its toll on the pro from Dover. I wished all of a sudden that I could send him home to sleep, but the trouble with that idea was we needed every last one of us to keep things rolling.

"How are you doing? Can I get you anything?" I asked.

"Do I look that rough?"

"You don't look great," I allowed.

"I can make it till this recording session is done, I think. Then maybe you and I could pop over to the food tent for some lunch. It will be ambient sound and archival recordings till four, right?"

I checked the schedule on the table, even though I knew it by heart. "Yep. We should be able to sneak off after seeing the next bunch onto the stage. You'd better tell Nathan about the crowd, and I'll get back to watching. I have to toss some hats after she's done."

It occurred to me to tell Woody about seeing Mary Montgomery, but I wasn't sure why it bugged me that she was there, and I wasn't sure I'd even mentioned her to him before this. I'd wait and try to remember to tell Steve when I saw him. For all I knew, Mary might have been the person I saw in the crowd yesterday, the one I thought I recognized from behind but then lost.

Had I told Steve about that person? Everything was starting to run together in my head. I heard a familiar phrase and turned back toward the stage. Ferron was starting my favourite song in the universe, her "Ain't Life a Brook." Woody came to stand next to me. He put a hand on my shoulder and I leaned back into him as the song washed over us. "But wasn't it fine ..." seemed to hang in the air, and the whole hillside took a collective breath before rising to their feet in an ovation. I grabbed an armload of hat platters and Woody did the same.

Ferron was flushed and triumphant, taking a third bow and smiling back at her adoring fans. Woody moved behind the tarp to stage left and I moved along the right side of the stage, and we began gliding our PR hats out into the crowd. Ferron took one from me, and pulled it onto her head.

"Long live folkwaysAlive! folks! We're going to be on a record! See you at the launch party!" The crowd roared its approval and she bounded off the stage.

Woody waved at the crowd and headed backstage. I finished tossing out hats and conferred briefly with the sound crew, who were already readjusting the cables and microphone stands for the next workshop, which would begin in five minutes.

I dashed backstage, but Ferron was already leaving. There wasn't all that much I wanted to say apart from gushing, so I sucked it up and got to work setting out water and snacks. The next folks were already waiting in the cool of the backstage tent. They were from Finland, and sang a cappella. That was all I knew about them, other than the fact that poor Paul Calihoo had been over the moon to hear that they'd been booked. It was all right with them that we only had five mikes, since they doubled up anyhow. I went back to tell that good news to the sound crew, who took one of the mikes off to the side. I looked out at the mikes with their little Muppet-nosed windsocks on, and wondered what it must be like to have a thin microphone stand as the only thing between you and the whole vast audience. Maybe performers weren't using it as a shield, though. That's likely what made them performers and me an academic.

I wasn't feeling all that academic at the moment. My jeans were a bit grimy because I wiped my hands on them each time before I grabbed water bottles for the performers. My hair felt thick and unruly, and I was pretty sure I was freckling from all the sun this weekend. Maybe I should try to think of it as field-work; I was certainly far more fashionable than anyone work-ing an archeological dig. On the other hand, I was never going to compete with the Finnish women walking on stage in their flowing dresses. This was the perfect time to get away from the backstage area, and to take Woody with me.

I spoke briefly to Nathan, telling him of our plans, and then waylaid Woody at the back end of the tent as he was re-entering from seeing Ferron off. "Want to head over for lunch now?"

"Sure thing. I could eat an entire steam table's worth of food. All I got at the police station was a bag of two-bit brownies and coffee out of a machine."

"I think they're called two-bite brownies."

"Don't be too sure of that."

We continued the superficial banter until we'd walked through the food line and found a place to eat away from most of the others. As usual, Woody had piled his plate into a pyra-mid point with every kind of food available. I wasn't feeling all that hungry, given the worry about everything, but then I hadn't spent the morning in the Big House, either.

"So, what did the police want with you, and why do they think everything is tied to the Folkways project?"

"That's what I love about, you, Randy, your delicate way of beating about the bush," Woody grinned. "First off, they called me in because the three deaths all involved Finsters, and Finsters mean money. If you follow the money, it ends up at Folkways."

"But that doesn't make a lot of sense. Why didn't they haul in Dr Fuller if that was their reasoning? She has more at stake than the Smithsonian in regards to the money."

Woody nodded thoughtfully. "That's true. And I wasn't even in the country when David Finster was trussed up and left on display, which I think is the main reason I'm sitting here with you right now instead of downtown trying not to drop the soap. On the other hand, Dr. Fuller doesn't pose any threat to a police officer's romantic relationship, so that might be part of the reason for the alternative focus."

"Are you accusing Steve of picking on you because you and I are friends?"

"Nope. I'm not accusing Steve at all, even if I'm not sure that friends are all we could be. I do think, though, that colleagues of Steve might perceive me as a threat, and they might have been doing their best to help him out."

I was glad the tent we were in diffused the light, since I had the distinct feeling I was flushing. As much as I was curious what Woody meant by us being more than friends, it wasn't something I felt like getting into right then, with a murderer loose on the hillside and my job in jeopardy.

"But they determined they couldn't hold you. Does that mean they don't think there's a Folkways connection anymore? Or just that you are squeaky clean? Did they tell you anything? It feels so frustrating to be completely in the dark about things."

"Are you channelling your inner Trixie Belden?" Woody chuckled. "I don't think there's much we can do, in any case. There are forensic tests ongoing, apparently, and the police are working as fast as they can under the circumstances. They are, I gather, just trying to make sure nothing more happens while they get all their ducks in a row."

"Well, if the Finsters are dead and Pia from the Barbara Shoppe is dead, I would say the next person to watch out for is that Audrey woman who runs the other shop. Where is she?"

"Audrey? You mean Holly Menzies? The manager of the shop that burned down? That's someone they were asking me about. Apparently no one has been able to contact her since the fire. They're looking at her as number one, I think. After yours truly, of course."

"If I didn't know better, I'd say you were enjoying this."

"I was, almost, up till the moment they showed me pictures of the victim on the hill. Pia? She had been drugged and then zipped into a plastic tent bag with duct tape over her mouth and nose. It must have been horrible." He shuddered in a way that made me realize that Woody Dowling was very likely claustrophobic. If he hadn't been before, he was now, at any rate.

"I can't imagine that Detective McCorquodale is going to get anything of use from Nathan's tapes if she was strangled to death," I said. "What sort of noises would that make, anyhow? Nothing that wouldn't be covered by crowd noises, eh?"

"Well, apparently they're going over the tent bag and tarp

that was left on the hill with all their CSI-styled wiles, and they hope to come up with a fingerprint or something that way. I still have a hard time believing that no one noticed a woman getting stuffed into a tent bag, when there had to have been people all around them."

"I don't know," I admitted. "It doesn't really surprise me. After all, it's dark, you're focused on the stage, or the video screens, or the people at your tarp. People are moving all over the place, wiggling into sleeping bags, helping each other into coats or sweaters, moving those low chairs around. Some people are canoodling, and you try to avoid watching that. Others are smoking pot, and you try even harder not to notice. All the murderer would have to do would be to wait till it was fairly dark and then treat Pia as if she were a paramour or a drunken friend being helped into a jacket, and no one would pay any attention. In fact, once it was all done, I would figure the murderer or murderers picked up whatever was incriminating and then just walked off as if heading to the porta-potties or the beer tent for a while, and didn't bother coming back. That way no one would pay much attention when packing up at the end of the night, if there was no one there to pick up the tarp."

"Apparently Security is really vigilant about tarp control, but they left a few of them till early morning to deal with, and unfortunately, Pia was one of those. Otherwise we might have had an earlier start on all of this. Of course, it might have meant me spending the night in the hoosegow, so on the whole I guess I'm grateful they left some."

"But none of this gets us any closer to why people are

murdering the Finsters and people connected to them," I sighed. "If it was just the Finsters, then maybe I could see a Folkways connection, or an anti-Folkways connection, because of the inheritance and all that. But murdering Pia sort of moves it toward a different level, doesn't it? It becomes about them instead of their mother's money."

"That's what someone involved with the money would like to see, though. I think the police are considering Pia's murder to be a possible red herring."

"Ooh, now that is awful."

"What?"

"To be murdered for no other reason than to deflect attention from some other venue of inquiry. If I ever get murdered, I would want it to be because of me, not expediency."

"Should I make a note of that?"

"Never mind. I'd settle for just never getting murdered, I guess. Speaking of," I said, looking at my watch, "we'd better get back to the stage or Dr. F will have plenty of cause to kill me."

We headed back into what had become a very bright, hot day. It was a relief to get into the backstage area, even if it meant shouldering the minute-to-minute crises that seemed to happen in what passed for show business in these parts.

Nathan stopped what he was doing to let me know that Steve had been in looking for me.

"Did he need anything in particular?"

"He just wanted to know where you were and who you were with and when you'd be back. You know, sort of half police interrogation and half *Father Knows Best*. He's in uniform with a bike, though, so he shouldn't be too hard to find."

Trouble was, I couldn't go looking for him. Dr. F expected me to be holding down the fort, since it was now her turn to head off for lunch. I think she was meeting up with Tom Paxton as well, to organize his recording session for the end of the afternoon. Meanwhile, I was flinging hats and helping to introduce the musicians for the "Bringing it Home" session. Jay Kuchinsky, a fiddler and banjo player, who had also brought along a guitar, an accordion, a mandolin and what looked like a saxophone case, was setting up for the set. Bill Bourne was tuning up, looking charmingly raffish this afternoon in his top hat and an orange T-shirt. Tim Tamoshiro was checking out the mikes, wearing a tuxedo jacket and Bermuda shorts. It looked like it was going to be fun. All three of these fellows used interesting ways to bring world music into their immediate forms. I'd heard Jay playing fiddle tunes and Ukrainian music on the banjo, Bill singing Caribbean-styled hymns set to bagpipe accompaniment, and Tim Tamoshiro crooning like Sinatra about cowboy romances. How Albertan could you get, putting these folks together? I thought Dr. F and Aric Skurdal were geniuses for thinking it up, and was looking forward to it. Now, I just wanted to get through it and get home where I'd be safe and sound.

Jay put on one of the Folkways hats immediately, and Tim did the same. Bill stayed with his top hat, but that seemed only fitting. I tossed some more hats out in the crowd. By now it felt like every seventh person should be wearing a Folkways sun hat, but I could still see quite a few Tilleys and peaked ball caps, and melanoma-baiting bare heads. I introduced the workshop with a lame pun about thinking globally while being a local act, and then headed backstage. Jay was already starting into a hopak on the banjo, which seemed so natural it was hard to believe that banjo wasn't the national instrument of Ukraine. This was one set I was going to take a dub from Nathan on for sure, partly because I liked these musicians so much, and partly because I couldn't pay the proper attention to them at the moment. I kept wondering about what Steve wanted, coming looking for me.

33

Since Woody was backstage and this was supposed to be his shift anyhow, I had no qualms about leaving things in his hands and heading out to find Steve. I still couldn't imagine what he had wanted. The last thing we talked about was him bringing his uniform to the tent to store for later, but according to Nathan he was already on duty and in uniform. I supposed he had either been seconded to the case of Pia's murder, or had been asked to spell off someone else who had been pulled onto the murder case.

Maybe he had a purely romantic reason for finding me; that was actually what I was hoping for. I had no real desire to think about the Finsters and their wake of bodies. For·one thing, I got a little bit nervous every time I did. I could still picture Paul lying there on the floor of the Centre in a pool of blood, and every time I thought about it I realized how easily that could have been me.

It was as if violence had been stalking me this entire summer. I could have been mugged at the Centre, or burned up in the Barbara Shoppe fire. What if that fire had started while Denise and were in there shopping? What if it had been me lying dead across the lap of Barbara Finster's Henry Moore statue? That put me in mind of the Murray McLauchlan song "Down by the Henry Moore," but I wasn't sure a murderer setting up "Tom Dooley" would aim for a relatively obscure Canadian pop tune for his next number. It might be a good idea to mention it to Steve, anyhow. If I could find him.

I trudged down the side of the mainstage, past the wall of volunteer names and the plate-washing station, down the lane of food kiosks. I didn't think it was likely that Steve had pushed his bike around the craft tent or halfway up the hills. I figured he'd either be patrolling the perimeter on the outside of the fence, along where the buses ran, or else down at the base of the hill near the food area or beer tent. On the whole, if there was going to be anything annoying happening during the day, it would most likely be emanating from the beer tent.

The place seemed to be hopping, even though you could only catch one segment of a single stage from within its confines. I swear there were people who paid their weekend pass fees just to come and swill overpriced beer at sticky picnic tables all day long. It made for some irritatingly loud people on the mainstage hill in the evenings, though the experience wasn't as bad as attending a concert in Rexall Place, the erstwhile hockey arena. Steve and I swore off attending concerts there, since the venue's yobbo factor was greater than at a British soccer match.

I just made it past the Funky Pickle pizza wagon when I ran into Mary Montgomery. If she looked startled or worried about seeing me, she hid it well.

She was holding a serving of sweet potato fries in one hand and a glass of freshly squeezed lemonade in the other.

"Randy! I figured I'd spot you sooner or later. I have to tell you, the Ferron concert was just sublime. You'll have to let me know when the record comes out. I'll buy it for sure."

She offered me a fry, and even though I was stuffed with free Festival food, I couldn't resist. As we chatted about all the nothing things people chat about when they run into each other in a different milieu, I examined her a bit more critically than usual. I was trying to gauge her body type and fit her into the memory shape of the person I'd seen walking away from me down the hill the night before. Mary was tall and elegant, with the look of an athlete, which was an irritating thing since I figured all academics should share my propensity for dumpiness. She looked like a swimmer, with broad shoulders and slim hips. In fact, if it weren't for her hair, which curled to her shoulders, she could be mistaken from the back for a man. Well, come to think of it, she could pass for a member of Tanglefoot without her hair all stuffed up in a hat. She could have been the person I saw on the hill. I'd sensed that person was a man, and just glimpsing Mary from a distance, with a hat, sweatshirt and stonewashed jeans, I might take her for a young man.

That realization didn't necessarily move her up the list of people I thought might be the killer, because even though I could envision her as someone out to scuttle the Folkways project, I couldn't necessarily see a key figure from the Orlando Project deliberately torching clothing stores and smothering women on the hillside in the dark. I believed Mary was capable of drugging and hefting Pia into a duffle bag, I just couldn't see any reason for her to do it. Not that madmen needed a reason to do mad things, but this series of events all felt like there was real reasoning behind it, not just random potshots of evil.

Mary took her leave and headed back toward Stage Two, and I moved on down the food lane toward the beer tent. I still hadn't spotted Steve, but it was all I could do not to bump into surging crowds of people balancing plates of tabouleh, or nachos, or huge Greek platters. Little boys trying to make money by returning the recyclable plates for the two-dollar deposit were annoyingly underfoot, as well. When I finally got to the beer tent gate, I nodded to the security volunteers, and headed left toward the porta-potties for a pit stop before searching for Steve.

Surprisingly, considering the location, there was no lineup. Maybe the drinkers were sweating out their fluids on such a hot day. I was in and out and squeezing sanitizing gel on my hands within minutes.

Then I walked the length of the beer tent, looking for Steve. I didn't expect to see him sitting at any of the tables, given the fact that he was in uniform, but I considered he might be close to the fence to keep people from wandering throughout the grounds with beer. No such luck, though. I did spot another officer, whom I didn't recognize, near the back of the enclosure, and the demeanour of the crowd was certainly mellow enough for just one uniformed officer, so perhaps Steve had biked up to the top of the hill the roundabout way. I decided I would be better off heading back to the Folkways stage and waiting there for Steve to return to me. At least it was one sure place. I decided to head back via the craft tent so I could wander through both it and the record tent before heading back to my duties. I didn't think I'd actually buy anything, but you never knew. I still had a fabulous brooch of Gumby and Pokey made out of Fimo that I'd bought at the craft tent a few years earlier.

I was watching some people try on funky woven hats made along the same principles as old-fashioned rag rugs, and wondering about the price of the silver spoon jewellery, when I spotted the same person I'd seen on the hill the day before. Again, the back was to me, but this time the distance was only half a tent away. Was it Mary? I had just seen her a few minutes earlier, but in the dimness of the tent, with the distance and the angle, I couldn't be sure.

You would think I was attempting to cross the Grand Canyon on a tightrope against monsoon winds, instead of trying to get through the tent heading westward. For some reason, the prevailing thought was that one entered from the west and moved east. I'd had the misfortune to come at things from the beer tent end, and I was paying the price in time consumed moving around people who had come to dawdle and window shop. The person I was following, who was also moving westward, seemed to have a much easier time of it. I was losing ground. It was dim in the craft tent, but as far as I could, tell he or she was wearing a loose denim shirt, white jeans, and a slouchy brimmed hat. Of course, they could have been very pale stonewashed jeans for all

I could tell. The diffused shade from the red and white tent roof made all the colours slightly off.

By the time I got to the halfway bend in the craft tent, the mysterious person had disappeared out of the tent and into the bright hillside of people. I stopped pushing my way through. The chances of spotting anyone outside in the milling crowd was one in eleven thousand, and I wasn't even sure why I was trying to nail an identity. I guess it had something to do with grounding any determinables at a time when so much was up in the air.

I found myself at the west door to the craft tent and looked up the hill to my left. I could see only the edges of Stage Two's audience from where I stood, but I could see lots of people moving about at the mainstage hill, even though there was no show happening there till six. For some reason, people just liked to return to their tarps at various points in the day.

Tarps. Damn. I had forgotten, in all the hell of the morning, to take a tarp up to the mainstage hill for the evening's concert. I wasn't sure I even wanted to stay for the evening concert, to tell the truth, though Steve and I were considering going to the volunteer after-show party that night. What with the murder and Woody's early morning call and all, I'd used up energy resources that should have seen me through the evening. I was blitzed already and it wasn't even four o'clock.

Maybe that's what Steve had been trying to see me about! Maybe he managed to put a tarp on the hill. If so, that would be great. If he hadn't, I decided I would fly the idea of our just heading home after we'd closed up the Folkways tent for the night. I knew Steve liked Tom Paxton; maybe he'd manage to get back to the Folkways stage by five for the concert. Speaking of which, it occurred to me that I should get back to the stage pretty quick myself. I took a quick detour through the record tent, saw seventy things I'd like to buy, watched Spirit of the West sign a few CDs and the back of one woman's shirt, ran into a former student whose name I actually remembered, and turned left past the CKUA broadcasting tent. Someone was interviewing Alison Brown, my absolute favourite banjo player. I listened for a few minutes, but she was talking, not playing, and while she was very erudite and intelligent, I couldn't really justify playing hooky unless she was actually picking. I checked my watch. Woody and Dr. F would be ticked with me if I didn't get back to the Folkways stage pretty dang quickly. I clumped along the wooden walkway and headed up toward the path to the further stages. More people were walking with me than against me, so I made pretty good time.

Bill Bourne had the entire hillside singing along, and all three musicians were jamming together along with Tim's pianist and bass player. The workshop vibe was really high, and you could tell the players were enjoying themselves just as much as their audience. I moved from the side of the audience to the entrance to the backstage before they ended their set, just to see if I could be of use. It turned out Woody had things set up for them, water laid out, orange slices in a bowl for a bit of energy replenishment, and towels ready. It looked like a race station for distance runners. In a way, that's what Festival performers were like: long-distance athletes, giving their all in the heat and the sun.

Woody greeted me with a smile and a nod, and spun me around in a polka step, in time to the music rolling in from the stage. "Have a good time?"

"So-so. It's hot out there, and full of people."

"Yes, and we are in our Arctic misanthrope mood today, are we? Lots of people means lots of potential Folkways fans. This is a good thing. Keep telling yourself, 'I am a people person, I am a people person.' And drink this." He handed me a cold bottle of water, which was a good idea. I ran it over the back of my neck and then cracked the lid open. I drank the entire bottle's contents in three gulps, which is not something I normally can even keep my throat open long enough to manage.

"They say that by the time you feel thirsty, you are already two or three litres dehydrated," Woody said. Where he came up with this endless supply of fascinating trivia, I wasn't sure. Maybe it came from working at the Smithsonian; all those amazing things housed together just had to rub off on a person eventually. Or maybe people who collected information by nature were drawn to working in places where collecting was privileged. It would be interesting to find out sometime. But not now. I was still down a litre or two.

Jay, Bill and Tim came off the stage looking flushed and happy. We gave them water and oranges, gushed approvingly, and helped them with their instrument cases. Meanwhile, Dr Fuller had arrived with Tom Paxton and his bass player, Richard Lee, and they, too, were chatting with the local fellows. Tom had such a personable way of engaging people in conversation. Jay and Bill asked if it would be all right to leave their cases backstage while they caught Tom's concert. I was planning to be there, anyway, and Nathan sure wasn't going anywhere, so we agreed, even though the principle was to make sure all instruments went to the huge trailer marked Instrument Lock-Up. Woody and Dr. Fuller went out to introduce the Paxton concert and to let people know that it was being recorded for folkwaysAlive! and would be available in record shops in the new year. The crowd agreed to rehearse their cheering quite happily. It was a beautiful summer day and they were about to be entertained by one of their favourite performers. Why shouldn't they cheer? Tom and Richard arrived on stage to a very happy ambience, and immediately made it more so.

They launched right away into Paxton's set, starting with some well-known standards like "The Marvelous Toy" and "Did You Hear John Hurt?" before segueing into a couple of the heavier political satire and social commentary songs he was so renowned for.

"I can see the headlines now: In his Dotage, Paxton Begins to Yodel," he commented after finishing a lilting song called "My Pony Knows the Way." Although his hair was white beneath his trademark poorboy cap, his comments on aging seemed odd. Perhaps it was because he always seemed like the elder states-man of the Edmonton Festival, appearing several times in the late Seventies and early Eighties. Maybe it had something to do with his connections to the heyday of the Village scene on McDougall Street that was spoken of reverently by Dylan and Pete Seeger and even Ramblin' Jack Elliott in various folk docu-mentaries. Whatever the case, Tom Paxton was an integral part of my vision of folk music, so much a part of it that I hadn't till now paused to consider that he was aging at the same rate as the rest of us.

My first urge was to have a Scarlett O'Hara fiddle-dee-dee moment. I didn't particularly want to think about getting old, although I was pretty sure it might have been an acceptable scenario to Pia Renshaw about twenty-some hours ago. The second thing I thought was far more along the lines of what Steve would consider the "Bad Randy" train of thought.

Tom Paxton had been around through the whole start of the folk scene. Wouldn't it stand to reason, then, that he had been acquainted with the Finsters? Surely he would have met Mrs. Finster when he first came through Edmonton in the time of the Hovel and early festival days. Maybe he could shed some light on all that had been happening, even if only to explain some of the antipathy the children had shown for the music their mother had loved. I still couldn't quite buy the idea that they'd been ignored by their mother in favour of folk music. That just didn't sound to me like the way folk music worked. You wouldn't ignore your children; surely you'd be hugging them to you and swaying along to "Kumbayah." Something didn't feel right about it all.

I sat on an empty silver case Nathan had set near the doorway to the backstage. From here I could guard the door against anyone wanting to steal Jay Kuchinsky's banjo—even though I knew that the joke was that people broke into cars to place banjos in them, not remove them—and still see part of Paxton's right arm beyond the bulk of Woody and Dr. F crowding the stage entrance. I could hear fine, though, and besides that, I had room to think things through.

I thought back to the time David Finster had surprised me at the Centre. He had been thoroughly disparaging of folk music, but even more so of academic practices on the whole. I tried to break the two apart, but it occurred to me that his dismissive attitude had been to anything that didn't have an outstanding monetary value. He was a man who only cared to read a healthy bottom line, but he couldn't find one in either the folk circuit or the ivory tower. No wonder he had been sneering. So maybe he just wanted the money for himself. Maybe it didn't have anything to do with beggaring the Folkways project. He would likely have been the same charmer if his mother had donated the money to MRIs for the homeless.

So was he killed by the folkies? Or by someone who just disliked him? Or someone else who valued money as much as he did? His sister was no screaming altruist either, but she was also dead. And Paul had been attacked, so there was a Folkways connection, there had to be. Of course, one of Barbara Finster's managers had also been killed, so maybe this was about her more than us, or her more than her brother.

Or maybe this was all some sort of chaos theory experiment gone awry. I could see possible links between the deaths, but no through-line to all of them. Apart from me, of course. I had spoken with each of the victims shortly before he or she died. Maybe someone was trying to make me stop conversing with people. Maybe Mary Montgomery and Bill Bourne were the next victims.

Maybe I'd had too much sun.

By the time he finished the final notes of "The Last Thing on My Mind," Paxton had the whole hillside in the palm of his hand. I swear I saw Dr. Fuller wiping tears from her eyes. I knew the song also signalled the end of the set. I got up from my perch to hurry over to the performers' table so I could lay out towels and water and fruit. Before I could make it there, though, I felt a hand clamp down on my shoulder.

34

've been looking all over for you. I've been back here three times."

I turned toward Steve, who was looking pretty sexy for someone who today was showing his knees. I tilted up my head to kiss him, working on the age-old theory that you can't stay really mad at someone you're kissing. He gave me a quick peck, and then followed me to the performers' table.

"Are you okay? Where have you been?" he demanded.

"I went for lunch with Woody, and then I went looking for you about an hour or so ago. Aside from that, I've been here all day. What's up?"

"I've just been a bit edgy about your safety, that's all." He took off his ball cap and wiped his brow. "This is all sort of weird, having three teams working on murders and not being sure if they're related or not. If you look at them one way, they have to be connected. If you look another, though, all the ties between them disappear."

"That's just what I was thinking," I replied, excitedly. Too excitedly, maybe, because Steve gave me that warning look he tends to get whenever he thinks about Staff Sergeant Keller and the talking-to's I've been given. "I'm not doing any digging, honestly. It's just been that same sort of day for me, wondering who the murderer is and whether or not I've been talking to him or her, and whether or not I'm next."

I told him about running into Mary Montgomery, about the Murray MacLauchlan song, and also about seeing someone I'd recognized on the hill the night before, but not being sure of who it was. "I think it might have been Mary. At first I thought it might have been a man, but now I'm thinking it was a woman, a tall woman. Thing is, you know how it is at folk festivals. Unless it's one of the watch-my-hands dancers in their bare feet and hippie gowns, most people tend to wear the same sort of thing on the hill at night—jeans and sweatshirts, or jackets and jeans. Hard to really tell from behind, sometimes, who you're seeing."

"Do you think it means something? After all, a good percentage of Edmonton was on the hillside last night."

"I dunno. It's preying on my mind. Maybe it imprinted as someone from some other part of this situation, or maybe I'm just paranoid. Thing is, I saw the person before I knew anything about Pia being killed, and it stuck with me."

Steve made a note of it, probably more out of kindness than actual need, since all I had to go on was some pretty vague description.

"Any news from Iain and the sound analysis?"

Steve shook his head. "Forensics are working full time on all sorts of angles, but they're still working the fire scenario, too. They are pretty definite that it was arson, though, so the push is on to determine whether she was confined there or killed accidentally. There was a real whack of insurance on all of the Barbara Shoppes, but that doesn't seem like a motive, unless we have someone who stood to inherit from Barbara Finster in the picture. As far as we can tell, the last will she made was in 2000, and there haven't been any changes. That's public record. Her lawyer is keeping pretty quiet, though, till all the forensic evidence is in, because the ID is still only tentative."

"It's all pretty complicated, eh?"

Steve sighed. "It seems more so when it's an ongoing investigation. There's this fear that the bodies might keep piling up if we can't figure out why things are happening and who's doing them. That's what puts everyone's nerves on purée. Every minute counts, and some elements of an investigation just have to be given time. You can't rush the lab coats."

"I was thinking about how so much of this connects to either folk music, Finsters or the university. If we wanted to pursue the folk music/Finster connection, you might want to talk with Tom Paxton when he gets back here. I'm betting he knew Lillian Finster personally."

Steve nodded thoughtfully. "You could be right. It might be good to get some sort of perspective on her involvement with the folk scene other than what you said David Finster went on about. After all, it's that bequest that brings you and the university into all this. That connection needs to be clarified."

"Here he comes now."

Dr Fuller and Woody were applauding the man as he stepped down into the backstage area, grinning at the joy of a set well done. Paxton looked over to where Nathan was sitting. The sound engineer gave him a big thumbs-up, and Paxton's shoulders seemed to relax an inch or two even though he had already looked perfectly composed.

"Good show, everyone. That's a nice crowd on that hill out there," Paxton commented. I handed him a towel and a bottle of water, while Woody took his guitar and set it reverentially into the open case.

"Tom," I interjected, "I'd like you to meet a friend of mine, Steve Browning." They shook hands. "Actually, Steve is working on the deaths of David and Barbara Finster, and the murder of the woman on the hillside last night."

"Yes, sir," Steve smiled. "I was wondering if I could take a few minutes of your time."

"You think I had something to do with murders?" Tom asked, his expressive eyebrows shooting up into his hat brim.

"Not the murders, no, but I think it would help us understand a lot more of the dynamics at work if you could tell us something about Lillian Finster, her involvement in the folk scene here in the Sixties and such."

Tom Paxton smiled. "I knew Lillian quite well. It was one of the treats of the circuit that you could be wined and dined like royalty when you hit Edmonton. She was a very nice lady who made you feel as if folk music was as valuable to the culture as opera or Philip Glass. Not everyone sees it that way, you know."

Dr. Fuller laughed knowingly. She had plenty of experience trying to explain the validity of her studies in esoteric music, too.

"So Mrs. Finster was well-known in the folk circuit?" Steve asked.

"Very well-known. Edmonton was one of the only places we folkies knew we had a great place to stay. Most of the time we stayed in what Tom Waits used to call 'an international hotel chain called *Rooms*.' Folk music, by its very nature, didn't pay all that well. It was difficult to sing Woody Guthrie songs and then get all hard case over your contract. Most of the time, you filled up on the food tray in the dressing room and made do between times. If you weren't driving yourself in a station wagon filled with guitars and equipment and sleeping bags, you were going from gig to gig on the Greyhound. You better believe Edmonton was a good place to play. Don Whalen would always have a basket of fruit backstage and he would take us out for dinner after the show. Lillian would make sure we had a place to stay, and if we hadn't been booked into a hotel, then she'd bring us back home with her. When a woman in a full-length sable picks you up at the bus station in a Bentley and drives you back to a mansion overlooking a forest of a river valley in the middle of the city, you better believe you appreciate it."

"Can you remember meeting any of her family?" Steve asked.

"I met her husband a couple of times, but he was sort of a distracted science type—pleasant but absent when people were around. Nowadays I'd probably say he had Asperger's. Then we called it being an absent-minded professor."

Tom was warming up in his reminiscences. Nathan had almost packed up his equipment behind us, and the festival techies were winding up mike wires and setting them in the cabinet beside my table, but Woody, Dr. F, Steve and I were rapt.

"The kids she had were sort of funny. She called them folkie names, as I recall, like Barbara Allen and Black Jack Davey. They were the oddest teenagers I met in the Sixties, I think. They stood out mostly because they looked like such throwbacks to my generation. You'd think that when your mother is into the folk scene, you'd have dispensation to grow your hair long and loosen up a bit, but David Finster had a brush cut well into the Seventies. At first, I thought it was rebellion against his mother, a sort of reverse thing from what the rest of the kids were doing, but then I had another idea. With all the girls and their long hair, he might have been worried he'd end up being mistaken for his sister if he had hair the same length as the other fellows at the time. They were as alike as twins, you know, but I don't think they were actual twins. Poor Barbara, even with hair down to her waist, I'll bet she was mistaken for her brother loads of times."

That was an interesting idea. Wouldn't it be funny if David Finster's reaction to folk music had been sartorial rather than musical? From my exposure to Barbara Finster as a well-dressed doyenne, I had to squint a bit in my imagination to see her as boyish, but I could sort of see what Paxton was talking about. Her broad shoulders had made her tailored suit drape elegantly, and of course, the fashions worked so much better with no hips to cut the line of the fabric. She might have been as tall as her brother, too, although it didn't occur to me at the time. For one thing, I was sitting down most of the one time I saw them together, and when a woman is dressed up, we tend to absorb quite naturally the idea that she may be wearing heels. That day in the Barbara Shoppe she looked long and elegant, but I was too worried about being recognized by her to spend a lot of time analyzing her looks and body type. Being tall myself, I generally only notice height if someone is about an inch or two taller than I am, and then I start stretching my spine up as I walk, in order to compete for superior airspace.

Nathan nudged me and indicated two of his heavy cases with a nod of his head. I poked Woody and passed the buck. Pretty soon everything was packed up on the golf cart. I managed to lock away the water bottles and unused towels, and loaded the bag of laundry on top of Nathan's equipment. There was no way I was hauling it back on my bicycle.

Tom Paxton and Dr. Fuller had decamped for Instrument Lock-Up and then the dinner tent. I thought about joining them, but decided that I wanted to be home more than I wanted lasagna and chocolate pudding cake, no matter how wonderful the food sounded. Steve had his bike with him, and his shift had ended twenty minutes earlier, so we decided to ride back together to my place. He had clothes enough to change into after a shower, and I figured I could whomp up a salad with the fixings in my fridge.

"Sounds good to me," Steve said as he leaned over and kissed my ear. We were halfway to the bike lock-up area, having shed Woody and Nathan at the performers and volunteers' gate. They were going to load up Nathan's van, and then he and Woody were heading out for some grain-fed Alberta beef, which Woody had pronounced superior to corn-fed American beef.

"I'm surprised that Woody can be so chipper, considering all he's been through today," I opined.

"Well, if he's a mass murderer, then he's likely used to this sort of thing. And if he's not, then it's probably something to do with his metabolism."

"Steve! You don't actually suspect Woody of murdering anyone, do you?"

"Why? You sound worried."

"Well, I would be worried if I thought I'd been working with a murderer all this time."

"You know what I mean."

"Are you asking me if I have feelings for Woody?"

"Well, yes. It has crossed my mind that you've been together a lot these past few weeks. I have to admit it's somewhat awkward seeing my girlfriend with a fellow who seems to be so connected to the same things that interest her. After all, you two speak the same language. Maybe he has more to offer you." Steve pushed his bike along morosely.

I stopped in the middle of the road. It would probably have made a greater impact if the road hadn't been closed to traffic, but you can't always have a Hollywood moment.

"Steve Browning, I can't believe I am hearing this from you. It seems so self-doubting, which is something I've never thought of in any context with you. Woody may be a funny, good guy to work with, but he doesn't speak my language any more than you do, and you forget the mundane fact that he's from Washington, DC. Is this really about Woody being a suspect, though, or is it about you and me?"

"What do you mean?"

"Are you really worrying about Woody and me, or are you worried about you and me getting too close? Maybe this is just a smokescreen because you're not sure about committing? I can sort of understand if that's what it is. Commitment is a big thing. I just don't want to muddy things up by attributing weight to red herrings like Woody and me."

"Sweetheart, if Woody is nothing more to you than an interesting co-worker, then I'm satisfied. And I'm not worried about commitment." He reached over to pull me close to him, since his bike was leaning up against his other side. I had to turn my head slightly to avoid getting the sun visor from his bicycle helmet imbedded in my forehead, but it was worth it.

35

I retrieved my bike from the lock-up with no troubles, although the volunteers there looked at me as if I were stark mad, leaving just before the evening concert was to begin. Let them. For me, it's always been the daytime workshop stages rather than the evening mainstage concerts that defined my Folk Festival experience. Although I've gleaned every moment of these wonderful music weekends I could get for years now, the times spent sitting in the dark on a bumpy hill with a bunch of strangers—some of whom are smoking pot, many of whom are visiting and chatting over the lyrics to my favourite songs—are not the best memories of the events. I just smiled and shrugged and pushed my bike out of the compound to where Steve was waiting for me.

He had to slow down from his usual gears to pedal along beside me. We drove along back the way I had come in the morning, then opted to push the bikes to the top of 99th Street hill and go home via Saskatchewan Drive.

We'd either have to push the bikes up now or later at Kinsmen Hill, and I figured I might as well expend energy while I still had some. The day I can pedal up a river valley hill is the day hell frosts up. Once we got to Saskatchewan Drive, it would all be level since we'd be up and out of the river valley—and therefore out of the few hills we could boast in this city.

Steve let me lead, since my bike would have to set the pace. I stayed on the road till we hit 103rd Street, also known as Gateway Boulevard. It was a one-way street that twinned with 104th Street, which, because it went south, was called the Calgary Trail. Past these two main thoroughfares, Saskatchewan Drive became a one-way street pointed easterly. Luckily, a bicyclist can pop up onto the sidewalk along the river valley, which is extra wide along this stretch for just that reason. That's what I was heading for when I heard Steve shouting my name. At the same moment, I heard a motor racing.

Out of nowhere, a huge cream-coloured half-ton truck loomed at me. It wasn't braking, and I was heading right into its path. I wasn't even sure if the driver had seen me. He or she made a wide turn into the space where I would have been if Steve hadn't called out and I hadn't pulled hard right into the gravelly grime on the edge of the road. Braking in that stuff made my rear tire skid out from under me and I pitched sideways onto the grassy verge between the road and the sidewalk. Thank goodness for bicycle helmets. My knee and inner calf weren't so lucky, scraping across the gears and pedal on the way to meet the rest of my tangled body under the bike. Mostly, though, I was shaking from the shock of seeing that big metal grille coming toward me, so fast and so impersonally. Why did people want to be so cut off from each other in those high, shiny boxes of trucks and SUVs? The height of the hood obviously must have made it impossible for the driver to see me, even perched up on a bike. While my leg was stinging along with the palm of my right hand, it felt better to just lie still than to try to untangle myself. I figured Steve would help me get to my feet soon. That would be soon enough for me.

He was on his cellphone when he hauled his bike up behind me. It sounded like he was calling in the bits of licence plate he'd managed to read on the receding truck. For such a shiny big vehicle, there was apparently a suspicious amount of grime on the first part of the licence plate. Finally, he snapped his phone closed and leaned over to help extricate me from my bike frame.

"Can you stand, babe?"

"What did you mean about a suspicious amount of grime?" I murmured.

"There was just enough dirt to obscure the letter portion and two numbers of the licence. That's not enough to haul the truck over for, but it's suspicious because the rest of the vehicle was so clean. I doubt that it's ever seen off-road conditions. That tells me that the licence was deliberately obscured, which makes me think that the driver is either a car thief staging a sloppy getaway or someone was aiming that three-thousand-pound weapon at you."

"At me? You've got to be kidding."

By this time, I was standing, picking tiny bits of gravel out of my knee. Steve checked out the skew of my front tire and pulled the handlebars back into alignment.

"It's workable, barely," he announced. "I think you need a new bike, kiddo."

"No way. I love my bike. I'll just take it down to the co-op and see if I can get some advice and help fixing up the front tire. Meanwhile, if you don't mind, I'm going to push it home instead of riding it."

"Good idea."

We set off down the five blocks to my apartment. Steve insisted on walking between me and the road. While I didn't actually believe his theory that I'd been targeted by the truck, it made me feel a bit better to be buffered from the slight amount of traffic we encountered. It also made me feel vindicated in a petty sort of way that Steve had been present to see me as the victim for once, instead of the prime suspect.

Once we crossed 109th Street and pushed through the alley by the Garneau Cinema, we were home, and I chained my poor little bike to the rack at the back of the building. Steve brought his bike into the building with him, since it was departmental equipment and probably worth more than several of the cars parked in the lot behind us.

Inside, I went to the bathroom to wash the grime off my leg and see if I could find some Mercurochrome while Steve headed for my telephone. I overheard part of his conversation to Iain.

"Just in case, run the numbers and description against vehicles owned by anyone connected. We'll be here at Randy's. You have the number, right?"

There was something warm and cozy about knowing your boyfriend gave your number to his workmates. Unless, of course, you were uneasy when your phone number was known by members of the police force as a useful contact spot during dangerous cases. I tried to remove that connotation from my head by concentrating on pouring stinging chemicals onto my knee.

I came out of the bathroom with gauze taped to my knee and shin, my hair pulled back and my face and hands washed clean of dirt and tear tracks. All in all, I figured I looked pretty darn good. Steve seemed to agree, although he was suitably ginger in his bearhug, not sure where I might be bruised from the fall. I leaned into the embrace, thinking I could do with a whole lot more of this and a whole lot less of murder, mayhem and bicycle spills.

"How are you feeling?" Steve murmured into my hair.

"Pretty good. Actually, I feel like making a couple of lists."

He laughed. "You must be feeling good. Okay, lists it is. You get the paper and pens and I'll make the tea."

"Oh God, marry me."

Steve laughed.

"Be careful, or I'll hold you to that. Lucky for you I don't hold anyone accountable for anything they say within twenty-four hours of a near catastrophe."

"What happened to 'anything you say may be used against you in a court of law'?"

"You've been watching too many American cop shows, oh aptly-named Miranda."

I rummaged in my desk drawer for a couple of pads of fools-cap and grabbed some pens from the can next to the computer. There was no way I was going to let Steve know I'd started a murder file on my laptop weeks ago, nor that I'd shared a list-making interlude with Woody. I had a feeling Steve would see that as an intimacy that went too far. He came back into the living room with two cups of steaming tea, which may have seemed inappropriate to anyone checking the thermometer but was exactly what I needed after a long day on the hill capped off by nearly becoming a traffic statistic. Bless Steve and his St. John's Ambulance training. I sat on the sofa, stretched out my grazed leg, and leaned into the corner. Steve sat on the floor, reclining against my end of the couch.

"All right. What are we going to start with?" he began.

"All the victims would be a good start, and then maybe we can make some connections."

"I'll do that in chronological order, then." He wrote in neat block capitals, in a column: David Finster (dead), Paul Calihoo (wounded), Barbara Finster (dead), Pia Renshaw (dead), Randy Craig (wounded).

"Hang on! Why are you putting my name there?"

"What if that wasn't some random bike-hating driver? We have to consider the possibility that your accident just now was an attack, too."

"You really know how to calm a girl down. You didn't mention that theory to Keller, did you?"

"Why?"

"I just think that man is going to kill me himself if he thinks

I'm involved in this investigation. Your boss doesn't like me, you know."

"It's not that he doesn't like you, I don't think. I think it has more to do with worrying about civilian involvement. Any time there's an extension into the community from the force proper, there is the greater possibility of vulnerability for all, especially the civilians. That's when it becomes Keller's problem."

"Well, I would rather he not think of me as being in his way and 'his problem.' I would also rather not be thinking of myself as a target for bad guys, so why don't we take me off that list for now."

Steve shrugged and added a question mark by my name, which I figured was as close a compromise as I was going to get.

"Is there anything to link the victims in terms of how they were attacked?" I continued.

Steve shook his head. "Nope, not unless we stretch things to your idea of song possibilities, and I think Murray McLauchlan is more country than folk, anyhow. We have someone knifed and garrotted and hung up on display. We have someone knocked on the head from behind. We have a business torched and a body burned to a crisp, and someone drugged and smothered on the hillside surrounded by thousands of possible witnesses. Then, we possibly have a hit-and-run scenario. All totally different MOs. Either these are completely separate crimes, which I just don't buy, or they are crimes of opportunity in which the murderer is pushed to improvise with materials and situations at hand."

"Everyone is connected somehow. David and Barbara Finster

are brother and sister. The Finsters are linked to the money bequeathed to the Centre where Paul works. Barbara Finster was Pia's boss at the Barbara Shoppes, although that isn't linked to David or to Paul. And I am linked to the Centre and, through proximity of the hillside, to Pia. I still don't see any sort of clear picture."

"Me either," Steve admitted. "Let's try a different list."

"Money?"

"That's a good one, but we're still not sure who benefits from Barbara Finster's death. We know there was a hassle between the Finsters and the university over the money to the Folkways Collection, and that it's possible whoever killed Pia Renshaw did so because she knew something about the arson or Barbara Finster's murder. Possibly Paul was attacked just because he was in the wrong place at the wrong time. He might have walked in while someone was robbing the Centre. Maybe Pia saw something she shouldn't have seen. Or maybe whoever set the fire that killed Barbara Finster was misinformed about which store Pia managed and was after her all along."

Steve let his head drop back toward me on the couch. Even from upside down, I could see the exhaustion around his eyes and the tension in his jaw.

"What time were you up this morning?" I asked softly.

"Same time as you, give or take an hour. It's been a long, strange trip today for sure."

"I promised you supper, didn't I? Maybe some food would help." I pushed myself up off the couch, cringing just a bit as I bent my sore knee. Steve pulled himself up onto the couch, asking if there was anything he could do to help. He looked relieved that my answer was negative.

I kept mulling over motives and connections as I chopped up some green onions, mushrooms and cheese to toss into a quick frittata. There was one very sad-looking tomato that I quickly chopped up into a bowl of bagged spring greens. I sliced up the last of a loaf of French bread and pulled a tub of margarine out of the fridge. Supper was ready in all of fifteen minutes. I set the table and went around the corner to call Steve. He had nodded off. I debated whether or not to just let him rest, finally deciding that food was just as important to a tired body as sleep. With the levels of tiredness coursing through my own body as a gauge, I didn't think he'd have any trouble falling back asleep once he was between cool sheets.

We ate quietly, both of us having endured enough sound-scapes for one day. Steve gathered up enough energy to help me wash the dishes, and then we moved back into the living room, having decided to go to bed as soon as he'd checked in with his partner, Iain.

I picked up Steve's notepad from the floor, looking at the lists of names and various arrows he'd doodled between them. There was a big question mark to the right of his list, with five arrows emanating from it toward the names of the victims, which included Paul and me.

That was the trouble in a nutshell: there was no one I could think of who could stand in the place of that question mark and have a need to hurt or destroy all the people on the list. Someone might hate the Finsters. Someone might hate the Centre or the Folkways collection. Someone might hate the Barbara Shoppes. But who would hate all three? Something just didn't add up. I stared at the names, not paying much attention to Steve's conversation, but hearing something in Steve's tone of voice get sharper. I idly rolled my pencil down the paper from the top, noting that it obscured an entire line of foolscap, wondering if that was an official measurement of line depth on paper—HB pencil diameter? I watched David Finster's name disappear, then Paul's and then Barbara Finster's. No long letters, so the names were completely obscured. Pia's name was, too. In fact, mine was the only name with a tailed letter in it.

Something gnawed at me. I rolled the pen halfway back up the list. That was it. I stared at the list now. I still didn't know all the whys and wherefores, but I suddenly had an idea about connections where before there had been none. I looked up at Steve just as he put down the phone and turned to me with an animated look.

"They finally found a dentist listed in Barbara Finster's home phone book, which they needed to check her dental records, and guess what?"

"Barbara Finster isn't dead," we said in unison.

41

Steve jumped into the shower as soon as he was off the phone. Iain was whipping by to pick him up on the way to the airport, after organizing the roadblocks on the Yellowhead both ways and the Queen Elizabeth II south. It was assumed she wouldn't be heading north. After all, fugitives didn't run from the police by heading north unless they had some sort of Albert Johnson fixation.

While he sluiced himself off and tried to find his second wind, I gently pulled some jeans on over my scraped knees and got ready to go along. Steve wasn't going to like it, but I had my reasons.

As he walked out to see me in jeans, T-shirt and a zippered hoodie, he started to protest, but I held up my hand. "I'm the only one of you who has seen Barbara lately, and she's in disguise. I am sure that's who I saw on the hillside."

"And you're saying Barbara Finster murdered Pia Renshaw?"

"Well, why not?"

"Let's start at the other end of the question: why? And if you're going to insist on coming along, let's head out to the front to watch for Iain. We've got to get to the airport to see if we can stop her. They're blocking the QEII just past the airport exit, this side of Leduc, but we need as many legmen as possible at the airport."

"What makes us so sure she's heading for the airport?"

"The direction her truck took after trying to run you down. I think that was just opportunity for her, not something she planned out. After all, we could just as easily have gone home through Skunk Hollow. She, on the other hand, had to come out of her condo parking garage and turn right on Saskatchewan Drive if she was going to connect with the Calgary Trail to the airport. She's on the move and I don't think driving to Kananaskis is on the agenda."

"So that was her truck?" I shivered, recalling the gold grillework bearing down on me. "Did Iain match the licence plate?"

"Make, model and last number of the plate match. That's enough for me. When a dead woman's truck starts aiming at my girlfriend mere hours after a third person connected to her dies, I make some room for circumstantial evidence. There he is," he said, waving at Iain, who was rounding the corner in an unmarked Crown Victoria.

Iain McCorquodale didn't look too pleased to see me clambering into the back seat, but he didn't say anything. He just checked quickly in all directions before pulling a u-turn in front of the Garneau School and heading back towards 109th Street. He had the dashboard light pulsing, which made the inside of the car resemble a patriotic discotheque. There wasn't all that much need for the siren, though, since traffic was low for a Saturday evening. With the Folk Fest on the hill and the Cariwest Festival downtown, and the weather being so nice, not too many people were getting into their cars just to cruise Whyte Avenue. Yet.

Iain drove capably while filling Steve and me in on the reports of x-rays proving that it hadn't been Barbara Finster in the Barbara Shoppe blaze. Apparently, Holly Menzies had been x-rayed for a heel spur a couple of weeks before the fire. I guess that's what comes from wearing those ballet flats day in, day out. Forensic x-rays showed the same spur on the deceased. So, two of the managers of her stores were dead, her inventory at one store torched, her brother murdered, and the second-in-command at the Centre for Ethnomusicology beaned, just so she could run away incognito? Something wasn't adding up.

"Another interesting thing about the fire was the lack of powdery ash at the scene. Seems there's no way a shop full of silk and wool and other expensive fabrics could burn without there being a higher percentage of residue left behind. Plus, the whole place should have been reeking of the smell of singed hair and feathers, which it wasn't. So, either the Barbara Shoppes were selling polyester masquerading as silk, or Finster moved a heck of a lot of inventory before she tossed the match."

I thought about my middy blouse, and the glorious feel of

the linen trousers I'd tried on. There was nothing cut-rate about Barbara Shoppe clothes.

"Maybe they should check the other stores. I remember there was only one of anything in any size at any Shoppe. If there were doubles of any sizes, wouldn't that indicate that she'd transferred clothes to the other stores before burning it down for the insurance?"

"Maybe," Steve said. "Of course, we have to determine whether Barbara was burning it down for insurance money and Holly Menzies just got in the way, meaning she died by accident, or whether Menzies was the intended victim and the fire a cover-up for the murder. Or maybe Menzies was just a convenient stand-in to make us all stop looking for Barbara Finster. But if Finster was going along with being thought dead, then how could she collect on the insurance?" Steve's mind was a thing of beauty. It would have taken me two lists and a spreadsheet to work all that out.

Maybe Iain was also taking stock of my limitations, because he clicked off his flashing light. As we turned onto the road to the Edmonton International Airport, he bluntly said to Steve, "What is she doing here, by the way?"

Before Steve could incriminate himself or slight me, I jumped in. "Neither of you has seen her in the flesh, and I think I saw her on the hillside yesterday as well. If she's in disguise, she's still registering on my radar. That's why I thought it would be a good idea for me to come along, even though God knows I would rather be soaking my wounds and resting after a hideously long day, thank you, Iain."

"I'm not the one who will take the heat for it," Iain shrugged. "Just thought you might like a dry run at a story since the first person we're likely to run into will be Keller."

"Never mind Keller," Steve shrugged. "We've got work to do, and Randy can help. That's good enough for me. Listen Iain: drop us at the departures level, and then you head back into the long-term parking lot and look for the Cadillac truck." He shuddered. "That's got to be the height of Alberta Crude, eh? A Cadillac pickup truck."

Iain pulled in behind a marked police car and two other Crown Victorias, and we piled out. We entered the international flights wing, mostly because that's where we'd ended up, but I guess it was a good idea. If you're on the run, run as far as possible.

Steve walked over to the small group of men surrounding Staff Superintendent Keller near the entrance to the Customs area. I figured if Barbara had made it inside, she was going to be effectively cut off. All the police had to do was stop any flights from boarding and work their way through all the people who had cleared customs. Maybe it was a stupid idea of mine to have tagged along. Keller was going to hit the roof when he figured out I was here, and besides that, my knee was really beginning to throb. I was suddenly hit by a wave of incredible tiredness.

I looked longingly at the coffee kiosk at the departures level, but thought better of it. Keller would spot me right away if I walked over there. Right down the escalator, near the arrivals, was a Tim Horton's outlet. I could head down there, grab a coffee and a Canadian Maple doughnut, and wait it out. Eventually

Steve would find me. Or he would find the doughnuts and see me by default. Cop instinct, right?

I imagined myself coming down the escalator with a carry-on bag, heading for the carousel and adoring fans or family. There was a nice setup for an entrance for sure. In fact, a flight must have been imminent, because there was a tow-headed young man in his early twenties waiting near the bottom of the escalator with a bunch of flowers and a huge teddy bear. He was polite enough not to look too disappointed to see it was just me.

I strolled over to the Tim Horton's line, glancing forward to make sure my favourite maple frosted doughnut was still plentiful. There were about nine or ten Canadian Maples on the tray behind the woman, but there were five or six people in line ahead of me. Talk about tense. The man and woman at the front of the queue were getting iced cappuccinos and crullers. The next customer, who looked like a businessman heading home, took a large coffee and a Canadian Maple. The next woman, who was pulling a hard-shelled, wheeled carry-on bag, ordered a coffee but no doughnut. I was poking through my wallet to see if I had enough change to buy Steve a doughnut as well while the man in front of me ordered. I looked up as the coffee-only woman excused herself to get by him and found myself staring directly at Barbara Finster in jeans and a Tilley hat. I was so flustered that I wasn't sure if my befuddlement even registered on her as more than jet lag. She kept walking and I stepped forward to buy my doughnut, which was probably the best thing I could do to keep from arousing her suspicions, right? Besides, I'd been in line for about ten minutes. If I was to step out of line at this point, she'd notice me for sure. There was no way, though, that I could now order a coffee … my hands were shaking too much to hold a cup of hot liquid safely. Damn, I wished I'd taken Steve up on his offer of a cellphone. What I wouldn't give to be able to surreptitiously text him right now.

By the time I got the doughnuts without any coffee, Barbara Finster had disappeared from view, but I figured she couldn't have gone far. I decided to try the washrooms situated beyond the luggage carousels for the local arrivals. If she was on this floor, it had to be because she was hiding out from the police, since she had a carry-on bag with her. It wasn't a bad idea. Even if it hadn't actually been her plan to elude police, the arrivals level was a whole lot more conducive to hanging out than the departure lounge. For one thing, there was the Tim Horton's. Then there were also the nice washrooms that you didn't have to navigate three hallways to get to. On top of all that, there were actually places to sit and wait for people you were picking up from delayed flights. While officials always instructed travellers to arrive two hours before international flights in order to clear customs, it usually didn't take more than ten minutes to wander through the big room with all the flags of all the States. And of course, that was only if you were going to the US. Anywhere else made you clear customs when you landed. So all in all, I was completely copasetic with Barbara Finster's decision to wait on the lower floor before her flight. It was just that pesky business about avoiding the police stationed on the upper floor that had me suspicious.

In fact, I was more than just suspicious. I was both suspicious and annoyed. The weird thing was that if she hadn't bothered to aim her truck at me earlier in the evening, I'd likely have been far more frightened than I actually was. Maybe my bike helmet hadn't protected everything from shaking loose up there. I was marching toward a cornered criminal who had probably murdered three people, and what I wanted to do more than anything was give her a piece of my mind. I felt the grip on my small bag of doughnuts tighten into a fist. The recollection of the doughnuts reminded me of Steve upstairs. Perhaps I should let him know where I was.

I veered left toward a bank of telephones outside the International Customs Arrival doors. I didn't want to have my back to the washrooms, but it was impossible to see the washroom doorway from the other side of the telephones. I settled for standing at a sitting booth, to the consternation of a nice man in a long robe who was talking passionately in another language in the booth across from me. I'm not sure why he thought I would be eavesdropping. Surely he'd figured out by now that most Canadians are woefully unilingual. He would have to have been gossiping very slowly about Monsieur et Madame Thibeaux for me to have cottoned on to much of what he was saying. I smiled at him apologetically as I fished for the change to make a call.

Steve wasn't answering his cellphone. With my luck, he'd be standing right next to Keller if he did. Instead I got his voice mail. I just hoped he'd would check his messages pretty quickly. and wondered if the location code of the payphone would come up on his call display as "airport" or merely as "payphone." I tersely said I was downstairs and that I thought I had spotted the target, but that I was now going to use the washroom. If the man across from me could codify his conversation, so could I. After all, I was sure he could speak English and probably seven other languages as well.

I hung up the phone, a little more nervous now than I had been before trying to check in. That's the trouble with sober second thoughts: they tend to take the adrenalin out of your sails. I walked toward to the washrooms, hovering slightly closer to the people congregating near the arrival doors. I looked like some-one about to welcome a Canadian home from afar, knowing that the first thing he'd want would be a hug and a Tim Horton's doughnut. Okay, so far, not a bad cover. Should I try to be a welcomer-with-doughnuts who had to use the facilities? Would that be a good idea?

I might as well check out the washroom. After all, what if Barbara Finster hadn't headed there? What if she'd left to catch a cab to take her away from the heavy concentration of unmarked police cars? But to where would she take said cab? Do people step off planes in one city and take cabs to another city? Not very likely. In fact, I didn't think I had ever seen a taxicab driving on the Queen Elizabeth II Highway to Calgary.

She had to be in the loo. I walked through the open concept doorway, thinking how good it was of the architects to preserve us from germs, leaving us open only to infestations of small boys daring each other to run through. A long line of sinks and mirrors ran along the right wall, and green toilet stalls along the left. The light was weirdly fluorescent, different than the light in the rest of the terminal.

I was hoping I could see if anyone was in the stalls, but all the doors hung uniformly closed. There was no one standing at the mirror or in the baby-change area, so if Barbara Finster was in here, she was in a stall. It occurred to me that if I made any noise kneeling down to check the stalls, I would be tipping my hand. I realized almost simultaneously that I really did have to use one of the stalls.

I pushed open the first door and locked myself in. I scrunched up the doughnut bag and set it carefully on the floor near the solid wall. Maybe I'd be able to check under the stall walls when I reached back down to pick it up? Or maybe I could drop something else, such as some change, and then reach down to pick it up?

I unzipped quickly and sat down, wondering if I was placing myself in one of the most classically vulnerable positions with a killer in the same room. It couldn't be helped, though. I stood to zip up and considered how I could peer under the stalls to see if she was holed up in one of the further cubicles. I just about jumped out of my skin as the automatic toilet flushed forcefully behind me, with the sound of a water cannon exploding into action. I realized the noise might cover me and dropped quickly to one knee. From that vantage point, I couldn't see much as the walls were lower to the floor than most public washrooms. Lucky for me, the stalls were made for people hauling luggage along, or I'd probably have hit my head on the latch of the door as I came back up. The toilet flushed again. I think I might have cried out. I know my heart started pounding. That infrared button on the flush mechanism was entirely too sensitive. I picked up my doughnut bag, pulled at the hem of my shirt to make sure I was presentable, and opened the latch.

The door swung open but there wasn't any space to walk out because Barbara Finster stood in my path. If she hadn't recognized me in the Tim Horton's line, that moment of grace was over now. She was glowering at me with an intensity I'd only seen once or twice in my lifetime. It was the look of someone who has gone beyond taboos and discovered she could still exist. That has to be the scariest look of all.

Before I could figure out a way to bluff my way out of there, she spoke. "You! I might have known. So I didn't manage to incapacitate you earlier? Pity."

I was already frightened, but her reminding me that she had nearly run me over—and was responsible for the gravel still smarting in my knee—put some iron back into me. "Sorry to disappoint you. Travelling somewhere?"

"Yes, as a matter of fact. It's been such a hot summer, don't you think? It will be good to get away."

"I thought you'd have wanted to stick around for your funeral, though."

She sniffed, which might have come across as a laugh if she weren't so scary and the stall weren't so cramped.

"Oh, no Tom Sawyer schtick for me. Besides, Barbara Finster has nothing to do with me any more. I've moved on to a whole new life. Soon, in fact, I won't even look the same."

"It's hard to hide your stature or your way of walking, though. I spotted you on the hill yesterday. You must have been leaving after killing Pia, right? I couldn't tell immediately that it was you, but I knew it was someone I had seen before. I wouldn't be so sure that you'll be able to disappear completely."

"Oh, you would be surprised what money can buy, dear. However, I am not interested in enlightening you. What I need to know is what you're doing here, and what you know about any police involvement. It would be too much to believe in two coincidental run-ins in one day, don't you think? You're not here to pick someone up from a Toronto flight, are you? You're here with that policeman."

It wasn't guile that made me dodge her question with a question of my own. "So that really was an accident this evening?"

"You mean on the road? Well, I admit I swerved, but I wasn't out hunting for you, if that's what you're intimating. You're not nearly as important as all that. I just noticed that ridiculous helmet and then saw it was you. I thought it would be a nice balance to the attack on the other fellow at the Centre where you work. I thought it might buy me some time, but now I see it was a mistake. That must be what has brought you here, right? Oh, dear. It just goes to show that a person should never act on instinct. Of course, one shouldn't go off exploring on one's own while there's a killer on the loose either, don't you agree?"

I was having trouble standing still. The confined space was getting to me, and Barbara Finster's glib attitude was doing a number on me, too. I couldn't see any remorse in her. Of course, aside from her just wanting to crush me like a bug under her huge tires or splatter me against her shiny grille, I wasn't clear on a motive for her killings either. But standing there with her looking straight at me with her passionless blue eyes, I had no doubt at all that she was the killer we'd been fearing and search-ing for all summer.

Since the attacks on the World Trade Center, security mea-sures in airports have increased exponentially. Nail files and umbrellas are routinely confiscated at check-in, and people are asked to remove their shoes and open their carry-on luggage with far more frequency than before. I was hoping that Ms. Fin-ster had packed accordingly and wasn't carrying a lethal knit-ting needle or garotte at the moment. She was slightly taller than I was, and probably in better shape if she had used a gym to defy time and look the ten-to-fifteen years younger than she logically had to be. On the other hand, I biked and walked everywhere, but was still achy and shaken from the collision earlier. On the whole, it would be better to keep her talking than try to take her or disable her enough to make a run for it. Maybe Steve had his messages by now. Maybe someone else would come into the washroom and I could get away. Maybe Barbara Finster would find God and turn herself in to the authorities.

"It won't do you any good to hurt me. They're already looking for you, so it won't deflect attention to anyone else. I'm assum-ing that's why Paul was attacked at the Centre, right? This didn't have anything to do with your mother's bequest to the Folkways collection. This was all about killing your brother and getting away with the loot, right?"

Barbara Finster laughed but there was no warmth in it. "Is this the part where I confess my motives and my actions to you while the police sneak up from behind and arrest me? I don't think so. I think this is the part where I add another notch to my rifle and ride off into the sunset. After all, one doesn't explain oneself to the hired help. You've been listening to too much folk music, my dear. Too much pie in the sky, by and by, right? Let's just settle for bye-bye, shall we?"

She moved her right arm toward her pocket, a movement I caught in the corner of my eye. I feinted left, pretending to try to rush past her. As I sensed her body move in response, I reached for the edge of the door to swing it shut.

It might not have worked, but the noise of the toilet flushing as it sensed my sudden movement was enough to startle her. I slammed the door shut and locked it in her face. It occurred to me that all she had to do was enter the stall next to me, stand on the toilet and kill me as easily as shooting fish in the proverbial barrel. I was clambering onto the toilet, ready to climb over the wall and close that door, too, when it also occurred to me that I had a moment's opportunity to run when she entered the stall beside. If I timed it right, I could do it.

I heard the door swing and leapt for the latch to my own cubicle. Once more the toilet flushed. I raced for the corner to the entrance, not looking back. I heard a whoosh and a ping close behind me, but it's not everyone who can hit a moving target when balancing on a wall-mounted toilet, and lucky for me Barbara Finster wasn't one of the happy few.

There were exhausted travellers from the late Toronto flight milling about and waiting for their baggage at the carousel to my immediate left, and lights flashing "ready" at the carousel just beyond. Two flights' worth of people and their attendants were between me and the stairs to the departures level where I could find Steve. Of course, one crazy murderer with a gun was behind me. I would cope.

Dodging in and around tired people with luggage carts is not something I'd recommend unless there are extremely pressing circumstances that dictate such behaviour. One older lady, who likely was a longtime and vocal member of the United Church Women, actually rammed my ankles with her cart because I had bumped her suitcase in my hurry. I mumbled an apology for bleeding on her cart and hurried on. I heard someone behind me shout, "She's got a gun!" and any attempt at good behaviour went out the window.

I ran directly at the second carousel, which had just begun to move and spit out mismatched luggage. I cleared the revolving black panels and teetered for a minute on the centre silver buttress. I was searching for someplace I could jump to on the other side that wouldn't involve colliding with bulky suitcases or more mean old ladies. Of course, my immediate objective was to jump *after* a huge dufflebag went past me on the moving carousel below me. As soon as the bag was to my left, I dove for a patch of floor, twisting my foot in the process.

The sound of a bullet whooshing past and exploding into the electronic sign above the luggage retrieval area was enough to keep me from dwelling on my ankle. I raced past terrified people who were now beginning to cower among their belongings. There was no way I was going to expose myself to Barbara Finster by taking the staircase in front of me. I ran toward the lost luggage office to my left and dodged into the lee of the doorway. Surely Steve and his bunch would have heard the commotion down here. There was no need to go any further. I slid to the ground in the archway. With luck I would be obscured from sight by the mound of suitcases stacked by the doorway. People were still shouting. I heard another couple of shots, but didn't look up.

When Steve found me, I was crouched down in the doorway with both arms over my head, as if I'd been told to assume crash position. Fitting, considering where I was. Also fitting was the fact that Barbara Finster had managed to shatter the illuminated sign welcoming people to "Canada's Festival City" just a few feet to my left.

Thank God for airport security, I guess. It seems you just can't pull a gun in the middle of a crowded airport and get away with it. Barbara Finster's body had six shots in it from two security agents and the first police officer responding to the commotion on the lower floor. She wasn't going to be available for questioning.

It was just as well. I was in no mood for any denouement. I just wanted to go home to bed for a month, which is about how long I figured it would take me to stop shaking. Steve helped me up to my feet and half carried me out to the car, where Iain was waiting for us. No one talked on the way home. Steve helped me to bed, told me he'd be by in the morning to take me down to the station for a statement, and kissed me goodnight.

I slept like the dead, which was as close as I wanted to come to the real thing.

42

The rest of the summer was a bit of a blur. The Festival ended with no more fuss. Woody took over my duties on the Sunday shift with Dr. Fuller pitching in. The university stood its ground against the Finsters' lawyers, who suddenly weren't all that interested in pursuing a claim made by two dead people, one of whom had been a killer. So the Collection still had its grant and I still had my job. In fact, I had Paul's job too for as long as I wanted it, since he was on extended disability leave. Of all her crimes, the most chilling to me was Barbara Finster's cold-cocking of Paul Calihoo. For the sake of deflecting attention, she had effectively removed his ability to speak and read. His memory seemed intact in other ways, but much like a stroke victim's recovery, it was going to be a long, slow process back to normal for him. In his graceful way, though, he was looking on the positive side that he had a route to follow.

Any potential chemistry with Woody had evaporated at the moment I'd actually suspected him of murder, so the rest of his stay was a bit stilted, although we were really too busy with winding up all the Folkways/Festival recording work to let it get awkward.

The police had determined, through a lot of forensic sifting and sorting through legal documents and paperwork on weird holding companies and such, that all of the crimes had been engineered by Barbara Finster in order to keep her brother from bidding on more LRT contracts.

Something in her mother's will had tied their money together so that investments made by one had to be supported by the other. That wouldn't be so bad if you were making money, but David Finster's desire to be as renowned in town as his father had been caused him to recklessly underbid on contracts that would net him some notoriety. Apparently, he spent a lot of the collective Finster pot on the teak awnings over the South Campus LRT station because the budget had already been used up on the essentials long before the accessories were tallied up. It was to his credit, I suppose, that forensic engineers could find no evidence of substandard materials used or shortcuts taken. Still, if he had kept this spending pattern up, the Finster millions would have been gone before the trains made it to NAIT.

So Barbara Finster murdered her brother after egging him on to bluster and complain about the Folkways bequest once he'd discovered it, figuring this tirade would muddy the waters, which it did. She then lured him down to the worksite after hours and murdered him in an intricately macabre, premeditated way.

None of the materials used to hang or display him had been from the worksite proper, and there was no evidence to show that she hired anyone else to commit the deed. The more I learned about this woman, the more amazed I was that I managed to get away from her.

Barbara Finster's real desire had been to run away with all the money she could filter into a holding company owned by Anna Ford, a non-existent person for whom she had created a long trail of paperwork over the previous several years. Her will left everything to this fictitious Anna Ford, which included all the money left to her by her late brother. The fire in the Barbara Shoppe had likely been for the additional money the insurance would kick in, and Holly Menzies' death appeared to be a tragic accident. I didn't think Barbara was all that broken up about it though, since she made sure to silence Pia Renshaw, the manager who could testify that excess inventory had been moved to her store the night before the fire took place. Pia had likely been willing to go along with insurance fraud, but unable to condone and cover up homicide. That's what happens when you start picking and choosing your principles.

Barbara Finster was travelling under her new name when she was killed at the airport, but they found a set of safety deposit keys registered under her real name in a money belt around her waist.

If she'd made it out of town, which she almost did, she would have been in the clear. Her fingerprints weren't on file anywhere. With some minor cosmetic surgery, she might have been able to exist quite easily and anonymously, a lifestyle that seemed to be her inclination, unlike her brother. No one would have been looking for a dead woman. Lucky for us, searching for the truck that caused my accident led us to her. Lucky for me, marksmanship wasn't one of Barbara Finster's primary talents.

Another lucky thing was that they hadn't yet interred the body found at the fire scene. So it really was Barbara Allan Finster who was placed beside her brother, Jack David Finster, at the Central Edmonton Cemetery in mid-August. I didn't go to the ceremony, but Steve and Iain attended it as part of the case. I jokingly asked Steve if they were planting a briar over her grave, as in the folk tune.

"Nothing like that, although it would have served them right," Steve laughed. "And if we're lucky, we're past the age where the bad guys are the ones who get the songs written for them."

"I think we are past that," I smiled back. "Folk music may have once been a way for the lower classes to vent against the higher orders, but now it's a social voice, urging us on to live together, to live simply, to live in harmony with nature and each other."

"The way you tell it, folk music will save the world," he teased. We were walking over to Remedy, a comfortable dive of a café kitty-corner from my place, for their pistachio chai tea and samosas.

He tickled me and began to sing "I've Been Working on the Railroad." It gave me a slight start, in that it was the same song Woody had chosen to sing to me, but it occurred to me that it may have been the only folk tune to which Steve knew all the words. I decided to write the choice of tunes off as a coincidence and focus on my man, putting his decorum and sensibilities to the side, for me. Plus, he wasn't half bad—he had a nice lyrical baritone. I joined in and the singing of it took us through the two sets of lights across the intersection. As he opened the door for me, we harmonized on the final lines, startling a fellow writing the great Canadian novel on his laptop in the comfy chair in the corner and causing some hipsters on the upper floor seating area to sit up and take notice, I'm sure.

"Strumming on the old banjo!"

Acknowledgements

I am enormously grateful to Dr. Regula Kureshi, who met with me, answered way too many questions about the Folkways Collection and then allowed me to install my fictional Dr. Fuller into her office, move everything around and re-imagine a Centre.

I extend special thanks to Tom Paxton, the patron saint of folk music, who generously agreed to appear in the nick of time to save the day. I may have put some words in his mouth, but the best lines belong to him. Thank you as well to each and every musician who allowed me to book them into my dream Festival. I would line up for two days to go to a festival that had all of you performing together. Some of you I know; the rest of you were so gracious when a perfect stranger bounded up and asked if you'd mind showing up in a mystery novel set at the Edmonton Folk Music Festival.

Please support your local folk musicians. Attend concerts of touring musicians and always buy the merchandise at the back of the hall. Listen to radio stations that play local and alternative music. And of course, keep buying books. Vote. Floss. Eat your vegetables.

I'd like to thank the friends who model for me, especially Kelly Hewson, and those who allow me to use their names for my characters, which makes the writing a less solitary experience. I've also actually met a very nice Randy Craig and Steve Browning since inventing mine, so it works both ways.

This is a much sleeker read, due to the diligent reading of Sharon Caseburg, Randy Williams and Madeleine Mant. Thank you so much for all your efforts.

And of course, my family—Randy, Maddy and Jossie—who put up with so much whenever I'm caught up in a book. Thank you for the laughter, the love and the laundry.

Sticks & Stones
by Janice MacDonald

How dangerous can words be? The University of Alberta's English Department is caught up in a maelstrom of poison-pen letters, graffiti and misogyny. Part-time sessional lecturer Miranda Craig seems to be both target and investigator, wreaking havoc on her new-found relationship with one of Edmonton's Finest.

The men's residence at the U of A wants to party and issues invitations to the women's residence, each with specific and terrifying consequences if female students don't attend. One of Randy's star students, a divorced mother of two, has her threatening letter published in the newspaper and is found soon after, victim of a brutal murder followed to the gory letter of the published note.

Randy must delve into Gwen's life and preserve her own to solve this mystery. Is someone trying to kill Randy, and if so, who? An untenured professor? An unknown student? Gwen's killer?

Janice MacDonald's intelligence and insight into human behaviour make her one of the most promising new writers on the Canadian mystery scene.—Gail Bowen

Spellbinding ... Janice MacDonald populates academe with real characters and puts the humanity back in the Humanities. Of course, she also picks one or two of them off / now and then, which is all right with me, too. Sticks and Stones is an up-all-night page turner with substance.—W.P Kinsella

Sticks & Stones / $14.95
ISBN: 9780888012562
Ravenstone

The Monitor
by Janice MacDonald

You're being watched. Former University of Alberta lecturer Randy Craig is now working part-time at Edmonton's Grant MacEwan College, and struggling to make ends meet. That is, until she takes an evening job monitoring a chat room called Babel for an employer she knows only as Chatgod. Between shutting down an online bookie and patrolling for porn, Randy begins to suspect a connection between a Texas woman having an online affair through Babel, and surfacing reports of a man killed at his computer in the same state.

Soon, Randy realizes that a killer is brokering hits through Babel and may be operating in Edmonton. The police are sceptical, as is Chatgod, and it seems that Randy's only ally is a mysterious fellow monitor who calls himself Alchemist. Randy doesn't know whom she can trust, but the killer is on to her, and now she must figure out where the psychopath is, all the while staying one IP address ahead of becoming the next victim.

Janice MacDonald has accomplished something no other mystery writer has done—she has managed to convey the inherent spookiness, the disembodied projection screen, that a social cyberspace can invoke. The Monitor is a cyberspace mystery that really works as both a tale of virtual social intrigue and a real life (and death) mystery tale. This is a community I can recognize and a world that, even if virtual, sparks with life.—Howard Rheingold

The Monitor / $10.99
ISBN: 9780888012845
Ravenstone

Janice MacDonald holds a Master's in English Literature from the University of Alberta where she has worked as a sessional lecturer, radio producer and bartender. She also spent a decade teaching literature, communications and creative writing at Grant MacEwan College and has held positions as both an online chatroom monitor, and distance course instructor. A consummate folkie, she plays five-string banjo, fiddle, guitar, and piano, wrote the music and lyrics for two touring historical musicals and has been a singer/songwriter. Janice lives in Edmonton with her husband Randy and is the proud mother of two glorious grown girls.